TENNESSEE
Weddings

TENNESSEE
Weddings

THREE ROMANCES LIFT BURDENS
IN THE VOLUNTEER STATE

JOYCE LIVINGSTON

BARBOUR
PUBLISHING

With a Mother's Heart © 2006 by Joyce Livingston
Listening to Her Heart © 2006 by Joyce Livingston
Secondhand Heart © 2006 by Joyce Livingston

ISBN 978-1-59789-849-2

All scripture quotations are taken from the King James Version of the Bible.

This book is a work of fiction. Names, characters, places, and incidents are either products of the author's imagination or used fictitiously. Any similarity to actual people, organizations, and/or events is purely coincidental.

Cover image: Walter Bibikow/Getty Images

Published by Barbour Publishing, Inc., P.O. Box 719, Uhrichsville, Ohio 44683

Our mission is to publish and distribute inspirational products offering exceptional value and biblical encouragement to the masses.

 Member of the
Evangelical Christian
Publishers Association

Printed in the United States of America.

Dear Reader-friend,

As you may know, my precious husband Don Livingston (who is now with the Lord) and I have a BIG family—six children and lots and lots of grandkids—and we've all had a great time growing up together. If you have read any of the other books I have written, I'm sure you have realized I put much of myself into them. Sorry, I can't help it. I not only like to share my emotional experiences but the fun and interesting things that happen in my life. I've included several of them in this book. For instance:

At the bottom of page 51, Judy prepares the Eggs in a Basket breakfast for Timmy and Victoria. I have fixed Eggs in a Basket for our children since they were tiny babies. We all love them and they are so easy to prepare. After Don and I became empty-nesters, I continued to fix eight or ten at a time, sealed the extras in a plastic bag, and put them in the freezer. You can take them directly from the freezer, pop them in the toaster, and breakfast is ready in a snap!

On page 145, Beemer spreads peanut butter on a slice of bread then submerges it in his bowl of potato soup. Next, much to Ginny's dismay, he sprinkles the whole thing with garlic salt! Yummy! Just the thought of it makes me want to run to my kitchen and whip up a pot of potato soup. Don and I love it this way, especially if the peanut butter is the crunchy type. Try it. . .you just may like it!

On page 245, Sammy meets Ted on Nashville's famous General Jackson Riverboat cruise. If you ever get to Nashville, you must take that cruise. It's wonderful.

On page 277, Sammy and Ted have dinner at the amazing Opryland Hotel then finish off their evening with a flat-bottom boat ride through the hotel's 4½-acre indoor garden. Don and I have done both of these things and thoroughly enjoyed them. And yes, Danny is a real fish! I didn't make him up!

Have fun reading *Tennessee Weddings*! I had fun writing it!

Joyce Livingston

With a
Mother's Heart

Dedication

I dedicate this book to my daughters Dawn Lee Johnson and Dari Lynn Leyba, and two of my daughters-in-law, Catherine Livingston and Tammie Livingston, all four whom I consider to be model mothers. And best of all, they each love the Lord. Like Judy, my heroine in *With a Mother's Heart*, I know should it become necessary, they would each lay down their life for their children. I am so proud of each one of you and can't praise you highly enough.

And, as with every book I write and ever will write, this book is dedicated to my beloved husband, Don Livingston, who is now with our Lord.

Chapter 1

Remember, your name is no longer Timmy Alexander. It's Timmy Smith now. And let me do all the talking, okay?"

Timmy nodded. "I will, Aunt Judy. I promise."

"Mom! Remember?" She gave him a shake of her head and a slight frown. "You have to call me *Mom* or *Mama*, Timmy, not Aunt Judy. It's really important, sweetie. I know it's hard to remember, but you have to try. Just pretend it's a game. Play like I'm your mother and we're off on an adventure, okay?" Her voice was gentle as she reached for the child's hand and gave it a reassuring squeeze. "I hate this as much as you do, honey, but we have to be careful. You do understand, don't you?"

Her loving demeanor seemed to placate the child, and he offered a weak smile in return. "Uh-huh, Aunt—Mom. I understand, but I wish we could go—"

"Sweetie, we both want to go home, but you know we can't. Not now. Maybe soon."

Timmy looked up hopefully. "Tomorrow, maybe?"

"No. Not tomorrow. But soon. As soon as it's safe, I promise."

"Can he find us here, Aunt Judy?" The child looked around anxiously, as if to see if the driver in the front seat of their taxi had heard his error.

"No, sweetheart, he can't find us here." She gave the eight-year-old a playful jab then leaned toward the man whose picture graced the sun visor. "This is the place, driver. Turn into the driveway, please."

Judy Alexander rechecked the address in the classified section of the newspaper before she and the boy exited the yellow taxicab. "Wait for us, please. We shouldn't be too long."

"Your nickel, lady. Take all the time you need. The meter's running."

The two walked slowly up the winding brick sidewalk of the lovely, but intimidating, rambling stone house in the Carson Hills suburb of Memphis. *Surely this isn't the right place. It's so—grand. Maybe the newspaper printed the wrong address.*

Judy tightened her grip on Timmy's hand before stepping up onto the wide porch, her free hand cupping his slim shoulder. "You don't have to call me Mom all the time. Call me Mama or Mom, just like you would your real mother if she were here. You and I are supposed to be a family, like your mom and dad and you were a family. But we're a pretend family, and if we're careful, no one will know the difference."

"I'm good at pretending—Mama." Timmy smiled confidently. "And I'm good at remembering. See! I called you Mama!"

She gave him a big grin. "I noticed, and I'm very proud of you. I knew I could count on you." Her expression grew serious. "I don't mean to frighten you, but our lives may depend on it. Just remember the Lord is with us."

"I—I know."

"Do you still have that shiny quarter in your pocket? The special one your dad gave you?"

The boy nodded. "Yep, right here."

"Okay, here we go. You want to ring the doorbell, or shall I?"

Timmy grinned and touched a fingertip to the button. From inside came the mellow sound of Westminster chimes bonging out their presence, then a baritone voice. "I'll get it, Max."

The heavy oak door swung open and a friendly male face appeared. "Yes? What can I do for you?"

Judy took a deep breath. Lying had never been easy for her. "I'm Judy Smith." She nodded toward her small companion. "And this is my son, Timmy. I called about the furnished apartment. Are you Mr. Bramwell?"

The man pushed the door open wide and stepped back to allow them entrance as he extended his hand warmly. "Oh, of course. Judy Smith. Yes, I'm Ben Bramwell. Come in, come in. I was expecting you, but you're early."

"I have a cab waiting," she said apologetically as she motioned toward the yellow taxi. "If you don't mind, I'd like to see the apartment. As the driver reminded me when I asked him to wait—the meter is still running."

"Then, by all means, let's go take a look at it." He turned and called out over his shoulder, "Max, I'll be back in a few minutes. I'm going to show Mrs. Smith the apartment." Closing the door behind him, he motioned toward the twosome. "Follow me; it's not far. It's over the garage, but I guess you knew that."

"Yes, you told me when I phoned."

He led the way as Judy and Timmy followed silently. "You don't mind that the apartment is furnished? If you'd rather use your own things, I think we have plenty of storage and can move whatever things you don't want out into the back garage."

"No, I'm glad it's furnished. This will save me having to shop for new furniture," she explained, trying to sound casual. *Although I don't really need any.*

Timmy listened, his big eyes rounded, making her feel all the more guilty.

"Will your husband be coming later?"

Judy flinched, her gaze quickly darting to Timmy, hoping the child's expression wouldn't give them away when she answered. She took on a sad look and hung her head slightly, hoping to avoid his eyes as she told another lie. "No, he—he died of a heart attack a few months ago."

Ben Bramwell placed a consoling hand on her shoulder. "I'm so sorry. I just supposed you'd come on to Memphis ahead of him, to find a place to live."

She gave him a guarded smile. "Thank you for your concern, Mr. Bramwell. Timmy and I are learning to live with it, but it's not easy."

"I—I know what you're going through. I lost my wife over a year ago."

"Losing a spouse is never easy. I'm sure you miss her terribly." Her heart went out to him. From the look on Ben Bramwell's face, he must have loved his wife very much.

"No, it's not. In some ways, I'm still recovering." Mr. Bramwell stopped before a covered doorway nestled between well-trimmed bushes and pulled a ring of keys from his pocket, inserting one into the lock. "I'll expect you to agree to a year's lease if you decide to take the place. My mother lived in this apartment. I wanted her to stay in the house with us, but she's a stubborn woman and didn't want to intrude on our lives, as she put it. I think she liked her independence," he explained with a smile.

"I guess we all do." Judy followed him up the thickly carpeted stairs with Timmy shadowing close behind.

Mr. Bramwell responded with a hearty laugh. "You know, I think you're right! That mother of mine gave me fits. I never knew where she was or when she was coming home. She hated it when I checked on her. I'd have to watch out my bedroom window to see when the lights came on in her apartment to make sure she was safely in for the night. That woman insisted on driving her own car until she was eighty-five."

"She doesn't want to live here anymore?"

He inserted another key in the heavy door at the head of the stairs then turned to face his prospective tenant, a wistful look on his face. "No. When it became impossible for her to climb the stairs, she agreed to move into the house with me. But then she fell and broke her hip and required more care than she thought I could give her. She insisted on moving into an assisted living unit, was there for a few months, and got along pretty good. But she's in a care home now and not doing too well. I may not have her with me much longer."

"Oh, I'm so sorry. I didn't—"

He gave her a kindly smile. "The Lord's been good to her. She's lived a full life and she's ready to go. She was happy in this apartment and I liked having her near me. However, when it became necessary that she move to the care home, she insisted that I rent the apartment to someone new. Mom, despite her wealth, is a pretty frugal old gal. She feels it's a waste to let it just sit empty. I resisted at first. I couldn't imagine having anyone else living here, but at her urging I've finally convinced myself it needs someone new to enjoy it again." He pushed the door open and stood aside. "And with that child of yours here, perhaps this place will be filled with laughter again. Mom loved laughter. She could see the bright side of any situation. Come in and have a look. See if it meets your needs."

Judy put an arm around Timmy and pulled him close as they moved past Ben Bramwell. The apartment was more than she'd hoped for. A large, thickly carpeted living room, with a wood-burning fireplace flanked by floor-to-ceiling bookcases, two nice-sized bedrooms, a full bath with rose-colored fixtures, and a compact U-shaped kitchen, just the right size for the two of them. And windows. Lots of windows.

"If the rent is the same as you quoted me on the phone and you're willing to rent it to us, we'll take it!" Judy said quickly, afraid someone else would snatch it up if she delayed her decision. It was perfect. She'd dared not even dream for this much when she'd responded to the ad.

"Well, you were the first one who phoned about it. At five this morning, I might add," he said with a mischievous wink.

Judy felt herself blush. "I'm sorry about calling so early, but when I saw your ad in this morning's paper, I knew you'd have quite a few people calling about it. I wanted to be first."

"Well, you were! I've probably gotten another fifteen or twenty calls since I first spoke with you, but I told all of them to call after nine o'clock, after you'd had a chance to take a look at the place. I never expected so many people to be interested in a furnished apartment." He moved to the window and glanced down into the spacious yard. "I think your cabbie is getting a bit anxious. He's pacing back and forth in the driveway."

"I have cash." She pulled a folded envelope from her purse and thrust it toward him. "I already have the first and last month's rent and the security deposit in here—in case your apartment was right for us and you agreed to rent it to us."

He took the envelope then reached for the lease agreements he'd left on the counter in the kitchen. "Here's my pen. Sign the lease. I'll write you out a receipt, and the apartment is yours. When do you plan to move in?" he asked when she handed him the lease.

Judy shook his hand eagerly while inwardly praising God for giving them such a safe and comfortable place to hide. "Today. Now."

Ben reared back in surprise. "You don't waste any time, do you?"

She had to smile. "Mr. Bramwell, we got off a bus yesterday morning. We spent last night in a hotel room next to noisy elevators that went up and down all night. We can't wait to get out of that place. Yes, we'd like to move in today, if that's all right with you. We're ready to settle down here in Memphis. The sooner, the better."

A broad smile broke across Ben Bramwell's handsome face as he surveyed his two visitors. "Mrs. Smith, welcome home." His voice was kind and sincere. He removed the two keys from his key ring and handed them to her. "It'll be nice having you and Timmy here. I had Miranda, our housekeeper, give the apartment a good going-over yesterday, so it's all ready for you. When you're settled, I'd like you to come to the house and meet my daughter. I think she's about Timmy's age. In the meantime, if you need anything, just let me or Max know. Max is my butler, but he's more like a father. Been with my family for years. You'll like them both, I'm sure; but just ignore them if they try to run your life like they do mine. They're good-hearted people, and they mean well."

"Thank you. I'm sure we'll enjoy living in your beautiful apartment. And we look forward to meeting your daughter and Max and Miranda. But right now, we need to do some shopping and stock up on supplies. We'll be back in a few hours." She grabbed Timmy's hand and made her way back down the stairs.

Ben closed the door and followed them. "Well, like I said, you don't waste much time. I guess I should have asked for references, but I doubt a newly widowed mother and her son have anything shady in their past."

Oh, Mr. Bramwell, if you only knew what we've been through these past few months and what we're going through now, I doubt you'd want to rent this apartment to us.

"The apartment is yours, Mrs. Smith. And you needn't tell me when you'll be back. I think you took my story about checking on my mother much too seriously."

Judy glanced back at him sheepishly as they descended the stairs and moved into the well-manicured yard with its lush growth of trees and flowers. "Maybe I did. Sorry." She and Timmy followed Mr. Bramwell around to the front of the big house where the taxi was waiting.

"You two have a good day, and remember, let one of us know if you need anything." Ben stooped to shake Timmy's hand. "Young man, you take care of your mother. I have a feeling she needs you."

Judy watched him step into the house and close the door behind him before she ushered Timmy to the waiting taxi and breathed a sigh of relief. They'd passed the first two hurdles in Memphis. She'd lied about her name and been believed, and they'd found a place to live. And although she'd agreed to a one-year lease, she hoped they'd be gone in less than a month.

∞

Ewald Bentley Bramwell III stood in the front hall of his sprawling mansion and peered through the beveled glass window at the mother and son who were crawling into the taxicab parked in his driveway. Why would she settle for a furnished apartment? She appeared to be a woman who appreciated nice surroundings. Judy Smith could be pretty, he thought as he watched them drive away. Although she was wearing sweatpants and a baggy shirt, they had a designer label embroidered onto them—even he could see that. And she seems to be well-bred, with her mannerisms and her perfect English. But why did she wear her long, red hair curled around her face like that? Between the hair and the heavy, horn-rimmed glasses he could barely see her face. *Well,* he concluded, *the place seemed right for her and her son, she had the cash to pay the rent, and renting it to her will keep me from having to string dozens of potential renters through the apartment.* Yes, he was glad he'd rented the apartment to her and her son. They should be good tenants and, hopefully, his daughter would be glad to have another child around.

"Sir? Will Miss Vanderbur be joining you and Victoria for dinner tonight?"

Max's question drew Ben's attention away from the window as the cab disappeared through the iron gate at the end of the long driveway. "No, Max. Tonight, there'll only be two at the table. Victoria and myself. Unless I can convince you and Miranda to join us."

"Sir, you know better than that. My wife and I appreciate your invitation, but you seem to forget we *are* servants. We'll have our dinner in the kitchen, as usual."

Ben nudged the pudgy man with his elbow. "Can Victoria and I join you?"

Max tilted his chin arrogantly. "Sir, that would be rather awkward for Miranda and me. I suggest you and Miss Victoria eat in the dining room."

"Good old Max. You never change. I've been trying to wheedle my way into a place at that kitchen table since I was three years old. You're a stubborn man, Max Reynolds."

"And you're a very kind man, Ewald Bentley Bramwell III."

Ben had to laugh at his butler's response. "Thank you, Max, but I think you're slightly biased."

Max took a step back from his employer and eyed him carefully as he adjusted his jacket over his rounded tummy. "Sir, if I may be so bold. . . Have you and Miss Vanderbur set a wedding date yet?"

Ben frowned slightly and pursed his lips thoughtfully. "Not yet, Max."

"It will be one of the social events of the year, sir. We'll need plenty of time to get ready. There'll be so much to do. And Miranda and I were wondering. . ." He paused.

"What, Max? You know you can ask me anything."

"Well, sir. We were wondering if you and Miss Vanderbur have decided where you will live as husband and wife. We were hoping it would be here at Bramwell House."

Ben appeared thoughtful. "We—we haven't come to an agreement on that yet, Max. Miss Vanderbur has her eye on a much larger house over in Brentwood. I prefer to live here. But we haven't made any concrete decisions yet."

Max started to say something but didn't.

"You're wondering about your employment, right?"

Max nodded.

"Well, don't worry about it, old friend. Of course you'll both be with me, wherever I live. I can't imagine life without you."

"Does Miss Vanderbur agree with that, sir?"

For the first time, Ben realized he'd never discussed the role of his servants with Phoebe. He had no idea how she'd feel about Max and Miranda working for them once they were married. In fact, there were many things the two of them hadn't discussed. Perhaps it was time.

∞

"I like our new place, Au—Mama." Timmy lowered his chin regretfully. "I'm trying to remember, Aunt Judy, honest I am."

She patted his knee gently as the taxi made its way down the street then cautioned him to keep his voice down to a whisper. "I know you are, but we have to remember. I don't want to frighten you, but you know what might happen if anyone finds out who we really are. I'm sure that man is looking for us, and he probably has other people looking for us, too. We can't take any chances. I know you're scared. I am, too. When I testified against him, I never dreamed he'd be able to escape. But if we're careful, and don't do anything foolish, we'll be okay."

With his face taking on a look of panic, Timmy's eyes rounded. "Do you think he can find us in Memphis?"

"I don't see how he could, not with all the different buses and planes we took to get here, and as long as we remember to use Smith as our last name." A chill of fear coursed through her body. *Dear Lord, please protect us from that evil man. I know he meant it when he said he'd find us and kill us when I testified against him. If I hadn't been able to identify Skitch Fallon as the man who shot my brother, he probably would have gotten away with it and never been found.*

"I know, Mama," Timmy responded with a smile that broke her heart. "See? I did it! I said it right."

"You sure did, honey. I'm very proud of you. It'll get easier the more you practice it. I know it will. It's a lot to ask of an eight-year-old." Judy focused on the passing scenery, her mind whirling with the inevitable consequences of what would happen if they were found. No, she wouldn't let that happen. She'd never let anything happen to this child. Not now. Not ever. A shudder ran down her spine as she glanced at the traffic around them.

"We could ask the taxi man to turn the heater on if you're cold," Timmy volunteered, his eyes showing concern. "Or maybe he'd stop so we could get a cup of hot cocoa."

"I'm not cold. Just a little tense." Judy smiled at the boy as the light turned red and the driver pulled the big yellow car to an easy stop. "We'll be at the grocery store soon and we can pick up a whole cart full of food, including a can of cocoa and a big bag of marshmallows. Then when we get back to our new apartment, I'll fix us big mugs of hot cocoa like I promised and you can add as many marshmallows as you'd like. How does that sound?"

She watched Timmy's eager eyes light up at the suggestion. He'd gone through so much in the past few months. They both had. It was nice to see him smile.

Timmy clapped his hands with glee. "Marshmallows? All right! And can we get some hot dogs to cook in that outdoor cooker thing on the deck?"

"Of course we can, sweetie. I think it already had some small twigs and logs in it, all ready to burn. Maybe we'll even get a couple of movies. I saw a video player in the apartment under the TV set. I might even be persuaded to pop a bag of popcorn in that little microwave in our apartment to go with our movies. Are you game?"

Excitedly, Timmy began to bounce up and down on the seat. "Oh, yes. Let's do it. I love popcorn!"

The driver flipped on the turn signal and made a right turn into the mall parking lot.

"I'm sure the grocery story has a video department. We'll select a few videos first, then our groceries. I think we'd better get a great big bag of frozen vegetables. Veggies, milk, and lots of apples, oranges, and juice."

Timmy frowned. "No ice cream?"

"Well—maybe. If they have any Rocky Road. That's my favorite."

"Mine, too!"

"I know! You're always after me to buy it."

It was nearly three o'clock before they arrived back at their new apartment. Their landlord was heading for a shiny black Porsche when their taxi turned into the driveway. He stopped to see who was arriving then awkwardly folded his long legs and lowered himself into the driver's seat of the sports car.

"Beautiful Porsche." Judy nodded and grinned at him as she grabbed hold of several grocery sacks and crawled out of the taxi. The fancy Porsche didn't seem to go with his conservative personality.

"My daughter hates this car. Actually, I never understood myself why I bought it but," he said with a shrug, "it seemed like a good idea at the time. My fiancée thought it would be the perfect car for me, but sometimes I feel a bit foolish driving it. Like an overgrown kid. All I need is a gold chain hanging around my neck and an earring in my ear."

Judy laughed. "Sometimes our ideas don't work out like we think they will."

"That's for sure. I'm afraid I can say I've had way too many such ideas, and this car was certainly one of them." He turned his attention to Timmy. "You like cars, young man?"

Timmy nodded his head.

"Well, I've never met a young man who didn't. There seems to be a love affair between a man and his car. When I was young, my dad bought. . ." He turned the key in the ignition and the Porsche roared into action. "But that's another story, and I know you two are eager to get settled. I won't keep you and your mom, but I do promise to take you for a ride in this thing sometime soon—with your mom's permission, of course."

"Cool." Timmy's face beamed his excitement.

"Are you going out for the evening, Mr. Bramwell?" Judy asked on impulse, wondering whatever possessed her to do so.

"No, just have to run back to my office for an hour or two. Why? What did you have in mind?"

"I just thought you and your daughter might like to join Timmy and me for hot dogs, cocoa, and a movie. We went grocery shopping and purchased a couple of videos." Why had she blurted out an impromptu invitation like that? He must think her terribly forward.

"I've already told Max that my daughter and I would be dining in tonight, but I'm sure Miranda can put whatever she's preparing in the refrigerator. We'd love to accept your invitation."

He revved up the engine. "See you this evening. About six?"

"Yes, six will be fine."

Judy and Timmy watched the black car as it whizzed down the driveway and disappeared through the gate.

"Looks like we're having company for supper. That okay with you? I guess I should have asked you first."

Timmy looked thoughtful, his gaze still pinned on the gate. "I'll bet he's a nice daddy."

Judy took his small hand in hers and stroked it gently. "Aw, honey. I know

17

how much you miss your daddy. He was the nicest man I've ever known. And he was the best brother a girl could ask for. He loved you so much. I wish—"

"He hadn't been shot?" Timmy asked softly as he wiped at his eyes with his shirtsleeve.

"Yes, I wish he hadn't been shot. We all loved him, didn't we?"

The boy gulped hard. "I really loved him."

"I know you did, baby. He knew it, too. Your mommy loved you, too, and she was the best mommy ever. Even when she was sick, all she thought about was you. I couldn't have asked for a better sister-in-law. I considered it a real honor when she asked me to help your dad take care of you after she was gone."

"Why did God take my mommy?"

"I don't know, Timmy, but He must have had a reason. But we'll see her again someday."

" 'Cause I have Jesus in my heart?"

For his benefit, she pasted on a smile, although the last thing she felt like doing at this moment was smiling. "Yes. One day, in heaven, we'll all be together again." *God, I don't understand this, either. Why would You allow my sweet, lovely sister-in-law to die from cancer? And why, only two years later, would You let my brother be shot and killed in a botched-up bank robbery? They were perfect parents and such good people—people who loved You with their whole hearts.*

She had to change the subject. She could barely stand to think about the trauma that had enveloped their lives. Losing Kayla and Jerod had nearly killed her. If it hadn't been for Timmy, she would have wished to die, too. Life had been hard and filled with too many sorrows for such a young boy. Now, it was up to her to raise this beautiful child and, with God's help, she'd do the very best she could to try to take Kayla's and Jerod's places. "Hey, you ready to help me carry all these groceries up to our new apartment?"

Blinking hard, Timmy smiled. "Sure, Aunt—Mom."

The two set to work filling the cabinets and refrigerator with their purchases. The place was in excellent shape. Apparently Miranda had complied with her boss's request. The dishes and pots and pans sparkled. The refrigerator was spotless. And there were clean dish towels in the drawer. Everything they would need was at their fingertips. *God, You are so good to us. Thank You for this place.* With Timmy's help, Judy built a fire in the little outdoor cooker, bent several empty wire hangers into shape, and soon they were ready to roast their hot dogs when their guests arrived later.

"I like this place," Timmy confessed with childlike enthusiasm as he carried a bowl of chopped onion to the table. "I think we're gonna be safe here."

"Me, too. I like being upstairs like this. We can open up the shades and no one can see in except the people in Mr. Bramwell's house, and I'm sure they're not interested in what you and I are doing." She gave him a grin as she opened the lid on the new bottle of ketchup. "And I like having the locked door up here and at the bottom of the stairs, too. Like you, I feel safe here. I'm sure God has been keeping this place just for you and me."

Timmy stared at the hot dog package. "I wish my mama could see our new apartment."

"I do, too, sweetie."

He frowned as he placed the paper napkin basket on the table. "I loved her and I really miss her. And I really miss my daddy."

She put a reassuring hand on his small arm. "I know. I miss them, too. I'm sure they're both up in heaven looking down on us. They knew how much I loved you and that I'd do everything I could to take good care of you."

Timmy raised his pale blue eyes to hers. "I love you, too, Aunt Judy."

She touched a fingertip to his nose and reminded gently, "Mama, Timmy. Not Aunt Judy."

"Sorry."

A few minutes before six, Ben rang the outside buzzer. Judy pressed the intercom.

"I goofed," he said, sounding as if he'd run all the way from the house. "My fiancée and I had plans for this evening, for dinner and a concert, and I completely forgot. Can we get a rain check on those hot dogs?"

Timmy frowned as he heard the man's words.

"Sure, that'll be fine." *Why did I ever invite him in the first place?* "It was probably a silly idea, anyway."

"No, don't say that! It's a great idea. My daughter and I both love hot dogs. Please say you'll invite us again. I can't tell you how disappointed she was when my fiancée called to remind me about our plans for this evening. I was disappointed, too. Actually, I'd rather have hot dogs with you than go to that concert, but my fiancée wants to go, and I'd promised to take her."

Judy had to smile. "Of course, we'll invite you again. I hope the two of you have a nice evening."

Timmy scowled. "Why didn't he tell her he'd rather eat hot dogs with us?"

She shrugged. "Don't know, but I'm wondering how a man could forget a date with the woman he plans to marry."

After they'd consumed their hot dogs, Judy and Timmy made themselves comfortable on the couch and started their first movie. She'd made sure the movies they selected were ones with happy endings. What Timmy didn't need right now were any reminders that things didn't always turn out okay.

"Can we have the cocoa and popcorn now?" he asked as the first movie ended and he stood and stretched his arms.

"Sure, honey. You pick out our next movie while this one is rewinding and I'll fix our snacks. I'm not sure it's wise to watch two movies in one evening, but this is a special occasion, so I think we can stay up late this once, don't you? It's not every day you get to move into such a nice apartment. We're celebrating!"

"Yeah!"

It was good to see Timmy happy, even if it meant sitting through two children's movies in a row. They'd settled back onto the sofa with their hot chocolate and popcorn, ready to hit the play button on the VCR, when the buzzer sounded.

Judy froze. *No one knows we're here, and this apartment has been vacated for some time. Who could be pushing the buzzer? It can't be Mr. Bramwell. He's attending a concert tonight.* She motioned for Timmy to keep quiet and moved toward the door. It was then she heard the crackling of the intercom. She pushed the button and spoke into the microphone, her heart pounding in her throat. "Who is it?"

Chapter 2

Sorry to bother you, Mrs. Smith. It's me, Ben Bramwell. My housekeeper, Miranda, made chocolate chip cookies for my daughter and me and she thought you and Timmy might like some. I've brought you a plate of them."

"I—I wasn't expecting you. You're back from the concert already?" Judy's flattened palm went to her chest as she let out a huge sigh and her heart settled back into its usual place.

"Actually, we had to end the night early. Phoebe got one of her migraine headaches so we didn't go to the concert after all. Just dinner." He let loose a slight chuckle. "Not that I minded, but I could have used the nap I missed. I usually have to struggle to keep from falling asleep at those things."

She tried unsuccessfully to muffle a giggle. "We'd love some cookies, Mr. Bramwell. I'll come right down after them."

She motioned for Timmy to remain on the sofa and made her way quickly down the steps and unlocked the door at the bottom. There, in the dim glow of the yard light stood Ben Bramwell, dressed in jeans and a pale blue sweater, holding a plate covered with a white linen napkin.

"Here you are, freshly baked cookies. Miranda is a terrific cook. You and Timmy are really going to enjoy these. She's been baking chocolate chip cookies for me since I was three years old. I think she's got the recipe down pat. They're my favorite, as well as my daughter's." His clean-shaven face beamed in the narrow shaft of light filtering through the trees.

"Thank you," Judy muttered, still shaken by the unexpected sounding of the buzzer. "Chocolate chip is our favorite kind, too. Thank Miranda for sharing them with us."

"You are most welcome. Did you enjoy your hot dogs?"

Judy felt herself blush again and was thankful for the shadowy doorway shielding her face. "Yes, now we're having hot chocolate and a big bowl of popcorn with our second movie."

"Then I won't keep you." He dipped his head and backed away with a salute. "Tell Timmy I hope he enjoys the cookies. When I told Victoria about your wiener roast, she said she'd much rather have had the hot dogs than the standing rib roast

21

Miranda had prepared for us. Remember you promised to invite us another time. We plan on holding you to that promise."

"Yes. Thank you. We will—invite you both, that is." Judy felt like a blubbering idiot. Why was she having so much trouble forming her words? Mr. Bramwell was no threat to their safety. "Good—good night."

"Good night," he echoed and was gone.

She quickly pushed the door closed and twisted the dead bolt. Living their lie was going to be difficult, especially when they had to lie to a man as nice as Ben Bramwell. But lie they must. There was no other choice. How she wished for the time when things would return to normal and they could go home.

"Aunt Judy?"

She turned quickly and began to ascend the stairs with a grin, her eyes fixed on the child standing at the landing above the stairway.

Timmy pulled a face. "I mean, *Mama*."

Her smile was warm and forgiving. "It's really hard to remember, isn't it? I have trouble remembering, too." She removed the linen napkin and held out the plate of cookies. "Cookie? That nice Mr. Bramwell brought them to us."

He frowned. "One?"

"Umm, okay. Two."

Eager eyes searched the plate before the boy lifted the two largest cookies from the freshly baked cookie stack. "Three? Please?"

Being a mother to such a winsome little boy was not an easy task, Judy decided as she stood holding the plate of calorie- and sugar-laden cookies in her hands. If she had her way she'd give him the entire plate and let him gorge himself, eating as many cookies as he'd like. But a loving mother would never let her child do such a thing, and neither could she. He was in her care now and she had to force herself to make sure every decision was the best decision she was capable of making. She smiled at the boy who was watching her with expectation. "How about two now and one with breakfast?"

"Aw. . ." He grinned sheepishly as he took his first bite.

"You nearly called me Aunt Judy, didn't you? But I'm proud of you. I know you're trying hard to remember, and you're doing a great job of it." She touched a fingertip to Timmy's nose. "Now, be a good kid and take this plate into the kitchen while I lock up, okay?"

He popped the remainder of the cookie into his mouth and took the plate from her hands. "Umm. These are good," he mumbled.

"No fair talking with your mouth full!" She watched as he skipped into the kitchen, enjoying the second cookie on his way, then turned the dead bolt and slipped the chain into the groove while feeling a comforting degree of safety.

This apartment was perfect for them, with its double locks on both the downstairs door and the door at the head of the landing. And with the height of the three-car garage beneath them, it would be next to impossible for someone to gain access to their living quarters through the windows. Yes, she felt secure living in the Bramwell apartment. She only hoped their stay would be a short one.

After she'd read her Bible and prayed, Judy lay awake long after the red numbers on the bedside clock passed midnight, even though she'd turned out the lights at eleven. If anyone had told her two weeks ago she'd be living in Memphis with this child, she'd have told them they were crazy. Never in her wildest dreams would she have believed her brother, Jerod, would have been shot during a robbery and Timmy would be both motherless *and* fatherless.

Lifting the sheet, she flipped over onto her stomach, her heart clenching with sadness. *Lord, I miss Kayla. No one could've done a better job raising this child than she did. She was the perfect mother. Why did she have to die so young? I've done all I could to help Jerod raise this wonderful child, but I'm not sure it was enough. And now Jerod is gone, too, and I'm totally responsible for Timmy's upbringing.*

Memories of both Kayla and Jerod filled her mind as tears gushed forth and cascaded onto the pillowcase. Jerod. Taken so quickly in the very prime of his life when he had so much to live for. So many people had loved that teddy bear of a man. Tall, burly, and wonderfully sweet for a guy who made his living as a police officer, Jerod had always been the first to offer when a friend needed help. He'd been the thoughtful, caring father who'd changed Timmy's diapers and given him his nightly bath since the day he'd first entered the world. Jerod had been a model father and Kayla the model mother.

Flipping back the quilt, she walked barefoot to stand at the window, absent-mindedly leaning her forehead against the coolness of the glass. Somewhere off in the distance she heard the faint sound of traffic moving on the interstate, but here, in this residential neighborhood of costly estates, everything was quiet. Peaceful. Serene. Safe.

She crossed her arms and wrapped them around her body as the cool night air sent a chill through her being. Somewhere out there was danger—danger for both her and Timmy. She had to keep a watchful eye at all times. No matter how safe this apartment seemed at the moment, she could never let her guard down. He was all she had now that his parents were gone. If it became necessary, she would gladly give up her life to protect him.

The floor creaked softly as she padded back across the thick carpet to where she slipped beneath the cozy, nine-patch quilt that topped the queen-sized bed. She checked the clock again. Still not even two. Would sleep ever come?

Ten minutes later, still wide-eyed, she clicked on the bedside lamp and pulled a paperback novel from the drawer, opening it to the page with a tattered bookmark, and began to read, hoping it would relax her and make her sleepy. Reading late at night usually brought sleep quickly, but no matter how hard she tried to get into the plot or appreciate the trials of the hero and heroine, she couldn't, and soon the book was placed back into the drawer and the light turned off. She'd just have to tough it out until sleep came naturally.

∞

Ben Bramwell stood at the window of his second-floor bedroom, staring into space, thinking about the two people who had moved into the garage apartment on his property. Why would a woman Judy Smith's age, who seemed highly educated and extremely independent, arrive in Memphis with her son and only a few items? Surely she'd accumulated more than that in her lifetime. And surely a healthy, normal boy like Timmy would have items like baseball bats, a skateboard, a bicycle, or a telescope—things all kids needed in their lives. He watched with interest as a light came on in the garage apartment, then glanced at the glowing red numerals on his nightstand clock. Was she having trouble sleeping, or was she a night owl like he was? Perhaps she was merely going to the bathroom or checking on Timmy.

He continued to stare at the lighted window. He'd told Victoria about their new tenants but, even though she'd finally agreed to the hot dog invitation at his insistence, she hadn't expressed any real interest in them. She wasn't interested in anything, and it broke his heart. How hard he'd tried to be both mother and father to his only child, but he'd failed. Failed miserably. She was an unhappy child. Other than the trips to visit her grandmother, nothing seemed to pique her interest. Not the new puppy. Not the huge dollhouse. Not the big-screen TV he'd placed in her room. Nothing. Since she'd lost her mother, she'd barely talked to him. Or anyone, except Granny. All Victoria did was sit and stare, locked in her own thoughts, whatever they might be.

The only thing he hadn't given her was a second mother. Not that her own mother could ever be replaced; he knew that would never be, but he could do the next best thing—marry a woman who would at least be a feminine presence in their home, and perhaps, eventually, with love and dedication, be accepted as Victoria's stepmother.

He shuddered at the word. Just the sound of it made his blood run cold. Whoever made up that term? Surely, there was another word, other than stepmother, to explain a woman who married a widower and became the child's substitute mother. Although Victoria seemed to resent Phoebe Vanderbur and avoided any conversation with the woman he intended to marry, surely once she'd moved into Bramwell House, the two would become good friends. *When she moved into Bramwell House?* The question hit him like a linebacker hits a quarterback when he's about to throw the ball. *What if Phoebe doesn't want to live at Bramwell House and insists on living in the big house she has her heart set on? Could I actually leave this place I've lived in all my life? And what about Victoria? It's the only home she's ever known. Could I even consider moving her to some strange place in her fragile condition?*

The window in the garage apartment went black. Ben stood in the darkness a few more minutes, listening to the scuffing sounds of the wind blowing a tree branch across the great house's facade and watching the twinkling of the stars before he turned in for the night.

Maybe, just maybe, when Victoria met Timmy she'd come out of her shell. And then again, maybe that was too much to hope for.

∞

It was nearly nine the next morning when Miranda motioned for Max and Ben to remain by the door of Victoria's room. She tiptoed across the bedroom and placed the breakfast tray on the table before taking a peek at the face resting on the pink satin pillowcase. "Time to wake up, honey. Your tutor will be here in an hour and I've got a nice breakfast fixed for you."

The tiny girl, who was barely making a bump in the big bed, raised her face toward the woman with a feeble smile.

"Victoria, please. Talk to Miranda." The woman sat down on the bed beside the child and stroked her cheek with the back of her curved finger. "We all love you, sweetheart. Your daddy. Me. Max. Your grandmother."

The child raised a brow as if in question.

"And Miss Phoebe, too, I think. She *says* she loves you." Miranda paused, as if questioning her own words. "Let's brace you against the pillows so you can enjoy a nice breakfast." She took a tiny hand in hers and slid her arm beneath the girl's shoulders and gave her an upward tug. "My, but you're getting big!"

Victoria nodded as she allowed Miranda to assist her.

"Wait'll you see what I've fixed for your breakfast. Your favorite. Oatmeal and brown sugar." She grinned at the little girl whose big brown eyes followed her about the room as she reached for the tray. "And I have the nicest bright yellow banana waiting for you, too."

Ben had been watching from the open doorway. Victoria picked up her spoon and idly twirled it in the oatmeal. "You need to eat, baby," he told her as he strode into the room.

She ignored his comment and continued to twist the spoon back and forth through the steaming contents of the bowl.

He moved to her side and seated himself in the chair next to her. "For Daddy?

Won't you eat it for Daddy?" he pleaded as he took the spoon from her hand and filled it with the smooth, sweetened oatmeal. "Miranda fixed it just like you like it."

She turned her head away from the offered spoon, her eyes downcast and sad.

"I know you miss your mommy. I miss her, too. But, Victoria, it's been over a year since Mommy left us. Mommy wants us to remember her, but she wants us to go on living, too." He caused his face to brighten as he touched his finger to the girl's chin and lifted her slim face to his. "I saw Mommy's star last night. Did you see it?"

The child's eyes widened a bit.

"Remember? We—you and I—decided that the brightest star in the heavens had to be your mom watching over us, taking care of us. She's up there with God. Someday, we'll be there with God and Mommy, but right now, we have to go on living. You wouldn't want to make Mommy sad, would you?"

He noted an almost undetectable shake of her head. "Then won't you please do what Daddy asks and eat your oatmeal?"

Two tiny lips parted slightly.

"Good. Here. Take this little bite and see how good it tastes." He carefully slipped the spoon between her lips. "Now, you have to admit, that tastes pretty good, doesn't it?"

When there was no response, he filled the spoon and offered it once again, hoping she'd eat at least a few bites. It seemed she was losing a little weight every day and he was worried about her. So was Miranda. But what could they do? Force her to eat? That would only upset her more.

The child sitting in the bed beside him was nothing like the little girl he'd spoiled from birth. That child had been filled with life. She'd been a joy to be around. He never knew when she'd slip up behind him and place her arms around his neck and kiss him until he begged for mercy. That little girl had played with her dolls from morning 'til night, savoring everything life had to offer to a child her age. Everyone loved her. Everyone said what a perfect child she was, with her tinkling laughter and her sparkling eyes. He remembered the way she would climb onto his lap with an armful of books and beg him to read to her. He thought of the finger-painted pictures she was so proud of and the way she would tape them all over the house. Even onto the expensive antique furniture, without a thought or care of the damage the sticky tape might do to the wood's finish. Love, joy, and laughter followed her wherever she went. She was a ray of sunshine. An oasis in a busy day. A lovely rainbow in a stormy sky. And he loved her with all his heart.

She was so like her mother. And he'd loved her, too, more than life itself. He would have gladly taken her place, but he hadn't had the chance. His wife's life had been taken so suddenly, and he'd been nowhere near her at the time. But Victoria was. Victoria had been in the car with her mother. Witnesses said a car crossed the centerline, clipped the Bramwell car, and sent it spinning over an embankment. For Carlotta, it was all over in a matter of seconds.

Her life was snuffed out, with Victoria, who had been strapped into her seat belt in the backseat, injured and pinned into the rear half of the crumpled wreckage. Though some said Carlotta might have lived if she'd been wearing her seat belt, it was something no one would ever know.

Ben's eyes misted over as he remembered. His heart had seemed to stop beating when the call had come that his wife was gone. He'd wanted to die, too. The agony was almost too much to bear. Then they'd reminded him his daughter, Victoria, was still alive, though hanging on to her life by a thread. At that moment, he'd known he had to live—for her.

He cringed at the remembrance then realized those big, innocent eyes were fixed on his face, waiting for another spoonful of oatmeal. He filled the spoon, making sure to include a small lump of brown sugar. "Victoria, you do understand why Daddy is getting married again, don't you?"

The child shoved at the spoon and turned her head away.

"I'm marrying Phoebe for you, baby. You need a mother."

Victoria crossed her arms, frowned, and lowered her head defiantly, avoiding his gaze.

"You'll learn to love Phoebe. Give her a chance, okay?"

"She doesn't like Miss Phoebe," Miranda volunteered as she began to clear away the breakfast tray.

Max stepped between his wife and his employer. "Miranda, be quiet."

Ben motioned him away. "Let her have her say, Max. I know Miranda loves Victoria." Ben motioned her toward the hall where they could speak without his daughter hearing their conversation.

Max moved away reluctantly with a be-careful-what-you-say look toward his wife of thirty years.

Miranda followed Ben then went on, "Victoria doesn't like her, Mr. Bramwell, and neither do I!"

Ben's eyes narrowed as he looked at the woman who'd been employed at Bramwell House since her youth. "How can you say such a thing, Miranda? Phoebe will make a wonderful mother for Victoria."

"You men can't see straight where a beautiful woman is concerned. Being beautiful won't make a woman a good mother. A good heart does. Maternal feelings don't come as naturally as those people who write those big relationship books would have you believe. Some women never have it, and I say Miss Phoebe

Vanderbur is one of them. She's too stuck on herself to be a good mother to our Victoria. She has no interest in that child. All she cares about is you, Ben." She shook a finger in her employer's face. "Mark my words. You marry that woman and you'll be sorry. She's nothing like Carlotta was. Are you in such a hurry to get married and bring a woman into this house that you can't see that?"

Max moved quickly to place a hand over his wife's mouth. "Miranda, you are way out of line." Then turning to Ben, he said apologetically, "Please forgive her. She's biased and overprotective where your daughter is concerned."

Miranda yanked her husband's hands away. "Yes, I *am* biased when it comes to Victoria and you had better be, too, Ben Bramwell. That child has already been through enough in her few years. That woman will—"

Max quickly clamped his hand tightly over her lips again. "Miranda!"

Ben stroked his chin thoughtfully. "I appreciate what you say, Miranda. I know you have our best interests at heart. I do value your opinion, and I want you to speak up anytime you have something you think I need to hear, but I must insist that you not speak negatively about Phoebe in my daughter's presence. Only to me. Is that clear?"

The woman stared at him with beady eyes. "Clear. But—"

Max shook his head and rolled his eyes. "Miranda! Stop!"

She turned toward her husband and waggled a finger at him. "Mark my words, both of you. Call it woman's intuition or call it meddling, but I see nothing but trouble if you marry that woman." With that, she spun around on her heels and went back into Victoria's room, her words hanging heavily in the air behind her.

"Sir—"

Ben held up his palm between them. "Forget it, Max. You, Miranda, and my mother are about the only people I know who really care about my daughter and me. And," he said good-naturedly as he cupped the man's shoulder, "I don't want you getting after Miranda for being truthful. Like I said, I value your opinions and I want to hear them anytime you feel I'm out of line with my life."

"But, sir, Miranda shouldn't—"

"Max! Didn't you hear me? Let Miranda have her say! You two may work for me, but you're like a second set of parents to me. You've taken the place of my dad since I lost him and my mom since she moved into the care home. Neither Victoria, nor I, could function without you two."

He moved back into the room to face his daughter, hoping she hadn't heard their conversation. "Isn't that right, honey? We love Miranda and Max, don't we, Victoria?"

For the first time, a slight smile broke across the slender lips as she barely nodded a response.

∞

Judy Alexander, alias Judy Smith, arose early despite the lateness of the hour when sleep had finally overtaken her busy, troubled mind. She had another problem to face. Thanks to her late aunt Margaret's generosity in her will, Judy could get along quite nicely without working for several years but, to keep from arousing suspicion, she needed to at least go through the motions of working like other women who were in the same boat and having to raise a child alone. Timmy hadn't been too keen on the idea of attending a strange school when she'd first mentioned it, so she'd decided homeschooling would solve that problem.

But how could she explain being home all day? One of her friends had worked at home for a national company that farmed out their customer service department to save the expense of maintaining office space. Yes, that was it. She could pretend to be working from home as a customer service representative. Good thing she'd brought her laptop with her. Now all she'd need would be a phone and an Internet hookup. It was the perfect answer. Having online access would also be a means of keeping tabs on the search for the man who'd killed her brother.

The aroma of pancakes browning in the skillet filled the kitchen as Timmy entered the room. He moved slowly to the table, his eyes still puffy from a good night's sleep, a frown on his face. "We're not gonna start homeschooling today, are we?"

The sad look on his face made her want to both laugh and cry. She placed the spatula on the spoon rest and gave his shoulder a pat. "Not today, but tomorrow for sure, so you'd better be ready. Trust me. It'll be fun. You'll like it."

His expression brightened as he sniffed the air. "Umm, pancakes. Can I have peanut butter on mine?"

Pulling the boy's slight frame toward her, she lightly tapped the face she loved. "If you want. Personally, I'd rather have warm maple syrup. But it's up to you."

Timmy grinned a silly grin. "Can I have both?"

"Together? At the same time?" She closed her eyes and crinkled her face. "Yuk!"

His small hand slid into hers. "It's good. You wanna try it?"

Stooping, she looked into the eyes of the child. "You miss them, don't you? Your mom and dad? As I recall, your dad liked peanut butter on his pancakes, too."

The small head dipped. "Uh-huh. I miss them really bad."

"Well, honey, remember, I love you, too, almost as much as your mother. And I know your mother wants to be with you, too, but she can't. God wanted her there with Him, and now your dad is with Him, too. Someday, in God's time, you'll be with them again." The sadness on his face ripped at her heart. He was so young. How was he ever supposed to understand why a loving God would take both his mother and his father from him? She'd been a Christian for years, yet she didn't understand it. How could she, or anyone, expect this eight-year-old boy to understand the mysteries of God's plan?

Judy shuddered, remembering the horrible day she'd lost her brother and the reason she and Timmy had been forced to leave Dallas. She had to be brave. Circumstances demanded it. But, right now, she didn't feel the least bit brave. Constant fear clutched at her day and night, strangling her with its grip.

Trying to put aside her fears for the boy's sake, she motioned toward a chair at the small table by the window. "You're such a good kid, Timmy. I'm so proud of you. Now, have a seat and I'll bring you your pancakes."

His eyes taking on a slight twinkle, Timmy sat down and tucked the napkin into the collar of his T-shirt. "Can I have my cookie first?"

With everything on her mind, she'd nearly forgotten. The chocolate chip cookie she'd promised the night before lay neatly wrapped in foil on the cabinet by the microwave. "I did promise you a cookie for breakfast, didn't I?" she asked with a loving nudge to his shoulder.

"Uh-huh. You did." Timmy reached for the foil packet and began to unwrap the cookie.

She smiled at the child. "Okay, the cookie is yours, but you have to promise to eat at least one pancake and drink a full glass of milk."

Timmy devoured the cookie then wadded up the foil and tossed it into the wastebasket. "That was good. But not as good as yours, Mama," he said with a grin.

"You remembered to call me Mama and I didn't even have to remind you! Remembering isn't easy, is it?"

He gave his head a shake then picked up his fork. "I'm ready for my pancake."

Judy pulled the lacy-edged pancake from the skillet and placed it on his plate then smeared the top with softened butter. "Sure you wouldn't prefer just syrup?"

He nodded. "Peanut butter *and* a little syrup, please."

The two had a pleasant breakfast. Judy did her best to sound cheerful. Timmy deserved it. Losing first his mom, then his dad, then being uprooted from his home was more than any child should have on his plate at his young age.

Timmy wiped at his mouth with the napkin then carried his dishes to the sink. Judy rinsed them and placed them on the rack in the dishwasher. "I know you'd rather go to school with your friends, but I promise I won't be too hard on you." She gave him a pat on his seat. "Now, go get dressed and we'll take a walk and check out the neighborhood."

∞

Ben kissed his daughter good-bye, grabbed his briefcase, and stepped out into the brisk morning air. The sun was shining brightly, foretelling a fall day designed to be enjoyed. As he headed around the house toward the garage, his gaze wandered up toward the window in the apartment where he'd seen the light burning late last night, and he wished he knew more about his new renters. *Why didn't I ask more questions before I rented that apartment to her? I didn't even see if she had references. Not that I think I did the wrong thing by renting to her, I'm just curious. Somehow, things don't quite add up.*

As he passed the apartment's downstairs door, he paused, wondering how the mother and son had fared their first night in their new place. He didn't have to wonder for long. The door opened and Timmy stepped out, followed by his beaming mother.

"Well, good morning, Mr. Bramwell. Isn't this a beautiful morning?" She pulled the door shut behind her and checked to make sure it locked before pushing the horn-rimmed glasses farther up her nose.

He tipped his head in acknowledgment. "Mrs. Smith. Timmy. Good morning to you."

"Timmy and I thought we'd take a walk."

Ben crawled into his car then fiddled with the knot on his tie. "I thought maybe you'd be enrolling Timmy in school this morning."

"Oh, didn't I tell you? Timmy is homeschooled. This is to be a nature walk. We'll be looking at the leaves and the trees, checking out the squirrels, the bushes, and flowers—that sort of thing."

"That's wonderful. Homeschooling has so many advantages. Victoria has a tutor, but I'm certain she won't learn as much from her as Timmy will from you."

Judy took Timmy's hand in hers. "Have a nice day, Mr. Bramwell."

"You, too, Mrs. Smith. Say, I have an idea. Why don't the two of you join my daughter and me for dinner tonight? We'll call it our get-acquainted dinner. To make up for last night."

Judy hesitated before answering, as if not sure getting acquainted was a good idea. "We—we wouldn't want to be a bother."

Ben was disappointed. "There's no way you could be a bother. Please say yes. Victoria has been rather down lately. I'm sure your presence will cheer her up. You must say you'll come." He jabbed Timmy lightly in the arm with his fist. "I'll even ask Miranda to fix hamburgers. Would you like that? She makes great burgers and terrific fries."

Timmy nodded with enthusiasm.

"Hamburgers and fries? You said the magic words. Timmy and I love hamburgers and fries, especially homemade ones." A smile curled at Judy's lips. "Okay. If you insist. What time?" Ben could feel himself smiling. After his conversation with Miranda and seeing how despondent his daughter seemed to be, he was hopeful meeting Timmy and Judy Smith would cheer her up. "Let's make it six, if that's good with you. I'm taking Victoria to see her grandmother this afternoon. I can hardly wait to tell Victoria you've agreed to come."

"We appreciate the invitation. Can we bring anything?"

"No. Not a thing. Believe me, Miranda will have plenty of food prepared. She loves company and, unfortunately, we've had very little since Victoria's mother died. But, please, call me Ben. Mr. Bramwell was my father's name."

"Ben, it is. If you'll call me Judy."

"Judy. Nice name. Short and sweet. I like it. See you tonight."

Judy and Timmy turned as a bright yellow Mercedes convertible whizzed into the driveway and pulled up alongside Ben's Porsche, its brakes screeching loudly as it came to an abrupt halt. Ben exchanged a few words with the driver, a beautiful blond, then waved at them and pulled out onto the street.

As the convertible made a U-turn in the driveway, Judy couldn't help staring at the driver—a woman attractive enough to grace the runways of the world's leading fashion houses. The woman stared back, her somber expression never changing even though Judy offered a friendly smile. She wondered who the woman was and why she was coming to Bramwell house. Could she be Ben's fiancée?

Chapter 3

Judy and Timmy arrived at the front door of Bramwell House at precisely six o'clock. She gave the boy a nod. "Okay, push the doorbell."

Max opened the door and stepped back to let them in. "Mr. Bramwell is bringing Victoria down from her room. Make yourselves comfortable in the living room. They'll be here shortly."

The two moved through the huge marble foyer into the pale blue of the formal living room where they found themselves surrounded by lovely period furniture that seemed to welcome them with its plush softness and the warm glow of several tall lamps topped by white pleated shades.

"Wow." Timmy ran fingertips over a shiny tabletop before scooting himself into a luxuriously upholstered wingback chair. "This is nice, isn't it, Au—Mama?" He blushed at his near error.

Judy stood in the middle of the room, mesmerized by its beauty, ignoring Timmy's near miss. She'd seen homes like this in magazines but never had she personally been in one this magnificent. "Nice isn't the word for it, Timmy. I—I can't even think of a word to describe it." So caught up was she, she didn't hear her host enter the room.

"So, you like my home?" Ben Bramwell asked as he stood in the huge arched doorway holding his frail daughter in his arms. "My wife did the decorating. She had an eye for color."

"I'd say she did," Judy agreed, feeling embarrassed that she'd been caught gawking in such an unbecoming way. "It's lovely."

"I'd like to introduce you to Victoria, my daughter, the light of my life."

Dragging Timmy with her, Judy walked quickly to join him. "It's nice to meet you, Victoria. This is my son, Timmy."

The young girl smiled sweetly but continued to hug her father's neck, ignoring Judy's extended hand. "Hi," she responded in a timid whisper.

"Your father invited us to dinner. I hope you don't mind." Somehow Judy got the feeling Ben's daughter was slightly less enthused about their presence than he was. "Timmy and I were eager to meet you."

"And Victoria was eager to meet you, too, weren't you, baby?" Ben gave his daughter a little squeeze as if to encourage her response.

"Yes," she said simply as she clung to her father's neck.

Why is he carrying her? Judy wondered as she watched father and daughter. *She's got to be about Timmy's age, and I certainly couldn't carry him around.*

"Well, I'm sure Miranda has dinner ready. Shall we go into the dining room?" Ben pivoted around and headed across the gleaming marble foyer.

Judy grabbed Timmy's hand and hurried to keep up with him.

"Why is her daddy carrying her?" Timmy whispered as he leaned close.

She gave him a be-quiet look and whispered back, "I don't know. Maybe she has a sore foot."

A gasp escaped Judy's lips as she followed Ben Bramwell into the formal dining room, all done in shades of pastel pink with a majestic crystal chandelier that splintered thousands of prisms of light in every direction across the magnificently furnished room. But it was not the room that made her gasp—it was what was sitting in the middle of the thickly carpeted floor.

A wheelchair, and Ben was lowering his daughter into it.

"I'm sorry, I—I didn't know," she stammered as she stared at the little girl being strapped into the chair.

"I should have told you," he explained quickly.

She hurried to Victoria's side, dropped down beside her, and began stroking the child's hand as it rested on the chair's padded arm. "Victoria, it is so nice to finally be able to meet you. Your daddy talks about you all the time."

Timmy stood frozen to the spot, his mouth gaping. Judy wasn't sure he'd ever known a child who used a wheelchair and didn't know if he'd make Victoria feel self-conscious by staring.

Victoria offered a weak smile, then covered her face with her hands.

"She's not being rude. She's just very shy." Ben pushed the little girl's chair up to the dining room table, which was set with a huge fresh flower centerpiece and four colorful tapestry place mats. "She doesn't talk much. Not even to me."

"Or me!" Miranda chimed in as she entered the room carrying a huge tray filled with luscious-looking hamburgers and fries, their enticing aroma filling the air. "This wee one is a sweetie, but she doesn't have much to say, do you, pumpkin?" She lowered the tray to the table then moved to place a napkin across the diminutive girl's lap.

Victoria peeked through her hands and gave Miranda a little grin, obviously meant only for her.

"But she's my girl!" the woman declared as she began removing the delicious-looking food from the tray and placing it on the plates on the highly polished tabletop. "I love this girl just like I do her father." She pointed an arthritic finger toward Ben. "That man right there—he was nothing like Victoria. He was an ornery young 'un, let me tell you."

Ben gave her arm a gentle swat. "Now, Miranda. Be careful what you say. My daughter thinks I was a perfect child. Don't burst her bubble."

"Perfect? Huh! Adorable maybe but, Ben Bramwell, take it from me, you were far from a perfect child. Shall I tell them about the gerbils?" She faced him squarely with her hands on her ample hips. "Or about the plastic snake in my flour bin?"

He put his finger to his lips. "Quiet, woman, or I'll call Max to take care of you."

"Did I hear my name?" Max entered the room toting an armload of colorful balloons filled with helium, which he began tying to the arm of each chair.

"Naw, Ben was just babbling, as usual." Miranda placed a big platter of sliced pickles, cheese, and fresh tomatoes in the center of the table.

Max gave his wife a stern look. "Really, Miranda. Must you talk about Ben that way? In front of the children?"

Ben responded with a hearty belly laugh as he grabbed his napkin and draped it across his lap. "Give up, Max. You've never been able to control our dear Miranda. What makes you think you can now? That woman will speak her piece anytime, anywhere. You should know that by now."

As the three bantered back and forth, Judy and Timmy watched and listened. And occasionally, even Victoria offered a smile. Eventually, Ben held up his hand for silence. "Enough of this. I think we'd better bow our heads and thank the Lord for our food."

Judy's heart sang as she listened to Ben pray. Though she couldn't understand why God had allowed her brother to die, she still loved the Lord with all her heart and was thrilled to know her landlord did, too. Her heart rejoiced whenever she met another Christian.

The big grilled hamburgers were good. Ben devoured two of them while his guests each struggled to consume one. Even Victoria nibbled away at her burger and seemed to enjoy it. Besides the burgers and fries there were baked beans and potato salad, the best Judy had ever tasted. She promised herself to ask Miranda for the recipes when she got to know her better, knowing some cooks were reluctant to share their culinary secrets. Somehow she suspected the congenial Miranda didn't fit into that category.

"Let's have our dessert in the TV room," Ben suggested when their plates had been cleared away. "I think the children will enjoy the new video I bought today."

Judy glanced at her watch. "It won't take long, will it? Timmy has to be in bed by eight."

"We have plenty of time. It's not a full-length movie." Ben stepped behind his daughter's wheelchair and began to push it across the room, motioning them to follow.

The TV room proved to be a massive audio-video center, complete with surround sound and individual chairs equipped with headphones. Once the foursome were seated, Miranda entered with a tray bearing big frosty mugs of ice cream topped with chilled root beer.

"Ooh," Judy sighed as her mug was handed to her. "This looks sinfully caloric. I'm not sure I should—"

Ben cupped his hand on her arm. "Please, Judy. Indulge with us. This is a special night. We're celebrating. I told you, we rarely have company."

She looked quickly toward Victoria who was holding her mug between her palms and sipping slowly on her straw while eyeing Judy's reaction. "Okay. Just this once; but I'll have to walk around the block six times tomorrow to make up for it."

Ben grinned and took a swig of the cold, sweet liquid. "Um, good. Just like Miranda used to fix me when I was a boy. Only my mother and father didn't know about these root beer concoctions of hers. We kept it a secret, didn't we, Miranda?"

With a wink, the cook tweaked his arm. "Tattletale."

He grabbed his daughter's frail-looking wrist playfully. "If Miranda tries to ply you with root beer floats behind your old dad's back, you come and tell me, okay?"

Victoria dipped her head with a slight smile and only nodded.

Ben gave her a wink. "Okay, everyone, here comes the video."

He was right; it wasn't a movie. It was a documentary designed for children, about all kinds of baby animals. While it wasn't a cartoon, it was funny and the two children laughed at the animals' antics. Victoria's laughter seemed to please her father immensely as he watched her with eyes filled with love and pride. Too soon it ended.

"We have to go home, Ben." Judy smiled to herself. She'd only been in the apartment one night and already she'd called it home. "We've had a great time. Thank you for inviting us."

"Our pleasure, wasn't it, Victoria?" He lifted the little girl from the padded chair and hugged her to him then led the way through the house to the front door where he handed her to Max.

"We'll say good night now, Victoria." Judy kissed the little girl's cheek as she lay in Max's arms. "You and your daddy must come and have supper with us soon."

"Okay," the child whispered so softly it was barely audible.

"Bye, Tory," Timmy said as Judy gently took hold of his arm and moved through the open doorway.

"I'm going to walk you to your door." Ben pushed a handful of the brightly colored balloons into Timmy's hand. "Here, Timmy, take these with you."

"Thanks!"

"Ben, you needn't walk us home. Stay with Victoria." She and Timmy tried to move past Ben but he cut them off.

"My mother taught me to be a gentleman. I *am* going to walk you to your door, whether you like it or not." His smile was infectious. Judy couldn't help smiling back.

"Okay, if Victoria doesn't mind." She glanced back at the child who was evidently more interested in the handful of balloons Max had given her than her father's presence.

Ben took her hand and slid it into the crook of his arm. "She doesn't mind in the least."

Timmy scurried on ahead of them, skipping and dipping as he went, allowing the balloons to soar in the wind and then pulling them back. When they were halfway across the yard, the familiar yellow sports car whirled into the long driveway, its headlights splaying across the lawn and coming to rest on the three of them as the car pulled up and stopped, and the blond woman Judy had seen earlier stepped out.

"Well, Ben," she said with a bittersweet tone as she flipped her long hair over one shoulder. "I thought you were staying in tonight to have dinner with your daughter. I hadn't realized you were having company."

She was as pretty in the soft glow of the yard lights as she'd been in the daylight hours, her coral jumpsuit emphasizing her slim waist and the curve of her hips. Despite Judy's good figure, she felt frumpy in the suave woman's presence.

Ben released his grip on his guest's arm and moved to take the woman's hand in his. "Phoebe, I thought you were at your parents' home tonight."

"I was. Earlier. But I was on my way home and figured Victoria would be in bed by this time and you and I could spend some time together. We have so much to talk about." She gave a sideways glance toward Judy and Timmy. "But I see you have guests."

"I'm sorry," Ben apologized quickly, as if realizing the two women hadn't yet been introduced. "Phoebe Vanderbur, this is Judy Smith and her son, Timmy. Remember? I told you they'd moved into my mother's apartment over the garage."

The socialite grabbed onto Ben's arm possessively, sidling up to him. It was obvious Phoebe Vanderbur didn't appreciate Judy's close proximity to Ben. "Oh, hello," she said coolly, her eyes scanning his new renter from head to toe. "I'm sure you won't mind if I take my Benny away from you. We're engaged, you know, and we simply must discuss some important decisions about our wedding."

Judy watched the twosome, a little amused at Ben's predicament. Had he purposely not introduced her as his fiancée, or had he actually forgotten about it? *Get a grip*, Judy told herself. *Why should he tell me anything? We barely know one another, certainly not well enough to discuss such personal things.*

"Stay here with Miss Vanderbur, Ben," Judy finally managed to say. "Timmy and I'll be okay. And thank you for a lovely evening."

"We'll have to do it again sometime."

Phoebe rolled her eyes. "Yes, Ben. Next time, you'll have to invite me. After all, I am your fiancée."

As Judy watched the young woman clinging to Ben's arm tightly enough to cut off the circulation, she could actually feel the chill the attractive woman was sending her way. "It was nice meeting you, Miss Vanderbur," she said, trying to make her voice sound enthusiastic.

"Soon to be Mrs. Bramwell," Phoebe injected coyly as she pulled Ben to her and kissed him fully on the lips.

"Well then, I guess congratulations are in order," Judy conceded, backing away and taking Timmy with her. Phoebe Vanderbur was not at all the kind of woman she'd expected Ben's fiancée to be.

Ben unwound himself from Phoebe's grasp. "I'm sorry, Phoebe. It was just an impromptu hamburger and fries dinner with the children. I know how you hate hamburgers." Ben smiled at his tenant. "But they were good, weren't they, Mrs. Smith?"

Judy grinned, knowing his words irritated his fiancée. "Yes, they were wonderful. Big, fat, juicy hamburgers, nicely browned fries, and smoky baked beans."

Phoebe grimaced as she turned to her fiancé with a look of abhorrence. "That is disgusting. How could you eat such ridiculous food? It makes me sick to think about it."

"And guess what we had for dessert?" Judy added, enjoying the jealous reaction of the haughty woman. "Big, thick root beer and ice cream floats in frosty mugs. Um, they were good, too. Weren't they, Ben?"

"Ben, you drank that awful thing? With all that butterfat and sugar?" Phoebe's free hand flew to her mouth, her other hand still holding a death grip on Ben's arm. "How could you? And you let Victoria drink that sugar-laden stuff, too? What were you thinking?"

Ben gave her a sheepish grin. "It was a special occasion, Phoebe."

"Oh? A birthday? Or a stock market coup?" she asked, her voice returning to its original sticky sweetness as her fingers ran seductively down Ben's arm and she gazed into his eyes. "And you didn't invite your Phoebe?"

Ben seemed uncomfortable as he struggled to put a little space between the two of them. "Neither, Phoebe. It was to welcome Mrs. Smith and her son to Bramwell House."

Judy took her cue from the penetrating look in the woman's eyes and decided it truly was time for them to exit. "Timmy and I will say good night now. Again, it was nice to meet you, Miss Vanderbur." She turned to Ben who was still being held hostage in his fiancée's grip. "And, Ben, thank you for a lovely evening."

As she and Timmy strolled up the walk toward the garage apartment she heard Phoebe's angry voice chastising Ben for not inviting her to their party, and she wondered how Victoria felt about having a new stepmother. Especially one like Phoebe. If there was anything Phoebe Vanderbur wasn't, it was mother material.

Once Timmy was tucked in for the night, Judy turned out the lights, moved to the window, and separated the curtains. The yellow sports car was still parked in the driveway. No doubt Phoebe was in the house with Ben, probably chattering at him a mile a minute. What an unlikely pair. Surely a man of his stature and standing could do better than that Phoebe woman. She seemed so—shallow. Yes, that was the word for it. Shallow. All tinsel and no tree!

Later, with a cup of hot tea and one of Miranda's chocolate chip cookies balanced on a saucer, Judy made her way into the living room and watched the ten o'clock news, all the while thinking about the improbable couple next door. And she thought about little Victoria. That child needed a mother, but not one like Phoebe Vanderbur. She couldn't help smiling as a thought made its way into her brain. What would God think of her if she attempted to pray that woman out of Ben's life?

When the news ended, Judy pressed the power button on the remote and headed for her bedroom, but the slamming of a car door and her curiosity took her once again to the window. There, in the dim glow of the yard light, she caught sight of Ben and Phoebe saying good night. She knew she shouldn't be watching them but even though she felt like a voyeur, she couldn't pull herself away from the window. She watched as Phoebe wrapped herself about him and kissed him with all her might. Did Judy imagine it or was Ben holding back? All the action seemed to be on the blond woman's part. When the headlights finally came on and the convertible wound its way down the lane, Ben stood watching as if fixed to the spot, his hands in his pockets. Judy pulled down the shade and flipped on the light on her nightstand. How could a wonderful man like Ben fall for a superficial woman like Phoebe? Hopefully, he would consider the impact marrying someone like her would have on his daughter and reconsider before it was too late.

She kicked off her shoes, pulled her pajamas from the closet, and was ready to move into the bathroom to cleanse her face when she heard a noise downstairs, then a slight rap on the door. Her hand flew to her mouth in fear.

Judy held her breath. Maybe she'd imagined the nearly inaudible noise. Moving stealthily across the carpeted floor to the door at the head of the stairs, she checked the dead bolt again. It was locked. She knew it would be. It was the first thing she did anytime she entered the apartment.

Pressing her ear to the door she listened and waited, her heart pounding wildly. Was this the moment she'd dreaded? The moment she and Timmy would be found?

Silence.

Deciding the noise had to have been her overactive imagination, she took a deep breath and headed for her bedroom. She had to get over this. She and Timmy were safe in Memphis. No one could have located them this quickly.

Then she heard it again!

A rap on the downstairs door.

Someone *was* there!

A frightened gasp escaped her trembling lips. Should she call Ben? What could he do? She couldn't expect a near stranger to come running to her aid, and calling him might put him in jeopardy, too. She could never do that to him—or to Victoria. What would that child do if anything happened to her father after losing her mother like she had? Her heart clenched within her chest and knotted into a tight ball.

Maybe she should call the police. But wasn't that the very thing she was trying to avoid? Bringing the police into their lives?

Terror seized her, and she began to shake uncontrollably as she broke out in a cold sweat. She had to do something. But what? She couldn't cower behind the door all night with a butcher knife in her hand, waiting for the dawn.

There! Another rap, this one more pronounced.

She had to take charge. Do something.

The intercom.

Warily she moved to the wall beside the door and pressed the button, asking in a shaking, halting voice, "Who's there? Answer me this minute or I'm going to call the police."

"Whoa, it's me, Judy. Ben Bramwell. I hope I didn't frighten you, but I saw your light on and. . ."

Her eyelids closed tightly as her body went weak with relief. It was Ben?

"I thought maybe you'd fix me a cup of coffee."

Relieved but still trembling, she pressed the button. "Sure. Yes. Coffee. Come on up."

"Do you mind if I use my key, or would you prefer to come down and let me in?"

"Use your key down there," she moaned softly. "I'll open the upper door for you." It was difficult turning the dead bolt with shaking hands but she finally managed.

"I saw your fiancée drive away," she confessed, feeling a little embarrassed that she'd admitted it. "I happened to be looking out the window—I wasn't spying on you. Honest. I. . ." She wished she hadn't mentioned it. Her words were jumbled and she knew it. What must he think of her?

A broad smile crept across his face. "I'm not keeping you up, am I?"

"No. I was just about to get ready for bed. I—I watched the news."

"I really don't need the coffee if you don't have any made. I guess what I really wanted was to talk—about Victoria. About Phoebe."

She tugged her sweater about her as she felt a chill course through her body. "I'll make the coffee. I could use a cup, too."

He followed her as she moved into the little kitchen, sitting down at the table. "I don't know why I'm bothering you like this. It's just that I'm concerned about Victoria and she seemed to warm up to you, which is rare for her. That's something she hasn't done since. . ." His head dipped, and he looked away.

"Since she lost her mother?"

"Yes."

"And you're worried about bringing another woman in to take her mother's place?"

Ben glanced at the coffeepot as the water surged through it and it began to gurgle. "Yes, to be honest, I'm terribly worried. It's been over a year since Victoria's mother died, and I'm concerned about my baby. You're one of the few people I know who realize how hard it is on a child to lose their parent. You've seen her. She barely talks to anyone. She doesn't eat. She stays in her room most of the time. Judy, I'm at my wit's end. You're a mother. You and your son seem to have such a great relationship. I desperately need your advice."

Judy nearly strangled at his words. She hadn't functioned as a single mother until shortly before she and Timmy came to Memphis. How could she offer him advice? "I—I think you need to talk to a professional, Ben."

"I have. Many times; but none of them seemed to be able to help."

When the coffee finished dripping, Judy filled two mugs and placed them on the place mats. "Sugar? Cream?"

He shook his head. "Black, thanks."

"It's really none of my business, Ben," she began as she seated herself beside him and cradled her mug between her palms. "But I was wondering. Has Victoria been in a wheelchair all her life?"

Ben's fingertip slowly traced the rim around the top of his mug. "No. Only this past year. Victoria was with her mother in the car when it went over the embankment. My wife died instantly. My daughter lived, but a number of bones were broken in her legs."

"Oh, how awful." She wished she hadn't asked; the wounded look on his face made her want to cry. *How sad,* Judy thought as she gazed at him, *that he and his daughter have suffered such a loss.* "Is there any hope for her? Will she ever walk again? Can they operate?"

Ben's hand moved to the dark shadow of his emerging beard, his fingers stroking it thoughtfully. "No one knows. I've taken her to a number of specialists, and they all say the same thing. There seems to be no physical reason why she doesn't walk. She's been through several surgeries and numerous physical therapy sessions, but other than her leg muscles being weak from not using them—"

"They think she doesn't want to walk?"

He lifted the mug to his lips and sipped slowly before answering. "They haven't been that blunt with their diagnosis, but basically, yes. A physical therapist still comes in three times a week to exercise her legs but she's always uncooperative, refusing to do what he tells her. The therapist ends up doing all the work, and she just lies there. It's very frustrating for both him and me. I don't know what to do. I've even taken her to a well-known psychiatrist. He says perhaps she was so traumatized by the accident and losing her mother that, mentally, she has decided she can't walk. I'm inclined to agree with him. For some unknown reason, my prayers on her behalf have gone unanswered."

"How does she get along with Phoebe?" she prodded carefully, wondering if she was treading on forbidden ground.

"She doesn't. That's it, pure and simple. She won't talk to Phoebe. She won't even have dinner with the two of us. She stays in her room when Phoebe comes to the house."

Judy pursed her lips and stared off into space before commenting, not wanting to offend this man who had opened his heart to her. "Have you considered the fact that Victoria might never accept Phoebe?"

Her words seemed to challenge his innermost thoughts. "Yes. I've considered that. I'm afraid that might be a distinct possibility."

Now what could she say? Should she tell him if he valued his relationship with his daughter he'd better break off his engagement to Phoebe? That if he didn't, he could be facing a miserable future of being torn between his wife and child? Actually, if she were honest, she would admit she didn't care much for Phoebe herself. She could sympathize with the child. The young socialite was as shallow as a pond with a leak. In her opinion, anyone who would believe Phoebe would ever put that tiny girl in first place in her life needed counseling.

Ben leaned back in his chair, grabbed the coffeepot from the countertop then, without asking, refilled Judy's cup before filling his own. "Do—do you think I should try to postpone our wedding? Give the two a chance to get better acquainted first?"

"Do you honestly think that would help? How long has Victoria known Phoebe?"

With the mug held securely between his hands, Ben met her gaze with a worried look. "She's always known Phoebe. Her father and I are partners in our architectural firm."

"Oh?" Judy was suddenly more concerned than ever. Had there been something going on between the two when Ben's wife was alive? Had the child suspected? Is that why she didn't like the woman?

He held up both palms and shook his head. "It's not what you're thinking. I loved my wife and although I've known Phoebe most of my life, I'd never had any feelings for her, other than that of a friend, until about six months ago. She was so good to me when Carlotta died, helping me answer the hundreds of letters and condolence cards I received, accompanying me to the hospital to be with Victoria, popping in here at the house daily to see if I needed anything, encouraging me to pick up my life and live again when I felt I couldn't go on. I owe her a lot."

And I'll bet she reminds you of that debt often, Judy thought as she listened to the troubled man talk. "So, were she and Victoria friends before the accident?"

He shook his head. "No. For some reason, Victoria has never liked Phoebe. Even when her mother was alive."

Smart kid, Judy reasoned. *She must have felt the same vibes I'm feeling. I don't like Phoebe Vanderbur, either. And I sure don't think she's right for the position of Mrs. Ben Bramwell. I've only known her for a day, but I've got that woman's number.*

He continued. "Actually, I never even thought of marrying again until Phoebe brought it up."

Judy stiffened and gave him an incredulous look. "She brought it up?"

"Well, her father actually, but she agreed. We were all at Carson Hills Country Club having dinner one night and I was telling them how withdrawn Victoria had become, how she stayed in her room most of the time and hated to come out, even for meals. Malcolm, Phoebe's father, said he thought the best thing for my daughter would be to have a mother again. Phoebe thought so, too, and the next thing I knew, they were talking about the two of us getting married."

"And you agreed? Just like that? Oh, Ben, what were you thinking?" She bit her tongue to keep from saying the rest of the things she'd like to have said. What right did she have to pry into his personal life this way, throwing out advice like she knew what she was talking about? "Sorry, I'm way out of line here. I barely know the two of you, and I'm being judgmental." She leaned back in her chair and watched for his reaction. She wouldn't blame him if he stormed out and told her to mind her own business.

But he barely reacted at all, just stared into his empty coffee cup. "You needn't be sorry. I'm the one who allowed myself to get into this situation. You see, I greatly respect Malcolm. He's been like a father to me since I lost my own father, but the man is blind when it comes to his only daughter. I guess I'm that way with Victoria."

"You haven't said. Is Phoebe a Christian? Does she love the Lord like you do?"

"She thinks she's a Christian because she's a good person. I've tried to explain the way of salvation to her, but she refuses to talk about anything that has to do with sin."

"Then maybe marrying her isn't too wise. You'll only be compounding your problems."

"I know you're right, but Victoria needs a mother." He rose to his feet, placed his cup in the sink, and absentmindedly filled it with water before leaning against the counter and crossing his arms over his chest. "I don't love Phoebe, Judy, but I have to admit I am lonesome for a loving, dedicated husband and wife relationship. I guess I've deceived myself into thinking I could have that kind of relationship with Phoebe. There aren't many women like my Carlotta. Phoebe says she doesn't expect me to love her, that she'll be content just being my wife. I guess you could call our pending marriage one of convenience. I'll get a mother for my daughter, and Phoebe will get a husband who can escort her to the many social functions she attends."

Judy rose to her feet and impetuously moved to stand directly in front of her guest. Looking squarely into his eyes, she took his hand in hers. "You can't marry for that reason, Ben. It's wrong! Think what God's Word has to say about marriage. You'll never be happy in that kind of arrangement. Neither will Victoria. You can't force a mother on her, no matter how badly you think she needs one. Especially one who doesn't share your faith. Oh, Ben, you are in for big trouble if you marry for the wrong reasons."

"But you've seen my daughter, Judy. You've seen how withdrawn she is. If she doesn't need a mother, what does she need? I've had her to every specialist worth his salt in Memphis. No one seems to be able to reach her. I'm willing to do anything—even marry Phoebe, if necessary. Giving her a mother is the one thing I haven't tried."

"Then, let me try." The words slipped out before her brain had a chance to consider the consequences.

"You?"

It was too late to retract her words; they'd already escaped. "Yes, me. Me and Timmy. Maybe we can reach her."

"How? No one else has been able to."

She released his hand and walked past the little table into the living room. "I can't explain why, but the more I hear you talk about your daughter, the more I think I can understand what Victoria is going through. I know Timmy can." She gestured toward the sofa. "Have a seat while I check on Timmy, and I'll explain. Okay?"

He nodded then seated himself in the corner of the comfortable sofa.

Within seconds, Judy moved back into the room and sat down beside him. If she was going to help him, she'd have to leave out much of the truth and tell big lies about some of the important parts. Each day she was finding it more and more difficult to keep track of the lies she was telling and whom she was telling them to. Hopefully, her charade would end soon.

"I—I haven't told you why Timmy and I moved to Memphis." She selected her words carefully. She couldn't give away too much. "Timmy's father was a successful salesman for a large pharmaceutical firm and he traveled all over the states to visit his clients. In the summertime, when school was out, we traveled with him. Many times to Memphis. I knew he had a weak heart, but with the medication the doctor had him on, he got along fine. Until about three months ago. He was here in Memphis when he was hit with a massive heart attack. Timmy and I flew here as quickly as we could and were able to spend two days with him, but he left us."

Ben slid an arm around her shoulders. "I am so sorry, Judy. I had no idea you'd lost him that quickly, and here I'm burdening you with my problems."

He was buying her story. Oh, some of it was true. Jerod, Timmy's father, had died three months ago, but not of a heart attack. He had been shot. And he wasn't her husband. Jerod was her brother. "Jerod was the kindest, most thoughtful man I've ever known. The perfect husband and the perfect father."

Visions of standing by her only brother's body at the funeral home as it lay in the casket flooded her mind and a tear slid down her cheek. "We miss him terribly."

Ben's arm about her tightened, his firm but gentle hand nudging her head onto his shoulder. "I'm so sorry, Judy. I know you miss him. There's nothing as horrible as losing the spouse you love."

She leaned into the security of his warm body and felt his head on hers, and she wished she could stay there forever. It'd been years since she'd allowed herself to get this close to a man. But Ben Bramwell was no ordinary man.

She lifted misty eyes to his. "Now do you see why I think Timmy and I might be able to reach Victoria? We've been there, too. We understand her pain because we've experienced it. At least it's worth a try."

His eyes met hers and he bent slightly, allowing his lips to graze her forehead. "You may be right."

She knew she should move away. He was so close she could feel the drumming of his heart, feel his breath on her cheeks. Instead she sat there, enjoying the nearness and wondering what it would be like to be married to a man as sweet and considerate as Ben.

"You're probably one of the few people who understand what Victoria and I have been going through. I'm one of those romantic kind of guys who has to have someone in their life to love and care for, and. . ."

His words stopped.

Neither of them moved.

"Judy?"

"Yes."

Without warning, his lips sought hers and he kissed her, his touch barely grazing her lips. It was the kind of kiss you would bestow upon the cheek of a child who'd fallen and hurt his knee, but to Judy it was much more.

She held her breath, not wanting to break the spell of this amazing, unexpected moment. Whether he'd done it out of sympathy or because he simply wanted to, she didn't care. All she knew was Ben's lips had touched hers and she never wanted the moment to end.

But the kiss that soon followed the first one was not the kind you would bestow upon a child. It was the kind of kiss young lovers steal when they first begin courting. The kind of kiss that makes your toes curl and your heart flutter. Ben Bramwell's kiss made her heart race with desire. The desire for another and another.

But this was madness. Whether he loved Phoebe or not, the two were engaged. And when you're engaged, you can't go around kissing other people like that.

Feeling a blush rise to her cheeks, Judy forced herself to pull back, her fingers touching her lips. "I—I think you'd better go. It's late."

Ben stood awkwardly to his feet, his cheeks flushed, his hair slightly mussed, as he attempted to apologize. "I'm so sorry, I—"

"It's—it's okay," she countered, tugging errant curls about her face. "We're both—lonely, that's all."

Without another word, Ben backed out of the room and disappeared down the stairway, leaving her alone with her thoughts as she recalled the thrill of their kiss. "Ben Bramwell," she said aloud once she heard the downstairs door close and the lock engage, "that wasn't the kiss of a man who is about to marry another woman! If my life weren't in such a mess right now, I'd give that Phoebe a challenge she'd not soon forget. You're too good for her, Ben. You deserve so much more. Someone who could love you like. . ." She swallowed hard. "Like I could! Don't settle for second best."

Drawing back the drapes on her bedroom window, she watched him cross the yard to the mansion, wishing things were different.

Wishing she could tell him of the love that filled her heart.

∞

When Ben reached the porch, he turned, looked up at her window, and waved.

She waved back.

In the dim glow of the yard light he could see her face framed in the window and he thought about their kiss. "Whatever possessed me to do such a thing?" he wondered aloud as he pulled the ring of keys from his pocket and inserted them in the lock of the big oak door. "I'm not an impulsive man. Normally, I think things through before taking any action. Yet, look what I just did! I kissed a woman I barely know, and I'm engaged. What's happening to me?"

He moved into the big marble foyer and headed for the circular stairs.

"You okay?"

Miranda's voice startled him, and he felt like a schoolboy sneaking into his own house. "I'm fine, Miranda. What are you doing up at this hour?"

"I forgot to put the roast out to thaw for tomorrow's dinner. I supposed you were already in bed sound asleep. You scared me when I saw that door open." The woman straightened the pink satin nightcap she was wearing then pulled her chenille robe tightly around her. "Didn't Max lock up?"

"Yeah, he did. I used my key. I was outside—getting a little air." He gave her a slight wave and continued up the stairs, not wanting to pursue this conversation any further.

He paused at the landing then moved quietly toward a sliver of light peeking out from under one of the bedroom doors. When he pushed it open, there was Victoria, propped up on a pile of pillows and she was staring at the portrait of her mother that hung on the wall across from her bed. "Can't sleep?" he asked in a whisper as he slid onto the bed beside her and kissed her tiny cheek. Her frailness frightened him.

"No."

"Tummy upset from that hamburger?" he prodded gently.

The diminutive child shook her head.

"What then?"

She pointed to the picture. "I was thinking about my mommy."

"We both miss your mommy, baby." He gazed at the lovely image of his wife, so like his daughter.

"Daddy, don't marry her."

He turned to face his little munchkin. "Phoebe? Why?"

"I don't like her, Daddy. And she doesn't like me."

"Oh, sweetie, she likes you. She's always telling me she wants to be your mother."

The little girl began to cry. "I don't want her to be my mother. I don't like her, Daddy. Please! Don't marry her!"

As Ben Bramwell gathered the tiny body in his arms, he remembered the advice of the woman he'd kissed so unexpectedly only minutes before. *You can't marry for that reason, Ben. It's wrong. You'll never be happy in that kind of arrangement. Neither will Victoria. You can't force a mother on her, no matter how badly you think she needs one. Oh, Ben, you are in for big trouble if you marry for the wrong reasons.*

In his heart, he knew she was right. But was it too late to turn back now? Their engagement had already been announced.

Chapter 4

"Hey, young man, what are you and your mother doing this fine Saturday morning?" Ben asked as he opened the door, stooped to shake hands with Timmy, and eyed the woman standing silently at his side.

Timmy grinned. "Can Tory come up to our apartment and watch cartoons with me? Me and my—mom are going to have spaghetti for lunch and we want her to eat with us, too. Can she come?"

"I don't think she'll say yes, but why don't you come in and ask her yourself?" Ben stepped out of their way and called out, "Victoria, you have company."

Tiny hands moved the small wheelchair into the foyer.

"It's me, Tory. I want you to come and watch cartoons with us. And eat spaghetti."

"I can't," the child offered weakly.

"Yes you can," Timmy countered as he hurried to the chair and began to push it in the direction of the door. "My mama said she'd carry you piggyback. You won't even need your chair. Come on, please?"

Victoria glanced at her father then gave Timmy a smile. "Can I, Daddy?"

Ben moved forward, surprise blanketing his face. "Of course, honey. You'll have a great time. Here, let me carry you."

Victoria shook her head. "I want Judy to carry me. Piggyback."

Grinning, Judy stepped around Ben and lifted the child's frail body from the chair, handed her to Ben, and turning instructed, "Put her on my back, please."

Ben, still stunned by his daughter's quick acceptance, did as he was told and soon the little girl was clinging to Judy's neck with all her might. "Are you sure you can make it?" he asked with concern.

Judy turned to him with a laugh. "With this tiny bundle? How weak do you think I am?"

"Hurry or we'll miss my favorite cartoon!" Taking the lead, Timmy headed for the door.

Ben followed close at their heels. "You will call me if you need anything, won't you?"

Judy turned her face toward him with a confident smile as she shifted the

49

child's position on her back. "Ben, we'll be fine. Relax. She'll just be next door."

He stepped into the open doorway and watched them go, utterly amazed that his daughter would let a near-stranger take her from the security of her home. "I'll bring her chair!" he called out.

"Forget it. We won't be needing it," Judy answered with a giggle. "We'll manage just fine without it."

∞

"Hang on, Tory," Timmy called out in his childlike voice as he gripped the handrail on the stairs leading to their apartment. "Don't wiggle or my mom might drop you."

"Don't listen to him, Victoria. I would never drop you." As Judy spoke, she felt the child's legs slightly tighten around her waist.

"I was just teasing," Timmy said, turning to watch them when he reached the landing. "Don't be scared, Tory."

She carried the little girl into the living room and plopped her onto the sofa. "There you go, little one. Safe and sound and I didn't drop you, did I?"

Timmy ran and bounced himself down beside his new friend, nearly landing in her lap. "Did you believe me when I said she'd drop you?"

"I knew you were teasing, Timmy." For the first time since they'd met the little girl, she actually said a complete sentence and laughed out loud. Not a slight obligatory chortle but a full-blown, hee-haw type laugh. Both Judy and Timmy stared at her with amazement and satisfaction.

Earlier, they'd discussed what they would do if Victoria didn't enjoy her visit to their apartment. After all, Ben said she rarely left the safety and sanctuary of her home. They'd wondered if she'd pout, demand to be taken home, have them call her father to come after her if she felt the least bit uncomfortable, or simply wouldn't like hanging out with them. Hearing her laugh set them both at ease in what otherwise could have been an uncomfortable and awkward situation.

"Have you had breakfast, Victoria? I was just about to make some for Timmy and me." *Of course, she's had breakfast,* Judy reasoned to herself. *With a doting father and two concerned servants to watch over her, there is no way their charge would have escaped breakfast in Bramwell House.*

Victoria ducked her head shyly. "Yes. But I didn't eat it. I—wasn't hungry."

"Well, I'm going to fix eggs in a basket. Can I fix you some?" Judy assessed the tiny body, remembering how light she'd been when she'd carried her up the stairs on her back. "Timmy loves eggs in a basket, don't you, Timmy?"

Timmy continued to bounce on the sofa, taking the frail child with him on each rise and fall. "Yum, yum, yes. Eggs in a basket are my favorite. Want some, Tory? They're good."

Victoria answered with a puzzled look. "I—ah—don't think so. I don't know what they are."

"She cuts the center out of bread and puts an egg in the hole. Then she cooks it. I love eggs in a basket."

Judy smiled at Timmy's sales pitch and hoped Victoria would buy into it. "Why don't I fix some for you and if you don't like them, you don't have to eat them. That sound okay to you?"

"With bacon?" Timmy questioned with big eyes as he rubbed his tummy with his palm.

"With bacon," Judy agreed, happy he was a fan of her cooking. "And orange juice."

"I guess I'll try it," the little voice answered through a slightly crooked smile.

"I'll have them ready in a flash." Judy picked up the remote control and handed it to Timmy. "Remember, you have company. Victoria gets to choose the cartoon she'd like to watch."

"It's okay, Mrs. Smith. I don't care which cartoon we watch. Timmy can choose."

The child's unselfishness surprised Judy. She'd expected to find a spoiled, pampered child visiting them this morning but Victoria Bramwell was anything but that.

"Naw, you choose, Tory." Timmy thrust the control toward his seatmate. "You're my company."

Judy leaned and first kissed Timmy on the cheek then Victoria. "You kids call me if you need anything. Okay? I'll be in the kitchen."

Two little heads bobbed in agreement as Victoria began pressing buttons. It was good to see both children happy and smiling. Even though Victoria didn't know it, the two of them had more in common than most children their age. They'd both lost their mothers, and Timmy had lost his father—losses no child should have to endure. Judy hoped in her own small way, she could be a comfort to both of them.

"That sure smells good," Timmy shouted over the raucous sounds of the cartoon as the aroma of bacon sizzling on the grill permeated the upstairs apartment.

"Won't be long now. They're nearly done. I hope you're both hungry." Judy flipped the browning strips over with a fork. Timmy was right. It did smell good. There was something about bacon frying that tantalized one's taste buds. She hoped it was having the same effect on Victoria. That child needed some meat on her bones.

She set about cutting big holes in the center of the slices of the whole wheat bread she'd purchased the day before. When the bacon was done she placed the browned strips between layers of paper towels to remove any lingering traces of grease then lined up the bread on the grill and broke an egg into each empty hole. While the eggs in a basket cooked, she prepared tall glasses of orange juice.

"The eggs in a basket are ready," she announced proudly as she entered the living room, carrying the big breakfast tray. "You two better be hungry. There's enough here for an army."

"We're gonna eat in here?" Victoria's big brown eyes shone with delight and surprise. "My daddy and I always eat in the dining room."

"Most of the time Timmy and I eat at the table, but this is a special occasion. You're here with us!" Judy lowered the tray to the coffee table in front of the sofa where the two children sat wedged into a corner. "Here is a napkin for each of you. Spread it on your lap and I'll hand you your plate. We can leave your orange juice on the tray until you're ready for it."

"Okay." Timmy spread the big floral napkin across his lap. "Want me to help you, Tory?" he volunteered, grabbing the girl's napkin and spreading it across her lap before she could answer.

"Would you like to pray, Timmy?"

The boy nodded.

A tiny hand slipped into his small hand and then reached toward Judy's as the two children bowed their heads and Timmy began to pray. "Thank You, God, for our eggs in a basket. And thank You for letting Tory watch cartoons with me. Amen."

Judy swallowed a lump in her throat as she eyed the two innocent children before her. Even very complicated lives were so simple for children. Surely, God heard and loved them for it.

"Oh, I forgot something. Wait," Timmy called out as Judy extended the first plate toward Victoria. "I need to add something else." He bowed his head again. "And please let Tory walk again. Amen."

Little Tory gazed at her intercessor as the corners of her tiny lips curled upward. "Thanks, Timmy."

With misty eyes Judy placed the plate on Victoria's lap, then one on Timmy's before taking the third one and settling herself into one of the nearby upholstered chairs, anxiously watching to see what the girl would do with the big breakfast she'd been handed.

"Eat it, Tory. You'll like it," Timmy advised her as he stuffed a much too large bite into his own mouth and began to chew.

Victoria looked first at Timmy then at her plate, then back to Timmy once again. "I'm not very hungry."

"Eat anyhow. That's what Au–Mama always tells me. Didn't your mama tell you that when she was alive?" He took a long strip of bacon, folded it, and shoved it in with the remains of his first bite as Judy cringed.

She struggled for something to say. She wished with all her might that Timmy hadn't brought up the subject of Carlotta Bramwell's death. Perhaps the little girl wasn't ready to talk to them about her mother. But instead of being upset by his question, she nonchalantly nodded, broke off a small piece of bacon, and began to nibble on it.

"Come on, Tory, eat your eggs in a basket," Timmy instructed with authority as he awkwardly used his knife to cut his own egg apart. "Eggs are good for you."

Judy cringed as he used his fingers to stuff the piece into his mouth but decided this was no time to make an issue of his bad manners.

Victoria nodded then began to mimic him with her knife, using it as awkwardly as Timmy had. It was obvious cutting up her own food was something she rarely did. Using her fingers, she picked up a small piece of bacon then chewed slowly as Timmy cut himself a second bite.

"You don't have to eat it if you don't like it," Judy offered, not wanting the child to feel as if she were being made to do something she'd rather not do.

"But she likes it, don't you, Tory?" Timmy chomped away on his third bite.

"Let's let Tory decide that for herself." She realized she had used Timmy's pet name for Victoria and wondered how the girl felt about being called by a nickname. Both her father and their servants always called her Victoria.

"I like it! It's good!" To Judy's surprise, Victoria folded a strip of bacon the way she'd seen Timmy do and shoved it into her tiny mouth.

Judy gasped. What if Tory did that at home and got in trouble for it? She started to mention it to her but stopped short of allowing the words to escape. At least Victoria was eating. That was something she hadn't expected her to do, even if she did use her fingers.

"Juice?" she asked as she held a tall glass of cold orange juice toward each of the children, who in just a few minutes had nearly cleaned their plates.

"Yes, please." Victoria wiped her mouth with her napkin and reached for the glass. "Thank you, Mrs. Smith."

"Judy. Not Mrs. Smith, Victoria. You must call me Judy." She handed the second glass to Timmy then seated herself once more and began sipping her own juice. "You kids are doing pretty good on that breakfast."

"Can I have another egg in a basket?" Timmy wolfed down the last bite on his plate and held it out to her. "And some more bacon?"

She nodded as she took it from him then glanced at Tory's plate. It was empty! So was her juice glass! "Would you like another egg in a basket, Tory?"

she asked out of politeness, certain the frail child's small tummy couldn't hold another teaspoonful of food.

Timmy nudged Victoria with his elbow. "You want some more, don't you, Tory?"

"If you're sure it's okay," she answered with a smile that tore at Judy's heartstrings. "I liked it."

"You bet it's okay. I'm so glad you liked it, Tory. You two kids sit right there. I have more in the kitchen. I'll be right back."

All three startled at the sound of the buzzer. Judy hurried to answer the intercom. "Yes?"

"I—ah—was wondering if Victoria is getting along okay?" came a male voice filled with concern.

It was exactly who she suspected it would be: Ben. "She's doing fine, Ben. Would you like to come up?" She pressed the button and waited, eager for him to hear how much breakfast Victoria was consuming.

"I don't want to intrude," he answered.

"Don't be silly. Come on up. Do you have your key for the downstairs door?" She placed her hand over the microphone and gave the children a grin. "It's Tory's father. Do you think we can get him to eat an egg in a basket with us?"

Little Victoria clapped her hands with glee. "Oh, yes. That'd be fun. He's never had eggs in a basket!"

"Yes, I have my key. I'm on my way up," he responded enthusiastically.

Within seconds Ben emerged through the open doorway, sniffing at the air. "Umm. Is that bacon I smell?"

"Uh-huh," Tory called out to him in her high-pitched voice. "Me and Timmy had eggs in a basket. Judy said you can have some, too."

He gave Judy a troubled look. "Oh, I hadn't realized Victoria was going to eat breakfast with you."

Judy's heart sank. Had she given the child something she was allergic to? Why hadn't she thought to ask? Would she end up sick? Maybe have to go to the hospital to be treated for a severe reaction? "Is there a problem?" she asked with great anxiety, her hand going to her heart.

Ben must have realized her concern for he rushed over to her, took her hand in his, and began to stroke it. "Oh, no, there's no problem. It's just that I couldn't get her to eat a thing this morning. I even begged her to eat a piece of toast, drink her orange juice, anything—but she refused just like she does every morning. I was just surprised, that's all."

Judy breathed a sigh of relief and pulled her hand away. "Whew. For a minute there I was afraid she was allergic to eggs or something."

"No, no! As far as I know, Victoria isn't allergic to anything! I'm just sorry to have worried you like that, especially after you've been so kind to my daughter."

"Daddy, I ate all my breakfast and Judy is going to fix us some more," Tory bragged to her father with a smile toward Judy. "And I drank all my juice, didn't I, Judy?"

"You sure did, honey, every sip," Judy answered proudly, now that she knew she hadn't caused the child a near mishap by feeding her breakfast.

"She did?" Ben asked in total surprise at his daughter's newly discovered appetite. "That's wonderful, sweetie! You don't know how much that pleases Daddy, but you mustn't call Mrs. Smith 'Judy.' It's not polite."

"She only did it because I told her to. Victoria and I are friends," Judy countered. "Now, can I fix you some breakfast?"

"Yes, Daddy, please. Eat breakfast with us," Tory begged from her place in the corner of the sofa. "Judy's eggs in a basket are really good!"

Ben shot a questioning glance toward his new tenant. "They must be good if my daughter is recommending them."

"They both wanted more, and I have extras ready to cook in the kitchen. It'll just take a few minutes. We'd love to have you join us."

"Actually, I had my breakfast hours ago."

She gave him a mocking laugh. "Then we'll call this brunch!"

"Please, Daddy. I want you to try the eggs in a basket. Judy fixes them real good."

He pursed his lips thoughtfully then looked from his pleading daughter to Judy. "I don't want to be a bother—"

"No bother at all. In fact, I have an idea. Why don't you help me in the kitchen? I found an apron just your size in one of the drawers."

Letting a slight giggle escape her lips, Victoria clapped her hands. "Oh yes, Daddy. Please do!"

"Okay, but only if Judy and Timmy will allow us to take them out for dinner. To return the favor." He turned questioning eyes toward Judy. "Agreed?"

Excited by Victoria's enthusiasm, she reared back her head with a laugh. "Agreed. We'd love to have dinner with you."

Judy grabbed his hand and tugged him into the kitchen.

"You'll have to give me instructions. I'm not very good in the food preparation department." His expression grew serious. "In fact, I really haven't been in a kitchen since. . ." His voice trailed off.

She pulled the apron from the drawer and tied it about his waist. "Since Carlotta died?" she asked softly.

"Yes." His voice was wavering. She could feel the hurt in his response. "Since Carlotta died."

"I can only imagine how much you loved her." Determined to bring the conversation back to its cheerful beginnings, she handed him a glass tumbler and gestured toward the loaf of whole wheat bread.

"What am I supposed to do with this?"

"You've never had eggs in a basket?" She removed the egg carton from the refrigerator and placed it on the counter.

"Guess not. Apparently from the look of enthusiasm on my child's face, I've missed a real treat." All traces of his smile disappeared as he moved closer to stand beside her while she began removing eggs from the carton. "Did she eat? I mean, really eat? Or was she just saying that? I've been so concerned about her, even to the point of trying to force food down her. She barely eats anything anymore."

It was obvious he was consumed with worry about his daughter. She'd noticed his deep concern the first time she'd seen them together. "She really did eat, Ben. An entire slice of bread with an egg and drank a whole glass of orange juice. Every bit of it. I think doing it with Timmy was what made the difference. Sometimes kids can reach one another when adults can't reach them."

He crossed his arms and leaned against the cabinet. "Guess I'll have to send her up here for all her meals. You two seem to have accomplished something Miranda, Max, and I haven't been able to do."

"She is welcome anytime. So are you."

"Be careful; we might take you up on that offer," he conceded with the raise of a brow.

She pointed to the loaf of bread. "Cut."

He obeyed with a salute and awkwardly began to cut. Soon five slices of bread with large holes in the center of them were stacked neatly by the grill where more slices of bacon were frying in regimented form. Ben watched as Judy flipped and turned the browning bacon.

Once the bacon was finished cooking he took the fork from her hand and began transferring the browned strips to the platter she'd set by the grill. "I'm sorry for mentioning Carlotta, but when you've loved someone like I loved her, it's hard to forget about them. My life revolved around her and Victoria, probably like yours did with your husband's. I—I wasn't prepared to let her go."

"I'm sorry, Ben." Her voice was nearly inaudible as her fingertips touched his arm. "I know how you feel."

Ben lowered the fork onto the spoon rest and turned to face her, his eyes filled with regret. Then, as if not knowing what to say, he slipped an arm about her and pulled her close. "What was I thinking? Of course, you know how I feel. You lost your spouse, too. I'm so sorry, Judy. Please forgive me for my insensitivity. Can you ever forgive me for being so thoughtless?"

She leaned into the warmth of his cashmere sweater, the musky scent of his aftershave wafting over her. He was right. She did know the feeling. But she ached over the loss of her brother, not her husband. She had never had a husband. If only she could be honest with this man she'd come to admire in such a short time. But that was impossible. No one could know their true identities. Just the thought of their identities being discovered caused a jolt of fear to run through her body, and she trembled.

"Are you cold?" Ben asked with concern, pulling her even closer.

"Just—just a little," she lied as troubling questions filled her mind. What if someone discovered where they were hiding? Would that discovery put Ben and Victoria at risk? Bringing those two people into her trouble was something she hadn't considered. She could never let that happen. Perhaps it was time for her and Timmy to move on—leave Memphis.

"I'm so glad you're here," he explained as his arms continued to enfold her. "Even though you've been here only two days, Judy, you've already become an important part of our lives. I'm amazed at how Victoria responds to both you and Timmy."

Smoke began filling the kitchen. "Oh, no! The bacon grease!" Judy turned to the empty grill still set on the high setting and quickly twisted the dial to the off position. "I can't believe I did that!"

"Hey, something smells funny and it's getting all foggy in here," Timmy shouted from the living room. "Did you burn our breakfast?"

The two adults attempted to stifle their laughter as they grabbed dish towels and began fanning them through the air to dispel the smoke as both answered in unison, "Everything's fine."

"Boy, some kitchen help I am," Ben acknowledged as he removed his apron. "Bet you'll never let me in here again."

Judy grabbed onto his arm. "Oh, no you don't! You're not getting off that easily. We still have eggs in a basket to cook."

"Burned eggs in a basket, if you put me in charge," he stated as his free hand covered hers. "Sure you want to take that chance? I warned you I was no good in the kitchen."

"Umm, you may be right. Maybe I'd better take over the cooking, although, after that trick I pulled by letting the bacon grease burn, I doubt I'm much better in the kitchen than you are! How are you at pouring orange juice? Think you can take care of that without getting into trouble?"

"If you point out the refrigerator I might be able to do it." He grinned as his eyes scanned the small kitchen.

"The big white box in the corner. The juice is the orange stuff in the gallon bottle on the top shelf. But be careful!"

"Oh, yeah. That big white box. I see it. I think I can handle that!"

Within minutes the tray had been replenished, and Ben was carrying it into the living room with Judy at his side. "Breakfast," he announced as proudly as if he'd prepared the entire meal by himself.

"*You* cooked it?" Victoria asked as he entered the room, with a sparkle in her eyes that apparently her father had rarely seen as of late.

"Well," he admitted with a backward look toward his compadre, "Judy helped."

The four enjoyed their breakfast together and once again Victoria cleaned her plate as her surprised father watched. The children went back to their cartoons and Ben carried the tray back into the kitchen with Judy close behind.

"Thanks, Ben, for coming over. I know Victoria loved having you here. She's a great kid. You must be very proud." She removed the dishes from the tray and placed them in the dishwasher. "And thanks for your help."

"I'm the one who should be saying thanks. It's been months since I've seen my precious child look this happy. I don't know how you accomplished it, but you and Timmy have worked wonders with her."

She felt his hands cup around her shoulders and the warmth of his breath on the nape of her neck and she froze in her tracks. Thoughtful, considerate Ben Bramwell was the kind of man she'd searched for all of her life. Now here he was, within kissing distance, and she couldn't even tell him her real name.

"Thanks, Judy. I'll always be grateful. I hope you and Timmy stay a long time."

Although her heart was pounding and she could feel a flush rising to her cheeks, she tried to ignore the grasp he had on her and went back to loading the dishwasher. "You are most welcome. The pleasure was all ours. Timmy and I love having Victoria here, and we hope you'll allow her to come often."

He dropped his grasp and leaned against the cabinet facing her. "Now, where would you like to go for dinner tonight?"

"Dinner?"

"Yes, dinner!" He nodded, crossed his arms, and cocked his head. "You agreed if I stayed for breakfast, you and Timmy would join Victoria and me for dinner. Remember?"

She placed the dishwashing capsule in the cup and locked the door before pressing the switch. "What about Phoebe Vanderbur? Will she be going with us?"

He lowered his arms and gave a slight whistle. "Phoebe! I nearly forgot! We have a date tonight."

How could he forget a date with his fiancée? Judy stuffed the dishrag under the faucet, alternately letting the hot water run through it and wringing it out. "Sounds like we'd better postpone our dinner to another time."

"We'll all go together!" He took the rag from her hand and began wiping the cabinet's surface.

"I'm sure Phoebe would love that!" she quipped with a slight sarcastic air as she watched the circular movement of his hand.

Letting out a sigh, Ben draped the dishrag over the center divider in the stainless steel sink. "You may be right. One child seems to be enough for her to handle; I'm not sure she could endure two. Not even one as nice and well-behaved as Timmy."

"Thanks anyway, Ben. We'll take a rain check. You go on and have a good evening with Phoebe."

"Sure you don't mind?"

She added the silk flower centerpiece to the table, doing everything she could to ignore his questioning eyes. Of course she minded. She'd like to see him tell Phoebe to take a hike. There was something about that woman that—

"You don't like Phoebe, do you?"

His direct question caught her off guard. She hadn't realized her face had betrayed her feelings about the irritating socialite. Ben was really nice and a wonderful father. He deserved better. Why were men so blind when it came to a beautiful woman? "What makes you think that?"

"Sorry, Judy. It just seems—well, you don't—I mean. . ."

She could tell he was fishing for words but as uncomfortable as she felt, she was also amused. Well-spoken, well-educated Ben Bramwell was having trouble finishing his sentence. "Okay, you're right." She threw both hands in the air in defeat. "You got me. I don't like Phoebe Vanderbur. Now I've said it. Are you happy?" She whirled around and rushed into the living room to join the children, not giving him time to respond.

Letting his question go unanswered, he followed quickly. "I think we'd better go home now, Victoria. Thank Timmy and Mrs. Smith for a wonderful morning."

"Aw, Mr. Bramwell, does she have to go?" Timmy asked with a scowl on his freckled face as he turned away from the TV. "We're having fun."

"We don't want to wear out our welcome." Ben moved to lift his daughter from the sofa.

"Daddy, not yet. Please?" she begged as she stiffened her body, making it difficult for him to lift her.

"Now, Victoria, mind Daddy."

As he struggled to lift the delicate child she placed a tiny hand on his cheek, beseeching once more. "Please, Daddy. Don't make me go. I like it here with Timmy and Judy."

Judy cleared her throat. "She's welcome to stay, if it's okay with you, Ben. I'll bring her over later. Timmy wanted her to stay for lunch and eat spaghetti with us, remember?"

Ben released his grasp and straightened. "That's right. I'd forgotten you mentioned spaghetti. Well, if you're sure you don't mind."

"Oh, goodie," Timmy chimed in as he began to bounce on the sofa again. "You can stay, Tory!"

"Are we going to have dinner with Timmy and Judy like you said, Daddy?" Victoria asked as she giggled aloud and joined Timmy in his bouncing.

He shook his head. "No, not tonight, pumpkin. Another time."

Seeming miffed, she quit bouncing and gave him a deep frown. "Why not? You said we'd go to dinner together. I heard you!"

Ben cleared his throat nervously. It was obvious he rarely denied his child anything she asked. "Daddy forgot. I already had a date set up with Phoebe to go to dinner at the country club. Sorry, kiddo. Maybe we can take them to dinner tomorrow night, if that's okay with Judy and Timmy." He turned to her as if he expected her to respond and in some way get him off the hook.

"Sorry, not tomorrow night. Timmy and I have plans for tomorrow. We won't be getting home until very late in the afternoon. We have a big day planned," she explained to the disappointed children. "Perhaps next week."

Ben gave her an appreciative smile. "Next week then. And if you're sure it's okay with you and she won't be in the way, it's fine for Victoria to stay for lunch."

"Once lunch is over, I'll bring her home."

After planting a kiss on the tip of his daughter's nose, he backed toward the door. "Thanks for the eggs in a basket. Victoria was right. They're very good."

Her conscience still bothering her, after hurriedly handing the remote control to the children, Judy followed Ben and grabbed hold of his sleeve to stop him before he moved on down the stairs. "Ben, I'm sorry. I had no right to speak out about your fiancée like I did. It's none of my business who you date—or marry—or anything!"

He swung around to face her. "I'm sorry for my behavior. I find I'm a bit touchy on the subject of Phoebe lately anyway. Call it premarriage jitters but, at times, I'm not at all sure I'm doing the right thing—for me, for Victoria, or for

Phoebe. Marriage is a big step, one that shouldn't be taken lightly. I have to ask myself when the doubts creep in, am I marrying Phoebe to give my daughter a mother? And to be honest—" He stared off in space, as if carefully considering his words before speaking them. "To be honest, I'm not real sure I could ever love Phoebe, although I am fond of her and grateful for her support. I've had none of the vibes I expected to go along with love. Like the vibes I had with Carlotta. Did you have those vibes with your husband?"

Now she was on the spot. Vibes! She'd never even had a husband! How was she to answer?

"You know what I mean, don't you, Judy? Those feelings that push you over the top when you're together. The goose bumps, that sort of thing."

She searched for something to say without giving herself and her deception away. "I know what you mean, Ben." *Like I felt last night when you kissed me.* "But more importantly, Phoebe doesn't share your faith, does she, Ben? As a Christian, it's something you need to consider," she said awkwardly, feeling she'd stepped over the proverbial line once again.

"I have to admit that has concerned me, but maybe once we're married I can get her to attend church with us and—"

She huffed. "That's pretty risky, isn't it? If she isn't interested in God now, what makes you think she will be then? And what about your values? Do you and Phoebe have the same values? If not, you may just be getting yourself into a real pickle."

"I know you're right, and I am concerned about those things. Would you tell me about your husband sometime? I'd like to hear about him. He must have been a wonderful man."

"I'd be happy to tell you about Jerod sometime," she hedged as her hand moved to brush a wisp of red hair from her face. Her lies weren't getting any easier to tell. She hated lying to Ben.

"Good. I'd like that. Well, I'd better be going. I'll talk to you later. Thanks for taking such good care of my baby."

"We love having her." She nodded and waved as he turned and moved quickly down the remaining steps, closing the door behind him.

Judy's fingertips touched her lips as she stood motionless, her thoughts going to the impromptu kisses they had shared, and she wondered if he ever thought of them, too. *Oh, Ben, if I weren't so tangled in this web I've woven, I'd go after you in a heartbeat. Please, please, Lord, don't let him marry Phoebe!*

∞

Ben Bramwell closed the door and paused on the little covered porch before striding across the lawn toward the big house. How did Judy ever get his daughter to eat two eggs and two slices of bread? Plus four strips of bacon! When he and Miranda had begged and pleaded with the child to eat the nutritious food they'd set before her and she'd refused? And Victoria actually laughed! Not once, but several times. Even giggled out loud. How long had it been since he'd heard those wonderful sounds? Too long!

And Phoebe. Had Judy been right about their relationship? He'd never confessed his apprehensions to another living soul, yet he'd opened his heart to this woman he barely knew—as if her opinion really mattered. She was his renter, not his psychiatrist. Shouldn't he be proud to have Phoebe Vanderbur for a wife? She was young. Beautiful. Had a gorgeous figure. She was intelligent. Well-educated. Independent. Everywhere she went, heads turned.

Still mumbling to himself, he opened the huge oak door and headed for his office off the entry hall. What about words like caring? Loving? Gentle? Maternal? Those were the words he needed in his life. A lot of women were beautiful. Even intelligent! But were they wife and mother material? Was Phoebe?

Dropping wearily into his desk chair, he leaned back, his fingers interlocked behind his head. He couldn't afford to make a mistake where marriage was concerned. The marriage vows might not mean much to Phoebe, but they did to him. When he took those vows, it was going to be for a lifetime.

He glanced at the framed photograph of his daughter. *What you want, Ben, old boy, is not important. Victoria is my life now that Carlotta is gone. She has to come first in every decision. My wants and needs have to be second place to her wants and needs.*

Suddenly he lunged forward, his palms coming down on his desktop with a thud. "Judy Smith, why did you have to come into my life? I may have had these same doubts about marrying Phoebe before, but you've made me see them for what they really are. Threats. Genuine threats to mine and Victoria's happiness."

He squared his chin, picked up the phone, dialed, then said coolly into the mouthpiece, "Phoebe, we have to talk."

Chapter 5

Judy rose early Sunday morning, although she'd had a difficult time going to sleep. She had no business caring what happened between Ben and his fiancée, but she did. She'd watched him leave for his date with Phoebe from the safety and security of her bedroom window the night before, wishing he hadn't looked so handsome in his navy blue blazer and tan slacks. Although he'd briefly glanced in the direction of her apartment as his sports car pulled out of the driveway, she couldn't be sure if it was accidental or if he'd purposely looked her way. Not that it really mattered. She was, after all, only his renter. A business acquaintance. A nobody in his personal life.

She'd lain awake until she heard his car return a little after midnight. By the way his tires squealed when he'd pulled into the driveway and screeched to an abrupt halt, things apparently hadn't gone well with Phoebe, and Judy was ashamed of the joy those thoughts brought her.

Now, this morning, as she stood in her pajamas, staring out her bedroom window at the black car parked in the circle drive, she couldn't help wondering about the man who lived in the big house with his invalid daughter.

"Is this a church day?" Timmy asked as he padded across the room, rubbing his eyes.

"It sure is, babe. And after church we're going to do something else you'll like." She gave him a teasing smile as she wiggled her fingers through his short hair.

He brightened as he wrapped his arms about her waist. "What? Tell me."

With a fingertip, she lifted his chin and asked, "How'd you like to visit the Memphis Zoo? Remember me telling you about all the animals that live there?"

"Yes, I remember!" Timmy began to jump around the room, waving his arms wildly. "Can we really go there?"

"You bet we can." She swallowed past the lump that rose to her throat as she watched the boy. He'd been so patient, more patient than she had ever expected he could be after being ripped from the only home he'd ever known and brought to this strange city, away from his friends, their church, and all that was familiar to him. Rarely complaining and doing whatever she asked of him.

He hugged her tightly, so tightly they both lost their balance and fell onto the bed. Giggling hysterically, Judy wrapped her arms about the child and pulled him close to her. "You're a sweet kid, Timmy. I love you very much."

He smiled up at her, the empty gap between his teeth making him that much more adorable. "I love you, too, Aunt Judy—er, Mama." Rising to a sitting position, Timmy crisscrossed his legs and tucked his ankles beneath them. "I wish Tory could go to church with us. She doesn't get to go many new places; she told me so. She doesn't even go to school. She has a tu—tu—"

"A tutor," Judy supplied.

"Yeah, one of those."

"She and her dad go to church. Maybe we can go to their church sometime, okay?"

Timmy nodded. "Okay. Should I get ready now?"

Later, as the two made their way outside, they were met by Ben Bramwell and his daughter. They had just arrived in a big sedan. Victoria's eyes brightened when she saw them.

"Good morning." Ben greeted them with a nod and a robust smile as he climbed out of the driver's seat. "On your way to church?"

Judy smoothed the hair around her face. "Yes, we are."

"Victoria and I went to the early service. We should have invited you two to come with us."

He unloaded the wheelchair and helped Victoria into it, then she and Timmy moved away from the adults toward a tree where a squirrel chattered noisily.

"Maybe next Sunday. Today, we're going to try one of the neighborhood churches."

"While I do attend church regularly," Ben admitted shyly, after checking to make sure Timmy and Victoria were out of earshot, "I'm ashamed to admit I'm not on as good a ground with God as I used to be. I still find it hard to believe He could—well, you know."

Judy felt obligated to step in, though she still had a few misgivings of her own on that subject. "You're not blaming God for Carlotta's death are you, Ben?"

He paused before answering, his voice lowered so the children wouldn't hear. "Let's just say I see no reason for Him taking my wife and leaving so many worthless people behind. Sometimes—"

"Ben, you can't blame God! He never does anything without a reason." *I'm a fine one to be telling you!*

"Did you understand why He took your husband? Don't tell me you weren't just a little bit bitter about losing him."

Think before you speak! "I was—at first, and sometimes, even now, I do feel pangs of anger, but I am trying to get victory over it. Like you, I don't understand the whys when someone we love is snatched from us into eternity, but prayer helps. I'm sure God realizes the horrible hole left in our lives when we lose a loved one."

"It's not so much for me, Judy. It's Victoria I'm concerned about. She's taken the loss of her mother so hard. You've seen her. She's been withdrawn, has had little interest in anything, barely talks, stares off in space. . . It's like she's been living in her own little world and would allow no one to penetrate it. Not even me, her father, the one she should be turning to for comfort. It's so sad. I think, in some ways, she blames herself for her mother's death since they were on their way to her ballet lesson when it happened."

Judy could feel the pain in his voice. If only there was something more she could do to help. "That would certainly help explain her withdrawal."

"She's been better since you and Timmy arrived, and that has brought me great hope. Pray for me, Judy. I don't want to harbor any anger toward God. He spared my daughter. I'll always be grateful for that."

"And you pray for me, Ben. I need your prayers." *More than you'll ever know. And for reasons I'm not at liberty to tell you.*

The children were coming toward them. A simple nod was his only response as he moved to the wheelchair and bent to button his daughter's sweater against the coolness of the morning Memphis air, then grabbed onto the handle grips. "You two enjoy the service."

"We will," Timmy called out enthusiastically. "We're going to church, and then we're going to the zoo."

Victoria reached back and grabbed her father's hand. "Please, Daddy, can we go to the zoo with Timmy and Judy?"

"Not today, pumpkin. Maybe another time."

Victoria frowned and lowered her bottom lip into a pout.

Though Judy was tempted to invite both Victoria and Ben to go to the zoo with them, thinking it best, she kept her silence.

"One of these days, I'd like to take the three of you to see the Peabody ducks," Ben offered as if hoping to change the subject.

Judy frowned. "Peabody ducks? Are they at the zoo?"

Ben let out a chuckle. "You haven't heard about the Peabody ducks? They live in the penthouse at Memphis's famous Peabody Hotel. Every afternoon at exactly the same time, they all get into the elevator with their keeper, ride to the main floor, then walk on a red carpet kept only for them and, with much pomp and circumstance, waddle to the huge fountain in the center of the hotel's magnificent lobby and take a bath. It's quite a treat to see them. I have to take you there. It's an experience you'll never forget. People line up on both sides of the ropes to see them. It's quite a show. The children will love it."

One of the biggest smiles Judy had ever seen on Victoria's face erupted as the child clapped her hands.

"Can we, Daddy? Can we take Timmy and Judy to see the ducks?" Victoria asked, tugging on her father's sleeve.

"Oh, Ben, that sounds like such fun. Timmy and I would love to go."

"Okay, it's a date." He hurriedly pushed the wheelchair around them and continued down the drive as Victoria waved her little hand good-bye.

"Maybe Tory can go to church with us next Sunday." Timmy grabbed Judy's hand as they began their walk to the church.

"Maybe." Judy adjusted the strap on her shoulder bag. "Or maybe we can go to their church. Would you like that?"

Timmy clapped his hand. "Can we?"

"We'll see. Next Sunday is a long way off. A lot can happen between now and then."

Judy was glad attending church was a regular routine for Ben and Victoria. Those two needed the love and support a church and its family could give them. She turned her head away, her own heart hurting. She hoped Timmy wouldn't notice the tear rolling down her cheek. *God, I'm sorry to admit it, but I know exactly how Ben Bramwell feels. I still experience moments of anger at You for taking Kayla and Jerod. Help me get victory over this. I know all things work together for good to those who love You, but I hurt. I miss them so much. Give me peace, please. I want to do Your will.*

The new church they'd decided on was everything she'd hoped it would be. The music was great, the message sound and scriptural, and the people friendly. Even Timmy commented on their friendliness.

After a quick lunch at an all-you-can-eat buffet near the church, they were in a taxi and on the way to the zoo. Timmy closed his eyes as they drove along and within seconds, he was sound asleep. She reached across and gave his small hand a slight squeeze, not wanting to wake him but not able to resist the sweetness and vulnerability of the sleeping boy. If anything ever happened to him she'd never forgive herself. His life was in her hands. She had to be careful. Letting her guard down, even for a minute, could mean disaster for both of them.

As she gave an automatic glance into the rearview mirror and caught sight of a black sedan about three car lengths back, occupied by two men in ball caps, fear seized her. Could that car be following them? Had she and Timmy been found already?

But the black car passed by and moved on down the street, with neither man even glancing in their direction. She pressed her forehead against the window and let out a deep breath. Was she getting paranoid?

A few minutes later, they arrived at the zoo. "Wake up, sleepyhead. We're here."

Timmy straightened in the seat and rubbed at his eyes with doubled up fists. "Already?"

"Let's go see the pandas. The Memphis Zoo is famous for its panda bears. Do you remember me telling you about Ya Ya and Le Le?" She picked up her purse and slung its strap over her shoulder.

Timmy nodded. "I remember; and I remember you telling me about the orangutan baby."

"The Memphis Zoo is also famous for its tropical bird exhibit, its herpetarium, aquarium, and a whole lot more. I'm not sure we'll have time to see all of it today but—"

He crawled out the door and, after she paid the driver, took her hand as she reached it toward him. "But maybe next time we can bring Tory?"

"Maybe. We'll see what her father says."

The two spent the rest of the afternoon exploring the zoo, laughing at the antics of the many animals, eating snow cones, and enjoying the beautiful day.

"Ready to go home, sport?" Judy finally asked after a quick glance at her watch. "We'd better call a cab then head back to the apartment. I think we've had enough zoo for one day."

"Umm, I guess so," he agreed reluctantly as she pulled her cell phone from her purse. "But can we come here again sometime? I know Tory would like it. I'll bet she's never been here."

"If it's okay with her father. They've certainly got excellent wheelchair access to the exhibits."

"I can push her."

"I know you can, but maybe we can take turns."

It was half past five when they finally got home. She herded the tired boy up the stairs and into their apartment.

"Hungry?" she asked once she'd closed the door and locked it securely. "I could fix us a sandwich."

Timmy shook his head as he threw himself onto the sofa and reached for his video game. "I'm too full."

Judy rushed to answer the phone when it rang. So few people had her phone number, it had to be Ben. "Hello," she said cheerily, hoping to hear his voice.

"This is the pizza man and his daughter. We saw you arrive and wondered if you've had dinner. I thought I'd call for pizza delivery—Victoria's idea—and have it delivered to your apartment. That is, if you think you and Timmy could put up with a cranky old man and his giggly daughter for an hour or so."

She had to laugh. "Of course, pizza man. Call for pizza and come on up. We'd love your company. You can even bring Phoebe if you want," she tacked on facetiously.

"I'm afraid Phoebe has other plans for tonight. A charity dinner or some such thing. It'll just be the two of us."

"Okay, as much as I'll miss Phoebe, I'll try to get along without her just this once."

When he didn't respond right away, she added, "Sorry, that was pretty rude. Just ignore me when I get this way. Good thing Timmy wasn't listening. I mean no disrespect. I have a tendency to plow right in where I'm not wanted or needed."

"Well," he said, politely ignoring her comment, "what kind of pizza shall I order?"

"Maybe I should eat humble pie after that remark. Timmy and I like any kind but we're partial to pepperoni with extra cheese."

"Done. We'll be right there."

She turned to Timmy. "Put your toys away. Tory and her dad are coming up for pizza."

"They are? Yippee!"

The two arrived in less than five minutes with Ben carrying his daughter on his back, much like Judy had carried her. "Nothing like inviting yourself, eh?" Ben placed Tory on the sofa beside Timmy and seated himself in one of the upholstered chairs. "Did you two have a good day?"

"We had a great time," Timmy announced with a broad smile that nearly covered his freckled faced. "We went to this really big church and then we went to the zoo. Can Tory come with us next time we go to the zoo?"

Ben winked at Judy before answering. "If you and Judy want to take her with you sometime and Tory wants to go, it's fine with me. In fact, if you and your mother will allow it, I'd like to go, too."

Timmy and Tory stared at the big man.

"Really, Daddy?" Tory asked with big eyes. "You want to go?"

"Of course, sweetheart, I just didn't think you were interested or I'd have taken you before now."

"We'd love to have you go with us, Ben. But really, it's not necessary. We can handle Tory's chair by ourselves." For some reason, Judy felt like she should give him a chance to get off the hook. "Maybe Phoebe would like to go."

"I doubt it," he countered with a mocking smile. "The zoo isn't exactly her thing."

"I didn't think so," Judy appended, shamelessly enjoying the bantering at Phoebe's expense.

The pizza arrived and after Timmy thanked God for their food, the four hungry people devoured it quickly. Even Tory seemed to enjoy it. His face showing both surprise and pride, Ben watched her then whispered to Judy, "What has happened to my little girl? Two days ago she hardly touched her food and we rarely saw a smile cross her face. Now she giggles at everything Timmy says, and she's eating pizza!"

"The company, perhaps?" She gestured toward Timmy. "Kids seem to gravitate toward one another. I think what she needed was the companionship of another child and people who treat her like she's human instead of a fragile doll."

Ben bristled. "Are you insinuating I treat her like that?"

"Don't you?"

It was a fair question. Ben appeared to look deep into himself before answering. "I do, don't I? I know I'm overly protective, but I can't help it."

Judy nodded. "Yes, you are overprotective, and so are Max and Miranda. I know you all mean well. Victoria has been through so much doom and gloom. What she needs is happiness. Encouragement. Laughter. She needs to get out into the real world, have some honest fun."

Ben moved closer to her. "I can truthfully say having you two here seems to have brought about the change. She loves being with you and your son. I think more than she enjoys being with me. You're all she talks about. It used to be we couldn't get her to talk at all. Now, thanks to you and Timmy, she talks nonstop."

"It's not us, Ben," Judy denied with a shake of her head. "I have a feeling she would have responded to anyone who treated her like a normal little girl instead of a breakable china doll. From my vantage point, and for what it's worth, I'd say you have to ease up on her. Give her some space, some breathing room. True, she's fragile but she won't break."

"You're right, but it's so hard." Lifting his sleeve, he checked his watch. "I think our conversation better come to an end. It's time for you two children to call it a day. Timmy has homeschooling tomorrow, and Victoria's tutor is coming at nine." He rose to his feet and lifted his daughter easily in his arms. "Say good night, Victoria."

The little girl reached out her arms toward Judy. "Good night, Judy."

Judy gave her a big hug then planted a kiss on the top of her head. "Good night, sweetie. Sleep tight."

"Bye, Timmy." Tory waved at her friend.

"Bye, Tory."

"Thanks for a lovely evening, Judy." Ben moved toward the door. "I mean it.

We really enjoyed being here, even if you did pin my ears back a few times."

She followed them to the door. "I'm sorry, Ben. I tend to blurt things out without thinking. I didn't mean to pick on your fiancée, but—"

He gave her a sideways accusing smile. "I know. You don't like her and you don't think she's right for me *or* Victoria."

"Exactly. So sue me for defamation of character." She playfully punched his upper arm with her fist.

"I may just do that." He gave her a sly wink. "I have to put my car in the garage later, after I put Victoria to bed."

She raised a questioning brow. "Oh? And why are you telling me that?"

"If you're up to it, I'd like to come back later so we could finish our discussion. About my future marriage—and other things."

"Well," she drawled with her Texas accent, pleased that he wasn't mad at her for meddling in his life, "I really don't have any plans for later. Say around nine o'clock?"

"Nine, huh?"

"I'll be listening for you."

He hurried down the stairs with Tory in his arms, leaving Judy feeling exuberant. Maybe he wasn't as interested in Phoebe as she'd thought. With Timmy tucked securely in bed, she freshened her makeup, ran a pick through her hair, and slipped into a fresh pair of jeans and her favorite baggy sweatshirt.

Nine o'clock came and went and no Ben. She assumed he was having trouble getting the keyed-up little girl into bed.

Nine thirty. No Ben.

Nine forty-five. Certain Phoebe had changed his plans, she gave up and decided to get to bed early for a change. As was her nightly habit, the first thing she did when she entered her bedroom was move to the window to close the drapery. It was then she saw it! Phoebe's convertible was parked in front of Bramwell House, and she knew instantly why Ben hadn't kept his appointment. That woman again!

She struggled over a book she'd intended to read for an hour then, giving up, turned out the light, all the while listening for the roar of Phoebe's engine, hoping for her departure. Finally, at half past midnight she heard the level hum of the expensive car's engine.

She told herself to stay in bed. There was no reason she should look out the window. What business was it of hers what time Phoebe arrived and left Bramwell House? But try as she may, she couldn't resist the temptation and found herself tiptoeing to the window. There was Ben, leaning into the driver's side of the yellow convertible, talking to his intended. She wished she could hear their conversation, not that it, too, was any of her business. Finally forcing herself away from the window, she backed into bed. Then the engine stopped and all was quiet.

What could be happening? Quickly, she tossed the covers back, hurried to the window, and drew back the drapes. Phoebe and Ben were standing in the driveway, and from the looks of things they were having a heated discussion.

Finally, Phoebe turned her back on Ben and began to cry. Ben pulled her into his arms. As the two talked, Ben continued to hold Phoebe, occasionally kissing her on the cheek. At one o'clock, he put Phoebe into her car and she drove off, leaving him standing in the middle of the drive waving good-bye.

Judy let the drapes fall back into their place and climbed into bed with mixed emotions. Was she hoping for their breakup for Tory's sake? Or her own? Even if he weren't engaged to Phoebe, what chance would she have with him? At this point in her life—what was she thinking? She had no life, absolutely none!

∞

Ben glanced up at the apartment's darkened window on his way into Bramwell House. He couldn't help wondering if Judy had been watching them. He'd told her he'd be back at nine o'clock, and he'd rudely left her waiting. She was probably furious. Especially if she'd seen Phoebe's car parked in the driveway or watched them as they talked. Upsetting Judy was the last thing he wanted to do. If she hadn't come into his life, his daughter would still be hiding in her shell. She'd made such a difference in both their lives. Even Max and Miranda had noticed. He'd always be indebted to her, and to Timmy. But he couldn't live his life the way his tenant wanted him to. What did she really know about him or his wants and desires? How could she possibly know what kind of a wife would be best for him? Just because she and Phoebe had a personality conflict didn't mean Phoebe wasn't right for him. Judy didn't even know Phoebe. She'd only met her that one time. She should mind her own business. Her red hair said it all. The woman had a short fuse.

He stood quietly on the porch thinking, his mind in a whir. Maybe Judy was jealous of Phoebe. After all, the woman looked like a fashion model, wore the clothes of a fashion model and had the figure to go with it. Oh, Judy was attractive enough, in a generic sort of way. He wished she'd pull her hair back like Phoebe's. You could barely see her lovely face with all that frowzy red hair pulled around it. And the clothes she wore did nothing for the figure she seemed to hide beneath them. From her delicate facial structure to her long, willowy fingers, it was obvious she was anything but overweight, but you could never tell it by the baggy clothes she wore. The woman seemed to have no sense of fashion or even care. Yet there was something special about her. Something that kept him thinking about her day and night. A magnetism that couldn't be denied.

As he stared at the darkened window, he continued to think about the woman who was sleeping in that room. Yes, Judy had been extremely critical of his fiancée, but there was no doubt Judy Smith had his and Victoria's best interests at heart.

Tomorrow would be another day. Perhaps he'd get a chance to apologize for not showing up as he'd promised.

∞

Judy lay awake staring at the ceiling and wondering how much was being done to find her and Timmy. How long would they have to stay in hiding before they could return to Dallas? She was tired of suspecting every car that followed her down a street. Every person who looked in her direction. Every noise she heard. Fearing whose voice it was when she answered the phone. This wasn't fair. She should be back home, grieving and adjusting to her brother's death, visiting his grave site. But instead, she was running. Not knowing who she was running from, or even if they were chasing her.

She was eager to get back to work, back to her job as a highly skilled, well-paid computer programmer. Eager to get back to their home and the closet of fashionable suits, evening gowns, and sportswear hanging there. Maybe they weren't as elegant as Phoebe's, but she'd always dressed in the most current fashions and felt she looked every bit as good as Ben's snotty fiancée. She was sick and tired of the red wig and the baggy clothes, but wearing them was the very camouflage she needed to keep Timmy safe. To do that, she would dress in rags if necessary.

And now she'd met Ben Bramwell, one of the nicest men she'd ever known and she couldn't even tell him her real name. She could feel the love building inside her for Ben, a love she must keep to herself. Not only because he was engaged to Phoebe, but because she herself would never be free to love until her ordeal was over, and at this point she had no idea when that might be. A week? A month? A year? Or never!

Her thoughts went to the child sleeping soundly in the next room. That child's safety was her prime responsibility now that he no longer had his father, and she'd gladly do whatever it took to keep him safe. Even if it meant denying her own future. She was prepared to make whatever sacrifices might be necessary for Timmy's sake.

Unable to sleep, she took a sip of water from the carafe on the nightstand then moved robotically to the window and drew aside the drapery. Across the courtyard, she caught a glimpse of a light that was surely the light in Ben's room. Was that his silhouette shadowed in the window? She pressed her head against the cool glass and closed her eyes, remembering his handsome face. But when she opened them, the light had gone out. The window was dark.

She crawled back into bed and pulled the covers over her head. She had to get some decent sleep. Morning would come all too soon.

But as she closed her eyes, a scream from Timmy's room pierced the darkness!

Chapter 6

Judy leaped from the bed and bounded into the child's room and there was Timmy, clutching his pillow to his chest with a look of terror etched on his young face and tears streaming down his cheeks. "It was that man! He was in my dream and he was chasing me, Aunt Judy. I was running as fast as I could but I couldn't find you! He was grabbing at me. I was really afraid!"

She threw her arms around the frightened boy, pulled him to her bosom, and stroked his tear-stained cheeks. "Aunt Judy is here, Timmy. Shh. You're okay. It was only a bad dream. No one is chasing you. We're safe here at Bramwell House. No one knows where we are."

Timmy was trembling from head to toe, his intense sobs breaking her heart. Perhaps they should have stayed and let the police protect them until Skitch Fallon was caught and put behind bars again. How long could they go on like this? The running was hard on her, too, but she was an adult. The decision to run had been hers. Timmy'd had no say in it. No, she decided as she nestled her chin against the boy's soft locks, running had been the only sensible choice. It was best this way. Hiding until they were sure they were safe had been their only option. True, the authorities would have done all they could to protect them. But would it have been enough?

"Can I sleep with you? I'm still afraid."

Judy wrapped her arms tightly around him and struggled to calm him down. He was still shaking, though not as violently as when she'd rushed into his room. "Sure, honey, but you don't have to be afraid. We're safe here in Memphis. It's a big city and a long way from Dallas. He can't find us here."

She took the boy's hand, led him into her bedroom and tucked him safely into her bed. As she lay there in the soft glow filtering in the window from the yard light, she remembered similar dreams she'd had as a child. So vivid, so real, of someone chasing her and nearly catching her, and she wished she could spare him the fear dreams like that bring to a child. But there was one big difference between her dreams and Timmy's.

Hers were only a figment of her imagination.

His were based on a real threat.

Her scattered thoughts went back to the car she'd assumed had been following

74

them as they'd driven toward the zoo. That incident had turned out to be a false alarm. Yet, had she and Timmy been followed or spied on at other times since they'd left home and not even been aware of it? She'd been careful to cover their tracks. The bus ride to Denver where they stayed overnight then bought a ticket. Another bus to Kansas City. Two nights in two different motels there, then the long bus ride to Memphis. As careful as they were, if they'd been followed wouldn't they have noticed? And if anyone intended them harm, surely they would have accosted them by now. Unless they were still searching and hadn't been able to find them. Though she tightly shut her eyes, she could still see Skitch Fallon's beady eyes peering at her through his shaggy brows as she sat in the witness box in the courtroom.

She shifted her position as she glared at the fiery red numbers staring back at her from the nightstand and wished she were back home in Dallas, in her own bed, living her own life. Everything had happened so suddenly. Without warning. If only they'd been fifteen minutes earlier, or fifteen minutes later to the bank, home in her own bed is exactly where she would be right now.

Well, if there was one redeeming factor in their situation, it was their opportunity to meet Ben Bramwell and his daughter. Seeing Bramwell House and all the other evidences of Ben's apparent wealth and knowing he'd give it all up in a heartbeat if his daughter was whole in both body and spirit, had given her a new appreciation for her own health and well-being, and that of Timmy's. Money certainly couldn't buy everything.

Money, and the love of it. That was what had brought the two of them to Memphis.

Someone else's need for money.

She and Timmy were simply pawns.

Eventually, sleep took over her thoughts.

At seven, Judy roused herself out of bed and tugged on Timmy's pajama sleeve. "Get up, sleepyhead."

Timmy's head popped out from under the covers, his face etched with lines from his night of cowering beneath the quilt. "Do I have to?"

Grabbing his hand, she tugged him into a standing position and headed him toward the bathroom. "We've got homeschooling to do. You don't want to be behind when we go back to Dallas, do you?" She gave him a gentle pat on his seat. "Go brush your teeth."

Although he was less than enthusiastic, he obeyed.

After a hearty breakfast of oatmeal, toast, and juice, the two headed out for their usual morning walk.

"So what are your plans for today?" a voice asked from behind her.

She turned to find Ben striding toward her, donned in a navy blue jogging suit with a beautiful black Lab at his heels. "I didn't know you had a dog."

"Misty has been at the vet's for several days. She had a nasty bout with some kind of virus that's been hitting the dogs in our area. But she's back now, aren't you, girl?" He stooped to pet the black Lab pup, who obviously adored him from the way she wagged her tail.

"Can I throw a stick for her?" Timmy asked, picking up a small fallen branch from the yard.

Ben grinned. "Sure, she loves to chase sticks." Once Timmy had hurried off with Misty, Ben asked, "You didn't answer me, Judy. What are you up to today?"

Her face squiggled up a bit. "Homeschooling and working at my job. Same as every day."

"You never did tell me much about your job. I know you work at home, but what exactly do you do?"

She wanted to say, "I'm a highly skilled computer programmer who is forced on hiatus," but she didn't. "I'm a customer service consultant for a large mail order house. The calls go into their eight hundred number and automatically get forwarded to me and several other people like me across the country."

"That was what you were doing before you moved to Memphis?"

"Pretty much, but I was more involved with computers there."

"I'll bet you make a terrific customer service rep." He kicked a rock off the driveway with the toe of his running shoe and lowered his head as if he didn't want to look her in the eye. "As one who hires a number of employees each year, may I make a suggestion?"

"Of course I wouldn't mind. I value your opinion."

His eyes still focused on his running shoe, he offered, "I think it might be a good idea to comb your hair a little—differently. You know, in a more stylish manner."

Her hands automatically rose to her red hair and she began to smooth it, pulling the tendrils close around her face.

"No, not like that."

She backed away as he reached out his hand.

"Away from your face. You're such a pretty woman, Judy. You shouldn't hide behind your hair. Let people see your lovely face—"

She wanted to shout, "But that's the whole idea! I don't want people to notice me. I don't want them to be able to see my face. I'm hiding!" But instead, she answered while still tugging at her hair, "I know you mean well, Ben. But—"

"But what?" His hand cupped her shoulder as he waited for her answer. "I wish you'd listen to me. I'm only trying to help."

"I like my hair this way," she stated firmly, appreciating his concern but wishing he'd back off.

He shrugged and pulled his hand away. "Okay, I'm sorry I interfered. I simply wanted to put in my two cents' worth as an employer."

"And I appreciate that, Ben. Honest I do. I know you mean well, but like I said, I like it this way." She hated herself for sloughing off his advice like that. "I guess it's a woman thing, like Phoebe wearing her skirts too short."

He threw up his hands. "Good grief, Judy. Do all our conversations have to come back to Phoebe? If I didn't know better, I'd think you were jealous of that woman."

Wow, that hit between the eyeballs. Jealous? Of course she was jealous. That woman was engaged to the nicest, kindest man she'd ever met, and totally unworthy of him. Jealous was a mild word for what she felt about Phoebe and her engagement to Ben Bramwell.

"Jealous?" she asked, her hands flying to her hips as she attempted to keep both her voice and her emotions under control. "That's absurd. What would I be jealous of? Her looks? Her money? Her social standing? Her engagement to you? The possibility of her becoming Victoria's mother? What?"

With a mocking move, he leaned into her face, his hands going to his hips. "Try all of the above."

"You think I'd change places with her if I could?"

With his hands still on his hips, he leaned even closer to her until their noses were mere inches apart. "You said it. I didn't. But yes, I think you'd love to change places with Phoebe."

Her eyes flashed with fire as she inched even closer. "Not me, Ben. If I changed places with that witch, I'd probably end up acting like her and I'd never want that to happen. Phoebe Vanderbur is not the kind of woman you need in your life!"

He inched even closer until his nose brushed against hers. "And what kind of a woman do I need, Miss Know-It-All? A woman like you?"

She pressed her nose against his. "Exactly."

"In my arms?" he repeated.

"Exactly."

"Then come into my arms, Judy," he whispered in a husky tone that sent shivers down her body. "Let me hold you."

She found herself helpless as his arms slid around her and pressed against her back. Without meaning to, she released a sigh of surrender. In her wildest dreams she'd never considered being held in Ben's arms like this. She lifted her face slowly to find his mellow gaze searching her face, as if for approval for what he was doing. What should she say? What could she say? This was the moment she'd waited for.

"I—"

His lips sought hers, silencing her.

Unable to control the knowledge that she shouldn't be doing this, she melded against them, savoring their softness as she basked in the wonderful scent of his woodsy aftershave. If only this moment could last forever.

Ben was right.

Absolutely right.

She *was* jealous of Phoebe Vanderbur.

"I'm sorry," he whispered into her ear when their lips finally parted. "Really sorry. I don't know what came over me."

"You—you're sorry for kissing me?" She rested her head against his shoulder, knowing she should back away, but it felt so good to be held in his arms this way.

"No, for giving you advice on your hairstyle."

She could almost see him smile as he trailed kisses down her cheek and sought her lips a second time.

"But I'm not sorry for kissing you."

"You're forgiven," she confessed dreamily. "For giving me advice." Her arms found their way around his neck, and she allowed her fingers to trail through the slightly graying hair at his nape. Even though she knew this moment couldn't last, she clung to it as tightly as she could. He belonged to another woman. Phoebe Vanderbur. And even if he didn't, she was in no position to seek a mate. Her complicated life wouldn't allow a relationship, not even a stolen one.

Now what do we do? she wondered as they stood in the middle of the blacktop and gazed into one another's eyes.

"I can't believe I kissed you like that." Ben broke his grasp and moved back a step. "Oh, Judy. I should say I'm sorry but—ah—you're—I—"

She could identify with his lack of words. She herself was speechless. And breathless, too, thanks to their impromptu kisses. "You—you don't need to say anything, Ben. I wanted you to kiss me."

His hands dropped to his sides as he gave her a nervous stare. "And I wanted to kiss you. What's wrong with me? I'm supposed to be engaged, yet I'm acting like a lovesick schoolboy with raging hormones. I wouldn't blame you if you slapped me." He stepped forward again and turned his cheek toward her. "Go ahead, take your best shot. I deserve it."

"How could I slap you—when I was as much at fault as you were? I was asking for it, and we both know it. You're only being a gentleman by offering to take the entire blame." Her head dropped to her chest as she realized how brazen she'd been. "Whatever must you think of me?"

"Think of you?" He took both her hands in his. "I think you are one of the finest women I've ever met. To be a single mom and have the great attitude you have, to love your son and take such good care of him, well, you're very special, Judy Smith. Any man would be proud to have you as his wife." He gave her hands an affectionate squeeze. "I know you're still recovering from your husband's recent death and you're probably not ready for a meaningful relationship yet, but someday you'll find another man as decent and loving as your husband was, and you'll be ready to commit again and love again. If you and I had met another time, in another place—"

"We might have been right for each other?" she asked with a heavy heart, her eyes misting over.

"Who knows?" Ben answered with a slight shrug. "I—I admit, I find you most attractive. You're a hard woman to resist, but I had no right to take advantage of you like I did."

Judy turned her face away as her tears rose to the surface.

The cellular phone he'd tucked in his pocket rang as he reached out to her. He stepped aside to answer it.

Judy rubbed her sleeve across her eyes, thankful for a moment to regroup and pull herself together. From his side of the conversation she could tell it was Phoebe and she hated the woman for interrupting the most precious, intimate time she'd ever had with a man—until she acknowledged the fact that he belonged to Phoebe, not to her.

"Yes, I'm planning on meeting you for lunch, Phoebe," he was saying into the small flip phone. "Yes, at the country club. At noon. No, I won't forget. I was thinking of bringing Victoria with me."

Judy listened as she stood gazing off in space, feeling awkward and confused as her fingertips touched her lips, the lips he'd kissed only minutes before.

"But why? The club is wheelchair accessible," he was saying. "I'll drive the sedan. Her chair fits in it just fine. It's a beautiful day. I thought she'd enjoy having lunch with us."

So? Phoebe doesn't want Victoria to join them. Why am I not surprised?

"Phoebe, if you're going to be my wife, you're going to have to get used to having Victoria accompany us. She's not a doll you can leave in her doll carriage when you get tired of playing with her, you know. She's my flesh and blood. I have—" Ben turned slightly away and fingered the phone nervously, shifting it to his other hand mid-sentence. "Okay. That's better. We'll meet you at twelve sharp in the lobby." He snapped the lid shut and stuffed the phone into his pocket with a deep sigh. "That was Phoebe."

"So I gathered. You and Victoria are going to have lunch with her today?"

"Yes, although I'm sure Phoebe would much prefer I leave my physically challenged daughter at home." He lifted his eyes to Judy, frustration written all over his face. "You know, when that woman says *handicapped*, it almost sounds like a dirty word."

Judy decided not to comment on his statement. He'd said it all. She had nothing to add. "Well, if I'm going to get any work done, I'd better get with the program. See you later. Enjoy your lunch." She turned and called for Timmy as she walked swiftly up the long drive toward her garage apartment. The boy appeared from around back with Misty at his heels.

Before Timmy was in earshot, Ben called out softly, "Judy?"

She stopped in her tracks but didn't turn to face him. "Yes?"

"I'm sorry."

Surprised, and not quite sure what he was sorry for, she spun around to face him. "That you kissed me or criticized my hairstyle?"

He paused, then smiled that crooked smile of his that sent her into orbit. "Guess."

∞

"Well, that's it for today. You're pretty good at math. Better than I was when I was your age. You can go outside and play for fifteen minutes, but stay close to the apartment and don't talk to strangers, okay?"

"Okay." Timmy smiled at her then grabbed a cookie and headed for the door. Judy folded up the math test she'd hand-written for him and placed it in the kitchen drawer. She'd barely closed the drawer when the phone rang.

"Judy," a tiny female voice said, "can Timmy come over and watch TV with me?"

No doubt about it, it was Victoria. "I'm sure he'll want to come, honey. He'll be real excited when I tell him you called and invited him. Did you have a good lunch with your daddy and Phoebe?"

"No," the little girl replied, a note of sadness in her voice. "Phoebe didn't want me to go."

Judy stiffened. "What do you mean, Phoebe didn't want you to go? I was with your daddy when he talked to Phoebe on the phone this morning. I thought it was all settled that the three of you were going to have lunch at the country club."

"Phoebe called me and said she didn't think I should go. She told me I wouldn't have any fun with all those grown-ups, and she said they might look at me funny since I was in a wheelchair."

A heavy ache rose in Judy's chest and she wanted to go pound Phoebe into the ground. The nerve of that woman, telling an already sensitive child something so ridiculous. It was obvious where such motivation had come from. Phoebe simply didn't want to be bothered with Victoria—today or any day. "Maybe you misunderstood her, sweetie," she said, remembering Ben's words and trying to give Phoebe the benefit of the doubt. "I know your daddy wanted you there."

"But she didn't," the child insisted. "I've told Daddy she doesn't like me, but he won't believe me."

You're right. He doesn't believe you, Judy wanted to say, but she held her tongue. "Well, when you love someone it's hard to believe something bad about them. Your daddy loves Phoebe, so it's hard for him to even consider that she might not love you as much as he does. Maybe, since she's never had children of her own, she doesn't know how to talk to little girls." Judy bit at her lip. Had she really said that? Was she actually making excuses for Phoebe's selfish actions? That was a first. She didn't like the woman any better than Victoria did.

"I know you like me, Judy. You're nice to me. I wish Daddy loved you instead of Phoebe. I'd rather have you for my mother."

Judy dropped onto the kitchen stool and stared with unseeing eyes at the toaster. "Ah—I'd like to be your mother. I mean—you'd be a wonderful daughter." She gulped at the prospect. "But your daddy has chosen Phoebe to be his wife."

"But I don't like her, Judy. Doesn't my daddy care?"

She could hear the tremor in Victoria's voice as she listened. "I'm sure your daddy cares, Tory. But he loves Phoebe, and he wants you to love her, too."

"Well, I don't love her," the little girl stated firmly. "And I'm not going to love her either. She's mean."

This conversation was going nowhere, and if Ben ever got wind of the fact that Judy and his daughter had been discussing the negative sides of his fiancée, he'd never forgive her. He might even ask her to move. "I have to get busy now, Tory. I'll send Timmy over right away. Maybe you can come over here and play tomorrow after you both get your schoolwork done. Would you like that?"

Victoria's voice perked up. "Yes, I would like that. I'll tell my daddy. Misty and I will be waiting for Timmy at the door. Bye."

"Bye, Tory." *Victoria is such a sweet child, and Ben is doing such a good job as a single daddy. I just hope Phoebe doesn't mess up that relationship when she becomes a part of their family—if she becomes part of their family.*

Judy leaned over the sink and parted the curtains on the window to make sure Timmy was staying close by as she'd told him to. What she saw made her heart sink. A dark sedan was parked in the driveway, and although she couldn't see the faces of the two men in the car she was sure they were the same two men she'd seen on their way to the zoo. But what scared her most of all, they were talking to Ben Bramwell.

How she wished she could hear their conversation. Were they asking about her? About Timmy?

"Timmy!" she said aloud, clutching the sink for support. "I'm sure he won't talk to them, not after I warned him." Should she go down and tell him to come inside? If she did, would they recognize her? If she didn't, would they snatch Timmy up and carry him off somewhere and she'd never see him again?

Her heart raced.

What should she do?

She glanced out the window again and there was Timmy, running across the drive toward Ben and the two men. She had to do something, but what? He was getting closer and closer to the car where Ben and the men were still in conversation.

Without stopping to retrieve the shoes she'd kicked off under the table when she and Timmy had been working on his math lesson, in her stockinged feet she raced toward the door, flung it open and hurried down the stairs taking two or three steps at a time, and rushed into the driveway flailing her arms and calling Timmy's name.

Timmy waved at her, a big smile beaming across his face.

Ben and the two men turned to see who Timmy was waving at. She had to reach him before the men could take him away from her.

She and Timmy connected with one another right beside the car. She pulled him into her arms protectively and held him tightly, nearly suffocating the poor child.

"Judy, where are your shoes?" Ben frowned as both he and the men stared at her feet.

"I—I was so excited to tell Timmy Victoria had called, I guess I forgot them." She looked past Ben into the curious faces of the two men. The two men she'd seen before. She was almost sure of it.

Ben nodded toward their visitors. "These gentlemen were asking directions, and we got to talking about the man who does the landscaping here at Bramwell House." He gestured toward Judy. "This is my new tenant and her son."

Ben! Be quiet! Don't tell them anything about us! she wanted to shout at him. Instead, she said a quick hello and excused herself and Timmy, dragging him toward the apartment.

"What's wrong, Aunt Judy?" Timmy asked once the door had been closed and locked behind them. "You're hurting my arm."

For the first time she realized how tightly she'd been clinging to him. "I'm sorry, sweetie. I didn't know those men, and we can't be too careful. I was just trying to keep you safe, that's all. Forgive me?" She tried to appear calm but inside, she was a raging jumble of nerves. *Who were those men really? They seemed harmless enough, but she couldn't take any chances.*

The next time she peeked through the curtains, she found the driveway empty. The dark sedan was gone and so was Ben. When she felt it was safe enough to allow Timmy outside, she walked him to Bramwell House where she knew Tory would be impatiently waiting for him.

With Misty at his side, wagging a greeting with her tail, Ben met them at the door. "Hi, Timmy. Tory has been sitting in this doorway for the past half hour waiting for you. Come on in." He ran his hand over the boy's red hair as Timmy passed by.

A delighted little girl smiled from her wheelchair.

Judy turned to go, but Ben caught hold of her hand. "Okay, lady. You have some explaining to do."

She put on the most innocent expression she could muster. "Explaining? About what?"

"You know. Running out to meet Timmy like that in your stockinged feet. No woman I've ever known would do such a thing. What was with you? I've never seen you so upset."

"I—I was embarrassed, that's all. I'd forgotten I'd taken my shoes off."

Ben tilted his head and searched her face. "Give me a break, Judy. That's about the feeblest excuse I've ever heard. Out with it! What really happened to send you tearing down the drive without your shoes?"

His hand still clamped onto her wrist, he waited for her answer and she knew she'd have to come up with a better story than forgetting she'd left her shoes in the apartment. "Answer my question first. Exactly who were those men, and why did they stop *here* for directions when there are so many other places they could have stopped?"

He gave her a mystified stare. "What difference does that make?"

She attempted to tug her hand away from his grasp with no success. "Just answer, please. Humor me."

"Actually, I don't know much about them. Victoria saw their car pull into my driveway and park while she was waiting for Timmy. I didn't recognize either them or the car, so I walked out to see what they were doing here."

"Did they tell you?" she asked, struggling to conceal her concern about what he'd said so far.

"Not really. They asked about the location of a building I'd never heard of then began asking about my landscaping and who did it. I thought that was kind of strange. The landscaping is great, but not that great. Then they asked about the garage apartment and wanted to know if anyone lived there. I—"

"Did you tell them?" she asked quickly, her heart pounding in her throat.

"Sure. I told them it was rented. One of the men said he had an attic over his garage he was thinking about turning into an apartment. He asked about the floor plan and the size of the rooms, that sort of thing. He seemed really interested. Why?"

Judy's free hand flew to her chest as she tried to get control of herself. His news had sent her blood pressure soaring and her palms began to sweat. "Did they ask any questions about Timmy and me?"

"No, not exactly, although they did ask if my renter was single or if I'd rented to a family. I think they were just making pleasant conversation," he said matter-of-factly. Then as if seeing the terror in her eyes, he asked, "Judy, are you in some sort of trouble?"

She lifted her chin defiantly. "Of course not."

He relaxed his grasp on her arm. "You're sure?"

"I'm sure."

"Because if you are, I'll do whatever I can to help you."

She offered a weak, appreciative smile to her benefactor. "Thank you, Ben, but I don't need your help." With that, she pulled away from him and moved quickly out the door, leaving Timmy behind.

∽

Ben watched her go. Something was wrong. He could feel it in his bones. He'd sensed it that very first day but hadn't listened to his intuition. But getting to know her this past week, spending time with her and Timmy—he knew, whatever trouble she might be in would not be trouble of her own making. She was an honorable woman and a wonderful mother. If only she would confide in him. But he had a feeling she was too proud, too independent to lean on anyone. Especially a near stranger.

And why had she been so frightened of the two men in the car? No woman runs outside in her stockinged feet and takes a chance on ruining them. There was more to this situation than she was willing to admit. Perhaps he could find out on his own—hire a detective to check out Judy Smith and her son, Timmy.

He shook his head to clear it. What was he thinking? This woman was his tenant. He'd known her less than a week, and he was considering hiring a detective to check on her? Ridiculous.

Ben turned as he heard two giggling children approaching. It seemed the only time Victoria wore a smile was when Timmy and Judy were around. He watched as Timmy spun Victoria's chair around in circles, with Misty barking at the wheels, until the two children were too dizzy to do it any longer, their joyous laughter filling the big house.

Then he thought about his lunch with Phoebe and how disappointed he'd been when she'd told him she called Victoria and the child had told her she'd rather not go to lunch with them. Was Victoria being a spoiled brat, as Phoebe called her quite often? Or did she genuinely dislike his fiancée?

"Mr. Bramwell."

Ben felt a tug on his trouser leg. "Yes, Timmy?"

"Did you tell those bad men about me?"

Chapter 7

The frightened expression on Timmy's face told Ben something was radically wrong. He'd never seen such fear on an eight-year-old's face before. "No, Timmy, I didn't tell them about you. What made you think I would?" *Something is going on with Timmy and Judy, something that's not good, but what?*

Timmy looked as guilty as if he'd stolen the Hope diamond. "I—wondered."

Judy appeared at the door an hour later. "Supper's ready. I've come for Timmy."

"Judy, Timmy asked me a strange question," Ben told her as he motioned her inside. "He wanted to know if I'd told those men about him. What interest would they have in knowing about Timmy?"

Judy reached out and pulled the boy to her. "He had a terrible dream last night and didn't sleep very well. I think he's overly tired. That's all."

Ben knew her excuse for Timmy's behavior was simply that—an excuse, and he wasn't about to believe it. "Look, Judy. I get the feeling you're hiding something. I don't know if you're in trouble or what, but I want you to know—whatever it is, I'm willing to help."

"Trouble? We're not in any trouble. I can't imagine why you'd say such a thing."

You're lying! I can see it on your face. Hear it in your voice. Ben placed a reassuring hand on her shoulder. "Just remember, Judy, I'm here for you."

"Thanks for your offer, Ben, but you needn't worry about us. We're fine." She latched onto Timmy's hand. "I'd better get Timmy upstairs before his supper cools off."

Ben kept his gaze locked on the pair until the door at the bottom of the apartment's stairway closed behind them. "Mark my words, Judy Smith. I don't give up easily. I *am* going to find out what's going on in your lives."

After supper, with Victoria on his back and a carton of Rocky Road ice cream in his hand, Ben made his way across the driveway and punched the intercom button. After hearing, "Come on up," from Judy, he made his way up the stairs.

"I didn't expect to see you two again today. Who's that little cutie on your back?" Judy winked toward Victoria.

"My precious daughter, who has all of a sudden turned into an ice cream

86

addict. She insisted we try to entice you and Timmy to indulge with us. We've brought Rocky Road." He reached out the carton to her then lowered Victoria onto the sofa. "Hope you don't mind us coming without an invitation."

The child's eyes lit up. "It's Timmy's favorite and now I like it, too!"

Eager to show her the picture he'd drawn during their homeschool session that day, Timmy sat down beside her and the two were soon engrossed in conversation.

Ben sent his daughter an adoring smile then followed Judy into the kitchen. "She's eaten more ice cream since the two of you arrived than she has in the past two years. I actually think she's putting on a bit of weight."

Judy pulled four bowls from the cabinet and began to dip the ice cream. "You're so lucky to have Victoria, Ben. She's a wonderful child."

"We nearly didn't have her. Carlotta couldn't have children."

Judy stopped dipping and turned to face him. "Oh, Ben, I'm so sorry. How awful for the two of you."

"We tried everything. Went to specialists in both New York and Chicago. Nothing worked. We finally gave up and decided on adoption. It took two years before we were able to find and adopt Victoria." With a shake of his head, Ben sat down at the table. "Can you imagine someone giving up a baby? Their own flesh and blood?"

"It must have been terribly hard on the mother."

He did a tsk-tsk. "That girl was only seventeen. I can't imagine kids that age having sex and getting themselves into that predicament. The attorney who handled the adoption told us the girl's boyfriend dumped her when he found out she was pregnant."

Judy went back to dipping. "At least she made sure her baby was given to a loving family. Does Victoria know she's adopted?"

"No. Both Carlotta and I decided it would be best if she didn't know until later. Maybe when she's eighteen. We know so little about her birth mother, except that she was promiscuous."

"How did you know that? Did you ever meet her? Meet her boyfriend?"

Ben rolled his eyes. "Come on, Judy. Any unmarried girl who has a baby at seventeen has been promiscuous. That baby didn't just happen."

"Do you think Victoria will want to find her birth mother?"

"I hope not. I really don't want Victoria to know she's the product of some careless teenager with raging hormones."

"If she wanted to find her birth mother, would you help her?"

He cocked his head to one side, thoughtfully considering the question. "I'm not sure. Guess I'll have to cross that bridge when I come to it. But I have to admit I'm thankful that girl decided to give her baby away. I can't imagine life without my sweet, precious Victoria."

"You are truly blessed, Ben. She had to have been a gift from God." After closing up the carton and placing it in the freezer, Judy handed the bowl with the most ice cream to Ben.

He took it, placed it on the table, then rose, his gaze pinned on her all the while. "I had more than ice cream on my mind when I decided to come up here tonight."

She turned her head away, avoiding his gaze. "I kinda figured that."

Ben grasped both her hands in his. "I know this isn't any of my business, but I like you and Timmy and I'm concerned about you. Come clean, Judy. What's troubling the two of you?"

"I've already told you. Nothing."

"You're lying. Why won't you tell me?"

"I—I can't."

"Why?"

"I—I don't want to get you involved."

"There was fear written all over your face when those two men were here asking for directions. Why, Judy? Why would you be afraid of them? I'm not going to quit asking until you tell me, so you might as well do it."

"I—I think they were following me."

Ben reared back, his brows lowered. "Following you? Why would they want to follow you?"

"I can't tell you, Ben. I'm afraid it's time for Timmy and me to move on. I couldn't bear the thought of anything happening to you because of us."

"Move on? You can't! You and Timmy have become an important part of our lives. Victoria needs you." Cupping her chin with his hand, he lifted her face to his. "I—I need you. Promise me you won't do anything rash without telling me!"

"You and Victoria will get along fine without us. Phoebe and you will soon be married and she'll have—"

"I'm not going to marry Phoebe."

Judy gasped. "You're not going to marry Phoebe? When did you decide that?"

"You've convinced me marrying her would be a mistake."

"Don't blame that decision on me! Who am I to tell you what to do? I don't even know the woman."

"I'm not blaming you, Judy. I'm thanking you for it. My little girl has never liked that woman. Actually, since you've come along, I realize I don't even like her. I've been trying to find a way to end this ridiculous engagement without hurting

Phoebe. The whole thing is going to be an embarrassment to her, unless—"

"Unless you can make it look like she dumped you."

"Exactly."

Judy sucked in a deep breath. Everything was happening so fast. She'd had no idea Ben had made up his mind about calling off their engagement. "Are you prepared to do that? What about her father? You have to work with him. Won't he be upset?"

"I'm sure he will, but I can't concern myself with that. Even if I loved Phoebe, which I don't, Victoria has never liked her. And, if I were honest, I'd admit Phoebe has never liked my daughter. She's gone out of her way to avoid Victoria. She even suggested we should consider sending her off to a special school for physically challenged children. I can't believe I let things go this far."

"I'm sure you thought you were doing the right thing."

"I did. How could I have been so stupid? So blind? Marriage to Phoebe would have been a nightmare. You saw through her right from the start."

"Ben, how I feel about Phoebe is of no consequence. It's how *you* feel about her that's important. You *and* Victoria. I had no business butting in like I have but I only did it because I want the best for you."

Her heart soared as Ben gazed into her eyes. "Maybe you're what's best for me. I—I think I'm falling in love with you, Judy."

Her breath caught in her throat and she found herself speechless.

"Say something! Don't just let me stand here. Do you think you could ever love me?"

"Hey, where's the ice cream?"

Judy and Ben parted quickly as Timmy came into the room carrying Victoria piggyback.

Feeling a blush rise to her cheeks, Judy hurriedly pulled the ice cream carton from the freezer and began dipping as fast as she could. "I'll have it ready in a minute."

"We'll talk more about this later," Ben whispered in her ear as he began gathering napkins and spoons for the tray.

"But—"

"I love you, Judy, and now that I've found you, I'm not about to let you go. I'll be back after I put Victoria to bed. Wait up for me."

After the ice cream had been consumed, Ben and Victoria bade Judy and Timmy good night. But Ben returned an hour later. "Put your jacket on and come with me. I have something to show you."

She checked on Timmy, who was sleeping soundly in his bed, then did as she was told. Soon they were making their way past the house to a thick grove of trees at the back of Ben's property, their path illuminated by a gorgeous full moon.

"Look," Ben told her as he parted a few branches and motioned her to step through the opening.

"A gazebo! Oh, Ben, it's beautiful!"

Taking her hand, he led her up the few steps to the built-in bench circling the outer edge. "I built this to memorialize my wife. She'd always wanted a gazebo but, somehow, I never got around to building it for her. Then—it was too late. I come out here sometimes, when I need to think. I—I've never shown it to Victoria."

Judy sat down and ran her fingers around the delicately turned post. "Why not? She'd love it!"

"I was afraid it might upset her. She's taken her mother's loss much harder than any of us anticipated."

"I'm so glad you brought me here."

Ben seated himself beside her and slipped his arm about her shoulders. "I brought you here so we could talk. I have to know what's bothering you."

"Okay, I admit I do have a problem, but I refuse to drag you into it."

"You're running away from something or someone, aren't you? Does it have anything to do with your husband? Was he in trouble? Do you owe money?"

"No, nothing like that. We just wanted a fresh start."

"Sorry, kiddo, your story doesn't hold water. You were terrified when those two men stopped by today. Out with it. What's wrong?"

She racked her brain for a valid excuse. "You hear so much about kidnapping these days. I guess I'm just a little jumpy where Timmy is concerned. That's all."

Ben pulled her close to him. "Look, Judy. I'm crazy about you. Totally in love. I know we've only known each other for a short time but for the first time in my life, I believe in love at first sight. I was drawn to you the day you showed up wanting to rent my apartment."

"You probably have feelings for me because Victoria and I are so close, that's all." She wanted so much to throw her arms around his neck, kiss his lips, and tell him how much she loved him.

"No, that's not it at all! You're drawn to me, too!"

"No, you're wrong!"

"Prove it! Kiss me, then tell me you don't feel the same vibes I'm feeling."

His words ripped at her heart because she was unable to accept his love, at least not until Skitch Fallon was captured and out of her life. How she longed to let loose all the emotions she'd held back for so long. "Ben, please. We have to end this now. I admit I have feelings for you, too. You're a wonderful man, but there can never be a future for us. My life is too complicated."

"I'll help you uncomplicate it!"

She rose and hurried down the gazebo's steps. "No, Ben. It can never happen. I have to get back to Timmy." *There's so much you don't know! If only I could tell you!*

With a look of defeat, Ben joined her and they walked back to the apartment in silence.

Before going to bed, Judy knelt and poured her heart out to the Lord, begging Him not only for safety, but for wisdom and guidance about her and Ben's relationship, and what she should do next.

∞

"You what?" Judy asked Timmy the next day when she returned from the grocery store and found him standing on the porch in front of Bramwell House.

"I—I accidentally told Tory our real home is in Dallas." The boy began to cry. "I'm sorry, Aunt Judy, but we were looking at the map in my library book and it slipped out. I asked her not to tell anyone."

She pulled him close. He'd done such a good job of hiding their true identity. Very few eight-year-olds would have done as well. "Don't worry about it. She's probably already forgotten it. Just try to remember, okay? Our lives may depend on us keeping our secret. Maybe we should have trusted the police after all and not run away and tried to hide on our own."

The front door to the big house opened and Ben strode out. "Timmy, Miranda sent me out to tell you the cookies are ready. Why don't you go inside and eat them while they're hot?"

Timmy sent a quick glance toward Judy. "Can I?"

She nodded. "Only if you bring me one."

They watched as Timmy raced up onto the porch, then Ben turned toward her, a small smile tilting at his lips. "Not still upset with me, are you?"

Struggling to put her anxieties aside, Judy gave him a shy smile. "Of course not. I want us to be friends."

His expression sobered. "Judy, I've thought, prayed long and hard, and I've come to a decision. I'm definitely going to tell Phoebe I'm breaking our engagement because I'm convinced she doesn't love my daughter and never will, but, most of all, because I don't love her and I doubt she loves me. There's never been a real emotional tie between us."

"Ben, are you sure about this? Take some time to think about it. Be sure it's the right thing. This isn't something that should be decided overnight. I'm so afraid my bias against Phoebe has influenced you."

"But I don't love her. I love you!"

Tears welled up in her eyes. "I—I love you, too. That's why I want you to take some time before doing anything rash, something you may regret later. Maybe if Phoebe and Victoria spent some time together, got to know each other a little better, they'd—"

"You know that'll never happen."

They both turned as the yellow convertible appeared in the driveway.

"Remember what I said, Ben. Take your time." Judy pulled away from him, her heart aching, and ran toward the apartment.

Standing behind the lace curtains, she watched from her window as Phoebe wrapped herself around Ben and smothered him with kisses. She felt like a helpless bystander who could only sit back idly watching her life slip away, at least until her brother's killer was apprehended and put back behind bars where he belonged, which could be years from now. Though she wouldn't admit it to a soul, ever since the robbery she *had* questioned her faith in God. Why would He let her wonderful, godly brother be gunned down so needlessly? In the prime of his life? *Oh, Ben, if only things could have been different.*

Judy held Timmy's hand the next morning as they took their routine walk about the estate. But something caught her eye. A black sedan parked on the street only a few hundred yards away. Panic set in. Could it be the same one? If it was, why were those men back? She and Timmy had to leave. They'd pack up their personal belongings and head for St. Louis, or Kansas City, or maybe even Chicago. But when she looked back a few minutes later, the car was gone. Had her paranoia set in again? Was she seeing ghosts around every tree? Flinching at the sound of a tree branch brushing across a window screen? Startling at her own shadow?

By the time she and Timmy had finished the lessons she'd prepared for that day, she had convinced herself it truly was coincidence that car had parked in that particular spot and allowed Timmy to go to Bramwell House to play Clue with Victoria. She almost didn't answer when the buzzer sounded, sure it was Ben, and she didn't know what they could say except what they'd said at the gazebo. But not answering would be rude. He had to know she was home.

"I have to talk to you," he told her, barging past her into the apartment. "I haven't been able to sleep a wink for thinking about you. You've got me in a quandary, Judy Smith. I don't know what to do. I don't want to marry Phoebe—I want to marry you—but you want no part of me."

"I told you—"

He held up a hand to silence her. "Let me talk, please. Like you suggested, I put off telling Phoebe I want to break our engagement. I've prayed and prayed about this thing, but no answers have come. This morning, when I told Victoria I was thinking about calling the wedding off, she actually giggled! I've never seen her so happy. She begged me to come up to this apartment right then and ask you to marry me. She had the crazy idea we could have our wedding at the church this weekend, after the morning service! It was all Miranda and Max and I could do to get her to calm down. She kept saying how happy she was that you were going to be her mother and Timmy was going to be her brother. How can I tell her you two are leaving? Walking out of our lives? Without even telling us why?"

"I'm sorry, Ben. I can't tell you why. Just know that if things were different, I'd jump at the chance to marry you. But they're not different, and I have no choice but to live with my situation."

"And you don't feel you can confide in me? Let me help you with whatever problems you're facing."

She bit at her lip. "No, I can't."

"So—in essence—you're telling me to get lost? Right?"

"I wouldn't exactly put it that way."

"But you're still saying there is no future for the two of us."

"Yes, that's what I'm saying."

He shrugged then backed toward the door, throwing his hands up in defeat. "Okay, then. From now on, I guess we're just landlord and tenant. Give me a call if the roof leaks, the plumbing stops up, or there is any other problem with the apartment. Those are problems I can fix. You and I may not have much to do with each other but, as long as you're here, I hope you'll continue to let Timmy come to the house to play with Victoria."

"I would never do anything to hurt Victoria. I hope you know that. I—I didn't want to hurt you, either."

He lowered his head, avoiding her eyes. "But you did hurt me, Judy, and I'm still hurting."

"I'm—sorry. I never meant to."

"I'm sorry, too. You and I could have a great life together." With that, Ben moved onto the landing at the head of the stairs and closed the door behind him.

Judy stared at the door, her heart breaking. *I'll always love you, Ben. There'll never be another man for me. I only hope you won't hate me for upsetting your life like I have.*

"What's the matter with Ben?" Timmy asked as he returned from playing Clue with Victoria. "He looked like he was mad or something."

Judy knelt and took Timmy's hand in hers. "We're leaving in the morning, Timmy, as soon as Ben goes to his office."

Timmy's eyes rounded and filled with tears. "But I don't want to go. I like it here."

"I'm sorry. I like it here, too, but we can't take a chance on staying any longer. Now, be a good boy and get your backpack out of the closet and put all your clothes in it, except the pajamas you'll be wearing tonight and a shirt and jeans for tomorrow. I'm going to pack up my things and the few other items we've bought since we've been here, then I'll come in and tuck you in."

"What about Tory? She'll miss me."

"I know, sweetheart, but you'll make new friends. Now scoot, and don't forget to brush your teeth."

"But—"

"I'm sorry, Timmy. I know you don't want to leave but we have to. Don't make it any harder than it is, okay?"

∞

She spent a sleepless night as all sorts of scenarios rumbled through her head. By morning's light, she felt like she'd been racing on a treadmill all night. After a simple breakfast, she and Timmy stood behind the covering of the lace curtains in the window waiting for Ben to leave for his office.

"Can I tell Tory good-bye?"

"I don't think it'd be wise, Timmy. Maybe we'd just better get in the taxi when it gets here and go."

Big tears welled up in his eyes. "Please?"

"Oh, all right, but we have to make it fast. It's a good half hour to the bus station from here. I've already purchased our tickets on the Internet. We don't want to be late."

As usual, Ben left for his office right on time. Once his car was out of sight, they walked across the lawn to Bramwell House. Victoria met them at the door. "How come you're here so early, Timmy?" she asked after glancing at the big grandfather clock in the foyer.

Timmy shook his head. "I came to say good-bye."

"We're leaving, Victoria," Judy inserted quickly. "We won't be back. Please tell your father good-bye for us."

Victoria began to sob. "Why? I—I don't want you to go!"

"We have to, sweetie. I'm sorry, but that's the way it is. I want you to know I love you and I'll be praying for you." She gestured toward Timmy. "Tell Victoria good-bye, Timmy."

Timmy ran to the little girl and wrapped his arms around her frail shoulders. "Don't cry, Tory. I don't want to go, either."

"Timmy, go on, say good-bye. We have to leave."

Timmy backed away slowly, his lips quivering. "Bye, Tory."

She reached out her hand to him. "Are you sure you have to go?"

He nodded. "Uh-huh. I'm sure."

Judy bent and kissed Victoria's cheek. "I love you, honey, don't ever forget it. You be a big brave girl and mind your daddy." Turning toward Timmy, she added, "I'm going to go find Max and Miranda to thank them for all they've done for us. Wait right here for me."

She found them both in the kitchen. "Something has come up. Timmy and I are packed and ready to leave Memphis, but I wanted to thank you—"

Miranda quickly set aside the vegetables she was cleaning and dried her hands on her apron. "You can't go! What will our little Victoria do without you two?"

"This is going to be very hard on her and on Mr. Bramwell," Max added.

Judy gulped hard. Lies. How she hated them! "I'm sorry I don't have time to explain, but I just wanted you to know how pleasant you've made our stay here."

"At least let me give you some freshly baked cookies to take with you. Chocolate chip. I know they're Timmy's favorites." She scurried across the kitchen, filled a plastic bag with the delicacies, then handed them to Judy. "May the Lord be with you and that precious son of yours."

"Yes, Mrs. Smith, we'll be praying for you."

Judy thanked them again then headed for the front hall.

Timmy was waiting for her, his head hung low. With a heavy heart, Judy took hold of his hand and ushered him out the front door, gently closing it behind them just as the taxi pulled into the driveway. With one final look at Bramwell House, they hurried toward the cab. Before she could pull open the door, the black sedan came roaring into the driveway with Ben's car right behind it, blocking her way.

Her worst fears had come true.

It was the two men who had been asking about the landscaping.

She and Timmy had been found!

Chapter 8

S tep away from the taxi," one of the men ordered as he slammed the door on the black sedan and hurried toward them.

She grabbed Timmy's hand and held it tight, her heart pounding a mile a minute. Were these two hit men sent by Skitch Fallon to do his dirty work? Were they going to shoot her and Timmy right in front of Ben's eyes, then shoot him?

The second man approached her with Ben at his side, his hands held up in surrender fashion, which confused her. "Please, Miss Alexander, we mean you no harm."

Judy glanced from one to the other, not sure whether to trust him. "What are you going to do to us?"

"Let me introduce myself," the taller man said.

Judy flinched as he reached into his pocket, pulled out his wallet, and flashed both an identification card and a badge.

"I'm Agent Marcum and this is Agent Stone. We're with the FBI."

The shorter man gave her a broad smile, exposing two gold teeth. "You're safe now, Miss Alexander. You can go home. We've caught him. Skitch Fallon can no longer harm you."

Feeling light-headed and reeling from the man's words, for the first time in months Judy felt herself relax. "I—I can't tell you how happy I am." Though she tried to hold them back, a trail of tears tumbled down her cheeks. "I–I've been so afraid he would find us."

Ben, who had been standing with his mouth open, stepped forward, his expression one of confusion. "I don't get it. You're with the FBI? What's going on? And why are you calling her Miss Alexander when her name is Judy Smith? And who is Skitch Fallon?"

Timmy climbed out of the car and ran to Judy, wrapping his arms about her tightly. "He's not going to shoot us?"

The second man stooped before Timmy and smiled at him. "No, young man, no one is going to shoot anyone. We're here to help you. That awful man can no longer harm you, thanks to your aunt, though she should have let us do the protecting. She did a good job of hiding the two of you. Good thing she left that note on her dresser saying you two had fled. Otherwise, we would have thought. . ." He paused with a quick glance toward Judy. "Thought something else might have happened to you."

Ben frowned at the man. "Aunt? Why did you call her his aunt? She's his mother."

"The whole thing is pretty complicated, Mr. Bramwell. I suggest Miss Alexander be the one to explain things to you."

Timmy reached out his hand. "Can I see your badge?"

The man pulled his wallet out again, displaying the shiny badge for the boy.

"Wow!" Wide-eyed, Timmy ran his finger over its surface.

"How *did* you find us?" Judy asked, once the blood started flowing through her veins again. "I thought we'd done a pretty good job of covering our tracks."

"Oh," the man said, "you did a fine job. If the clerk at the bus station in Kansas City hadn't recognized you when we sent out an APB with your and Timmy's pictures on it, we might never have found you."

Ben impatiently tapped the man on the shoulder. "Could someone please explain to me what's going on? I think I deserve to know."

Judy nodded toward him. "Oh, Ben, I'm so sorry all of this had to happen. I promise I'll explain everything later. Right now I need to hear everything these gentlemen can tell me. Trust me, okay? Believe me, it was necessary that I keep this from you."

Ben gave her a disgruntled nod. "You have a lot of explaining to do, and I want a full account of everything."

"And you'll get it, I promise."

The agent went on after a quick glance at the two. "You were the key witness that sent Skitch Fallon to prison. We had to do everything we could to find you before he did. That man had nothing to lose by carrying out his threats. Good thing that man at the bus station remembered you when we showed him your pictures."

"But those pictures look nothing like I look now. How did he recognize me?"

The man chuckled. "No, you don't look anything like your pictures with that red wig on and wearing those ridiculous glasses! But, despite the short hair, Timmy looks like himself. It's hard to disguise a face full of freckles. The clerk said Timmy made an impression on him because of his freckles and because he'd been so polite, even offered the man a piece of his bubble gum. He phoned our Tennessee office immediately. By the time you and Timmy climbed off of that bus here in Memphis, we were at the bus station waiting for you."

"Why didn't you say something? Take us into custody?"

"We considered taking you to one of the shelters here in Memphis, but we figured that if by some weird chance Skitch Fallon did find out you'd come to

Memphis, the first place he'd probably look would be a women's shelter. Though we do all we can to keep the location of those shelters a secret from the general public, it's impossible. If he'd asked the right person, offered them enough money, or simply threatened them, they probably would have given him the location. We decided the best thing to do would be to follow you to wherever you ended up then keep you under surveillance."

Ben blinked hard and gave his head a shake. "Who is Skitch Fallon?"

"The man who killed her brother. She testified against him at his trial," the taller agent explained. "Then, after threatening to kill her, he escaped. Walked right out of the courthouse. Heads rolled over that one, believe me."

"That's why you stopped at my house and asked all those questions?"

"Yes, Mr. Bramwell. Your place seemed to be the perfect hideout for these two. But you needn't worry. You were in no danger. We kept a constant eye on you and your family."

Ben stepped up and wrapped his arm protectively around Judy. "No wonder you were running."

Still feeling a bit shaky from their ordeal, Judy turned toward the two men. "Where did you find him?"

"He got as far as Oklahoma City. A buddy of his took him in. I think you had him baffled. It appeared he had no idea where you'd gone and all he had done during the time he was loose was spin his wheels. Eventually, his buddy turned him in for the reward money."

"Reward money?"

"Yes, the company you worked for in Dallas as a computer programmer placed half-page ads in several Texas and Oklahoma newspapers, offering twenty-five thousand dollars to anyone who gave the FBI information that resulted in his capture. No honor among thieves, you know."

Ben grabbed her arm. "You're a computer programmer?"

"Yes, Ben, I am. I'm sorry to have lied to you, but I had to protect Timmy." She reached up and touched her hair. "Well, I guess I don't need this anymore."

Ben gasped loudly as Judy pulled off the frowzy red wig, and let her long hair fall softly to her shoulders. "You're a blond!"

She tugged off the horn-rimmed glasses and smiled up at him, her blue eyes gleaming. "Even these ridiculous oversized glasses were part of my disguise. I don't even wear glasses."

"This is too much!" Ben leaned back and appraised her from head to toe. "You—you're beautiful, Judy."

"I'm so sorry, Ben. I never wanted to deceive you." Judy frowned. "What are you doing here?"

"While you were in the kitchen talking to Max and Miranda, Victoria called my cell phone and told me you were leaving. She was upset and crying so hard I could barely understand her. She begged me to keep you here. I rushed back home as fast as I could."

The taller agent cleared his throat, as if trying to get her attention. "Do you want us to take you somewhere, Miss Alexander? Get you a hotel room? Plane tickets?"

She sent a quick glance toward Ben. "No, I think I need to stay here for a while. Mr. Bramwell has been so good to us, it's only fair that I give him the whole story. As long as I know Skitch Fallon is locked up tight and this time he won't get away, I'll be fine. I promised Timmy we'd take a real vacation when this thing was over. I think I'll rent a car, drive to Branson, Missouri, on the way home, and spend a couple of days doing anything Timmy would like. I understand it's a great place to take kids. After all he's been through, he deserves some real joy in his life. It'll be nice to not have to look over our shoulders for a change."

The shorter man pulled a card from his wallet. "Then I guess we'll be leaving. Here's my card. If you need anything, and I mean *anything*, call me."

"I can't thank you enough for watching out for Timmy and me. I just wish I'd known the two of you were—"

"I wish we could have told you we were here, but the fewer people who knew where you were and that you were under surveillance, the safer you were. I'm just thankful everything turned out like it did." He shook Judy's hand then Timmy's. "You take care of your aunt, young man." Then turning to Ben, he reached out and shook his hand. "She was mighty lucky to have a landlord like you."

"I'm the lucky one." Ben thanked the man then once again circled his arm around Judy's shoulders as the black sedan moved out of his driveway and onto the street. "That man kept calling you Timmy's aunt. I don't get it. Why would he call you his aunt when you're his mother? I have a lot of questions that need answering, Judy. All I know is that someone murdered your brother and was out to get you for testifying against him. The rest is a total blank." He reached out and stroked her hair. "No wonder you've been wearing that awful wig. You must have been terrified."

"Oh, Ben, now I can tell you everything." *Well, not everything, but as much as you need to know.* "I've wanted to confide in you the entire time we've been here, but I just couldn't get you involved. Cancer took Timmy's mother's life a couple years ago. I was only posing as his mother to throw off anyone who might be looking for us."

Timmy tugged on Judy's hand. "Can I go see Tory?"

"Good idea, Timmy. I'm sure she'd love to see you. You have no idea how upset she was when you two told her you were leaving town." Ben took hold of Judy's hand. "Let's all go in the house. Maybe we can talk Miranda into making us some hot chocolate."

After the hot chocolate had been devoured and the children had busied themselves putting Victoria's new puzzle together in the den, Ben seated himself on the living room sofa beside Judy. "Now, how about starting at the beginning and telling me everything? I want to hear all of it, Judy, every little detail."

She knew if anyone deserved to hear the truth, it was dear, sweet, concerned Ben Bramwell. "I guess the best place to start is with Kayla, my brother Jerod's wonderful wife, Timmy's mother. Like I said, she died a little over two years ago from uterine cancer. She was the perfect mother and she loved the Lord with all her heart. We were all devastated by her death. I can't tell you how much we loved her." Judy dabbed at her eyes with her sleeve.

"A few days before she passed away, Kayla made me promise I would help Jerod raise Timmy in her place. The day after her funeral, I moved in with Jerod and Timmy."

"You can tell Timmy loves you," Ben interjected, handing her a tissue from the box on the end table.

She took it and blew her nose. "Jerod was a police officer. He'd wanted to be a police officer since he was about Timmy's age. To make extra money so Kayla could be a stay-at-home mom, he was moonlighting on his days off as a bank guard."

Ben shook his head. "Now I'm beginning to get the picture."

"I banked at the same bank, so after Timmy got out of school one afternoon, I took him to the bank with me to make a deposit. We visited with Jerod for a few minutes then went back out to the car to wait until his shift ended so the three of us could go out for pizza. I never dreamed something was going on inside the bank until two men came running out with ski masks on and leaped into a car parked several spaces down from us. Then the third man came bursting through the doors brandishing a gun in his hand. He jerked off his mask as he climbed into their car and—"

Ben drew in a quick breath. "You saw his face!"

"Yes, I saw his face."

"Did he know you were there?"

"No. He was more interested in getting into that car and making his get-away. Timmy and I actually heard him shout to the other two men to get out of there fast because he'd had to shoot the bank guard. We sat there paralyzed, knowing Jerod had been shot but not sure what we should do. Within seconds, police cars came from every direction, and officers jumped out with their guns drawn and entered the bank."

"And your brother?"

"I didn't know Jerod had died until one of the officers noticed us sitting in the car, recognized us, and came and told us Jerod had been shot three times, once in the heart, and had died instantly." Judy couldn't help it. Reliving that horrendous day was overwhelming and she began to weep openly, sobbing from the depths of her heart.

Ben wrapped his arms securely around her and nestled his chin in her hair. "I'm so sorry, sweetheart. If only I'd known. No wonder you seemed so worried and frightened all the time."

"Those men thought they'd gotten away scot-free, but when given several mug shot books, I picked Skitch Fallon out right away. There was no doubt in my mind he was the one who had shot my brother. Several witnesses in the bank, though they hadn't seen his face like I had and heard him boast he'd shot the bank guard, testified it was him. He was a good six inches taller than the other two men, much more muscular, and the only one of the three who seemed to have a gun. At the trial, those witnesses' testimony was good, but the lawyers all agreed it was my testimony that had convicted him."

"It's a good thing he pulled that mask off."

She clamped her eyes tightly shut and slowly nodded. "Yes, it was. At least my brother's life was avenged. But when the guilty verdict was read, Skitch Fallon looked directly at me and shouted a few obscenities, saying he was going to get even—it was my fault he was probably going to spend the rest of his life in prison and he was going to make me pay."

"No wonder you were terrified, but how did he escape? Surely, being a murderer, they locked him up. The agent said he walked right out of the courthouse."

"They did lock him up. We all thought that was the last we'd ever hear of him. But the day of his sentencing, there were a number of other trials going on in the courthouse and, due to being shorthanded, a young, inexperienced deputy was assigned to watch Skitch Fallon in a side room until it was time for him to enter the courtroom for sentencing. Normally, I learned later, leg irons are kept on prisoners even though their handcuffs are often removed. I guess this is because prisoners are allowed to wear street clothing in the courtroom instead of those awful orange jumpsuits. But he talked the deputy into removing one leg iron, claiming he'd broken his ankle, it hadn't healed, and the leg iron was rubbing it raw. The man complied because he figured being in the courthouse with so many officers around, it would be okay. He didn't realize what a desperate and dangerous man Skitch Fallon was."

"He overpowered him?"

"Yes, pinned the man down, knocked him unconscious, took his gun from its holster, and just walked down the hallway and out the front door. No one knew what happened until the bailiff went into the room to escort Fallon and the deputy into the courtroom. By that time, he was long gone."

"Oh, man. I'll bet that deputy got fired. What a stupid thing to do."

Judy leaned her head against the back of the chair and relaxed. It was good to feel safe again. "Yes, I'm sure he did. There was quite a hubbub about the whole thing. Even made the national news. Several people got into big trouble. That inexperienced deputy should never have been left alone with a desperado like Skitch Fallon. They no longer allow prisoners to be unshackled before it's time for them to enter the courtroom. I doubt something like that will happen again."

"And it shouldn't," Ben agreed.

"Because of the threat Skitch Fallon had made toward Timmy and me, the court assigned officers to stay at our house twenty-four-seven. We were the ones who were prisoners while Skitch was running around free. It was terrible. Timmy couldn't go to school. I couldn't even shop for groceries."

"Is that when you decided to leave? To hide out on your own?"

She shook her head. "Not at first. I was too frightened to be more than five feet away from those officers. I was hoping they would find Skitch and put him in prison where he belonged, but that didn't happen. He'd been on the loose for one week when I got a phone call from him. I was so scared my teeth rattled when I heard his voice. He told me I could run and I could hide, but he was out to get both Timmy and me. And when he found us, he was going to kill me in front of Timmy and then torture him to death!"

"Oh, Judy, I can't imagine how frightened you were. Did you tell the police?"

"Yes, I told them. They doubled the guards at the house, but I could tell from that man's voice, he wouldn't quit until he found me. I decided I couldn't just sit there, waiting like a sitting duck, for him to come for me. I had to take Timmy and get out of there."

"Didn't the police offer to move you to another location?"

"Yes, they offered, but I was afraid somehow word would get out as to where we were. I guess I watch too many detective shows on TV, where someone leaks information inadvertently and witnesses die. I had promised Kayla I would take care of Timmy and protect him, even if it meant giving up my own life to do so, and I meant it. I just never dreamed I might have to do it."

Ben gave her a questioning stare. "So what did you do? How did the two of you get out of Dallas?"

Judy pulled away from him, rose to her feet, and began to pace about the room. "I knew we had to walk out with only the clothes on our backs, otherwise, we'd raise suspicion. I called my bank and told the bank president I was leaving and would be in to withdraw a big part of the money from my savings account. I had no idea how long I would have to be in hiding, but I knew it would be expensive. My aunt was a wealthy woman and had left Jerod and me everything she had, and then there was the money from Jerod's insurance. I knew it would be difficult to draw that much cash out if I didn't call the bank first and let them know I was coming. I got the officers to drive us there, saying I needed to make a withdrawal and pick up the box of newly printed checks I'd ordered. While they watched Timmy for me, I went to the cashier. The president had told her I would be coming, so there was no need for her to question such a large withdrawal. It was counted out and all ready for me. I signed the withdrawal slip, assured her there was no need to count it out, thanked her, and placed the money in the large tote bag I'd taken with me. Then, trying to appear casual, I walked back to the officers who were waiting only a few yards away."

"Wow, that was pretty gutsy! Carrying that much cash around in a bag."

She gave him a weak smile. "I was scared to death going through those bus terminals knowing I had all of that cash with me. But, praise God, we made it without incident."

"So how did you get out of the house?"

She continued to pace. "That was the hard part. When the officers changed shifts at eleven each evening, they usually visited a few minutes in the kitchen over a cup of coffee, relaying the day's happenings. That seemed to be our best chance to slip away unnoticed. When I put Timmy to bed that night, I had him leave on his street clothes. I called a taxi and asked that the driver meet us on the corner at exactly five after eleven. As soon as I heard the men talking in the kitchen, I woke Timmy up, grabbed my purse, laptop, and the tote bag. Then the two of us climbed out my bedroom window, closing it securely behind us, and walked to the corner and got into the taxi. From there, we headed for the bus station. Since the officer coming on duty thought we were in our rooms sleeping, we weren't missed until seven the next morning when the next officer came on duty. By that time we were miles away from Dallas."

Ben huffed. "You *have* been watching too many detective stories."

"It's hard to explain but, even with protection, I just didn't feel safe staying in Dallas, not with that man on the loose. I wanted to get out of town, as far from that man as I could go." Judy wearily seated herself again, the relaying of the events taking its toll on her.

"That's some story! I hope this means you'll reconsider my proposal and you and Timmy will stay in Memphis and let me take care of you," he told her, moving toward her and pulling her close.

Afraid he might kiss her and she'd weaken, she turned her head away. "No, Ben. I'm not staying. I'm going back to Dallas."

The look of rejection on Ben's face made her want to cry. Why had she ever allowed their relationship to get this far? She'd never wanted to hurt Ben. Nothing would be sweeter than to be able to throw herself into his arms and let him know how much she loved him. But she couldn't. *Lord, this is so hard, but I can't tell Ben the whole truth.*

Determined to stick with her plan even though her heart was breaking, Judy pulled away, afraid if he kissed her even one time she might weaken and do the wrong thing.

"I—I don't understand. I—I thought you loved me. Now that this horrible ordeal is over—"

Placing her trembling hand on his arm, she lifted misty eyes to meet his. "You don't know the real me, Ben, the me who can tell lies without the bat of an eye. There's so much you don't know and if you knew—you'd hate me."

"Hate you? I could never hate you. I love—"

"Let me finish. Please. I do have feelings for you—you're a wonderful man and you'd make a marvelous husband—but. . ." She paused. "There's someone else."

"How could that be? It's only been a short time since your husband passed away. Is this another lie, Judy? Are you telling me this because you never really loved me? You only used me as a cover-up?"

"A cover-up? No, Ben. No, nothing like that! I honestly did, and still do, have feelings for you, but that's all they are. Feelings, not love. The love of my life's home is in Dallas. I have to go back."

Dangling his long arms at his sides, Ben frowned. "This doesn't make any sense, Judy. From the way you've talked, I thought you'd loved your husband like I did my wife. Surely you weren't carrying on with another man while you were married to him! That's not like you. You're a Christian!"

"I think you'd better hold on to your chair. What I am about to tell you will shock you."

Chapter 9

Shaking his head, Ben let out a long, slow breath of air. "I can't imagine what you could tell me that would shock me more than what you've already said."

"I've never had a husband, Ben. I—I've never been married."

Ben leaned forward quickly, his eyes blazing. "But you said your husband—"

"I lied. I didn't have a husband. I made up that story about him. You already know I'm Timmy's aunt and you know I promised my sister-in-law on her deathbed that I would take care of Timmy for her and raise him to love God like she did. After Skitch Fallon escaped and threatened me on the phone and it became necessary for us to run, I posed as Timmy's mother, thinking the two of us would be harder to trace if we changed our last name to Smith and everyone thought we were mother and son."

Ben stared at her. "What a nightmare that must have been for you, but—"

Judy trembled just thinking about the problems she had caused. "Oh, Ben, I should never have come to Memphis and rented your apartment. It wasn't fair to get you involved in my troubles."

"But you did come, and now I'm in love with you and you're telling me you love someone else?"

"I've known this person for a long time, Ben. Long before I met you, and I've always loved him. Because of that love, I must return to Dallas. His happiness is my happiness. My number one priority."

Ben shifted his position, looking her straight in the eye. "And I'm just supposed to forget about you? Go on with my life as if you never existed? And what about Victoria? What am I supposed to tell her? That a woman who waltzed into our lives, claiming to be a Christian, was lying to us the whole time?"

She lowered her gaze, unable to stand the pain on his face. "Regardless of what she thinks of me, she deserves to know the truth. Just make sure she realizes this entire deceptive plan was mine. Timmy had nothing to do with it. He only lied because I told him to."

"There's no chance you'll change your mind? About us?"

"No, Ben. I can't. There's too much at stake."

He frowned. "At stake? What does that mean?"

"I can't explain. Just know that I'm making the right decision to return to Dallas." She rose quickly, hoping to end the conversation before she broke down in tears. "I'm going to tell Victoria good-bye and then we're leaving."

∞

Ben watched as she moved out of the room, his heart aching. *God, why did You have to let this happen? Let Judy and Timmy come into our lives? You had to know I'd fall in love with her. Was it so I'd come to my senses and break off my engagement to Phoebe? I love this woman! I need her! So does Victoria. How could something like this have happened? Oh, God—help me to understand. I've prayed so many times about this. I was so sure You were leading the two of us together, now this has happened. I'm so confused. I want Your will for my life, but how am I to know what Your will is?*

Within minutes, Judy came back into the room, her hand holding tightly to Timmy, her eyes filled with tears. "You'd better go to Victoria, Ben. She's upset and crying. I–I'm sorry. I wish I could have spared her this—spared both of you—but it had to be done. I've called for a taxi. It should be here any minute."

His heart breaking, he reached out for her hand but she backed away. "You could change your mind, stay here with us."

Blinking hard, she shook her head. "No, I can't stay. Good-bye, Ben." She tugged Timmy toward the door.

Sniffling, Timmy lifted his hand and wiped his nose on his sleeve. "Bye, Ben."

Bending down quickly, Ben wrapped his arms around the boy and gave him a hug. How nice it would have been to have Timmy as his son. He'd always wanted a son. "Good-bye, Timmy. Take care of your aunt. She loves you very much."

Timmy stuck his hand into his pocket and pulled out the shiny quarter and reached it toward Ben. "My daddy gave this to me. It's a special quarter. Would you give it to Victoria for me?"

Ben felt a lump rise in his throat. "I'd be happy to, Timmy. I'm sure Victoria will treasure it because it's from you, but are you sure you want to part with it?"

"Uh-huh. Victoria is my friend."

Judy tugged on the boy's hand again. "Timmy, we have to go. Our taxi is here."

Ben moved quickly to open the door. "I'll walk you to your taxi then—"

Pushing past him, Judy held up her palm between them. "I think it'd be best if we'd just say good-bye here. Your daughter needs you."

Not knowing what to say to keep Judy at Bramwell House any longer, Ben nodded. "I'll be here if you change your mind."

"I—I won't change my mind. I can't. But thank you for being the wonderful man you are. I'll never forget you." Stopping on the doorstep long enough to turn back and face him one last time, Judy dabbed at her eyes with the tissue he'd given her. "I'll be praying for you and Victoria. Good-bye, Ben."

She nearly ran to the taxi, dragging Timmy behind her.

"Aunt Judy, do we have to go?"

The flood of tears she'd been trying to hold back erupted, momentarily blocking her vision. "Please, Timmy, just get in and fasten your seat belt, okay? We need to get going if we're going to rent a car and get checked into a hotel before dark."

"But—"

"Just do it, okay? I don't want to leave any more than you do but—"

"Then why can't we stay?"

After rubbing her tears away with her sleeve, Judy reached across and gave Timmy's shoulder a loving pat. "I know you don't understand, and right now I can't tell you. Just know that I love you and I'm trying to do the right thing for both of us." Forcing an enthusiastic smile, she gave his arm a gentle pinch. "You and I are off to Branson. I think it's about time we had some fun, don't you?"

She was relieved when Timmy nodded then settled down and trained his eyes on the road. *Thank You, God,* she prayed as the taxi made its way out of the driveway and down the street. *Thank You for keeping Timmy and me safe while that evil man was on the loose. Ben's apartment was the perfect hiding place. Please, Lord, help Ben to understand and not have hard feelings toward me for lying to him. He's such a wonderful man. He didn't deserve all the lies I told him. I love Ben with all my heart. He has every attribute I'd want in a husband. He loves You and he loves his daughter.* She bit at her lip and suppressed a tear. *And, wonder of wonders, he loves me! But why, God? Why did You let us fall in love when there was no hope the two of us could be together? I need Your touch, God. Comfort my heart. Let me know I'm doing the right thing.*

∞

Three days later, after an enjoyable stay in Branson, Judy and Timmy reached Dallas and the home they'd shared before their terrible ordeal. Feeling much relief to be back home, she angled the rental car into the driveway and turned off the engine before reaching over and gently shaking the sleeping boy beside her. "Wake up, sweetie, we're home!"

Timmy sat up straight and rubbed his eyes.

She gave him a smile. Though she'd hated to leave Ben, it was nice to be home. "Can you get your backpack from the backseat and carry it into the house?"

He stretched one arm, then the other, before climbing out and opening the rear door. "I'm hungry."

"We'll go to the store later. Maybe we can find something in the freezer."

Timmy's face lit up. "Ice cream?"

She gave him a gentle swat. "No, silly, not ice cream. I was thinking more along the lines of a frozen TV dinner."

Timmy pulled a face. "Yuk! I don't like TV dinners."

"Then how about—"

"Hi, Judy."

Immediately recognizing the voice, Judy whirled around, her heart thumping wildly. "Ben! What are you doing here? How did you find us?"

Smiling, Ben pushed Victoria's wheelchair a bit closer. "You weren't very hard to find. I already knew you lived in Dallas. The rest was easy."

Timmy rushed to Victoria's side and gave her a hug.

Judy hugged her, too. "It's nice to see you again, honey."

Ben took Judy's hand and gave it a squeeze. "Aren't you the least bit glad to see me?"

Though her heart was overjoyed to think he'd followed her all the way to Dallas, her smile faded as she pulled her hand away. "You shouldn't have come, Ben. You're only complicating matters. Nothing between us has changed."

Ben grinned shyly. "Can we come in?"

She longed to throw herself into his arms and tell him how much she loved him. "We've said our good-byes. I just don't understand why you would follow us here like this."

"I'll tell you when we get inside." Moving past her, he pushed Victoria's chair toward the porch.

Judy let out a long, slow sigh. Though the sight of Ben had sent her heart skyrocketing, he was the last person she expected to see when they reached Dallas. Her hands trembling, she unlocked the door then stepped aside while Ben rolled the little girl into the living room.

Timmy grabbed onto Victoria's chair. "Can I show Tory my Transformer collection, Ben?"

After shooting a questioning look toward Judy, Ben nodded. "I'm sure Victoria would love to see your Transformer collection."

"Would you like some iced tea?" she asked Ben out of courtesy and for something to do other than look at his sweet face once the children were out of the room.

His grin made her spine tingle. "Actually, I'd like a cup of coffee."

"I–I'm not sure I have any in the house."

"You could look."

Allowing a smile to escape her lips, she made her way into the kitchen.

Ben followed. "I broke my engagement to Phoebe."

Her heart did a leap, but she immediately ordered it to behave. "You did?"

"Uh-huh. Just like I told you I was going to do, and you know what? Though I hated to hurt her, breaking off our engagement actually felt good. You were right. The two of us were never intended to be together. After the initial shock and a screaming tantrum, she actually admitted she hated being around Victoria and had planned to talk me into sending her away to a special school for disabled children as soon as we were married, just to get her out of her sight. I can't believe I was so blind."

Judy filled the coffeepot with water then turned to Ben. "What about her father and your partnership?"

Ben sat down at the table. "After you left, I closed myself up in my room and prayed like I've never prayed before. I just couldn't settle for losing you, Judy. You mean too much to me. I couldn't imagine God bringing us together like He did and then letting you walk out of my life. I made a few calls to my accountant then called Phoebe's father, offering to buy out his half of the business. From what he said, he was ready to retire anyway and decided the best thing to do was to break all ties with me and, to my surprise, he accepted my offer without even making a counteroffer. The business is all mine now. I should have bought him out years ago. Architectural Concepts is now Bramwell Architectural Concepts."

Judy couldn't help sharing his joy. "Ben, that's wonderful! I'm so proud of you."

"I'm really excited to be out on my own, in full control of my business. It's something I've always wanted."

"I'm sure you'll do very well. I wish you the best."

After filling the basket with coffee and pouring the water into the reservoir, she reached into the cupboard and pulled out two mugs.

"My head is swimming with ideas, but it's you—"

She paused, mugs in hand. "Stop, Ben. I've already told you there is someone else in my life."

"Don't lie to me, Judy. I know better."

Confused by his words, she raised a brow and tried to remain calm. "I—I don't know what you mean."

Ben rose and ambled slowly toward her, his eyes focused on her face. "I talked to your neighbor, Mrs. Groundage. She said in all the years you've lived next door, she'd never seen you with anyone other than your brother. If there was someone in your life as important as you've led me to believe, why wouldn't she have seen him? I have a feeling that nice old lady knows everything there is to know about her neighbors."

Judy fumbled for words. "Maybe she—"

"You're lying again, Judy. I can tell by your eyes. Why can't you be honest with me? I love you!"

She swallowed hard. "I already told you. If you knew the truth, you'd hate me."

Ben took her hand in his, pulled it to his lips and kissed her fingertips, all the while lovingly gazing into her eyes. "I could never hate you. Come on. Give me a chance. Tell me the truth, sweetheart."

"I can't."

Warily, Ben slipped an arm around her shoulders. "Let me help you get started."

Judy's heart raced. Whatever could he mean?

"When you left Memphis, I figured I'd never see you again, but I couldn't let it end that way. I loved you too much to let you go without a battle. I thought over the things you said before you and Timmy left. They didn't add up, honey. Your story was too full of holes."

"Holes?"

With his forefinger, he lifted her face to his. "Yes, holes. I know you love me, Judy. Tell me that you don't."

"I—I admitted I have feelings for you but—"

"Those *feelings* are love, like the love I have for you. I'm convinced of it. I got to thinking about what you said. Your exact words were, 'I've known this person for a long time, Ben. Long before I met you, and I've always loved him. Because of that love, I must return to Dallas. His happiness is my happiness. My number one priority.' You didn't say you'd known this wonderful man, or your sweetheart, or the man who makes you feel complete. You said *person*, Judy. No one refers to the love of their life as *person*. I love you and I could never refer to you in a conversation to someone as simply *person*. I'd call you Judy, or my girlfriend, or the one I want to spend the rest of my life with. You said none of those. Not only that, you referred to that *person* as your number one priority. Is that any way to talk about the one you loved enough to pull away from me and my love for you? And the feelings you said you had for me? No, I think not. Something was wrong with your story. Radically wrong. I couldn't accept it. I won't accept it."

"I think you misunderstood, Ben."

"Look, Judy, until I meet this person face-to-face and am convinced that you love him more than you love me, I have no intention of leaving Dallas." Pulling his cell phone from the holster on his belt, he held it out to her. "Why don't you call and ask this person to come over? I'd like to meet him."

∞

Judy stared at the phone. "He's—he's out of town."

"You might have lied to me before and gotten away with it, but I know you better now, and your eyes, those beautiful blue eyes I love so much, say you're not telling me the truth. Call him, Judy. Now."

Timmy came bounding into the kitchen, startling the pair. "Can we have some ice cream?"

Releasing Judy's hands, Ben quickly knelt in front of the boy. "Timmy, is your aunt's boyfriend out of town?"

Timmy's mouth gaped. "What boyfriend? She doesn't have a boyfriend."

Judy nearly choked. "Sure, you can have some ice cream. Chocolate chip or strawberry swirl?"

Timmy quirked his head thoughtfully. "Chocolate chip."

She sent a quick glance Ben's way as she opened the freezer door and pulled out the ice cream carton. "I'll have it ready in a minute."

"Ice cream sounds good. Why don't we all have some?" Ben stood and after checking behind three different cabinet doors, located the bowls. "Want me to dip?"

Avoiding his gaze, she reached into the drawer and pulled out the ice cream scoop and four spoons.

When Ben finished dipping, he handed two of the bowls to Timmy. "Here ya go. Two bowls of ice cream for two great kids. Your aunt and I are going to eat ours in the kitchen."

He waited until Timmy was safely out of earshot then turned to Judy. "Well, it appears your nephew doesn't think you have a boyfriend. If I were a lawyer, I'd rest my case. I think you have some explaining to do."

Judy felt sick in the pit of her stomach. This was the moment she'd hoped to avoid. The moment of truth. Knowing Ben and how determined he could be, she was sure he wouldn't leave until she gave him a satisfactory answer. Covering her face with her hands, she began to sob.

"I'm not going to leave until you tell me." He pulled her close and after kissing first one cheek and then the other whispered, "Whatever it is, babe, I'm here for you. I love you. You can tell me anything."

Gasping for a deep breath of air, Judy leaned into the strength of his arms. She was sure once he heard her story he wouldn't be able to stand the sight of her. But, like he said, he wasn't going to leave until she told him. Should she invent another lie or tell him the awful truth? Maybe it was time the lying stopped.

Chapter 10

J udy. I'm waiting." His voice was kind and understanding. "I have to know the truth. Please, just tell me."

Though it gave her great pain to even think about the truth, let alone reveal it to another living soul—especially the man she loved, adored, and respected—she knew it had to be done. Trying to prolong the inevitable, she slowly pulled away from him and moved to the window where she could stare out into the yard, avoiding his eyes. "All right, Ben, I'll tell you. But, believe me, it's not going to be pretty. When you hear my story, I doubt you'll ever want to see me again."

"Whatever it is, sweetheart, we'll deal with it, I promise you. Nothing you could tell me could keep me from loving you."

"We have to keep an eye on the door. I don't want the children to hear this." Judy lifted her eyes heavenward. *God, help me, please! This is so hard.* "Re–remember when I came to your apartment claiming I was Timmy's mother?"

"Of course I do."

"Though nearly everything else I told you was a lie, that part was the truth. I—I am Timmy's mother."

Ben reared back, holding her at arm's length and stared at her. "What? You're Timmy's mother? I thought your sister-in-law, Kayla, was his mother and your brother was his father!"

"Jerod and Kayla were his parents—his adoptive parents—but I was, and still am, his mother."

"You mean, after Kayla died you became his mother in her place?"

She had to say it. "No, Ben, I'm Timmy's birth mother."

The look on Ben's face ripped at her heart and shredded it into little pieces. She wanted to rush from the room, throw herself on her bed, and pull the covers over her head. But she had to go on. There was no turning back. "It's a long story, Ben."

Though his expression was one of shock and all the color had drained from his face, he gave her a weak smile. "Go ahead. I have all the time in the world."

She motioned him to sit back down at the table, then sucked in a cleansing breath and began her story. "It may be hard to believe since I'm such an old prude now, but I was a pretty rebellious kid when I was in high school. All the really popular kids were using drugs, having drinking parties, and doing all sorts of things my old-fashioned parents objected to. All my friends were being intimate with their boyfriends, even bragging about their conquests. I wanted to be popular, too, so I. . ." Judy swallowed at the lump of guilt that nearly strangled her. "I did something very foolish, and I'm spending my life paying for it."

"No wonder you were so protective of Timmy," was all Ben said, but she could tell from the look on his face he was shocked by her admission—and she wanted to die of shame. How could she have done the things she'd done? Had she honestly thought she could do those things and not become pregnant?

"My folks tried everything to get me to see the destructive path I was going down, but I was too stubborn and having too much fun to listen."

Ben gave his head a sad shake. "Knowing you, it's hard to imagine you would take part in any of those things. The Judy I know is much too responsible."

"But I did, and I ended up pregnant."

"With Timmy."

"Yes, with Timmy. I never thought anything like that could happen to me, even though I'd heard all the lectures at school, as well as the warnings from my parents."

Ben blinked hard, as if trying to comprehend what she was saying. "Surely you weren't a Christian then."

"No, I wasn't. Actually, with what I'd done and the disrespect I'd had for my parents and everyone who'd tried to help me, I didn't think God would be able to forgive me. The guilt was unbearable. I was so ashamed. I—I still am. I live with that guilt every day of my life. Even though God has forgiven me, I can't forgive myself."

She moved back to the window, pressed her head against the coolness of the glass, and closed her eyes, hoping to dispel the headache she felt coming on. "My parents weren't Christians, either, but my brother was. Jerod was nearly ten years older than me, married to Kayla, already working as a police officer in Dallas, and very active in his church. I can't tell you how many times he'd lectured me, begging me to wake up before it was too late, but I wouldn't listen to him, either. I accepted Christ later on, when I finally came to my senses."

"You were lucky to have a brother who cared about you," Ben said simply, his voice filled with emotion.

"Yes, I was, and I can't begin to tell you how I miss him." Judy rubbed at her temples. She felt both drained and exhausted, but she had to go on. Ben deserved to hear it all.

"Anyway, when I found out I was pregnant, all my so-called friends tried to talk me into an abortion. A number of them had done it and thought it was a cool way to deal with things. I don't know if it was God dealing with me or what, but in my heart of hearts I knew abortion was wrong. Even though I was young, alone, and afraid, and wouldn't be able to provide for my baby or give him the kind of future he deserved, I knew I could never willingly throw away his life."

She paused long enough to join Ben at the table. "When my pregnancy became impossible to hide, I told my parents. Although they weren't Christians, they were good people and it nearly killed them. They agreed abortion would be taking my baby's life and that my plan to let it be adopted by some loving couple would be the best thing for everyone—especially the child. It was only after my brother told us the doctors had confirmed that he and Kayla would never be able to have children that we came up with the idea that my baby should be given to them."

"What about the father?" Ben prodded softly, shock still etched on his face. "What did he say about it?"

Tears trailed down Judy's cheeks at the sad remembrance of Timmy's real father. "He—died of an overdose before Timmy was born. His name was never on the birth certificate."

"And his parents? Weren't they interested in adopting Timmy?"

Judy huffed. "My boyfriend's father was in prison, and raising a baby was the last thing his mother was interested in doing. She wanted no part of him and made it perfectly clear she had no intention of paying any doctor or hospital bills."

Ben leaned back in the chair and locked his hands behind his head. "Whatever a man sows, that shall he also reap."

"You're right, Ben. I asked for everything that happened to me. All for popularity. My life was a mess. I went against God's laws and I paid the price. My baby, perhaps the only child I'll ever have, had to be given to someone else to raise. He doesn't even know I'm his mother."

Ben let out a long, slow whistle. "So you're Timmy's mother! Amazing! I never would have suspected. So when *did* you become a Christian?"

Judy felt a slight smile curl at her lips. "Becoming a Christian was the one bright spot in my life. When I decided to give my baby to my brother and his wife, Kayla was overjoyed, but my brother was apprehensive about the whole thing. You see, as Jerod's sister, I would become Timmy's aunt, and Jerod felt, with my rebellious lifestyle, I might be a bad influence on him. He was also concerned that my drinking and drug-taking might have caused damage to the baby. I'd always looked up to my big brother, so his words really hurt. I told him I had quit those things the day the little tester showed I was pregnant, and I had. Being told I was going to have a baby was a real wake-up call. I'd seen on TV what those things can do to a baby, and I wasn't about to let it happen to mine."

Ben pulled his handkerchief from his pocket and handed it to her.

She dabbed at her eyes then went on. "I don't know if it was the reality of being pregnant or, once again, the touch of God, but suddenly all my friends seemed stupid and immature. I couldn't stand being around them, and they felt the same way about me. When Jerod and Kayla finally decided to adopt my baby, I made them agree to let me come to Dallas so I could watch him grow up. In return, I promised I would never tell Timmy I was his birth mother if they would just let me be around him. The only way my brother would accept my terms was if I regularly attended church with them. Three days after Timmy was born, I packed my bags and we moved to Dallas."

"You lived with them?"

"At first, but when the little house next door to them went up for sale, Jerod bought it for me. I moved in, and Timmy grew up thinking I was his Aunt Judy. It was the best thing for all of us. Timmy had two wonderful, godly parents and I got to be with my son as he grew up."

Still wide-eyed, Ben moved to the sink and filled a glass with water, drinking nearly all of it before returning to the table. "You became a Christian after you moved to Dallas."

"Yes, the following Easter Sunday. I responded to the invitation at the close of the service. My heart had never been as touched by God's Word as it was that day. The plan of salvation had been explained to me time and time again, but it was that morning when the pastor talked about Christ's sacrifice on the cross— for me—I finally confessed I was a sinner and in need of a Savior. From that day on, my life did a complete turnaround. Each time I looked at my precious son, I knew I'd done the right thing by refusing to abort him and giving him to my brother and his wife, who were absolutely wonderful parents. Most women who allow their children to be adopted never see them again. Thanks to the graciousness of the Lord, I've been able to see my child every day of his life."

Ben's eyes misted over. "And now with them gone, it's up to you to raise Timmy. Are you going to tell him you're his birth mother?"

Judy glanced toward the living room, making sure the children were still engrossed in their ice cream. "No, like you and Carlotta, I may tell him when he's eighteen. Maybe not even then. I plan to keep Kayla and Jerod's memory alive for him as long as I can. I may be his birth mother, Ben, but they were his parents. I could never take that away from them." She rose, rubbing at her eyes with her sleeve. "Knowing the way you felt about the girl who gave birth to Victoria, I'm sure, after hearing my story, you feel the same way about me. Thank you for listening without condemning me."

Ben stood. "I never forgave that girl—"

"I know, and I don't expect you to forgive me." Grasping the edge of the table for support and fighting back tears, Judy took one final look at the man she loved before turning her head away. "Please, Ben, not another word. Just get Victoria and go." With that, she ran from the room and into her bedroom, slamming the door behind her.

∞

"What's wrong with Judy?" Victoria turned her head toward her father with concern as he rushed through the living room. "Is she sick?"

Even though his insides were churning, Ben forced a smile. "Don't worry, honey, she's just a bit upset. It's nothing for you and Timmy to worry about."

Timmy's big eyes rounded. "I think she was crying."

"Girls do that sometimes." Ben tried to sound casual. "I'll check on her. Why don't you kids watch one of those videos Timmy told you about when he was in Memphis?"

Ben waited until the children had selected a video about wild animals and had inserted it into the VCR before guardedly moving toward Judy's closed door.

"Judy," he whispered, rapping softly on her door. "Let me in, please. We have to talk."

"Please, Ben, just go. I know you hate me for what I did, and I can't blame you. I hate myself."

"I could never hate you, sweetheart. I love you." Gently turning the knob, he pushed the door open a crack. When she didn't respond, he stepped into the room and stood there, his long arms dangling awkwardly at his sides. "I'd do anything for you, don't you know that?"

No response.

Her sobbing broke his heart. He slowly moved toward the bed, not sure what to do or what to say. "Honey, I admit I said those things about Victoria's birth mother, and I thought I meant them, but after hearing your story and all the things you went through to make sure your baby would live and be adopted by a loving family, I realize how wrong I was. Oh, not that I condone what she did, I don't. I know I said I never wanted Victoria to know she was the product of some careless teenager with raging hormones. I had no right to talk that way about that young woman. Who am I to judge her? That girl was God's child. He loved her every bit as much as He loved me. Instead of making crude comments about her, I should have been praying for her."

Judy raised herself to a half-sitting position and stared at him with tear-filled, mascara-stained eyes. "She may not have been a promiscuous teenager, Ben, but I was. I admit it. I'm still so ashamed, even though I know God has forgiven me. He loves me, Ben, but how could you love me?"

Ben dropped down beside her and gathered her in his arms, holding her close. "I was a fool living in a glass house, Judy, with very little patience for those who didn't share my same set of values and convictions. Though I've been grateful to that teenage girl for giving us Victoria, I never fully realized what she went through and how hard it must have been to give that precious baby away. I'm ashamed to admit I don't even remember her name, but if it hadn't been for her. . ." He paused, suddenly overcome with guilt. "Carlotta and I would never have had Victoria. I—I owe that girl so much, yet I've never been man enough to try to find her and thank her. And I owe you, too. How I must have offended you when I spoke about her that way and your experiences were so similar."

A tear rolled down her cheek. "Your words did hurt. You weren't talking about me, but I deserved them. I was a promiscuous teenager. But praise the Lord, He took my sin upon Himself and paid the price and I'm forgiven."

Suddenly, he kissed her forehead.

"Dear, dear Judy. I can't imagine going through what you've gone through, but I am so proud of you. You have the heart of a true mother for facing up to your responsibilities when you found out you were pregnant. Instead of taking the easy way out you chose life for your baby, nine months of ridicule, and what had to be an uncomfortable pregnancy. Then you gave your brother and sister-in-law the sweetest, greatest, and most sacrificial gift only a caring and loving mother could give. Your own flesh and blood son—Timmy."

She lifted misty eyes. "You're proud of me? You—you don't hate me?"

"Hate you? No! You've shared the most trying time in your life with me. If anything, I love you even more for telling me."

"But—"

Ben put a finger to her lips. "Shh, no more buts. I love you and you love me. Plain and simple. Now that I know there isn't another man in your life, there's nothing to keep us apart." Taking both her hands in his and gazing at her with eyes filled with love, Ben knelt before her. "Judy, will you be my wife? Will you let me love you, care for you, provide for you, and protect you for the rest of our lives?"

Judy smiled up at him. "Oh, Ben, my handsome, caring, loving Ben—I love you. I'm crazy about you! I want nothing more than to be your wife but—"

"But? But what? Is there another obstacle to conquer?" His face contorted with frustration. "Something else I don't know about?"

"Oh, Ben, no! Nothing like that! I just thought, before we decide to spend our lives together, we need to make sure it's okay with Victoria and Timmy."

Ben's grin spread from ear to ear. "Whew! There for a minute, you had me worried. Of course, we'll ask the children, but I have a feeling they're both going to like the idea. But before we tell them, we have something else to take care of."

She stared up at him. "Something else? What?"

He leaned so close to her she could feel his warm breath on her cheeks. "This!"

As his lips claimed her, she melted into his arms. At last, she was free to fully and openly declare her love for him. "I love you, Ben Bramwell. I've loved you from the moment I rang your doorbell that first morning," she murmured against his lips.

When they finally parted, Ben closed his eyes and lifted his face heavenward. "Lord God, Judy and I come before You, praising You and thanking You for bringing us together as only You could do. And, with Your help and guidance, we promise to do our best to bring our children up to love You as much as we do. Father, I love this woman with all my heart. Help me to be the kind of husband she deserves."

Judy quivered as she rested her forehead against Ben's. "God, I'm so unworthy of Ben's love and in total amazement that he wants to spend the rest of his life with me. Please, Lord, help me to be the wife this good man is worthy of and the kind of mother Victoria and Timmy deserve. I love You, Lord."

Ben added an amen then sealed their commitment with another kiss. "I think it's time to talk to the children."

"We can never tell Victoria the truth, Ben. I don't want to continue to lie to her, but she can't know I'm Timmy's mother. And I know you don't want Victoria to know she's adopted."

"The decision to tell Timmy is up to you, my love, but I definitely don't want to tell Victoria. Not yet, anyway. We won't be lying to the children, Judy. We'll just avoid telling them the truth, for their good, at least until they are both old enough to understand why we did what we did. It would serve no purpose to tell them now, except to hurt and confuse them."

"I know you're right, dearest, but I just want this lying to end."

"Look at it this way, sweetheart. All we're doing is delaying the truth. Our two children have had enough tragedy in their lives. Telling them would only add more. I can't put Victoria through that, and I'm sure you feel the same way about Timmy." Ben dipped his head shyly. "Can you believe it, honey? Despite our lack of trust in Him, in His own way and His own time, God has answered all our prayers. I hate to admit it, but I was beginning to wonder if it would ever happen."

"Even though I know I can never take Carlotta's place and I don't expect Victoria to call me Mom, I promise you I will love your precious child as if she were my very own daughter and I truly was her mother." Smiling through her tears, Judy cupped Ben's cheek with her palm. "I love Timmy with all my heart but, like probably every woman, I've longed to have a daughter. Now I'll have one. That is, if Victoria will accept me as her stepmother!"

With the tip if his finger, Ben wiped away a tear as it trickled down her cheek. "And if Timmy will accept me as his stepfather. Or would I be his uncle?"

Judy smiled up at him, her joy obviously uncontainable. "Timmy loves you already, Ben."

"And Victoria loves you. Maybe it's time we brought them in on this. Whatcha think?"

She slipped her hand into his and gave it an adoring squeeze. "I think they're going to love it! Let's tell them!"

After Timmy and Victoria were summoned, Ben, standing before them, filled with excitement asked, "How'd you kids like to be a family? If it's okay with the two of you, Judy and I are going to be married."

In unison, their eyes sparkling, both children shouted, "Yes! Yes!" Timmy grabbed onto the handles of Victoria's wheelchair and began to spin her about in circles. Then, coming to a sudden halt, he turned to Judy. "Aunt Judy? You're gonna be Tory's mother? That's cool!"

Victoria clapped her hands excitedly. "Yippee! I'm so happy! I've always wanted you to be my mother! Not Phoebe."

Ben tapped the end of his daughter's nose affectionately. "So does that mean you two are okay with Judy and me getting married?"

Again, the children shouted, "Yes! Yes! Yes!"

With a gigantic grin, Ben turned to Judy. "Looks like it's unanimous. We're gonna be a family, my love!" Wrapping her tightly in his arms and gazing into her eyes, he lowered his lips to hers and lovingly kissed them like he'd longed to kiss her since the first day they'd met.

"Don't look, Tory!" Making a face, Timmy turned his head.

Giggling, Victoria covered her eyes with her hands.

"I'm actually going to be Mrs. Ben Bramwell," Judy said dreamily, her face shining with joy and happiness.

Looking back, Timmy wiggled his nose. "Does that mean Tory will be my cousin?"

Judy froze as she shot a quick questioning glance toward Ben. She evidently had no idea how to answer him.

He gave her a wink. "Actually, after Judy and I are married, if it's all right with you, I'm going to adopt you. That'll make you and Tory sister and brother."

"Are we going to move to Memphis and live with Ben?"

Judy sent an adoring glance Ben's way. "Oh, yes, Timmy. We'll all live together as a family." Although that was something they hadn't discussed, she was sure he would expect them to live in his lovely home in Memphis.

Timmy nodded. "Can I take all my Transformers?"

Ben's hand cupped Timmy's shoulder. "You can take anything you want. Bramwell House is going to be your home. Nothing would make Victoria and me any happier than having the two of you live with us."

Victoria tugged on her father's sleeve. "Can we call Miranda and Max? I want to tell them Timmy and Judy are going to live with us."

"Of course you can. We'll call them later tonight. But first, I'm going to take the four of us to Dallas's famous Pierre's By The Lake for dinner. We have something to celebrate!"

After the excitement died down, Timmy announced proudly, "Me and Tory have a secret." His face aglow, he turned to Victoria. "Go ahead, Tory. Show them! They're gonna like our secret."

With a giggle, her little face shining like an angel's, Victoria nodded. "Okay, but you have to help me."

With a mischievous smile, Timmy grabbed onto the handles of her wheelchair. "Ready?"

She nodded then, holding tightly to the armrests, scooted to the front of the chair. "Watch, Daddy! Watch, Judy!"

Ben grabbed for her, afraid she might fall. "Careful, baby! Daddy doesn't want you to get hurt!"

"She's okay," Timmy said confidently. "You don't have to worry about her."

Victoria lifted one foot from the footrest and placed it on the floor, then the other and stood.

Ben reached for her again but Victoria leaned away and shook her head. "No, Daddy, don't help me. I can do it by myself."

Ben backed away.

Bracing herself on the armrests, Victoria rose to her feet and took two steps toward him.

"Victoria!" Ben lunged for her, grabbing her up in his arms and whirling her about. "That's wonderful! You stood by yourself and took two steps, sweetheart." Turning to Judy with tears in his eyes, he said, his voice filled with deep emotion, "She walked, Judy. My baby walked! Praise God, she actually walked!"

Timmy grabbed onto Victoria's hand and tugged her away from Ben. "She's not through, Ben." Then turning loose of the little girl's hand, he said, "Show them, Tory. Show them what you can really do!"

Victoria nodded, sucked in a deep breath then, smiling at her father, walked across the floor toward Judy at a rapid pace, her steps steady and secure.

Weeping openly, Ben rubbed at his eyes. "I can't believe she's walking. She hasn't walked since her mother died. It's a miracle. A true miracle."

Judy reached out her hands. "It is, Ben. The miracle we've been praying for."

When Victoria reached Judy, giggling merrily, she spun around and walked back to her father, her eyes shining, her delicate mouth quirked up in a smile.

"Me and Tory have been practicing," Timmy said proudly. "She wanted to surprise you, Ben, or am I supposed to call you Dad?"

Ben wrapped his arm around the boy. "There's no way I could ever take your father's place. You can call me Ben, or anything you want."

"I'll just call you Ben." Timmy gestured toward Victoria. "Show them how you can run, Tory."

Ben grabbed tightly onto Victoria's hand. "No, Timmy, she might fall."

Victoria let loose another giggle, pulled away from her father's grasp, then ran around the room in circles, her voice a merry tinkle filling the room. "Look, Daddy, I can run! I can run just like Timmy!"

His jaw dropped, Ben stared at her in amazement. "You *are* running!"

Judy slipped her arm into the crook of Ben's elbow. "Oh, Ben, this is wonderful! God has been so good to us."

Timmy responded with a casual shrug. "She could run for a long time, but we kept it a secret. Victoria didn't want you to know."

Ben's smile disappeared as his brows raised in surprise. "But why? Why didn't you tell Daddy? You knew how much I wanted you to be able to get out of that wheelchair and walk. Didn't you want Daddy to be happy?"

"She didn't want you to marry Phoebe," Timmy stated matter-of-factly. "Phoebe was mean to her when you weren't around."

His heart filled with remorse, Ben sat down and pulled Victoria onto his lap, his arms circling her tightly. "Is that the truth, Victoria? Was she really mean to you or was it just that she didn't know how to behave around children?"

The little girl nodded. "She said she didn't like any little kids. She told me she was going to marry you then send me off to a school in another city, far, far away from you. I thought as long as I was in my wheelchair, you wouldn't send me away, so I played like I couldn't walk and my legs got really weak."

"Oh, pumpkin, I'd never send you away! It breaks my heart to know she told you such a thing."

Victoria wrapped her arms about Ben's neck and kissed his cheek. "When I told Timmy I really could walk but my legs were getting weak, he said I needed to get some exercise or maybe someday I really wouldn't be able to walk, and he made me get out of my chair. Sometimes, when you weren't home, he'd push me out into the yard behind his apartment where Miranda and Max couldn't see us and I'd get out of my chair and we'd play hide-and-seek. Now I can run."

Timmy nodded in agreement. "Her legs were really weak."

Again, Ben's eyes teared up. "Oh, sweetie, I'm so sorry. That was a cruel thing for Phoebe to do. Daddy would never, ever, ever send you away, for any reason. Can you ever forgive me for being so blind? I should never have tried to force Phoebe on you."

Judy placed a comforting hand on his shoulder. "Don't feel bad, Ben. You were only doing what you thought was best for your daughter. Obviously Phoebe wanted you and put on her best behavior around you."

"But you saw right through her!"

She grinned. "It's a woman thing."

"Whatever it was, you had Phoebe's number right from the start. I should have listened to you."

"Ben, I was a stranger!"

He tapped the tip of her nose playfully. "But you were a woman, and women know those things. You said so yourself." His expression turned serious. "If the Lord hadn't led you and Timmy to Memphis and to my apartment, I might have married Phoebe, and Victoria may have never walked. I shudder at the thought."

She pulled his hand to her lips and kissed his palm. "That's something we'll never know, my love."

"Now that our children have given their approval, don't you think it's about time you answered my question?" Again, Ben knelt before her, his heart overflowing with love. "Are you ready to take on the job of being my wife and Victoria's stepmother? Will you marry me, my darling, my precious one, the one God so graciously sent into my life?"

Bending, her eyes shining with love for Ben and gratitude toward God, Judy threw her arms around his neck and pressed her lips to his. "Oh, yes, Ben. I'd love to be your wife. I've waited a lifetime for a man like you, and I'm not about to let you get away."

His face all screwed up, Timmy yanked on Victoria's hand. "Yuk! Come on, Tory, let's get out of here. They're kissin' again!"

Epilogue

Two months later

"Would you stand still?" Judy rolled her eyes at her matron of honor. "Miranda! Stop fussing over me! You're so fidgety you'd think you were the one who was getting married today instead of me."

Miranda paused, her hand holding the hair-pick mid-air. "You really don't want that little wisp of hair sticking out of your headpiece, do you?"

"No, of course not, though I doubt anyone but you would even notice."

Miranda placed the pick on the dresser and stepped back to appraise the bride. "Okay, let's go over the list I made."

"Again? We've already gone over it twice."

She responded with a roll of her eyes. "Sorry, but as Ben's housekeeper I'm used to making lists and checking and rechecking them. It never hurts to be sure. Okay, the something old is the little gold pinkie ring you're wearing on your right hand."

"Right."

"The something new is—"

"This beautiful eternity necklace Ben gave me." Smiling at the woman who had become as close to her as her own mother, Judy lovingly fingered her necklace.

"Something borrowed is—"

"The safety pin I borrowed from you."

"Check. And your something blue? You still haven't told me what you've selected for your something blue."

"That's because I didn't know myself until a few days ago. When I told Timmy and Victoria about the old-new-something borrowed-something blue tradition, they asked me if they could provide my blue thing. They wanted to pay for it with their own money. I thought that was such a sweet idea."

"So? What was it? What did they give you?"

Judy glanced toward the door making sure it hadn't been left ajar then, turning toward Miranda, lifted her skirt to just below the knee.

Miranda's hand flew to her mouth, and she gasped as her eyes widened. "You got a tattoo? Oh, Judy, I hope you asked Ben about this before you did it. I'm not sure he'd approve of his wife wearing a tattoo."

Judy gave her a mischievous grin. "It's not very big, only a small blue flower. I kinda like it. Besides, like I told you, it was a gift."

The outspoken Miranda gave her head a disapproving shake. "You'll never be able to wear a dress or a shorter skirt without it showing. I wish you'd thought this through before getting it. Do you have any idea how hard and how expensive, not to mention how painful, it is to have one of those things removed." You should never have listened to those children and let them talk you into something so foolish."

A coy smile tilted at Judy's lips. "So you think I should have rejected Timmy's and Victoria's blue gift?"

"You could have explained there were other gifts they could have given you, rather than paying to have your leg tattooed."

Noting Miranda's concern, Judy decided it was time to come clean. "I'm sorry, Miranda. I didn't mean to deceive you. It's not a real tattoo. Just a temporary one. The kind you can peel off a paper, press onto your skin, and then remove when you want to. The kids thought it would be fun for me to wear a tattoo as my something blue, and I agreed. No one will see it but the three of you, and later on tonight, Ben, when we reach the honeymoon suite. I know he'll get a real laugh out of it."

Miranda let out a sigh of relief as her hand went to her forehead. "You really had me going. I thought that thing was real, but I had no business spouting off at you."

"Don't worry about it." Judy lifted her skirt again. "It does look real, doesn't it? But it's not, I promise you."

A rap sounded on the door as the wedding planner's head appeared. "The rest of the wedding party is in their place, Judy. Are you ready?"

"Oh, yes, more than ready."

Flo Driscoll smiled at Judy approvingly. "That magnificent white gown is perfect on you. The seed beads and pearl trim, the empire waist, the sweetheart neckline, all look as if they were made for you." She turned to Miranda. "Don't forget to take Judy's bridal bouquet from her when she reaches the altar."

Miranda nodded. "I won't forget, and I'll make sure her train is laid out straight like you told me."

"Good. And, please, both of you remember to walk slowly. The audience wants plenty of time to look at your beautiful faces, gowns, and your flowers."

Judy let out a nervous snicker. "What if I trip?" Why had her hands all of a sudden become clammy?

"Take it from me, you won't. I've always thought that was one of the reasons fathers, or their stand-ins, are given the privilege of walking the bride to the altar so they have someone to hang on to, so they wouldn't trip or fall from sheer nervousness and excitement. I'm sure, with Max holding on to you, you will make it to the altar in fine style."

Judy was glad she'd asked Max to give her away. Both he and Miranda had been of such importance in her life since she'd met Ben. The fact that the two of them felt so unworthy of the tasks made it even more special that they had finally accepted her invitations.

As Flo led the bride and matron of honor into the foyer to join those who were already in place, two precious children rushed to Judy, circling their arms around her, both asking at once, "Are you wearing our blue present?"

Without answering, Judy pulled her skirt to her knee. Both children clapped their hands with glee.

Frowning, Flo, who as the wedding planner seemed concerned that they would wrinkle Judy's satin gown with their hugs, reached out and gently pulled Victoria and Timmy back into position before nodding to the organist.

The music swelled and the wedding began.

One by one, she started those she'd assembled down the aisle; first Victoria, with her flower basket filled with rose petals, then Timmy, bearing the ring pillow, and lastly, the two lovely bridesmaids, both friends from Ben's church, before reaching out her hand to Miranda.

"Those four have prepared the way for the bride, but your job is of even more importance. It is your appearance as her matron of honor that signals the audience the bride will soon appear." She latched on to Miranda's ample hand. "By the way, you look lovely in your pink satin gown, Miranda. Smile and lift your head proudly as you make your way."

"Are you sure this gown doesn't make me look too fat?"

Judy shook her finger at her. "No, it makes you look adorable."

Miranda smoothed at her hair. "Not many women my size look adorable, but thanks for saying it." After a grateful smile toward Judy, Miranda turned and started down the aisle.

Hoping to settle the butterflies in her stomach, Judy swallowed hard then sucked in a deep breath of air. Why was she so nervous? This was the day she'd waited for, planned for, and had looked forward to all her life. She hadn't been this nervous since she'd testified in court. *Lord,* she breathed out in prayer while lifting her face upward, *help me. I'm so weak I can barely stand.*

She had no more than uttered the words when she felt strong fingers circle her arm. "Are you ready?" a kind male voice asked.

Feeling a wave of confidence at the sound, she turned to face Max. "I am now." *Thank you, Lord.*

Max slipped her hand into the crook of his arm then smiled down at her, his presence giving her the strength and encouragement she needed.

As they rounded the doorway and she caught sight of Ben standing at the altar, in front of the flower-laden arch of pink roses, white lily-of-the-valley, and wandering trails of ivy, her heart nearly burst with joy.

∞

Ben felt his heart lurch. Never had he seen a woman as beautiful as Judy at that moment as she headed toward him holding onto Max's arm. How could he have been so blind as to even consider marrying Phoebe, simply to give his daughter a mother—a mother she didn't want? Judy was the perfect woman for him and the ideal mother for Victoria. And if that weren't enough, Timmy was going to be the son Ben had wished for and never had. Why hadn't he turned the whole thing over to God when he lost his wife, rather than trying to handle it himself? God's plan was always the best. He'd known that from the day he'd accepted Christ as his Savior, but, in his foolishness and self-confidence, he hadn't let God have full control of his life. Well, no more. From now on things would be different. God would be first in his life, with Judy second, then the children. His own wants, work, hobbies, sports, everything else in his life would come after them. What a privilege it would be to be the head of this new family God was giving him. Though it was an awesome responsibility, it was one he accepted gladly and with eagerness.

"Who gives this woman to be married to this man?" Pastor Green asked as Max and Judy joined Ben and Miranda at the altar.

Ben smiled at Max. Good old Max. He was glad Judy had insisted Max be the one to give her away. If he had his way, Max and Miranda would be with him and his new family until God took them home to be with Him.

"In the absence of Miss Judy's father, I do," Max said proudly before taking Judy's hand and placing it in Ben's.

Ben felt himself beam as his fingers circled Judy's hand and he gazed into her sweet face. *This lovely woman is actually going to be my wife!*

∞

A delightful tingle surged through Judy's body as Ben's fingers tightened around hers. All nervousness suddenly disappeared and all she could think about was Ben, dear sweet Ben, the man with whom she would be spending the rest of her life. If anyone would have told her a year ago that she would be marrying such a wonderful godly man, would become the step-mother of a lovely child like Victoria, and would be raising her very own son, she would have called them crazy.

Something like that could never happen.

But it was, and God had made it happen. He'd taken the bad things in her life and had turned them into good. What an awesome Father He was.

To Judy's amazement, she remembered every word of the vows she'd written and memorized. Perhaps because they had come directly from her heart. And she would never forget Ben's vows and the sincerity in his eyes as he recited his to her.

"Ben. Judy," Pastor Green said when the soloist finished her song, "marriage is not to be entered into lightly. It is not something that should be done on a whim, because the other person makes you feel good, or because of some personal gain or gratification. It is an honest pact entered into by two people, before God and those who witness their wedding. As God has told us in His word, He doesn't look favorably on those who break vows taken in His name. Remember the vows you have taken today, recite them to one another on your anniversary each year. Use them as a guide to build the happy marriage you both desire. Another way we mortals use to remind us of our vows are the rings we exchange on our wedding day." He motioned to Timmy who, grinning a grin nearly as wide as his face, extended the ring pillow toward Ben.

Ben tugged on the satin ribbon then lifted the ring and turned to Judy. "I love you, Judy, with all my heart, and promise to be the husband you deserve and desire. I give you this ring as a symbol of my love."

Through tears of happiness, Judy glanced down at her finger as he placed the ring on it. The glow of the flame from the candles on the candelabra reflected in the diamonds, fracturing the light and sending it into countless shards of color. Like the eternity necklace Ben had given her, the circle of that ring had no beginning and no end. She prayed their love would be the same way.

Timmy stepped in front of Judy and lifted the pillow, his face shining with expectation. She pulled the remaining ring from its moorings then bent and kissed his cheek. As Timmy backed into his place, she turned and accepted Ben's outstretched hand.

"Ben, my love and my best friend, you are the person I have been waiting for all my life. With God's help and your encouragement, I will do all I can to be the wife you deserve. Please wear this ring as a symbol of my unending love for you." She slipped the ring on his finger then reached up to lovingly touch his cheek. "I love you, Ben."

∞

Ben knew he should wait until the Pastor Green pronounced them husband and wife, but he couldn't. Though, as an architect, he had always followed instructions to the letter and knew the importance of planning and structure, he couldn't help himself. He had to hold Judy in his arms and kiss her. His lips ached to kiss her.

So, kiss her he did, much to her surprise, the pastor's surprise, Miranda and the bridesmaid's surprise, and the audience's surprise, and even to his surprise, fully on the lips with a long and tender embrace. To his delight, Judy melded into his arms and willingly participated. When their kiss finally ended, Ben, feeling somewhat foolish for his impetuousness, turned partway toward Pastor Green and partway toward those assembled and uttered, "Sorry, folks, that part was unplanned, but I was so moved by Judy's words I just had to kiss her."

Most gaped at him, a few even applauded, but everyone smiled.

"I think we all understand," Pastor Green said, as if to get Ben off the hook. "At least those of us who have been privileged enough to enjoy the love of a good woman. In fact, I'd like to encourage you to show that same kind of spontaneous love to your mate every day for the rest of your life. It never hurts to let those you love know it."

Gesturing toward Judy, he added, "As your pastor I have no doubt your marriage will be quite successful—in every way, so if you and Ben will turn to face your family and friends, I'd like to officially introduce you to them."

Ben wrapped his arm about Judy and pulled her close then pivoted them both toward the audience. Was his face red? It had to be. Rarely in his life had he done something so impetuous. His actions had been totally out of character, but he didn't care. He wanted the world to know of his love for his bride.

Pastor Green moved up beside them and, after reciting the usual legalities about the power vested in him by the State, with a swoop of his hand, he added, "May I present to you the Bramwells, Mr. and Mrs. Ewald Bentley Bramwell, the third."

Ben lifted his hand to get the pastor's attention. "Judy and I are only a part of this new family, Pastor Green. There are two more members. I'd like to have Victoria and Timmy join us. Without those two and their conniving, Judy and I may never have gotten together."

With a "Yippee!" Timmy grabbed on to Victoria's hand and dragged her to Judy's side before taking hold of Ben's hand.

Feeling as if he had been suddenly appointed king, Ben reached out his arms and circled his little family of four. "God has blessed me beyond belief."

Then smiling, he added, "This the new Ben Bramwell family."

Listening to Her Heart

Dedication

As I'm writing this dedication, it is nearly midnight. I'm sitting on my bed in my pajamas, my computer resting in my lap. The house is quiet since I no longer have my hero, my dear departed husband Don with me, yet I am so thankful. Thankful for a man I could *trust* with my life. What a blessing, yet I know that many women have either not experienced that kind of trust or have had a very special someone disappoint them by breaking their trust. As Aunt Margaret states in this book, "You can fall in love, but you can't fall in trust. Trust has to be earned. And once it has been broken it can rarely be restored." I dedicate this book to Don and all the other men who are worthy of a good woman's trust. Thank you, Don, for being you.

Prologue

Dressed in the pretty pink, lace-trimmed gown the nurse had helped her slip into after her shower, eighty-five-year-old Margaret Douglas sat perched on the edge of her bed at Hendersonville, Tennessee's medical center waiting for Dr. Mechan. "I'm sorry, Margaret," he told her as he entered her hospital room, clipboard in hand. "I wish I had better news, but you've always told me you wanted me to be straight with you and tell you the truth."

He placed the clipboard on the nightstand, then stood gazing at her, his fingers cradling his chin thoughtfully. "We've run out of options. There's nothing else we can do. I'd like you to stay another night to make sure this new medication continues to agree with you. Then, if there are no more problems, you can go home tomorrow."

Her palm flattening against her chest, Margaret drew in a deep breath and stared at Dr. Mechan. "How long do I have?"

Clasping her free hand in his, he looked deeply into her eyes. "Six months at the most. Maybe less. I'd suggest, if you haven't already done so, you get your affairs in order."

Though she'd hoped for better news, Margaret wasn't surprised by the doctor's report. When she'd learned nearly ten years ago she had liver cancer, she hadn't expected to live this long. In fact, at that time she had begged God to give her five more years. He'd done that and more. She'd had a good life with Harold, her husband of more than twenty years, and now that he had gone home to be with the Lord, she was ready to go, too.

Except for two things.

Number one. To make sure her brother-in-law's son, Beemer Douglas, who had lived with her and her husband since he was a young boy, had made his peace with God.

And number two. To see Ginny Markham, her beloved niece, her sister's only child, and Beemer united in marriage.

I have to figure out a way to bring those two together, she told herself the next morning as her nephew drove her to 223 River Road, the beautiful, Victorian-style home she'd lived in for nearly three decades. *But how? Beemer lives here in Hendersonville, and Ginny lives in St. Louis. They haven't seen each other in nearly*

133

twenty years. But in my heart of hearts I know they're perfect for one another.

"Lord," she whispered in her heart as she watched Beemer turn the key in the lock to her front door, "my time here on earth is short. Please give me a plan."

Chapter 1

"Stay in the van, Tinkerbelle. I'll be right back." Ginny Markham slammed the door on her old van then headed up the sidewalk leading to the house at 223 River Road. Knowing how ill Aunt Margaret had been, she hated to ring the doorbell, but without a key she had no choice.

"Hey, you made it." An athletic-looking man, who could easily have been mistaken for a Tennessee Titans' linebacker, pushed open the storm door and smiled down at her. "Come on in. We've been expecting you."

Both surprised and shocked by his greeting, Ginny backed away, hurriedly glancing toward the numbers mounted above the mailbox, thinking perhaps she had the wrong house. But how could that be? She'd been to Aunt Margaret's beautiful home dozens and dozens of times. But, if this was her aunt's house, who was this man? And why was he here?

He leaned out the door and reached for the small suitcase in her hand. "Hey, I won't bite. Come on in."

She took two quick steps backward, nearly catching her heel on the welcome mat. "I've come to see Margaret Douglas. Is she here?"

The man squiggled up his face. "Sure, she's here. Where'd you think she'd be? She got out of the hospital more than a week ago."

Still keeping her distance, Ginny scrutinized him carefully, not about to go into her aunt's house alone with this giant of a man. For all she knew, he could have broken into Aunt Margaret's house and, perish the thought, be holding her captive. Or maybe something even worse. She shuddered at the thought of her helpless, frail aunt being someone's victim.

"You don't recognize me, do you? I'm Beemer." The big man let loose a slight chuckle. "I guess I've changed quite a bit since we last saw each other. How long has it been? Ten years? Twenty? But you sure haven't changed much." He eyed her from head to toe. "You've grown up to be a pretty good-lookin' little gal."

"You're Beemer?" She couldn't remember exactly how many years it'd been since she'd last seen her aunt's nephew by marriage, but it had been a long time. He'd gone into the Marines right after graduating from high school and had been career military, with most of his time spent overseas. Though he had come back to Hendersonville a number of times for a visit, their paths hadn't crossed.

Trying not to be obvious, she sized him up. He was right. He had changed. As far as she was concerned, for the better. Much better. Being a Marine had added both weight and muscle to his already big-boned body. His face was tanned, and he appeared to be freshly shaven. A handsome man indeed. Not at all like the pictures she'd seen of him on her aunt's mantel, but those had been taken years ago.

His smile broadening, he nodded. "Yep, it's me. I'm—"

"Ginny? Is that you?"

The question came from somewhere inside the house. Ginny recognized the voice immediately. "Yes, Aunt Margaret, I'm here!" She pushed past him and into the house in search of her aunt. She found her in the family room, stretched out on a sofa, looking pale and drawn.

Her aunt reached out a trembling hand. "I'm so glad you made it, dear. I've been praying for your safe arrival."

"St. Louis is only five hours away, but thanks for your prayers. That must be why I made it without incident." Ginny bent and kissed her wrinkled cheek. "How are you feeling, Aunt Margaret?"

"Much better, now that you and Beemer are here."

Although concerned about her aunt's loss of weight and the frailness of her body, Ginny forced a smile. "My boss granted me a leave of absence. I'm here as long as you need me."

"I've been taking good care of her. She's my little sweetheart." Beemer's voice boomed out from behind them. "But I'm not very good at giving her sponge baths."

Aunt Margaret motioned him toward her then grabbed on to his hand. "Beemer has been a godsend. He moved in with me about a month ago. I didn't tell you because I was afraid you wouldn't come if you knew someone was already helping me."

Ginny cast a glance toward Beemer then back to her aunt. "Of course I would've come, but I'm glad he's been here. You shouldn't have been alone." She glanced back at her cousin. "Thanks for staying with her until I could get here. I'd have come right away if she'd let me know she needed help."

"No *problemo*. I love this old gal almost as much as my uncle Harold did. She's a great lady. We've had a good time together."

Aunt Margaret gave his hand an affectionate squeeze. "Beemer has been wonderful to me. I can't thank him enough for coming."

Ginny, feeling a pang of guilt for not recognizing Beemer and for being so standoffish at his warm welcome, gave him one of her most pleasant smiles. "Thanks, Beemer, for being so good to our aunt, but I'll take over now. I'm sure you're anxious to get back to your life."

"This *is* my life now. At Aunt Margaret's request I locked up my apartment and moved in with her. I'm here to stay as long as she wants me to. Took me awhile but I've got all my electronic gear set up, and I'm actually operating my business from here now." He sent a smile his aunt's way. "Just like Uncle Harold would have wanted me to."

Aunt Margaret's demeanor took on a seriousness. "A dying woman wants as much of her family around her as possible. You two *are* my family. Everyone else is gone. I need both of you here, Ginny. I refuse to go to a hospital, and caring for me is not an easy task. You could never lift me and carry me around as Beemer does."

Ginny gave Beemer a grateful smile then patted her aunt's shoulder. "Don't you worry about a thing. We're both going to take good care of you."

"I've got the bedroom opposite Aunt Margaret's ready for you. Mine is at the far end of the hall," he explained, picking up her suitcase. "Give me your keys, and I'll get the rest of the stuff from your van while you two visit."

Before she could warn him her sweet little pregnant cat was locked up in the van, a gigantic bundle of fur came bolting down the hallway and hurled itself against her, its huge paws nearly knocking her to the floor.

Beemer grabbed Ginny and wrapped her protectively in his arms. "Mortimer, down! Bad dog!"

At the sight of the big St. Bernard, Ginny clung tightly to Beemer's arm. Having never owned a dog, or even liked them, she had no idea what to do next. "He's *your* dog?" she was finally able to ask, the sound of her heart pounding in her ears. "He's living here with you?"

Aunt Margaret smiled up at her as if nothing had happened. "I told him it would be all right. Mortimer is such a gentle dog."

Gentle dog? Is she kidding? That dog is a monster!

Beemer loosened his hold on her and bent to rub the dog's ears. "He'll be better once he gets to know you. Go ahead. Pet him. He's harmless."

Ginny backed away, her eyes pinned on the dog. "I—I don't like dogs."

"You'll like this one." Beemer gave her a confident smile. "He's really a pussycat."

"Cat!" Ginny sucked in a deep breath. With the appearance of that dreadful animal, all remembrance of Tinkerbelle had escaped her mind. "Oh, no! I brought my cat with me. She's in my van."

Beemer threw back his head with a laugh. "This should be interesting. Mortimer has never been around a cat, except in a fight."

His comment set Ginny's teeth on edge. Even with those sharp claws of hers,

Tinkerbelle would never be able to defend herself against his enormous dog.

"I hope that cat of yours doesn't like birds."

Ginny turned to stare at him. "What do you mean, doesn't like birds? Birds are their natural prey."

Beemer shrugged. "I've got a couple of little blue finches in my room."

A big dog? Finches? This is never going to work. Ginny lifted her chin defiantly. "Then you'd better make sure they're locked in their cage."

He laughed, the sound deep and rich, then reached out his hand. "I'll make a deal with you. You keep your cat away from my birds, and I'll try to keep Mortimer away from your cat."

Ginny put her hand on her hip and looked at him sharply. "And how do you propose to do that?"

"Mortimer's a fast learner. But it'd be wise to keep her away from him."

"Her away from *him?* There is no way I can keep Tinkerbelle locked up in my bedroom all day, nor do I want to. She's used to having free rein of the house."

"So is Mortimer," he countered.

"Can't you keep him penned up in the backyard?"

He shook his head. "He's never been penned up. He'd bark his head off, and the neighbors would turn in a complaint."

"Can't you tell him to be quiet?"

"Yeah, and I can stop a speeding train. He's a dog. Dogs bark when they're cooped up. Can't you pen up your cat?"

"You can't pen up a cat unless you put a cover over their pen. They can climb over anything. Besides, cats are independent creatures. They're used to being free to roam wherever they choose." Ginny stood firm, her eyes pinned on Beemer. She was not about to back down.

He shrugged. "Well, then, I guess we've got a problem."

Aunt Margaret rubbed at her forehead. "I'm sorry. I knew Ginny would be bringing Tinkerbelle. I should have thought about you both having pets when I asked you to come here."

Her aunt's weak voice, and the look of disappointment on her face nearly broke Ginny's heart. "I'll try to keep Tinkerbelle out of Mortimer's way," she told the big man, though not sure how she'd do it, but she was determined to try. "I know Aunt Margaret wants us both here."

"And I'll do all I can to keep Mortimer from eating your cat."

Ginny froze at his choice of words. Surely he could have said it another way. "And I'll try to keep my cat from *eating* your birds," she shot back, hoping he'd get the message.

"Touché. I deserved that. Guess I should have worded that sentence another way and said I'd do my best to keep Mortimer *away* from your cat. I've never actually seen him eat one, although he has had a few tangles with cats. Nothing serious, though. The cats lived through it."

Was that comment supposed to be reassuring?

"Tinkerbelle has had a few unpleasant experiences with dogs, too. Nearly scratched one dog's eyes out," she flung back, trying to sound as casual as he had.

Beemer let out a roar. "Well, then, I guess we'll just have to let them duke it out."

"I think you're both worrying needlessly. They'll be fine," Aunt Margaret offered from her place on the sofa. "Mortimer is a good dog, and I'm sure Tinkerbelle is a good cat. I'll pray and ask God to help those two get along."

Beemer let loose a chuckle. "You think that will work? If there is a God, I'm not sure He'd be concerned about little things like dogs and cats getting along."

Ginny was appalled by his remark. *"If* there is a God? You mean you don't believe there is?" She'd assumed the man was a Christian simply because her aunt and uncle had raised him.

He tilted his head thoughtfully. "I don't know there is a God, but I also don't know there isn't! I just know I've never heard from Him."

Aunt Margaret reached out and touched his hand. "Beemer, dear, as I've told you so many times, please don't shut your mind to God's existence. He is real, and He wants *you* to know Him, too."

Beemer turned his attention to Ginny. "I suppose you believe in that God stuff, too?"

She was glad he'd asked. She loved being a witness for the Lord. "Yes, I do. He's very real to me. My faith is important to me."

He gazed at her for a moment, as if thinking over her words, then laughed and nodded toward Mortimer who had sauntered across the room. "Hey, old boy, you'd better not go after that cat. God is watching you."

Ginny struggled to hold back the words that just begged to be said. At least she knew where Beemer stood. She was disappointed he didn't love God as she and her aunt did.

"My God is able to do wonderful things. Even cause your pets to get along." Aunt Margaret sent them each a sweet smile. "Let's not invite trouble by worrying about something that may never happen."

Beemer bobbed his head. "Sounds like a good plan to me." He reached out his hand to Ginny again. "Keys, please. We need to get you settled in."

She handed him the keys then followed at his heels as he walked through the house and out the front door, still not sure this situation between their pets was going to work. But who was she to doubt her aunt's prayers would be answered? She'd promised she would stay as long as she was needed, and she was going to keep her word, whether Tinkerbelle and Mortimer got along or not. She only wished Aunt Margaret hadn't asked Beemer to move in, too. Then she'd have no dog to contend with. Surely, no more than her aunt weighed, she could have handled her by herself.

"Better let me open the door," she told him as he turned the key in the lock. "I don't know what Tinkerbelle will do when she smells dog on you."

Without a word he obliged and stepped out of the way. Ginny carefully opened the door then gathered the cat up in her arms, speaking softly to assure her nothing was wrong.

Beemer leaned toward her for a better look. "She's a fat one. You must feed her well."

"She's pregnant."

"Pregnant?" He reared back, lifting his hands in surrender. "How long's she have to go?"

Now it was Ginny's turn to shrug. "Don't know. Probably not too long. It's been some time since I've taken her to the vet."

Staring at the cat, he scratched his head. "So now I not only have to keep my dog from eating a cat, I have to keep him from eating a pregnant one."

"And I have to keep my cat from eating your birds," she reminded him with a slight grin. "But I'm willing to do whatever it takes to make my aunt happy."

"Me, too." Beemer's hand went out slowly. "Does she like to be petted?"

Ginny nodded. "She loves it. Go ahead. She's a pretty gentle cat."

Using a single crooked finger he cautiously stroked the cat's back. "I think she likes me."

"I guess she does." Ginny was surprised Tinkerbelle hadn't seemed to notice the dog smell on Beemer. She'd half expected her to scratch at him or at least raise the hair on her back.

"Maybe she'll like Mortimer."

She had to laugh. "Don't count on it. Most cats are afraid of dogs, and from what I've heard most dogs don't like cats."

He snorted. "Maybe these two will be the exception."

"I hope you're right." Cradling Tinkerbelle in one arm, Ginny pulled out the bag that contained the sack of her cat's favorite food and bowls. "If you were serious about helping me unload, could you please grab that large suitcase and the bag of kitty litter?"

"Sure, I'll get those two smaller suitcases, too."

Once they were in the house, Ginny filled both the water and food dishes, then locked Tinkerbelle in the bathroom while she and Beemer unloaded the rest of her things.

"You women sure have a lot of stuff," he told her with a teasing grin as they carried the last few boxes into the house. "Looks like you're planning to stay for a while."

"As long as Aunt Margaret needs me. My boss was kind enough to give me a generous leave of absence, but if I have to stay longer than expected, I will. I can always find another job if I have to, but I can't replace my precious aunt."

He nodded, then stacked the boxes neatly in a corner. "That's exactly the way I feel. I was in grade school when my mom and dad decided they no longer wanted to be parents, handed me over to Uncle Harold and Aunt Margaret, and took off for South America. Even though my aunt and uncle had only been married a short time, they found it in their hearts to take me in and raise me until I was old enough to join the Marines. Aunt Margaret may not have been a blood relative, but I love her as much as if she had been. I'd do anything for that woman."

Ginny bobbed her head. "That's exactly the way I feel."

"Too bad, with you off living in St. Louis and me tied down playing football and other sports here in Hendersonville, we never got together. Seems folks get so busy with their own lives, they don't have time to get to know their relatives."

"I know. My mom wanted so much to drive down here and visit Aunt Margaret; but she didn't drive and my dad had so many responsibilities with his job that he rarely took a day off, so we never made it. By the time I began coming down on my own, you were already in the military, serving our country."

He stuck out his hand. "Well, it looks like we're gonna have time to get acquainted now, Ginny."

"Yeah, I guess it does." Smiling, she grasped it, cringing at his strength when he gave it a vigorous shake. Maybe all of them living together wouldn't be as bad as she'd expected.

When they walked back into the living room, Aunt Margaret asked them to sit down in the two chairs opposite her, saying she needed to talk to them. Something in the tone of her voice frightened Ginny.

"Could you please prop me up a bit higher, Beemer?"

Beemer quickly moved to his aunt's side and pulled her into a better sitting position while Ginny plumped several pillows and positioned them at her back.

"Thank you. That's much better." Aunt Margaret adjusted the shawl Ginny had placed over her lap then gazed at first one then the other. "I'm sure you both thought it was a bit extreme, being asked to put your lives on hold and move in here to care for me."

"You needed someone to care for you. I wanted to come." Ginny nodded toward Beemer. "I'm sure Beemer did, too. We love you, Aunt Margaret."

"I love you, too." She paused for a moment, as if trying to compose her thoughts before continuing. "I asked you to come—because I'm dying. I have advanced liver cancer."

Ginny let out a loud gasp as her hands flew to cover her mouth. "Your cancer has come back?"

Beemer stood with his mouth open, his long arms dangling at his sides.

"Yes. It never really went away, just into remission for a time. Dr. Mechan has given me all sorts of tests. It's progressed rapidly this past year. I've known for some time and have been making preparations for my death; but I couldn't face being alone at the end, and I didn't want to die in a hospital. I—I wanted to die at home, right here in this house, surrounded by the people and things I love and know best. That's why I needed you two. Without you it would be impossible for me to stay."

"Are you sure?" Ginny asked, her heart aching with sadness and grief. "Maybe you should go to Mayo's or Sloan Kettering or M.D. Anderson, or one of the other—"

Her aunt held up her hand. "Believe me, dear Ginny, I've exhausted every possibility." Her face took on a slight smile. "But I don't want you to feel sorry for me. I've lived a long, good life. I'm ready to go meet my Lord, and your uncle Harold is there waiting for me."

Finally finding his voice, Beemer whispered, "I love you," then bent and kissed his aunt tenderly on the forehead. "I don't want you to go. Surely there's something that can be done. Can't they do surgery? Remove the cancerous portion of your liver?"

"My cancer is inoperable, Beemer. It's far too advanced. What they call a Stage IV. It's too close to the area where the liver meets the main arteries, the veins, and the bile ducts. It's also spread to the lymph nodes. It's just a matter of time. As you can see, I'm nearly bedfast. My doctor has already contacted hospice. In a few days they'll be bringing in a hospital bed and the other items I'll be needing."

Weeping, Ginny sat down beside her aunt and threw her arms about her frail body. "Why didn't you tell me? I'd have been here weeks ago."

Beemer rubbed across his eyes with the back of his hand. "She never mentioned any of this when I visited her, and I've been living right here in Hendersonville since I left the Marines. I had no idea things were this bad, or I would have moved in weeks ago."

"I didn't want to ask either of you to come until it became absolutely necessary."

Ginny released her hold and backed away. "Are you in pain?"

"The medication the doctor gave me helps, but I'll have to be on morphine before long."

Beemer breathed out a long sigh. "She's a plucky old gal. She's probably in pain right now, but she'd never tell us."

Ginny took her aunt's hand in hers and gently stroked it. "So what can we do to make you comfortable? Is there anything you need?"

Aunt Margaret smiled at her then at Beemer. "The only thing I need is having you both here. I can't thank you enough for coming." With a nearly inaudible groan she shifted her position slightly. "Maybe you'd better take the pillows from behind my back, Beemer, dear. I'm getting a little tired."

"Your wish is my command." As if she weighed no more than a rag doll, Beemer scooped her up in his arms and headed down the hall toward her bedroom. "But if I'm gonna cart you around, you'll have to lay off the Twinkies and ice cream. I could barely lift you."

The tinkling melody of her aunt's laughter brought tears to Ginny's eyes. Though she'd assumed her aunt wasn't well when she'd phoned and asked her to come, she'd had no idea her illness was terminal.

She followed them into the bedroom, pulled back the covers, then stood watching Beemer carefully lower their aunt onto her bed, impressed that a man of his size could be so gentle. "Thanks, Beemer. I'll take it from here."

He gave her a wink and a salute. "I'll bet you're hungry. I fixed a pot of potato soup this morning before you got here. I'll go warm up some for us. Aunt Margaret can eat later, after she's had a nap."

"I can heat it up after—"

"Nope, cuz. You had a long drive from St. Louis. Besides, you have to unpack. I'll do it."

Ginny helped her aunt take a sponge bath and get into a fresh nightgown then tucked her in and, after closing the door, made her way to the kitchen. "It sure smells good in here. Soup ready?"

Before he could answer, the doorbell rang. "Want me to get it?" Ginny asked.

"Sure, if you don't mind. It's probably a neighbor checking on Aunt Margaret. They come by pretty often."

Ginny hurried into the hall then flung open the door to find a gorgeous blond, clad in a pair of white shorts and a red halter top, standing on the porch, a huge smile blanketing her face.

The smile quickly disappeared when she saw Ginny. "Who are you?"

Ginny returned her question. "Who are you?"

The woman lodged her hand on her slim hip. "Where is Beemer?"

"Beemer? He's in the kitchen."

The woman pulled open the storm door and, sidestepping Ginny, made her way to the kitchen with Ginny at her heels.

Beemer smiled at her as she entered. "Hey, Rosie, what's up?"

After giving Ginny a backward glare, Rosie hurried toward Beemer and threw her arms about his neck, planting a kiss on his lips. "I've been missing you. Why haven't you called me?"

"I've—ah—been busy." Beemer shot Ginny a quick glance before tugging the woman's arms from about his neck. "Want some soup?"

Rosie latched onto his arm and gazed up into his eyes. "What I want is for you to go to the health club and play racquetball with me like you promised."

Beemer frowned. "Oh, was that today? I forgot all about it."

Rosie pivoted toward Ginny with a look that could have curdled cream. "Forgot? Or been busy with someone else? You haven't introduced me to your friend."

He chortled. "Oh, yeah, I didn't, did I? Rosie, this is Ginny. Ginny, this is Rosie."

Rosie stared at her. "I don't remember seeing you around. Are you—?"

"Ginny is going to help me take care of my aunt," Beemer inserted. "I'm not too good on the female stuff."

"Does that mean *she'll* be living here, too?" Rosie's words were so cool they made Ginny shudder.

Smiling, Beemer nodded. "Yep, my aunt insisted on it. It'll be nice for Aunt Margaret to have another woman around."

Why doesn't he explain I'm his cousin? Ginny wondered.

"I hope *she's* not the reason you haven't called me," Rosie said, smiling sweetly and running her fingertip down his arm. "Rosie has missed her Beemer."

Grabbing onto Rosie's arm, Beemer headed her toward the hall. "I'm sure sorry I can't go to the health club with you, but I've got to help Ginny unpack. I'll call you in a few days, and maybe we can reschedule that game."

Ginny could still hear Rosie trying to talk Beemer into spending the evening with her as they moved down the hall then Beemer cutting her off midsentence and telling her good-bye before he closed the door.

He was sporting a smile when he reentered the room. "Sorry about that. Now where were we? Oh, yes, the soup." He hurried to the range, lifted the lid on the soup pot, and began to stir.

"Why didn't you tell her I was your cousin?" Ginny asked, still puzzled by his obvious omission.

He gave her a mischievous grin. "'Cause I thought it'd be more fun to let her think otherwise. I like Rosie, but sometimes she gets a little too possessive."

"She's really pretty. I love her thick, blond, curly hair and her flawless complexion. She should enter beauty pageants."

He huffed. "She does, all the time, and usually wins. Her goal is the Miss Universe Pageant. Unlike you, she's pretty stuck on herself. She knows she's a knockout, and, take it from me, she works it to her best advantage."

"She seems to think a lot of you."

"She's a fun date, but I could never get serious with a woman like her. I've learned by experience, outward beauty is not always a reflection of what's inside." He gave the soup a final stir. "Soup's good and hot. Grab a couple of bowls and spoons. I already put the garlic salt, bread, and peanut butter on the table."

"Are there any crackers?"

He nodded toward the cabinet. "In there. First shelf."

After grabbing a hot pad, Beemer carried the pot to the table and ladled out generous portions of soup into each bowl. "You're gonna like this. I don't know much about cooking, but I make a mean pot of potato soup."

Ginny filled two cups with the coffee Beemer had made, carried them to the table, and sat down. "If it's half as good as it smells, it's going to be wonderful." She hesitated until he had settled in a chair then, when he plowed into his food, bowed her head and prayed silently. While Beemer's heart seemed right where his aunt was concerned, it was certain he didn't share her faith.

When she opened her eyes, she couldn't believe what she was seeing. "What are you doing?"

He gave her a questioning stare. "Getting ready to eat my soup."

"You just spread peanut butter on your bread and put it in the bowl with your soup then sprinkled garlic salt on it!"

He shrugged. "Yeah. So?"

"You're going to eat it that way?"

"Sure, I always eat it this way. It's great. You ought to try it." He filled his spoon to overflowing and stuffed it into his mouth. "Umm, umm. Delicious."

Ginny turned her head away and made a face. "That sounds awful! Peanut butter, bread, and garlic salt? Yuck!"

Beemer filled his spoon again and waved it toward her. "Don't knock it until you try it. You'd be surprised how those flavors meld together. I've been eating my potato soup this way since I was a kid. It's the way Uncle Harold always liked it. I learned it from him."

She reached for the crackers then broke several into her bowl. "Must be a family thing. Thanks, but I think I'll stick with crackers."

Beemer's expression turned serious. "I can't believe we're going to lose her. I knew Aunt Margaret was sick, but I had no idea things had progressed this far."

"Me either, but I'm glad you've been here for her. When did you decide to retire from the Marines?"

Beemer grabbed the garlic salt container and gave it another generous shake over his soup. "It was a hard decision. I joined right after I graduated from high school then spent most of my military years overseas. I was one of the lucky ones. I was able to get my college degree while in the service. Got a master's in computer science. Most of my time overseas was pretty exciting, and I enjoyed it, until some of the crazies in those far-off countries decided to turn the world upside down. I lost several of my closest buddies because of those madmen. Came close to getting it myself once. I considered staying in for another five years but decided against it. Giving as many years of your life as I did is a long time to give to anything. Besides, I missed being in the good old USA. As far as I'm concerned, we've got the best country in the world."

"I can't imagine what it must have been like over there. It had to be awful for you, to live from day to day, knowing each one could be your last." Though she'd known Beemer had been in the service and had been serving out of the country most of the time, she hadn't realized he'd been that close to the action.

"I had it pretty easy compared to those infantrymen. They put their lives on the line every day. They encountered some real dingbats over there, with some warped ideas. I spent most of my time sitting behind a computer." He placed the lid on the garlic salt container and screwed it on tight. "If you don't mind I'd rather not talk about it. Even listening to the nightly news gets me stirred up. Let's talk about something more pleasant." He smiled then wiggled his eyebrows. "Like what are we going to have for dessert?"

She didn't want to change the subject. In fact she had many more questions she wanted to ask him, but those could come later. "If I eat all of this, I may be too full for dessert."

"We've talked enough about me. Tell me about yourself, cuz. I was out of the country all those years, and I've been so busy with my own life since I got back that I barely know anything about you."

"Not much to tell. I've lived a pretty boring life. As you know, my dad got a job offer in St. Louis right after I graduated from high school, so I moved there with him and Mom and opted for business school rather than college. I took a job at Larsen's Investment Company and have been there ever since."

"You like living in St. Louis?"

"It's okay. The work is enjoyable. I go to a great church. That's important to me, and I like my apartment."

Beemer slathered another slice of bread with peanut butter. "You're really into this Christian stuff, aren't you?"

"It's my life, Beemer. My faith is what keeps me going, especially during the hard times."

"I don't get it. Seems to me if you believe in God, you wouldn't have *any* hard times. I thought He was supposed to answer prayer or something."

"He does answer prayer. Just not the way we want it sometimes or when we want it."

He gave an indifferent shrug. "Then why bother praying? Why not just let things happen?"

"God never promised to give us what we wanted, but He did promise to supply our needs. Sometimes the things we want most may not be the best for us. Besides, prayer brings us closer to God." She chuckled. "He loves to hear from us, even if it's to complain. He's interested in every phase of our lives."

"Would He let our aunt live if you asked Him to?"

"If prolonging her life was in His will."

Beemer scrunched up his face and lifted his hands in the air. "Too complicated for me. I think I'll just keep struggling along without His help. *Qué será, será.* Whatever will be, will be. I'm a big boy. I can handle it."

"Just because you don't understand Him doesn't mean He isn't real." Ginny placed her hand on his wrist and smiled up at him. "Please don't rule out God, Beemer."

His gaze covered her from head to toe. "You're a good-lookin' chick, cuz. How come you never married?"

Though he'd given her a compliment, she was sure his words were a ploy to change the subject. "I almost did once, but it didn't work out."

"I'd say that was some idiot's loss. Any guy who would let you get away would have to be *loco.*"

She felt herself blush. "I'm the one who was *loco.* Turned out he wasn't the person I'd thought he was. Life with him would have been unbearable."

"So you gave him the boot, huh?"

"No, he ran out on me."

Beemer's eyes widened. "Oh, cuz, I'm so sorry. I didn't have any idea that—"

"Could we not talk about it? I'm—I'm still hurting over it. It's tough to be rejected by the person you thought you'd spend the rest of your life with."

"Sure, we'll quit. If that's what you want."

Ginny broke another cracker into her soup then filled her spoon. "What about you, Beemer? No wife for you?"

His face took on a somberness. "Like you, I nearly got married once. I'd only been in the Marines about a year and was stationed at Marine Corps Base Hawaii. I spent most of my free time at Kaneohe Bay where I met this gorgeous little Hawaiian gal. She was everything a guy could want. I thought! Smart, sassy, athletic, and had a body that would stop—" He paused and gave Ginny a sheepish grin. "Let's just say she looked great."

"Did she have a pretty Hawaiian name?"

He nodded. "Yeah. Maylea, which means wildflower. She was rightly named. That girl was as wild as they come, but at the time I thought her wildness was cute. She came on to me like a moth to a flame, and, dumb me, a twenty-year-old who thought he was God's gift to women, I bought it all. All my buddies told me how lucky I was to catch such an attractive little gal. Eventually I pulled every cent out of my savings account and bought her a diamond engagement ring. I thought I was sittin' on top of the world."

"But things didn't work out?"

"Oh, they worked out all right—for her and one of my best buddies. Two days before our wedding I caught the two of them making out in his pickup. That little episode cancelled the deal. I grabbed her hand, yanked off that ring, and told her to get lost. I'd never felt so hurt and deceived in my entire life. From what I heard later, I guess he wasn't the only guy she'd been cheating with. Like you, I was lucky she didn't go through with the wedding. Life would have been miserable."

Ginny sighed. "Looks as if we've both been there, done that."

"Yep, it looks like we have. I don't know about you, but that experience kinda soured me on the big M. Not that I don't like female companionship, 'cause I do, but anytime a woman begins to get serious or a bit too possessive I'm cuttin' off the relationship and gettin' out of there. No marriage for me. There're too many fish in the sea to put up with a female with marriage on her mind. I've seen too many guys ruin a perfectly good relationship by letting some little gal talk him into getting married. Once a couple says I do and the honeymoon is over, it's all downhill."

"That's a pretty cynical attitude, isn't it?" Ginny asked, though in some ways she agreed with him. "There are a lot of good marriages around. Wouldn't you like to find the right girl, settle down, get married, and raise a family?"

He appeared thoughtful. "Yeah, I guess so, but finding the right girl could take some searching, and she may never come along."

"Maybe you're looking for her in the wrong places," Ginny suggested.

A frown settled on his forehead. "Could be, but I thought the health club would be a good place to start. I sure wouldn't want a wife who didn't work out and love sports."

"Okay, so you want a woman who works out and loves sports. What else?"

A grin tugged at his mouth. "Umm, she'd have to have more on her mind than winning beauty pageants."

"And?"

"And she'd have to love me as much, or more, than herself."

Ginny nodded. "That's reasonable."

"She sure couldn't run around on me. I'd want her to be faithful."

"Definitely reasonable."

"She'd have to be interested in creating a homey atmosphere. A man likes to have his home be his castle."

She couldn't help but grin. "With a queen to do all the chores?"

He grinned back. "I wouldn't mind helping out when needed. I'd expect her to make time for the two of us. If I had a wife, I'd want us to be together as much as possible. You know, share dreams, visions, work together toward a common goal. None of that we're-too-busy-to-spend-time-together stuff."

"And you'd make time for her?"

Without hesitation he nodded. "You bet I would. If the right woman came along, I'd devote my life to her."

"What about money?"

"Hey, I make decent money. Not a fortune, but I could take care of a wife in pretty good style. If she wanted to work or had a career, and it didn't interfere with our home life, that'd be fine; but if she wanted to stay home I'd like that, too."

"And you'd want children?"

"Oh, yeah. At least two. Four'd be even better."

"What if your wife didn't want children?"

"Then she wouldn't be my wife! We'd iron all that stuff out before we were even engaged. Every man wants a son. I'd want that, too, and at least one daughter."

Ginny smiled. "I can see you've given this marriage thing some real thought, but you've missed one very important element."

He lifted his brow. "Oh, what?"

"God."

Beemer sat silently, mulling over her words. "So you think God is the magic ingredient in a happy marriage?"

She nodded. "In my case, yes. He would definitely be the magic ingredient in my marriage because my life is dedicated to Him. I knew in my heart I was asking for trouble when I dated and got serious with a man who didn't share my faith. Thank the Lord, our wedding never happened. I'm sure there are a number of happy marriages in which neither the wife nor the husband loves God. But, when and if I ever decide to marry, I'm going to make sure the man is a Christian *before* making any kind of commitment. The odds of a happy marriage are much greater if that marriage is centered on Him."

He threw his hands up in the air again. "Don't ask me what it takes to have a happy marriage. I never even got past the engagement stage."

"I saw some vanilla ice cream in the freezer. How about a scoop or two of that for dessert?"

"Sounds good. How about a little—?"

Breaking in, she gave him a teasing grin. "Oh, no. Don't tell me you're going to put peanut butter and garlic salt on that, too."

He raised his brows and chortled. "Hey, I never thought of that. It might be pretty good. I'll have to give it a try."

Ginny giggled. "Not with me watching, I hope."

"Okay, coward. Just for you I'll stick with plain vanilla, but I may be missing the taste treat of a lifetime."

Ginny pulled the ice cream carton from the freezer then dipped two generous bowls full of the sweet concoction, sprinkling on a few chopped nuts and adding a maraschino cherry on top before placing them on the table.

The doorbell rang again. This time Beemer answered it. Within seconds he was back in the kitchen, accompanied by a redhead in a form-fitting, plum-colored pantsuit. "Ginny, this is Dora. Dora, this is Ginny. She's going to be helping me out with my aunt."

Ginny nodded, tempted to go ahead and explain she was Beemer's cousin but decided against it. What he did with his friends was his business.

"I was explaining to Dora that I couldn't go to a movie with her tonight because I had to help you unpack."

"I really don't have that much—"

"And we have to figure out a place for your cat," Beemer said, interrupting her. "Plus Aunt Margaret hasn't had her supper yet."

Dora lowered her lip into a pout. "But, Beemer, you said we'd go to the movies this week."

Beemer patted the woman's shoulder. "I know, but duty calls. Maybe another time, okay?"

Still pouting, Dora leaned into him and snuggled up close. "I miss you, Beemer." Then gesturing toward Ginny she added, "You didn't need to move your little friend in. I could have helped you with your aunt. I even have the nurse's hat I wore in a play once."

"It's nice of you to offer," Beemer told her, slowly leading her toward the hallway, "but Ginny and I have things under control."

Dora gave Ginny the kind of look she'd never want from her friends. "I do hope she won't be taking up *all* your time."

Beemer laughed. "I'll still find time for you, babe. Just be patient. Maybe we can catch a movie next week."

Ginny couldn't resist. "Maybe I could come along. It's been ages since I've been to a good movie."

Dora's look exceeded the first. "I'm sure that would be nice, but shouldn't someone stay with Beemer's aunt?"

Ginny snapped her fingers. "Oh, that's right. Maybe I won't be able to go after all."

Beemer turned long enough to give her a mischievous wink before moving Dora along at a quicker pace. "Yeah, it's too bad someone has to stay with Aunt Margaret. I'm sure the three of us would have had a great time together."

"Ta ta." Muffling an amused laugh, Ginny waved as the couple disappeared into the hall.

While Beemer bid his guest good-bye, Ginny busied herself in the kitchen. By the time he appeared again, she had everything in order and a clean bowl and spoon on a tray on the counter, ready to fill with soup when Aunt Margaret woke up. She was surprised the ringing of the doorbell hadn't wakened her.

When Beemer walked back into the kitchen, he had a silly grin on his face. "I know what you're going to ask me, and the answer is the same. I didn't tell Dora you were my cousin because I thought it would be more fun this way. I like to keep my women guessing."

"How many more women are there?"

"A few."

"Three?"

"More."

"Five?"

"More."

"Ten?" she asked facetiously.

"A few more. I've lost count."

"Beemer!" Ginny exclaimed. "For a man who has no interest in getting married, you sure have a lot of girlfriends. Do you think it's fair to lead them on like you do? When you have no intention of ever becoming serious with them?"

He pulled a clean glass from the cabinet and filled it at the sink, took a few sips then poured the rest down the drain. "I've never deceived any of them. I've let them know right up front I am not interested in a permanent relationship. But that doesn't seem to bother any of them, and we have a great time together. It's all perfectly harmless."

She sat down then gestured toward his bowl of ice cream, which had, by now, begun to melt. "To you maybe, but I'm not sure about them. They hang on you like ivy to a brick wall. Both Dora and that Rosie woman look at you like you're an Adonis. Can't you see it? Those women are crazy about you. I'll bet each one of them thinks they're going to change your mind and drag you to the altar."

He filled his spoon with ice cream. "No chance of that happening. You know why? Because I only date the kind of girls I'd never marry."

"What? That's crazy!"

"No, it's not. Think about it. These girls are beautiful, have great bods, like to have a good time, and treat me like a king; yet they're all conceited airheads, obsessed with themselves and their wants and desires. We have a little fun for a few hours, and I'm the envy of all my guy friends—then I take them home and forget about them until the next time. No strings. No commitments. Just the way I like it."

"Did it ever occur to you that they may be using you, the same way you're using them? What girl wouldn't like to have a night out on the town on the arm of a handsome hunky guy with him paying the bills?"

"Would you?"

She rolled her eyes. "No, but that's different."

"Why?"

"For starters, I'd never lead a guy on like that unless I had honorable intentions. To me, dating is not a game; it's a way to get to know what a person is like. To see how much we have in common. To check out his value system. What he wants out of life. What his goals are. His hobbies. His frustrations."

He huffed. "You make it sound like a job interview."

"In some ways it is."

"Would you ever date me?"

She stared at him, surprised by his question. "Of course not. You're my cousin."

"Not really. You and I aren't blood relatives."

She huffed back. "Well, you seem like my cousin. I could never think of you in any other way." His silly grin made her laugh.

"Well, don't worry about it. You're too goody-goody for me anyway. I could never live up to your standards. They're way too high for me."

"I'm awake," a feeble voice said from the bedroom wing. "Is that Beemer's famous potato soup I smell?"

Beemer gave Ginny's arm a playful pinch. "You make a great cousin, but I'm afraid you'd be a boring date. Why don't you take your cat for a walk while I fix Aunt Margaret's tray?"

Rising, she hurried to the range and filled the bowl she'd already set out on the tray. "No, I came here to help. You've been taking care of her for several weeks now. Go take your dog for a run. That, or go find Rosie or Dora and tell them you've changed your mind."

He grinned that silly grin again. "I'll take Mortimer for a run. I'll be back in an hour or so."

Ginny prepared the tray and, remembering her aunt loved fresh vegetables, added a few celery stalks and a couple of baby carrots, plus a cup of hot tea, and carried it into the bedroom.

"Are you and Beemer getting acquainted?" Aunt Margaret asked once she'd finished her meal. "He's such a nice boy. I just knew the two of you would get along well."

"We had an interesting visit."

"I heard the doorbell ring. Was it one of Beemer's girlfriends?"

Ginny pulled the paper napkin from the tray and dabbed at her aunt's chin. "Two different women stopped by. Rosie and Dora."

A smile tipped the corners of Aunt Margaret's lips. "I wish Beemer would find himself a nice girl and settle down, but I'm afraid his tastes run more to the flamboyant type."

"I've noticed. That description certainly fits Rosie and Dora."

"He needs someone like you, Ginny. Someone pretty but with her feet on the ground. Someone who loves God."

Ginny reached for her aunt's hand and cradled it in hers. "Beemer likes his life the way it is, Aunt Margaret. He has no desire to change it."

"Did he tell you about his fiancée?"

Ginny nodded. "He told me a little about her."

"That girl really hurt him. It took him years to recover. I think he's still recovering. He just won't admit it." Her aunt adjusted her position. "My back is getting tired. I can't sit up very long now. Maybe I'd better lie back down."

"A few more bites first?"

"Not now. Maybe later."

Ginny pulled the pillows from behind her and gently lowered her to a reclining position. "Would you like me to read to you?"

Aunt Margaret's face brightened. "Would you, dear?"

"I'd love to read to you." She pulled the worn Bible from the nightstand, opened it to the book of Psalms, and read until her aunt's eyelids began to droop. Beemer had warned her the medication they were giving Aunt Margaret had affected her appetite and made her drowsy much of the time.

Ginny glanced at the clock as she entered her own room, surprised at how late it was. Poor Tinkerbelle had been locked in that bathroom for nearly three hours. The cat nearly leapt into her arms when she opened the door. She stroked her a few times then placed her on the bed. "I forgot to lock up the van after we finished unloading it, and my automobile title is in the glove compartment. You stay right here while I go lock it, okay?"

Tinkerbelle meowed in response then leaped up into her arms again.

"Didn't understand me, huh?" Ginny stared at the cat. "I guess I could take you with me. That big, awful dog went for a run with Beemer." Cradling the cat close to her, she moved quietly through the house and out the front door. She'd nearly reached the van when Tinkerbelle arched her back and her fur went up. Ginny turned in time to see Mortimer coming toward them at full speed, with Beemer doing his best to catch up with him.

Chapter 2

Before Ginny could gather her wits about her and prepare herself, Mortimer was crouched in front of her, ready to pounce on her precious cat. She tried to hold Tinkerbelle over her head, out of his reach, but Tinkerbelle had other ideas and jumped from her arms, leaving several long scratch marks, and headed for the nearest tree, with Mortimer just inches behind. Fortunately for the cat, she made it to the tree and was already on her way to the top before he got there.

"Mortimer! Leave that cat alone!" Beemer ordered, bending over, panting and out of breath from his unexpected sprint. He grabbed onto the big dog's collar and tugged, but Mortimer wouldn't budge. He had cat on his mind and continued barking and clawing at the tree trunk.

"He could have killed her!" Ginny screamed at him while vying for space at the base of the tall tree. "Why did you turn him loose like that? Couldn't you see I had Tinkerbelle in my arms?"

"I didn't turn him loose!" he growled back, nearly as loud as the dog. "He pulled away from me. See—the leash is still attached to his collar. What were you doing with that cat outside anyway?"

Ginny was growing more furious with each moment. "She'd been cooped up in that bathroom for more than three hours, Beemer. I brought her with me so I could lock my van."

"You could have waited until I got back."

"Why? So your dog could eat my cat?"

Beemer tugged on Mortimer's collar again, to no avail.

Ginny grabbed hold of the trunk and stared up into the tree, trying to locate the frightened cat, but the branches were so close together and the leaves so thick she couldn't see her. "My poor, poor cat. She'll never come down. She must be frightened out of her wits."

Beemer gave her shoulder a slight pat. "Don't worry. I'll go put Mortimer in the backyard, then I'll come back and we'll figure out a way to get her down." His voice had changed to kind and gentle, even reassuring.

Ginny had hoped that once Mortimer was out of sight Tinkerbelle would come down out of the tree and she could take her back to the safety of the bedroom. But, even though she called the cat over and over, Tinkerbelle was not to be seen.

Beemer returned a few minutes later with a ladder and a length of rope.

Ginny gave him an incredulous stare. "What are you going to do with those things?"

"I'm going up after her."

"You can't go after her. We can't even see where she is."

He gently pushed her aside then leaned the ladder against the tree. "It'd help if you'd steady this thing for me."

She tried to wedge herself in front of him. "I'll go up after her."

"She's up there because of my dog. I'm the one who should go after her." He grabbed hold of her arm. "She scratched you?"

Ginny pulled her arm away. "She didn't mean to. She was scared to death."

"You need to put something on those. Looks like they're pretty deep. But first you need to hold on to the ladder for me."

"You will be careful, won't you?"

He gave her a playful nudge before starting up the ladder. "Hey, you're talking to an ex-Marine. Climbing a little tree is child's play. I'll have that cat down in a flash."

She watched him deftly scale the tree. "Can you see her yet?"

"Nope," his voice uttered from somewhere among the leaves and branches.

"How about now?" she asked a few seconds later.

"Nope. Still nothing."

Ginny's heart tied itself in a knot. What if Tinkerbelle had gone clear to the very tip top of the tree where the branches were small and yielding? She might fall. And even if she landed on her feet, what about her unborn kittens?

"I think I see her! There're some branches moving up near the top. Call her. See if she'll come down to you."

"Here, kitty, kitty. Tinkerbelle, come to Ginny. Here, kitty. Is she moving?"

"Umm, doesn't look like it. I'll have to go farther up."

"Oh, Beemer, please be careful." She watched as he worked his way up the tree, in and out of the thick leaves, cautiously moving from branch to branch. "It'll be dark soon. She has to come down. She's pregnant. Her kittens could be born anytime. She can't stay up there all night."

He shifted his position, parted a few leaves, and stared down at her. "I'm doing the best I can, Ginny."

She released a heavy sigh. "I know. I'm worried about her."

"Trust me, cuz. I'll get your cat down. One way or another."

One way or another? Was that supposed to be reassuring? She held her breath as he moved even higher then disappeared out of sight again, her vision blocked by the dense growth. "Are you sure those branches are big enough to hold you?"

He harrumphed. "Guess we'll soon find out. Whoops, one of them just cracked."

"Beemer! Be careful!"

"I see her! She's just out of my reach. I'm going to have to go up a bit farther, but I see her now, cuz. I'll have her down before you know it."

Ginny stepped from one side of the trunk to the other, but it was no use. She couldn't catch sight of him. He was up much too high. "Be gentle with her, and be careful she doesn't scratch—"

"Ouch! Ow, that hurts! You dumb cat! I'm trying to help you!"

"Beemer! Are you all right?"

"If you can call bleeding all right—then I'm great. You really ought to have this furry monster declawed. Your stupid cat won't let me take hold of her. She's out on a tiny branch. I don't dare climb out any farther. I'm hanging on for dear life now."

"Talk to her. Maybe it'll quiet her down."

"Maybe you'd like for me to sing, too. I don't know what to say to a cat."

"It's not what you say; it's how you say it. Just say something in a nice soft voice. Maybe it'll soothe her. That's what I do when she gets upset over something. It's worth a try."

"Okay, if you say so." There was a slight pause; then in the kindest of voices she heard Beemer say, "Come on, you ugly stupid kitty, before I wiggle that branch and send you flying to the ground. Let's see how many lives you have left. Come on—come to Beemer. I hate cats, but I'll try to be nice to you because that's the way Ginny wants me to be."

Despite the seriousness of her cat's dilemma, Ginny couldn't help but laugh. His voice was kind, but his words were cruel. She knew Tinkerbelle wouldn't care what he was saying, though, as long as it sounded soothing. "Is it working?"

"I'm not sure. At least she hasn't tried to go out any farther on that twig of a limb she's clinging to. Get ready to catch me if I fall. I'm going to try to inch out a little bit more. Maybe I can kinda lunge and grab hold of her."

"Lunge? What if you fall? Oh, Beemer, please hang on. You're a long way up. You could break your neck, maybe even your back if you fall from that high."

"You don't want me to leave her up here, do you? I'm not sure she could get down by herself, even if she wanted to, with that big tummy of hers."

"No, I don't want you to leave her there, but I don't want you to get hurt either. Just be careful. Okay?" She watched as the leaves at the top of the tree began to move around.

"Okay, I'm getting ready to grab for her. The way that cat's eyeing me, I doubt she's going to cooperate. You'd better ask that God of yours to protect me. I'm more afraid of her claws than I am of falling."

Ginny sent up a quick prayer, ashamed she hadn't thought to pray before.

A shout of pain and the fierce loud meowing of a cat split the air simultaneously as a rain of leaves and twigs filtered to the ground. "She got me good that time, but I have hold of her," Beemer called out excitedly. "We're coming down."

Thank You, Lord. Ginny stood at the base of the trunk, staring up into the tree as Beemer began to descend, painstakingly locating each lower branch before carefully placing his foot on it.

"Stop scratching me, you dingbat cat! I'm trying to help you!"

Ginny flinched at his words and could only imagine how many times Tinkerbelle had scratched him. Maybe she should have had her cat declawed, but then she would have been almost helpless. At least with those claws she could defend herself. "Please calm down, Tinkerbelle. Beemer is only trying to help," she called up, knowing her advice was futile.

"Man, I wouldn't have a cat for anything. Give me a dog any day."

"Cats are great pets," Ginny responded defensively. "You just have to get to know them. You're about halfway down."

"A dog will obey when you give them a command. Cats do exactly what they want and couldn't care less about what you want. Ooowww! She just clawed my face!"

Ginny flinched. "Oh? Like Mortimer quit chasing Tinkerbelle when you ordered him to stop?" she shot back.

"It's only natural for dogs to chase cats." His voice betrayed his impatience. "It's an instinct. Talk to your God about it. He's the one who made them that way."

"I didn't think you believed in God."

"I only said that for your benefit, 'cause I know you believe in Him."

Ginny snickered to herself. "You're right. I do. You only have about twenty more feet to—"

A loud crack and then a yell sounded as a dead branch came hurling itself toward the ground. Ginny ducked out of the way in time to avoid being hit by the branch—and Beemer—as he tumbled past her and hit the ground with a loud *thump,* Tinkerbelle still cradled in his arm.

"Aaaggg. Ohhhh." He lay on his back, trying to catch his breath, then moaned and groaned in obvious pain.

Ginny grabbed her stunned cat from his grip, cradled her close, then bent over the would-be rescuer, taking stock of the deep scratch marks across his cheek. "Are you hurt? Should I call an ambulance? Oh, Beemer, I'm so sorry. It's all my fault."

"My hand—I think it's broken," he was finally able to say between groans.

Aunt Margaret's next-door neighbor, Mr. Morton, appeared out of nowhere. "Ambulance is on its way. I saw the whole thing from my front porch. That was quite a fall."

Beemer struggled to sit up, but Mr. Morton's strong hand subdued him. "Better not move around, young man, until they have a chance to look you over. The way you hit the ground, you might have broken your back or at least a few ribs. I think you'd better stay right where you are until the EMTs arrive. You might cause even more damage if you move."

"But I'm—"

Ginny stooped and placed her free hand on Beemer's shoulder. "He's right. Please, Beemer, don't move until they get here."

"You guys are making way too much of this. Other than a bunch of cat scratches and a hand that feels broken, I'm okay. I'd know if I wasn't."

The wail of sirens shattered the stillness of the evening. Within seconds a fire truck pulled up to the curb, followed by an ambulance. A fireman leaped out of the engine's door and hurried to Beemer, kneeling down. "Hear you fell out of a tree."

Beemer rolled his eyes. "Next you're going to tell me I'm too old to be climbing trees, right?"

The man gave him a slight smile. "I considered it."

One of the EMTs knelt beside them and opened his medical case. "Where do you hurt?"

Beemer held out his arm.

The man gave him an incredulous look. "You got all those scratches falling out of a tree?"

"My cat did it. He was rescuing her," Ginny admitted.

"The scratches hurt, but I can live with those. It's my hand that really hurts. I think I fell on it when I hit the ground."

The man took hold of Beemer's injured hand, rotating it slightly. Ginny could tell from the look on her cousin's face that he was in agony.

"No back pain?" the man asked as he continued to examine his hand. "No pain in your ribs?"

Beemer shook his head.

The EMT turned to Ginny. "How high was he when he fell?"

She tried to stop trembling but couldn't. "About twenty feet, I guess. He hit the ground pretty hard. It was all my fault. He was rescuing my cat."

The man gave Beemer a smile. "Well, that explains what a man your size was doing climbing trees."

The fireman snorted. "We've already covered that. I'd say he's mighty lucky if that hand is all he broke. That had to be a pretty nasty fall."

The EMT rose and stared at Beemer. "You need to have that hand looked at, and they'll probably want to take an X-ray. We'll take you to the emergency room."

His face scrunched up with pain, Beemer pushed himself into a sitting position. "No way am I going to ride in an ambulance for a simple broken hand. I'll drive myself."

The man shrugged, then reached out to assist Beemer to his feet. "Your choice, but it might be a good idea to have someone else drive you. They ought to take a look at those deep scratches, too."

"I'll take him." Ginny moved a step closer to Beemer.

Cradling his hand, Beemer glanced at Tinkerbelle. "Keep that monster away from me. I don't want any more confrontations with her."

One of the firemen reached out and stroked Tinkerbelle's head. To Ginny's surprise the nervous cat settled down and began to purr.

"My family loves cats," the man told her, continuing to stroke Tinkerbelle. "They make great pets. She's pregnant, isn't she?"

Ginny nodded, still impressed with the way he'd been able to calm Tinkerbelle with only a few strokes. "Yes, I think her kittens are due anytime. That's why it scared me when Beemer's dog chased her up that tree."

"Cats have a way of bouncing back from any ordeal. I'll bet she'll be just fine." He gave her one final pat then backed away. "Guess you have no need for us now. We'll be heading back to the station."

Both Ginny and Beemer thanked them for coming so quickly.

"You're lucky if you come out of a fall from that distance with no more injuries than a broken hand." The two EMTs smiled at Beemer. "Sure you don't want us to take you to the hospital?"

He smiled back. "Naw, but thanks, guys. I'm sorry to have caused so much trouble."

"No trouble. We were getting kinda bored sitting around waiting for something to happen. Get that hand taken care of, okay?"

Beemer nodded. "Okay. Thanks again."

He and Ginny stood watching as the fire truck pulled away from the curb followed by the ambulance.

"I'll tell Aunt Margaret what happened, lock Tinkerbelle in the bathroom, grab my keys, and be right back. You need anything from the house?"

Beemer dolefully shook his head. "You know what this means, don't you?"

She gave him a mystified look. "No, what?"

Chapter 3

It means I can't work. Remember—I'm a computer analyst. I won't be able to type."

She'd felt terrible that her cat, along with *his* dog, had been the cause of this ridiculous fiasco, but now the gravity of his comment hit her. "Oh, Beemer, I am so sorry. I was so worried about Tinkerbelle and her babies that I didn't think about what this was doing to you. Due to my stupidity I've taken away your livelihood. I should have known better than to carry Tinkerbelle outside until I was sure you and Mortimer were back from your run."

He let out a long sigh. "It was as much my fault as yours. I should've had better control over Mortimer. Sometimes he listens to me about as much as your cat listens to you."

She gestured toward her van. "Let's take my van."

"The truck would be a lot more comfortable."

"I've never driven something that big. I'm not sure I could handle it."

He paused thoughtfully. "Okay. I guess I'm in no position to argue, but I'm sure I can drive myself. No need for you to go."

"Get in the van. I'll be right back." She gave Beemer a smile, then headed toward the house to tell Aunt Margaret and lock Tinkerbelle in the bathroom.

∞

"Well, the X-rays show you have two broken fingers," the emergency room doctor said after examining the pictures the technician had taken. "Fractures on both your index and middle finger showed up quite clearly."

"Of course it had to be my left hand," Beemer told the man. "I'm about as left-handed as you can get. Feeding myself is going to be a real problem. Probably won't even be able to hit my mouth with my fork."

The doctor smiled. "It's going to be awkward for you for a while. I'll have to splint your fingers together. You'll probably be bumping them on everything, so they need stabilization." When he finished splinting Beemer's hand, he made a few notes on his clipboard. "With a fall from that height your injuries could have been much worse. I've seen guys fall from a six-foot ladder and do more damage than you've done. I'd say you're a mighty lucky man."

Ginny's heart went out to her cousin. If anyone had to go up that tree after

Tinkerbelle, it should have been her, not Beemer. What a day this had been.

∽

By midnight the house was quiet, except for the steady rhythmic snoring that seeped out from under Beemer's bedroom door. Though it was keeping Ginny awake, she was glad he was able to sleep, especially since he'd refused the pain pills the doctor had tried to give him. As she lay awake staring at the ceiling, she took stock of her life. *God?* she asked, crying out silently from the depths of despair. *Surely You have a purpose for me, but what is it? Other than the few mundane tasks I've volunteered for at my church, I haven't any idea what I am to accomplish for You. When I was growing up, I was sure You had called me to be a wife and mother. Maybe even be married to a missionary. But the man I thought I could trust with my life let me down and wiped out all my savings. I guess that's what I deserved for getting involved with someone who didn't know You. But now what? Other than stay here and take care of Aunt Margaret as long as she needs me, what am I supposed to do with the rest of my years?*

Tinkerbelle jumped up on the bed and snuggled close to Ginny, the steady hum of the cat's purr giving her comfort. "You're a poor substitute for a husband and children, but at least you love me. That's something."

Her thoughts turned to the man snoring across the hall. Even though Beemer had been a part of Aunt Margaret's and Uncle Harold's lives for a number of years, she'd seen him only a few times and not once since he'd joined the Marines and gone overseas. Other than having a passion for birds and dogs and a hatred for cats, her cousin seemed like a nice guy. It was easy to see why those women were crazy about him. Great physique. Good personality. Terrific sense of humor. And handsome in a hunky sort of way. She smiled as she thought of Rosie and Dora and wondered how many more there were like them. Probably many. From all appearances Beemer was a good catch. Obviously a number of women agreed.

Tomorrow would be another day. In addition to caring for Aunt Margaret, Beemer would need all the help she could give him. Being careful not to crush Tinkerbelle, she flipped over onto her side and closed her eyes.

∽

Ginny had the table set for breakfast when Beemer appeared the next morning, his face looking as though he'd slept on it and bearing scratch marks. "Rough night?"

"Not bad, but my hand throbbed some." He pulled out a chair and sat down at the table. "Something smells good."

"Bacon and French toast. Aunt Margaret said it sounded good, but she barely ate anything when I took her tray in to her." Ginny opened the oven door and lifted out the platter of toast and bacon she'd kept warm for him. "I hope you're hungry."

He gave her a grin. "Starved."

She filled his cup with freshly brewed coffee, then sat down beside him. "I'm a pretty good typist. I'm going to help you all I can, Beemer. I don't want you to get behind in your work."

She watched as he struggled to cut his slice of French toast. "I'd be happy to cut that for you."

"You wouldn't mind? I feel like a baby. You should have seen me trying to brush my teeth with my right hand. Good thing my razor is electric, or I might have done more damage to my face than your cat did."

She flinched as she stared at the deep red marks on his cheek. "I can't tell you how sorry I am about those scratches, Beemer. If I'd had any idea what—"

He waved his good hand. "Forget it. What's done is done. No big deal. I'll recover." He looked around the room. "Where's Dumbbell?"

She rolled her eyes. "It's Tinkerbelle."

"Oh, yeah. I remember. Where is she?"

She gestured toward the hall. "She's still locked in the bathroom."

"She doin' okay?"

"Slept as if nothing ever happened."

"You can let her out, you know. No sense in keeping her cooped up in the bathroom all day. Mortimer spends a good deal of his time in the backyard. I promise I'll give you warning before I let him in."

Ginny stared at him. "You mean that? You don't mind her running loose in the house?"

"Naw. I'll get used to it." He forked a wedge of French toast then struggled to hit his mouth with his fork. "Besides, Aunt Margaret likes cats. She'll enjoy having her around."

Ginny hung her head. "You're a nice man, Beemer. I never did tell you how much I appreciated your climbing that tree to bring Tinkerbelle down."

"No problem. If I hadn't been such a klutz—"

"You weren't a klutz. That dead branch broke. You were doing fine until you put your weight on it. You never even dropped Tinkerbelle. I'm in awe of what you did."

He gave her an impish wink. "Hey, after all I went through shinnying up that tree, getting tangled in the branches and leaves, and enduring her scratching and clawing at me, I wasn't about to let her get hurt. I knew how much you loved that cat." Using his fingers instead of a fork, he picked up a slice of bacon and waved it at her. "Not another word on the subject, okay? I don't want you making me out to be some kind of hero for doing what any guy would have done. Besides, I can't stand to see a grown girl cry. If you want to reward me, maybe you can name one of Dumbbell's kittens after me. Beemer the cat. I like that. Sounds like a cartoon character."

His words surprised her. "Name a kitten Beemer? You're kidding, right?"

"Why not? The name was good enough for me. Now go let your cat out."

She nodded, grateful for his cheerful attitude, then walked down the hall toward the bathroom. Tinkerbelle shot right past her when she opened the door and began snooping at her new surroundings. "You stay out of mischief," Ginny warned her, stooping to stroke her soft fur when she caught up with her. "I'll be back later to check on you."

By the time Beemer finished his breakfast, he had powdered sugar all around his lips from where he'd missed his mouth. "I must look a mess," he told her, mopping at his face with his napkin. "Guess I didn't do so great with my right hand. I'd better go wash up."

Ginny tried to withhold a grin, but it escaped. "I'll clean up in here then help you with the typing." She placed the leftover toast and bacon on a plate, covered it with plastic wrap, then carried it to the refrigerator. After that she loaded the dishwasher and put the rest of the kitchen back to readiness. She was about to carry out the trash when Beemer called out from his room.

"Ginny, you'd better come in here! Your cat is sleeping in my bed."

She hurried down the hall, and, sure enough, Tinkerbelle was curled up in perfect comfort in the middle of Beemer's unmade bed.

"Now I gotta sleep with cat hair." He gave a disgusted shake of his head. "I never thought about Dumbbell coming in here. Guess I'd better start closing my door."

Ginny sighed. "I'm sorry, Beemer. I'll keep her locked in either my room or the bathroom. I should never have let her run loose."

"That's not fair to you or the cat, Ginny. The easiest thing is for me to remember to shut my door. That's the least I can do. If I forget, it's my fault, and I'll live with the consequences. Aunt Margaret needs you here. I'm willing to do all I can for her, but you can do some things I can't."

"She needs us both, Beemer. You're every bit as important to her as I am. I'll make a deal with you. When I get ready to let Tinkerbelle out, I'll check your room first to make sure the door is shut. If it isn't, I'll close it."

He stuck out his good hand. "Sounds like a deal to me. I'd better get to work. Are you sure you wanna help me?"

"Absolutely. Give me a second to check on Aunt Margaret, and I'll be right there."

Aunt Margaret was awake and watching her favorite news channel when Ginny entered her room. "Would you please bring me that quilt on the top shelf of my closet?"

"Sure." Ginny opened the door and lifted the beautiful blue and white quilt from its place and laid it on the bed, amazed at its beauty. "Did you make this one, Aunt Margaret?"

Her aunt stroked the quilt's surface with her twisted, arthritic fingers. "I made three quilts last year before I got so bad. I keep one on my bed, I gave one to Beemer, and this one is for you."

Ginny gasped. "For me? Really? Are you serious? I've never owned a quilt before." She unfolded the elegant quilt and fanned it out across the bed. "It's magnificent. Such an intricate pattern, such tiny even stitches. I can't believe you did this and that you're giving it to me."

"It's my original design," her aunt said proudly. "I started with Jacob's ladder then used paper to make the tiny diagonal pieces. I love blue and hoped you did, too. I can't tell you how many shops I visited to find that many shades of blue."

"And you embroidered the little navy blue roses?"

"Yes. As you know, roses are my favorite flower."

"It must have taken you forever to make this quilt. It should be in a museum."

A smile lifted the corners of the older woman's colorless lips. "It's not *that* good, but it was a labor of love. I wanted to leave you something to remember me by. At the time I didn't realize my liver was going to give out on me. But with my age I knew I didn't have too many more years. I'm glad you like it."

Ginny refolded the quilt. "I love it." After setting the quilt aside, she bent and kissed her aunt's cheek. "I'll cherish it always."

"I was hoping you would. Every time you look at that quilt, Ginny, remember how much I love you."

Ginny kissed her again. "I will, Aunt Margaret. I promise. Now, if you don't need me for anything, I'm going to help Beemer for a while."

"Go, dear. I'm fine. Don't worry about me. Beemer needs you more than I do right now."

"Ring that little bell if you need anything, and I'll come running." She lifted the quilt and cradled it in her arms. "I love you, Aunt Margaret."

"I love you, too, sweetie."

The doorbell rang as she moved into the hall. "I'll get it."

She pulled open the door and stared at a model-like creature standing on the porch. *Another blond? How many of these women are after Beemer?*

"I've come to see Beemer," the woman said, opening the door wider and stepping inside. "Is he here?"

Feeling plain and ordinary in comparison to the blond beauty, Ginny nodded then led her down the hall to Beemer's room. "In there."

When the woman saw the scratch marks and the bandage on Beemer's hand she rushed to him, throwing her arms about his neck. "My precious little Beemer! You have a boo-boo?"

Ginny wanted to throw up.

Beemer backed away, trying to break her hold on him. "I broke a couple of fingers, Mitzy. That's all. I'll be fine."

"Don't you need Mitzy to take care of you?"

Beemer flinched when she grabbed hold of his hand. "I can do pretty well on my own."

"Let Mitzy kiss her Beemer's hand and make it all well."

He sent a sideways embarrassed glance toward Ginny. "Don't worry about it, Mitzy. I'm sure it's healing just fine."

"My poor baby." Mitzy pulled a chair next to Beemer's desk and leaned her head on his shoulder. "Mitzy's going to cook you supper."

Another glance went toward Ginny. "That's really not necessary. Ginny's here now."

Mitzy gave Ginny a look that would have melted an igloo.

Suppressing an outright laugh, Ginny pasted on her sweetest smile and gave the woman a wave. "Hi. I'm Ginny."

"Ginny and I are taking care of my aunt Margaret."

The hostile expression on Mitzy's face deepened. "She's surely not living here."

He winked at Ginny. "Yeah, she is. It makes it convenient."

"I'll just bet it does." Mitzy glanced at her watch. "Sorry. Gotta go. I have an appointment for a pedicure, but I insist on cooking you supper, Beemer. It'll give your little friend a break. Maybe she can go shopping or something. After I get finished up at the beauty shop, I'll go to the grocery store, pick up a few items, then come back and cook for you. See you about five."

Beemer rolled his eyes. "Okay. But make it simple."

Mitzy planted a kiss on Beemer's cheek. "I will. See you around five, sweetie."

Ginny followed Mitzy through the house to the front door and closed it behind her. *Whew! Glad that one is gone.* "Exactly how many women do you have in your harem?" she asked Beemer when she returned to his office.

He spun around to face her and grinned. "Never counted."

"Are you expecting any more ravishing beauties today?"

He gave her the impish grin that always made her laugh. "Who knows? I'm a popular guy with the ladies. Must be my animal magnetism."

Ginny felt a grin spread across her face. "You're impossible."

He bent and placed a playful, smacking kiss on her cheek. "And you're cute."

She put her hand on her hip. "Is that a joke?"

He reared back with a laugh. "No, it was a compliment. You are cute."

"No wonder you're so popular with the ladies, you flatterer. You've got a line a mile long. I think we'd better get to work."

They worked for a full two hours, with Beemer calling out numbers and designating columns, before the phone on his desk rang.

"Douglas Computer Solutions," he said into the phone, taking on a businesslike manner. "How may I help you?"

He listened a moment, then grinned. "I think that'll work. Hang on a sec." He covered the mouthpiece with his bandaged hand. "A couple of my friends heard about my accident and want to come over. That okay with you?"

She nodded. "Of course it's okay. You don't have to ask me. This is your home now, too."

"Sure, come on over." He hung up the phone. "They'll be here soon. They're only a block away. No sense doing any more work until they leave. Let's take a break."

She glanced at her watch. "Good idea. I need to fix a bite of lunch for Aunt Margaret. You and I can eat after your company leaves."

As she started for the kitchen, Beemer grabbed onto her wrist. "Thanks for helping me, Ginny. I was beginning to wonder how I was going to get a couple of my more important jobs out on time, but with you helping me and your expertise on the computer, it'll be a cinch."

"I'm glad you're letting me help. I owe you a lot, Beemer. You wouldn't be having this problem if it weren't for me."

Beemer's expression sobered. "Look, Ginny. You owe me nothing. Believe me, I've done worse things to myself than break a couple of fingers. You should have seen the condition I was in after I drove my motorcycle down the side of a steep, sandy hill on a dare. Not a pretty picture. I still have the scar on my leg from the exhaust burn and skid marks on my shoulder. That idiotic trick was the reason I sold my motorcycle."

Ginny started at the sound of the doorbell. "Must be your friends. I'll be in the kitchen if you need me."

After preparing a fresh green salad and heating up a can of chicken noodle soup, Ginny arranged everything attractively on a tray, added silverware and a napkin, and was about ready to head for her aunt's room when she heard female giggling coming from the living room. Were all Beemer's friends women?

"Ginny?" Beemer called out. "Can you come in here? I want these people to meet you."

"Be right there." Carrying the tray into the living room, Ginny put on her best smile.

"Patti, Deirdre, Gloria. This is Ginny. She's helping out with my aunt."

Oh, oh. He's still playing his little game.

"Ginny is also doing the typing for me while"—he held up his injured hand—"while these are healing."

Three heads nodded; then the redheaded one of the group gave him a smile a mile wide. "You should have called me, Beemer. I'd have been happy to help you."

One of the two blonds elbowed her in the side. "You can't type."

The redhead elbowed her back. "Neither can you."

"I didn't say I could."

"I can type," the second blond inserted. "And I could have helped with Beemer's aunt, too. I took a Girl Scout first-aid course when I was twelve."

Beemer held up his hand to silence them. "Girls, I appreciate your willingness to help, but it's really not necessary now that Ginny is here. She's a fantastic typist and a good cook, and she gets along great with my aunt." Giving Ginny a wink, he gestured toward the tray. "Just look at that luscious-looking lunch she's prepared."

Taking that as her cue to exit, Ginny told them how nice it was to meet them then excused herself and trod down the hall toward Aunt Margaret's room, amazed that Beemer still wasn't explaining their relationship.

"That's cruel," she told him an hour later, after his guests had left and the two of them were enjoying their soup and salad at the kitchen table. "Not telling those women I'm your cousin. They're going to be furious with you when they find out."

A grin tugged at his mouth. "I like keeping you my mystery woman."

Ginny shrugged. "Mystery woman?"

"Yeah, couldn't you see the jealousy in their eyes? They can't figure out who you are or where you came from. You're an unknown quantity."

Her jaw gaped. "You really enjoy playing games with your women! Shame on you."

He let out a chuckle. "Just having a little fun, that's all. Those gals are always in competition with each other. Now they have you to worry about."

"Me? You must be kidding. I'm no competition. Those women are gorgeous."

"And you're not? Have you looked in the mirror lately, Ginny? They've got good figures. In fact they've got great figures. But take away their makeup and their fancy clothes and they're nothing. You're a natural beauty."

"Me? A natural beauty?" Ginny glared at him. "Now you're playing games with me."

He raised his right hand. "No, no games. Just the truth. You *are* a natural beauty whether you think so or not, which, by the way, only makes you more attractive. I'm a man, Ginny Markham. A connoisseur of beautiful women. Take it from me, *you* are a beautiful woman. Part of your charm is your unassuming shyness and lack of conceit. The three women you just met, and Mitzy and Rosie whom you met earlier, are the queens of conceit. You're nothing like them. They're all Barbie dolls. Plastic robots. Their appearance means everything to them."

Ginny wadded up her paper napkin then leaned back in her chair. "And you're telling me you're not serious with any of them? It's obvious they all like you."

"And I like them, too, but serious? No, not in the least. I love being around beautiful women, and we have a good time together, but that's it. As I told you before, I have no interest in another serious relationship. I'm still chaffing from the last one. I may never recover."

Though Ginny didn't have a string of men after her, she understood his feelings. She wasn't sure if she'd ever be able to trust again. The scars on her heart were still deep and painful and slow to heal. Whoever said it was better to have loved and lost someone than never to have loved anyone at all should have had his head examined.

Beemer took hold of her hand and cradled it with his long fingers. "You and I have a lot in common, dear cousin. We're both a couple of losers."

Struggling against the tears that welled behind her eyelids, Ginny smiled up at him. "I guess we are."

Beemer put the things in the refrigerator while she loaded the dishwasher, and soon the kitchen was back in shape. "Ready to get back at it, cuz?" He held out his hand.

Ginny smiled as she slipped her hand in his. "You betcha, cuz."

By the time Mitzy arrived with her sack of groceries, Beemer and Ginny had completed one project and begun another.

"Let me know if you need anything," Ginny told her, excusing herself. "I'll either be in my room or my—Beemer's aunt's room."

Beemer hooked his thumbs into the waistband of his jeans, concern marring his brow. "Aren't you going to eat with us?"

Ginny shook her head. "No, Aunt Margaret and I are going to call for pizza. We'll eat it in her room. You two enjoy yourselves."

"But—"

Mitzy grabbed onto Beemer's arm. "Let her do what she wants, Beemer. I've been looking forward to having you all to myself."

Ginny zeroed in on Beemer and allowed a mischievous smile to creep across her lips. "You two have a lovely evening, okay? And don't worry about us. We'll be fine."

"Which girl is cooking Beemer's supper?" Aunt Margaret asked when Ginny entered her room. "I do wish that boy would find a nice girl and settle down before I'm gone. I worry about him."

"This one's name is Mitzy."

"He needs a girl like you, Ginny, not one of those prima donna–type women."

Ginny sat down on her aunt's bed and stared at a family portrait on the wall. "Like me? You must be kidding. I have nothing to offer a man like Beemer. He's smart. Funny. Talented. Good-looking. Educated. Traveled the world. Me? I'm a nobody."

Aunt Margaret let out a small gasp. "Don't say that. You're a child of the King. God loves you. You're very special to Him. Your name is inscribed on His palms. He has a purpose for your life—a purpose only you can fulfill."

"If I'm that important to Him, why did He allow me to be hurt like that? I lost everything, Aunt Margaret. I was a fool."

"No, dear. You thought you were in love with that man, but I think, instead, you were in love with the idea of being in love. Love makes us do strange things. It blinds us to others' faults and the warning signs God places in our way. Had you sincerely prayed for the Lord's guidance before committing yourself to that man? Did you honestly have peace about your relationship with him? As much as I hate the hurt you went through, I'm thankful you found out about him before you two were married."

Ginny struggled with a threatening tear. "I am, too. I can't imagine how hurt I would have been if he'd become my husband, though I doubt that would have happened. He had his deception planned right from the start. I was his target. Too bad I was too dumb to realize it."

"My dear niece, don't close your heart to true love. I pray constantly that the right man for you will come along and that you will learn to trust again."

Ginny huffed. "Trust again? I'm not sure I'll ever be able to do that, Aunt Margaret. Not after what I've been through."

"Just listen to your heart, dear one, and listen to God. He wants only the best for you. So do I. I'm constantly in prayer for you." The older woman turned her head aside. "I'm tired. That medicine takes all my energy. I'm really not hungry. Would you mind if we called it a day?"

"I wouldn't mind at all." Ginny rose and straightened her aunt's bed, pulling the quilt up close around her before bending to kiss her good night. "Sleep tight, dear Aunt Margaret."

"Good night, my sweet."

Ginny tiptoed to her bedroom and, after checking Tinkerbelle and the litter box, donned her pajamas and crawled into bed with one of the romance novels she'd brought with her. *These days my romances are lived vicariously through the novels' heroines. Their lives always turn out right. I only wish mine would, too.*

She read until eleven and was about to turn out her light when someone rapped on her door.

"Ginny? Are you awake?"

Pulling on her robe she hurried to the door and opened it, fearing something was wrong with Aunt Margaret.

Beemer gave her a shy grin. "Is there any pizza left?"

"Sure. Quite a bit. We ate less than half of it. Why?"

"I'm hungry."

She eyed him carefully. "I thought Mitzy was cooking supper for you."

"She did. That's why I'm hungry. It was awful, Ginny. She fixed some kind of weird oriental dish that tasted like motor oil, and the rice stuck together in one big wad. Pizza sure sounds good."

Ginny glanced down at her bare feet. "Want me to heat it up for you?"

"Would you?"

After putting on her slippers, she padded quietly down the hall and into the kitchen with Beemer at her heels.

He pulled a chair away from the table and sat down, grinning up at her. "I could've heated it up myself, but I thought maybe you'd eat a piece with me."

She grinned back. "I could do that. I love pizza."

"Me, too."

She busied herself placing the pizza on a glass plate then popped it into the microwave and filled two glasses with iced tea from the pitcher she'd placed in the refrigerator earlier. "Guess Mitzy wasn't too good at cleaning up after herself. This kitchen is a mess."

"She had no idea what she was doing, Ginny. I doubt she'd ever fixed a meal in her life. I even had to show her which knob to use to turn on the burner." He glanced at the grains of cooked rice stuck to the range's surface and the sauce that had spilled onto the countertop and shook his head. "Pity the poor guy who marries her. It sure ain't gonna be me."

Ginny stifled a snicker. "I guess you know you're going to have to clean up this kitchen."

He let out a long sigh. "Yeah, I know. I plan on doing it before I go to bed.

It's a real mess. I only hope I can get that burned sauce out of the pan."

When the microwave dinged, Ginny pulled out the plate and placed it on the table. "I'll help you. I'm a real sucker for guys in distress."

He grinned again then picked up a slice of pizza. "You're gonna make some man a great wife. I just hope the guy realizes how lucky he is."

Ginny selected a slice then swung her head to stare at him. "*If* that right man ever comes along and *if* I'm brave enough to trust again, which is doubtful."

"We're some pair, aren't we?"

She nodded. "Yeah, we are."

They finished eating their pizza then, working together, cleaned up the kitchen and said good night.

The next two weeks flew by as Ginny spent as much time as she felt she could allow away from her aunt working at Beemer's side, typing, filing, and doing whatever else she could to help him. Though his sense of humor was always present, when he was working on a client's project, he was all business. His hand was doing well, and he'd soon be able to get along without her help, something she was almost dreading. Working with him was not only fun and educational, she was enjoying every minute of it.

"Thanks," he told her, stretching first one arm then the other, one evening when they'd worked especially late. "Do you realize you've put in nearly ten hours today helping me on this project? Not counting the time you've prepared meals and taken care of Aunt Margaret. You must be exhausted."

She yawned. "But we got it done, didn't we?"

He shut down the computer then stood, reaching out his hand. "Thanks to you. Now go. I'll look in on Aunt Margaret."

She yawned again. "You don't have to tell me twice. Good night."

Ginny fell asleep right away, only to be awakened at four when Beemer burst into her room without knocking. "Come quick. Tinkerbelle needs you."

Chapter 4

Ginny rubbed at her eyes. "What? Tinkerbelle needs me? Where is she?"

"In my room. In the closet. I think she's having her kittens."

Ginny leaped out of bed and yanked on her robe before rushing into the bathroom. "Oh, no! I was so tired when I went to bed I must have left the hall door open. She's not here."

Beemer grabbed onto her arm. "Ginny! Wake up! Didn't you hear me? I said she's in my closet. You'd better hurry. She may need you. I know nothing about cats."

The message finally reaching her addled brain, Ginny hurried past him, down the hall, and into his room. "Tinkerbelle, oh, Tinkerbelle, are you all right?" Dropping onto her knees and pushing aside the garments hanging from the rod, she leaned into the closet. There in the corner, lying on her side on a quilt, looking agitated and totally exhausted, was Tinkerbelle. And beside her were two tiny newborn kittens already trying to nurse. The scene was so beautiful that Ginny couldn't help but cry. "I wanted to be with you when this miraculous birth happened, but I missed it. Oh, Tinkerbelle, you handled it all by yourself."

Beemer huffed. "Looks like she did a good job of it, but did she have to do it in my closet?"

"I'm so sorry, Beemer." She gazed at the two puffs of fur. "I should have realized she was going into labor. She's been fretful and restless all day."

"Guess she was looking for a private place. Can't get any more private than the back of my closet."

After tucking her hair behind her ears, Ginny leaned closer to Tinkerbelle. "Your kittens are beautiful, but only two? I thought sure you'd have three or four," Ginny whispered softly as she lightly stroked Tinkerbelle's soft fur. "But why did you come into Beemer's closet to have them? You should have stayed in the bathroom in the maternity bed I made for you. It was nice and private in there."

Beemer squatted down beside her and peered into the back of the semidark-ened closet. "Oh, no! She had those kittens on the quilt Aunt Margaret made for me. Look at that mess she made. Those stains will never come out."

For the first time Ginny noticed the quilt. It was magnificent. Hand-pieced with bits of fabric in the Inner Cities pattern and quilted with Aunt Margaret's trademark, tiny even stitches. Like the one she'd given Ginny, it was truly a work of art. Aunt Margaret had to have put months and months of painstaking work into that quilt, and, horrors, her cat had ruined it! Despite her joy at seeing Tinkerbelle's newborn kittens, she began to cry. "Why would you ever store that precious quilt on the floor?"

Beemer glared at her then pointed to a sturdy box marked Tax Papers. "It wasn't on the floor. It was neatly folded on top of that box. She must have dragged it off with her claws."

Ginny reached out and gripped his arm. "I'm sorry, Beemer. I should have known you wouldn't be careless with that quilt. It's just that I'm so upset to think my cat ruined it for you. I'm sick about it."

Beemer slipped his arm around her and pulled her close, cradling her head against his chest. "What's done is done, cuz. We can't undo it. Maybe it's not as bad as it looks. I'll take it to the dry cleaners. They've usually got stuff that'll take out weird spots."

Ginny wiped at her tears with her sleeve. "You really think they can get it out?"

"I'm counting on it."

"You're a great guy, Beemer. Why couldn't I have met someone like you?"

He threw back his head with a laugh. "Hey, I'm still available."

Ginny couldn't help smiling. "That would raise a few eyebrows. Cousins dating cousins."

He rolled his eyes. "Ginny, you keep forgetting. We're cousins, but not blood cousins. There would be nothing wrong with the two of us dating."

"I doubt that harem of yours would think it was acceptable."

"Who cares what they think. I'd be proud to be seen with you."

She pulled away from him, then shrugged. "Well, that's something we'll never have to worry about."

"Oh? Why?"

"Well, I mean—you know. You're used to dating glamour gals. Not the likes of me. More important, we don't share the same faith. That could cause a big problem, and—"

"Haven't I told you I could never be serious about any of them?"

"Yes, but you also said you weren't sure if you could ever be serious with *any* woman again."

Placing his finger beneath her chin, he lifted her face to meet his. "Didn't you tell me the same thing? That you weren't sure you could ever trust another man after your fiancé hurt you?"

"Yes, and I meant it."

"Do you think you could ever trust me?"

"Of course. You're family."

"I'm a man, Ginny. A man who finds you very attractive."

Tinkerbelle let out a loud *yeowl*.

Beemer quickly backed away. "What's the matter with her?"

Ginny stared at her cat. "I'm not sure, but I think she's having another one."

"Another kitten?"

"Looks like it, from the way she's acting."

Beemer wrinkled his nose and turned his head away. "I've never seen a cat give birth, and I'm not so sure I want to now," he confessed as Tinkerbelle began to pant and make a sound almost like crying. "My pets have always been male dogs. They don't have babies."

"That may be true, but they *are* the ones who create those babies." Ginny clamped onto his wrist. "It's a beautiful thing, Beemer. A miracle, the way God created the mother cat to know what to do and how to handle things all by herself."

As the two continued to watch, Tinkerbelle dropped onto her side again and, after an almost grunt, delivered a third kitten.

Remembering how repulsed she was the first time she'd seen a mother cat give birth, Ginny couldn't help but grin.

Apparently fascinated by the entire process, Beemer turned back and stared at the scene playing out before them. "How long will it be before they open their eyes?"

"Around ten days."

"How do you know so much about cats?"

"I used to spend my summer vacations on my grandparents' farm. People would dump their pregnant cats on the road near their house. My grandma felt sorry for them and always took them in, so there were dozens of cats and kittens running around their place. Not wanting to contribute to the growing cat population, she found homes for many of them. The others she had spayed."

"But you didn't have Tinkerbelle spayed?"

Ginny gazed at the kittens, knowing full well, despite their cuteness, she wouldn't be able to keep them. "No, she was already pregnant when she showed up on my doorstep. Like Grandma, I couldn't turn her away. But, believe me, as soon as it's possible, I will have her spayed."

He frowned. "What about her kittens?"

Ginny shrugged. "I hope I'll be able to find homes for them, but only if the new owners agree to have them neutered or spayed."

"Maybe a couple of them will be males. That would solve your problem."

"Not really. Very few people want to own an unneutered tomcat, or even tolerate him, because he fights other people's pets, male *and* female, and marks houses and gardens with an intolerable scent. The male population needs to be controlled as much as the female." She narrowed her eyes. "You have had Mortimer neutered, haven't you?"

He nodded. "Yup. I got him at the humane society. That was one of their requirements."

Ginny smiled. "Smart move. He's one mighty lucky dog to have you as his owner."

Beemer let out a chuckle. "And I'd say that cat of yours is one mighty lucky cat. Don't worry about Mortimer bothering her. I'll make sure he stays in the backyard. I sure don't want him upsetting this new little mother."

"Thanks, Beemer, and thanks for being so understanding about the quilt. But don't worry about taking it to the dry cleaners. I will. After all, it was my cat that did the damage."

He shook his head then glanced at the clock on his nightstand. "Naw, I can drive with one hand. I'll take it when she gets to the point we can take it out from under her. Think there're gonna be any more kittens?"

"I don't know. We'll just have to wait and see." He rose and yawned. "If you think you and Tinkerbelle can get along without me, I'm going to sleep the rest of the night on the couch. You stay here with her. You can even curl up on my bed if you want to."

Ginny gazed up at him, amazed at how well he was taking Tinkerbelle's interference in his life. "You sure you don't mind?"

"Don't mind a bit." Grabbing a blanket from the foot of his bed, he grinned at her. "Holler if you need me."

"I will."

"Good night."

"Beemer."

"Huh?"

"You're some great guy."

He turned, giving her one last glance before exiting into the hall. "And you're one neat lady. Thanks for sharing this experience with me. See you in the morning."

Ginny stretched out her legs, leaned her head against the open closet door then gazed at the three kittens nuzzling their mother peacefully, in complete awe of what she'd seen. Though she'd witnessed dozens of births while visiting her grandparents, none of them compared to the thrill of seeing her very own cat give birth. *Thank You, God, for being with Tinkerbelle and for letting Beemer witness this miraculous birth with me. Speak to him, Lord. Whether he knows it or not, he needs You in his life. I know Aunt Margaret has been praying for him. Nothing would make her happier than to see him turn his life over to You.* She swallowed at the lump of emotion that swelled in her throat. *Please let this happen before You call her home.*

Ginny watched over Tinkerbelle for one more hour then slipped down the hall, checking on Aunt Margaret, then Beemer. He looked so cute sleeping on the sofa with his long legs folded up so he would fit into the space, with one arm dangling to the floor. If she'd had a camera handy, she would have taken his picture. She'd never expected to see this soft caring side of him. His gentleness with both her and Tinkerbelle touched her heart deeply. *You're quite a man, Mr. Douglas. Yes, quite a man indeed.*

She decided her cat had probably given birth to all the kittens she was going to have, but she wanted to be near her in case she had more. Stepping back into Beemer's room she crawled onto his bed, and within seconds she was fast asleep.

She was awakened several hours later by a slight tugging on her hand.

"Ginny, wake up. I think we have a problem."

Sitting up quickly and rubbing her eyes, she gazed into Beemer's unshaven face. "What? Is it Aunt Margaret?"

"No. It's one of Tinkerbelle's kittens. I think it's dead."

Ginny leaped out of bed and hurried to the closet. Looping a strand of errant hair over her ear, she squatted down close to the soiled quilt Tinkerbelle still claimed as her birthing bed. One kitten, the last one to be delivered, lay on its side, its body limp and lifeless.

"I woke up and decided to come in and check on you," Beemer explained, extending his hand toward the still kitten.

Ginny grabbed onto his wrist. "Don't try to touch it! New mother cats are terribly protective. She might scratch you." Grateful for his concern, she released his hand then gave it a pat. "Let me try. She trusts me." Keeping her gaze focused on Tinkerbelle, all the while talking to the cat, explaining in soft tones that she simply wanted to help, Ginny slowly reached out and lifted the lifeless body from the quilt.

"Is it—dead?"

Before answering, she began massaging the kitten's abdomen with her thumbs as she'd seen her grandmother do so many times when trying to get a newborn kitten to breathe, hoping somehow it would respond. But it didn't. "It's gone, Beemer."

"You sure?"

"Yes." Still moving slowly, she stood and, fighting tears, backed away from the closet, the tiny body cradled between her palms.

He reached out his good hand. "Want me to take it?"

Ginny gazed at the form. "Would you? I'd like to stay here with Tinkerbelle."

He gave her a gentle, understanding smile. "Sure, be glad to."

Determined not to cry, she carefully placed the kitten in his palm. "Thanks, Beemer. I—I don't know what I would have done without you."

He bent and kissed her on the cheek. "The pleasure was all mine." Turning, he added, "Tell Tinkerbelle I'm sorry her kitten died."

"Tinkerbelle?" Despite her sorrow a slight smile curled at her lips. "What happened to Dumbbell, the pet name you had for her?"

"Somehow, after seeing all she went through delivering those kittens, the name no longer fits her. I'd say she's one smart cookie." He gave her a shy grin then nodded toward the little bundle in his hands. "Don't worry about this wee one. I'll take good care of it for you."

She smiled in return. "Somehow I know you will."

"Stay with Tinkerbelle. I'll keep watch on Aunt Margaret. I'll even fix her breakfast." He chuckled. "Sure glad she likes cold cereal."

Ginny stayed with Tinkerbelle most of the morning, making sure the cat had plenty of food and water, the importance of which she'd learned from her grandmother. She could almost hear her say, "That mother cat has worked hard to deliver those kittens. She needs her nourishment to be able to provide good, healthy, abundant milk for her babies."

Beemer came back into his room just before noon. "Do you think you can leave her for a little while?"

Ginny glanced at the sleeping Tinkerbelle. "Sure. She's doing fine, and she seems to be resting comfortably. In fact, I think if we're careful we can move her out of your closet and back into the bathroom. That way we can get your quilt out from under her so it can go to the cleaners."

He held out his hand. "Come on then. I need you outside."

Ginny took hold of his hand and allowed him to pull her to her feet then followed him down the hall, through the house, and out the sliding glass door onto the patio. "Why are you bringing me out here?"

"You'll see." He tugged her across the patio to a place out near the fence where Aunt Margaret had grown her prize roses. Beemer bent and picked up a large rectangular tin, much like one filled with cookies at Christmas time, and carefully opened the lid.

Chapter 5

Ginny leaned forward for a look at its contents. "Oh, Beemer, it's Tinkerbelle's kitten. How thoughtful."

He hung his head slightly, as if embarrassed by her praise. "I figured we could bury her here in the rose garden."

Ginny eyed him suspiciously. "Her? How do you know this kitten is a girl?"

"I don't. Just guessed." With the toe of his shoe he kicked a board aside from beneath one of the larger rose bushes. "I dug a grave. I knew you'd want to bury her."

"I do want to, but I wasn't sure where I could do it." She gaped at the preciseness of the hole. It was just big enough to hold the tin with a bit of room to spare. "How did you dig this with one hand?"

"Used one of those long-handled, stainless steel stirring spoons from a kitchen drawer. Guess I'll have to buy Aunt Margaret a new one. That one kinda got bent."

In awe of his thoughtfulness Ginny watched as Beemer dropped to one knee and carefully placed the tin in the hole. "Maybe we could give her a little funeral. You know—say a few words about how sad we are that she didn't make it."

Ginny's mouth dropped open. "A funeral? What a nice idea. I'd like that."

He reached up and took hold of her hand, pulling her down beside him. "I've been to a bunch of funerals but never a cat's. What should we say?"

"I think we should thank God for allowing us to witness this kitten's birth, even though she didn't make it, and thank Him for the safe delivery of the other kittens and for protecting Tinkerbelle."

"Sounds good to me." Beemer gave her hand a squeeze. "They usually have music at a funeral. Want me to sing?"

"You're kidding, right?"

"No, I'm not kidding. Ask Aunt Margaret. I sing to her sometimes when she can't sleep."

When he didn't smile, she realized he was serious. "What would you sing?"

"Aunt Margaret taught me a couple of her favorite songs. Sometimes she and I would harmonize on them. You know 'The Old Rugged Cross'?"

She bobbed her head. "Yes, I love that hymn."

He grinned. "Okay. You pray, and then I'll sing it."

Still in awe of his kind gesture, Ginny bowed her head and prayed aloud, being sure to include each of the things they'd discussed. When she said amen, Beemer began to sing. His beautiful voice and the tenderness with which he sang the words reached deep into her inner being and twanged at the strings of her heart. He remembered every word. *Oh, Beemer, dear sweet Beemer, if only you believed the words you're singing.*

When he finished, using his bare hand, he manipulated the loose dirt into the areas around the box, covering it completely, tamping down the surface. Once he finished, he took a nearby garden stake and anchored it securely into the ground to mark the spot. "Maybe we should put some flowers on it," he told Ginny, standing and pulling his knife from his pocket then gesturing toward three perfectly formed pink roses on a nearby bush. "It looks kinda bare."

She nodded then took the knife from his hand when he offered it. "That's a lovely idea. Here—let me cut them."

"You put them on the grave. You're better at this kind of stuff than I am."

Making sure to avoid the thorns, Ginny cut two roses and crisscrossed them over the little mound of dirt then placed the third rose down the center. "They're beautiful, aren't they?"

He nodded. "Yep, they sure are."

Taking his outstretched hand, she rose and stood beside him, twining her fingers through his. "Thank you, Beemer. The funeral was a wonderful idea. I couldn't stand the idea of simply putting Tinkerbelle's kitten in the Dumpster."

He smiled at her as his grasp tightened. "I'm getting to know you pretty well. I figured you'd rather bury it."

Ginny gazed up into his face. She no longer thought of him as her cousin but as the kind of man she had dreamed all her life of marrying. Shaking her head to clear it, she realized the foolishness of her thoughts. She might not think of him as her cousin, but she was sure he thought of her that way. And she was nothing like the women Beemer chose to hang out with, who, much to her dismay, continually showed up at their door. Not only was she gun-shy when it came to men, but, plain and simple, Beemer did not share her faith. That alone was enough to keep her from falling in love with him. She'd committed herself to another man who hadn't shared her faith and look where it got her. No, she'd never do that again. Not ever! Besides, Beemer was a confirmed bachelor. Hadn't he made that clear?

"You okay? You kinda spaced out on me there for a second."

"I–I'm fine. Just a little sad, that's all." Hoping her face hadn't betrayed her thoughts, she felt a warmth rise to her cheeks. "Thanks, Beemer, for everything.

I'd better go check on Aunt Margaret then see how Tinkerbelle is doing."

She could feel his gaze on her as she walked to the house. She wondered if what they'd just done, burying and having a funeral for a dead kitten, was a joke to him and he was laughing behind her back. Or if Beemer Douglas was really the wonderful man she believed him to be. Either way she'd best protect her wounded heart.

"How're you feeling, Aunt Margaret?" Ginny pulled the cord, tilting the blinds in her aunt's room, letting in the brilliant sunlight.

"Weak and tired. God didn't intend the human body to stay in bed all day."

Ginny slipped her arm about her aunt's shoulders and tugged her to a sitting position, propping pillows behind her back. "That better?"

"Much. Did you and Beemer bury that precious kitten?"

"He told you about that?"

A smile of satisfaction worked its way across her aunt's face. "Yes, he felt really bad about Tinkerbelle's baby dying. He knew you did, too, and he wanted to do something nice for you. Something to make you feel better. He's a marvelous man, Ginny. I know you've been hurt. I learned a long time ago you can fall in love, but you can't fall in trust. Trust has to be earned, and once it has been broken trust can rarely be restored."

"Oh, Aunt Margaret, you're so right about that. I doubt I'll ever be able to trust again."

Aunt Margaret reached out her hand. "You must forgive the man who hurt you, dear. The hatred you feel for him is eating you up inside."

Ginny sat down on the edge of the bed. "I can't forgive him. He ruined my life."

"Ginny, until you learn to forgive, you'll never be happy. You're the only one who is suffering. Do you want him to control your life forever? The way he treated you and took advantage of you, I doubt that man ever gives you a thought. What you need is a man like Beemer."

Ginny's eyes widened. "Beemer? You'd want me to get involved with another man who doesn't love the Lord?"

"He doesn't love our Lord"—with a slight squeeze to Ginny's hand she paused, her eyes twinkling—"yet."

"But, Aunt Margaret, you and I both know Beemer could have his pick of women. You've seen how many beautiful females fall at his feet. I could never compete with them. Besides, he thinks of me as his cousin, not as someone he'd want to spend the rest of his life with."

Aunt Margaret smiled. "Believe me, sweetie, he thinks of you as more than his cousin. Beemer is a man. I've seen the way he looks at you. He's well aware you two are related by marriage, not by blood."

Ginny winced. "I'm Beemer's buddy, that's all. The only thing holding us together is you. He loves you, Aunt Margaret. He'd do anything for you."

"And for you. Didn't he just dig a grave for your cat's dead kitten? Sing at the funeral? I think you're selling yourself short. Give him a chance. Give your relationship a chance. You might be surprised how much the two of you have in common."

"I'll be honest, Aunt Margaret. I love being with Beemer. He's kind. He makes me laugh. He treats me like a lady. But aren't you still forgetting he doesn't share our faith?"

"No, dear. I haven't forgotten. I've been praying for Beemer ever since Harold brought him into our family all those years ago, and all that time he's resisted God's call. But am I about to give up on him? No. Beemer has a good heart, but like you he's been hurt. He needs to see and feel the healing love of Jesus. Though you've been hurt, Ginny, you still love the Lord. I know you can't understand why God allowed you to be duped by that man. I can't understand it either. But think of it this way. What if he hadn't duped you until *after* you had married him? Then what? You knew that man didn't share your faith; yet you accepted his engagement ring and set a wedding date. It seems to me that, instead of letting you down, God saved you from making a terrible mistake. I think He did the same thing for Beemer by allowing his fiancée to run out on him as she did. God can see the end from the beginning. We can't."

"So what am I supposed to do, Aunt Margaret? Even if Beemer were interested in me, which I know he isn't, are you saying I should encourage a man who doesn't love the Lord?"

"I'm saying we should both pray for Beemer. God has placed you and me in Beemer's life as a witness for Him. We need to let God's love shine through us. Beemer is seeking, Ginny. He wants a purpose in his life. You and I need to help him find it."

"Hey, Ginny? Where are you?" Beemer's voice echoed down the hallway.

"In here, Beemer, in Aunt Margaret's room!"

"Remember, Ginny, dear, let your light shine before Beemer. Let him see God in you, and pray, pray, pray."

Ginny bent and kissed her aunt's cheek. "I will, Aunt Margaret. I promise."

Beemer appeared in the doorway, cell phone in hand. "You left your phone in the kitchen. It was ringing, so I answered it. The guy says he's your boss."

Chapter 6

"My boss? Why would Mr. Larsen be calling me? Something must be wrong." Ginny hurried to retrieve her phone. "Hello."

"Ginny, I have good news. They got him. They want you to come here and make a sworn statement."

She smiled into the phone. For months she'd hoped and prayed to hear those words. Now that she was hearing them, they hardly seemed real.

"Our attorney has set up your time for the day after tomorrow at his office at nine in the morning. It should only take you a day. Can you be away from your aunt for that long?"

She glanced toward Beemer. "I think so. Yes, I'm sure that time will work. Tell him I'll be there."

"You have the address, right?"

"Yes. I've been there before. I can't believe this is finally happening. It's time that man pays for what he did to me and those other people."

"I wish I could tell you more, but it'd be best if you heard everything from the attorney."

She thanked Mr. Larsen then snapped the phone shut, cutting the connection.

"I guess that was good news."

Slipping the phone into her pocket, Ginny smiled at Beemer, then at her aunt. "Yes, but I need to go back to St. Louis. They want me to make a sworn statement. Will you two be okay while I'm gone? It's important that I go."

"We'll be fine, dear. Don't worry about us."

"I'll leave tomorrow afternoon and come back as soon as I can. If all goes as planned, I'll be gone no more than two nights. But right now I'm going to put our lunch on to cook. It's already past one."

Beemer followed her into the kitchen. "Can I help?"

"Not with that sore hand, but you can watch me peel the potatoes. I thought I'd reheat the chicken and noodles I made yesterday. I love chicken and noodles over mashed potatoes."

"Sounds good to me."

Once Ginny had set the pot of potatoes on the burner and the temperature to high, she turned toward Beemer. "As soon as those are cooked I'll mash them while the chicken and noodles heat in the microwave, and our lunch will be ready."

Beemer eyed her for a moment then leaned toward her. "Ginny, is something wrong? I know what you do is none of my business, and I hate to pry, but is everything okay? You seemed surprised when your boss called, and now you have to make a trip back to St. Louis. You would tell me if anything was wrong, wouldn't you?"

"Nothing is wrong—now."

"What does that mean?"

Ginny searched her heart and decided it was time to come clean with Beemer. After all, hadn't he opened his heart to her?

He shrugged. "We both know how unstable Aunt Margaret's health is. She's been going downhill for days and could take a turn for the worse any moment. The way you've been so concerned about her, I was surprised you agreed to leave town so readily. Whatever that call was about must be important."

"It is important, Beemer." She sat down at the table and motioned toward the empty chair next to her. "I think it's time I told you the whole story."

He pulled the chair away from the table and angled it toward her before seating himself. "I'm listening."

"All my life I waited for that one special man, the one God intended for me. I envisioned him sweeping me off my feet with a wonderful whirlwind courtship, followed by a fairytale wedding, an adorable cottage, the white picket fence, beautiful children, the whole enchilada. But that man didn't come along."

Ginny paused. Voicing this to Beemer was even harder than she'd thought it would be. "I dated a number of men from my singles' group at church; but, even though they were nice guys, our relationships never progressed beyond friendship. Then about two years ago Steve Conrad, one of the top investment counselors at the firm where I work, asked me out to dinner. I knew he wasn't a Christian, but he was fun and witty and a great conversationalist. I figured there wasn't any harm in it since we were going with one of his clients and his wife, so I accepted. I had a great time, so when he asked me to go to a musical the next weekend, I said yes. He treated me like a queen, showered me with flowers and little presents, and made over me like I was the greatest thing that had ever happened to him." Hoping to relieve the knot forming in her stomach, Ginny drew in a deep breath.

Beemer leaned forward in his chair, a frown on his face. "Go on."

"I realized I was doing the very thing I'd said I'd never do—getting involved with someone who didn't share my faith—so I tried inviting him to church. He kept saying he'd come sometime, but that sometime never arrived. He always had one excuse or another to keep him away. But just the promise that he'd eventually go with me kept me encouraged, and I let our relationship go further and further. Three months later he asked me to marry him and slipped the most beautiful engagement ring I'd ever seen onto my finger. I was convinced that once we were married I could lead him to the Lord and everything would be fine. So I ignored God's still small voice, and we became engaged." Ginny rose, pulled the big glass bowl of chicken and noodles from the microwave, and gave it a stir.

"But you didn't marry him, right?"

She gave her head a shake. "No, Beemer. But if what I am about to tell you hadn't happened, I might have married him. At the time I thought I was in love with Steve. Now, looking back, I realize I was in love with love, not with him."

Ginny returned the bowl to the microwave, closed the door, and punched the timer, then checked the pot of potatoes boiling away on the range's front burner before settling down again in her chair. "Being an only child, when my mom and dad passed away I inherited everything they'd built up over their nearly fifty years of marriage, which came to a sizable amount. Especially after I sold the big house they'd built on prime land. You would have thought that since I worked for an investment firm I would have invested it with them, but I hadn't. Instead I'd left everything in a savings account in the same bank where my parents had kept it all those years. Since Steve was going to be my husband, I confided in him about the money. He said he had no interest in it. As far as he was concerned, I could leave it there forever. He claimed he had made a number of wise investments over the years and would be able to provide everything we'd ever need or want. He even said we should have children right away. And he wanted me to be a stay-at-home mom, which was another one of my dreams."

Beemer leaned back in his chair and straightened his long legs. "You make him sound like a great guy."

"I wasn't the only one who thought so. Everyone who worked for the firm, including Mr. Larsen, loved Steve and respected him. He'd been there for years and had a list of clients three times as long as any of the other investment counselors. Top salesman every month. Everything was going along fine. I'd purchased a beautiful wedding dress, selected the bridesmaids and their dresses, and the tuxedos had been fitted—everything. The wedding was only a week off when Steve came over to my apartment one evening all upset."

She paused. This was so hard to talk about. "At first he wouldn't tell me why—just kept pacing about the room raking his fingers through his hair. When I begged him to tell me what had him so upset, he told me he had a problem but didn't want to burden me with it and started to leave. I'd never seen him in such a state, and it worried me."

Dreading what she had to say next, Ginny hurried to the refrigerator, pulled out the pitcher of iced tea she'd made for their supper, and filled two glasses, setting one before Beemer and the other at her place at the table before sitting back down.

"What was wrong with him? Don't tell me he had some terrible disease."

"No, nothing like that." Ginny took a sip of iced tea and let the cool liquid slip slowly down her throat. "It took a bit of convincing, but I finally talked him into telling me. It seems he'd gotten an insider tip on a stock that was going to go over the roof in value the next day. So he'd not only taken every penny of his own money he could get his hands on and invested it in the stock, wanting to make a great showing for his clients, but he'd also, without their permission, invested their money as well. It turned out his insider tip was a fluke, and the rise in the stock didn't happen. In fact, the value plummeted, taking all of Steve's money with it and his clients' money, too. What he'd done was unlawful, and he was in big trouble if he couldn't cover his clients' debt."

Beemer rolled his eyes. "So he asked you for your money to cover it."

Ginny hung her head, avoiding his gaze, the stupidity of what she'd done still ripping at her. "No, he didn't ask me for it. I volunteered it."

Beemer's eyes widened. "Why, Ginny? Why would you do such a thing? Your parents had worked nearly fifty years for that money!"

His accusatory words angered her. "You've been in love, Beemer. What right do you have to criticize me? You trusted your fiancée and your best friend, and look where it got you!"

"But I didn't lose my shirt," he countered. "I hope you're going to tell me he refused to take it."

"After much convincing on my part, he agreed to take it. We went to the bank the very next morning, and I drew it all out, even the certificates of deposit—and had to pay a penalty on them for early withdrawal. Steve promised to pay it all back as soon as he could sell some valuable commercial property his parents had left him."

"So? Was he able to sell it? Did you get your money back?"

Ginny swallowed at the emotions that threatened to choke her. "I don't know if he ever sold the property or not. As soon as I gave him all that money, he kissed me, then headed out the door to cover the investments he'd made, with the promise he'd meet me at my apartment at six and we'd have a nice, quiet dinner at home, just the two of us."

Beemer rubbed his chin thoughtfully. "You came out on the short end of the stick, but at least his clients must have been able to get their money back."

"No, they didn't. And neither did the firm or a number of other people he'd swindled. None of us has seen or heard of him since that day I gave him the money. When he didn't show up for work and I admitted to Mr. Larsen what he had done, my boss searched the files on Steve's and the company's computers. He found Steve had been doctoring files and swindling money for over five years, transferring it to several banks in other states. They checked with those banks and discovered he had drawn out all the funds and closed the accounts. Counting what he took from me, the amount was well over two million. The SEC and the authorities figured he'd left the country."

"Did he?"

Ginny shrugged. She was so excited when she received the call from Mr. Larsen that she hadn't asked. In fact, she hadn't even asked about the money. "I don't know. I guess I'll find out when I go to St. Louis. That's what the call was about. They've found him, Beemer. They've found Steve! That's why I have to go to St. Louis. For over a year I've waited for this news. I was beginning to wonder if they'd ever find him."

A huge smile blanketed Beemer's face. "No wonder you were excited when your boss called." He reached out and took her hand. "Don't worry about Aunt Margaret. I'll take good care of her. You go to St. Louis and do whatever you have to do to make that guy pay for what he did to you and those other people. Guys like that need to be locked up for life."

Ginny suddenly remembered her cat and the new kittens. "I'll call the vet. Maybe I can leave Tinkerbelle with him until I get back."

Beemer grinned. "What's the matter? You don't think I can take good care of her? That cat and I have bonded, which is probably why she had her kittens in my closet."

"In your closet! Oh, Beemer, I was going to help move Tinkerbelle off that quilt and into the bathroom so you could take it to the cleaners. With Mr. Larsen's unexpected phone call coming as it did, I completely forgot."

Beemer stood and pulled her up with him. "I have an idea. Since Tinkerbelle seems to enjoy my closet, and it's nice and warm and protected in there, why don't we take the quilt out from under her and her babies? We can put an old blanket in its place and leave her there until you get back. That way I can keep a closer watch on her. I think she'd much rather stay in my room than go to the vet's."

His unselfish offer surprised her. "You'd do that? You wouldn't mind?"

He cuffed her chin playfully with his good hand. "Not in the least."

"What about your hand? Can you manage doing everything for Aunt Margaret with one hand?"

"It'll be a little awkward, but I'll get along. Several restaurants in the area deliver. We'll do fine. The doctor said I should be able to get rid of these cumbersome splints today or tomorrow. I think I'll call him and ask him if I can go ahead and take them off myself."

"Why doesn't that surprise me?" She gestured toward the range. "I think the potatoes are done."

"Ginny, I'm glad you confided in me," Beemer told her once lunch was over and the kitchen cleaned up. "I know it was hard talking about it, but what you told me explains a lot about you. When you arrived here, it was pretty obvious you'd been hurt. I just didn't realize how deeply. You deserved so much better. No wonder you're afraid to trust anyone."

"I was pretty stupid."

"I prefer to call it naïve. You're anything but stupid."

"I was out of the will of God."

"You really think He expects you to toe the mark? I've heard it said that no one can keep the Ten Commandments."

Ginny gave him a smile. "You're getting pretty biblical on me."

He slipped his arm around her shoulders as they exited the kitchen. "I know a thing or two about the Bible."

"Then you know everyone has sinned and come short of the glory of God? Even you?"

A playful, unexpected kiss landed on her cheek. "Let's go get Tinkerbelle off that quilt. Then we'll fix Aunt Margaret's lunch tray."

Ginny spent the better part of the afternoon with Aunt Margaret, giving her a good bath, massaging her back, arms, and legs, and rubbing her dry, wrinkled skin with a wonderful, lemony-scented lotion. After that, she made her aunt's favorite gelatin salad and chocolate cake, hoping Beemer would remember to give them to her during the time she was gone. After supper she spent over an hour reading the Bible to her aunt. Then, before retiring to take her shower and prepare for the trip to St. Louis, she sat on the floor with Beemer in front of his closet, watching Tinkerbelle care for her kittens.

"I'm going to miss you," he told her, giving her shoulder a gentle nudge. "I've kinda gotten used to having you around."

She smiled up at him. "You'd be crazy to miss me, after all the trouble Tinkerbelle and I have caused you."

He glanced at his watch as the doorbell rang. Bracing himself with his good hand, he stood and hurried to answer it. He was back in less than a minute. "It's Dora and Mitzy. They want me to go to a movie with them."

"So go."

"You don't mind?"

"Why would I mind? I have plenty to do if I'm going to drive to St. Louis tomorrow. I want to leave by nine. It'll take only about five hours, but I want to get in early enough to stop by my office and see how things are going. Catch up on what's been happening since I've been away."

"Okay, then I guess I'll see you in the morning. I'll check on Aunt Margaret and make sure she takes her medicine before I go."

"I'll give it to her."

He shook his head. "Naw, I'll do it. She's kinda used to me kissing her good night. I'll see you in the morning before you leave. I'd better get back to Dora and Mitzy."

Ginny waited until she heard the giggling in the living room stop and the front door close before giving Tinkerbelle one more pat and rising to her feet. It had been a long day, and she still had to pack her overnight bag and take a shower. The best part of the day had been the phone call saying they'd found Steve. The worst part was having to admit her stupidity to Beemer, but at least she'd told him. She'd gotten the whole sordid thing off her chest and felt better because of it. It was as if a wall had come down between her and Beemer, and it felt good. Really good. She hated secrets.

Ginny rose early the next morning, taking care of last-minute details before making sure Aunt Margaret had a good, nourishing breakfast and had taken her morning round of pills. She shuddered as she thought of what might lie ahead for her aunt. The doctor had told them the time would soon come when hospice would take over and she'd have to be on morphine, something they all had dreaded. But for now the pills seemed to be doing the trick. That, or Aunt Margaret wasn't telling them how bad the pain was getting.

"You will be careful driving, won't you, dear?" Aunt Margaret asked as Ginny peeked into her room for one last good-bye. "I wish you had flown here instead of driven. There are so many weird, irresponsible people out on the road."

Ginny smiled at her, grateful for her concern. "I could have flown, but last-minute airfares are so expensive. Besides, it'll be nice to have my car there since I'll be spending both nights in my apartment."

"Beemer said the two of you had a good talk yesterday."

"We did. We talked about many things. We know each other a whole lot better now." Ginny wondered how much he'd said. For fear of worrying her, she'd never given her aunt all the reasons why she hadn't married Steve or told her how he'd absconded with her money and so many other people's. Just that there had been problems between them and he'd broken her trust.

"I'm glad. I want the two of you to get along." She gave Ginny a dismissive wave of her hand. "Run along. I don't want you driving fast. And don't worry about me. I'll be in good hands with Beemer. He fusses over me even worse than my husband did. And don't be concerned about Tinkerbelle. I think Beemer has taken a real shine to that cat."

Ginny planted a loving kiss on her aunt's warm cheek. "Are you running a fever?"

"Don't be such a worrywart, Ginny. It's probably from the hot tea I drank for breakfast. Now go."

Still concerned but accepting her aunt's reasonable explanation, she smiled, waved good-bye and headed toward the front door. Beemer was waiting for her in the living room, her overnight bag in his good hand.

"I'll walk you to the car," he told her, slipping his arm about her waist.

"I'm only going to St. Louis. The way you and Aunt Margaret are carrying on, you'd think I was off on a six-month safari."

Beemer placed her bag in her backseat then stood staring at her.

"Why are you looking at me like that?"

He wrinkled up his nose. "I'm trying to decide."

Not having any idea what he was talking about, she frowned. "Decide what?"

A slow grin crept across his face. "If I should kiss you on the cheek like this"—he bent and lightly touched his lips to her cheek—"or if I should—"

Without warning Ginny found herself gathered up in his arms, his lips pressing against hers. Her brain told her to plant her hands on his chest and push away from him, but her heart told her to enjoy his kiss, to respond.

Her heart won out, and Ginny found her lips pressing against his, her arms circling his broad shoulders, her fingers touching the short stubby hair at his neckline.

When they finally parted, Beemer uttered a low growl, then added a whispered "Wow. I've been wanting to do that ever since you walked in that front door."

His kiss had not been a cousinly kiss. The one he'd given her had sent her heart into orbit and back again. She found herself speechless and not sure what to do next.

Beemer solved that problem by kissing her again, and again her heart went into orbit. She'd never felt this way before. Not even when she'd deluded herself by thinking she was in love with Steve.

When Beemer backed away, his gaze locked with hers, and he smiled at her. "I could make a habit of kissing you. You'd better get out of here before I do it again."

"You—you have my phone number if you need me, and I'll be calling to check on Aunt Margaret and Tinkerbelle." Her hands were shaking, and she felt as if her words were slurring. "Don't forget Aunt Margaret's medicine."

He pulled her into his arms again, and this time she went willingly. "Don't worry about us," he whispered into her hair. "Just come back as quick as you can."

"I—I will," she murmured, her mind in a whir. Lifting her face toward his, she closed her eyes and waited, her heart doing a marathon, as the kiss she hoped would come fell softly on her lips.

Pulling herself back to reality, Ginny slowly backed away. "I–I'll see you in two days."

"I don't want to let you go," Beemer said in a low, husky voice as she turned and walked toward her car.

She wanted so much to forget her trip, run into his arms, and stay there, but she held her breath and resisted the temptation. "I'll be back—soon." Keeping her eyes straight ahead, she walked to her van, climbed in, and started the engine.

What am I doing? I can't let myself get involved with Beemer, she told herself as she took the 386 ramp onto Vietnam Veterans Boulevard and merged into the traffic. In her confused state she'd almost forgotten Vietnam Veterans Boulevard was actually I-65. *I let myself get involved with Steve, knowing full well he didn't share my faith. Thank the Lord I didn't marry that man. Even if he hadn't run out on me with my money, what kind of life would I have had with him?*

Taking her eyes off the road for only a second, she punched the button for her favorite inspirational radio station, and the car was filled with music.

More important, what kind of life would I have with any man who didn't put God first in his life? She had seen women like that. Women married to good men who loved their families and provided well for them but refused to go to church with them or have anything to do with Christian activities of any kind and certainly not pray with them. Women like that had attended her home church in St. Louis, sitting alone with their children on Sunday mornings, no husband by their side. She had seen them wipe the tears from their eyes when the pastor talked about godly homes and the importance of raising their children to love the Lord.

The palm of her hand came down hard on the steering wheel. *No! That kind of life is not for me. I'd rather spend the rest of my life alone than have a husband who refused to share the most important thing in my life with me.* Beemer was a wonderful man. She could so easily fall in love with him, but, no matter how much she cared for him, she couldn't let herself succumb to his charms and ignore the fact that he openly claimed he wasn't a Christian and had no interest in having God in his life. Unless he acknowledged he was a sinner and in need of a Savior, there could be no future for them.

She blinked hard at the tears begging to be released. *Who am I kidding? I'm already in love with the guy.*

Please, God, help me to be strong.

∞

It was nearly three o'clock when Ginny reached the investment firm's offices. After warm greetings from the members of the staff, Mr. Larsen motioned her into his office. "I didn't know much when I phoned you, but since then some things have come out that I knew you'd want to know. They found Steve living in Galveston. One of his clients was on vacation there, saw him in a restaurant, and called the police. He gave up without a struggle. When they searched the beachside cabin he'd leased, they found about half of the missing money stuffed under his mattress. Smart guy, huh? So, rather than deal with a lot of legal ramifications and the embarrassment of facing his accusers, he agreed to tell them where the rest of the money was if they'd offer him a plea bargain. I received a call a few minutes before you arrived, saying he'd taken them to a shed not far from his cabin where he'd buried a steel box. When they opened it, there was the rest of the missing money. Apparently he'd spent very little of it. Isn't that amazing? He'd worked so hard to cover his tracks all those years, duping you and me and people who trusted him, then didn't even spend the money."

Ginny stared at Mr. Larsen. How many times had she dreamed Steve had been caught and the money had turned up, only to wake up and find it was all a figment of her restless mind? Now it had happened. It had really happened!

"Ginny, did you hear what I said? You're going to get most of your money back."

She shook her head to clear it, the reality finally soaking in. "You have no idea how hard I've prayed this would happen."

He rose, smiling. "Well, I guess God heard your prayers. The lawyer tells me they'll still want your statement in the morning, but that should be the end of it. Now go visit your coworkers. I'm sure they'll be glad to see you. We've all missed you and are looking forward to your return."

Ginny felt as if she were walking on air when she left the office and drove toward her apartment. *Thank You, God. Only You could have made this miracle happen. Steve's finally been found, and he still has the money!*

Once she reached her apartment, she phoned Beemer with the news.

"I'm thrilled for you, Ginny," he told her, but something in his voice didn't sound thrilled.

"What's wrong? Is it Aunt Margaret?"

"She hasn't felt good all day. I've never seen her this weak." Ginny's heart clenched. "Have you called the doctor?"

"He stopped by on his way home from the hospital. We may be losing her sooner than we expected. He said it's time to call hospice and get her started on morphine. She's been in more pain than she's let anyone know."

"Oh, Beemer, I wish I were there. They still want me to do the sworn statement in the morning. I'd planned to stay in St. Louis again tomorrow night, but I'm not going to. As soon as I'm finished with the statement, I'm heading back there. You will let me know if there's any change, won't you?"

"You know I will. Ginny, be careful driving. I don't know what I'd do if anything happened to you."

"I will. I'll call you first thing in the morning to see how Aunt Margaret is. I hope Tinkerbelle isn't being any trouble."

"No trouble at all. All she has on her mind is those kittens. She's a good little mother. You'd be proud of her. Good night. Try to get some sleep, and don't worry about us. We're doing okay."

Ginny's hand was shaking as she hung up the phone. She should never have left Aunt Margaret. She glanced about the room. Maybe it'd be best if she just hopped in her van and took off for Hendersonville. She could be there in a little over five hours. But it was already after nine. It'd be nearly three in the morning by the time she got to Aunt Margaret's house, and she hated driving alone on the highway at night. Besides, she was already exhausted. She'd not only made the five-hour drive to St. Louis, she'd been up since before dawn. It'd be dangerous to drive when she was so sleepy. If she could finish her sworn statement and get on the road by ten o'clock, she could be in Hendersonville by three in the afternoon.

Though she wanted desperately to get back to Aunt Margaret's as soon as possible, she opted for staying, giving her statement, then driving back in the morning.

She had expected to fall asleep immediately, but it didn't happen. She watched as the hands of the clock ticked their way to eleven, then to midnight, tossing and turning, praying and feeling very much isolated from those she loved in Hendersonville. The last time she looked at the clock before drifting off, the hands were nearly at one o'clock.

The ringing of the phone wakened her five minutes later.

Chapter 7

"Ginny, I'm at the hospital. It's Aunt Margaret. She's taken a turn for the worse."

"No! Oh, no, Beemer, not while I'm gone. I need to be there with her." Ginny felt weak, as if all the blood had drained from her head.

"I heard her cry out a little after midnight. I rushed into her room and found her lying on the floor by her bed, unconscious. It looked as if she'd tried to get up and then fell. She must've hit her head on the nightstand. There was blood everywhere. I called 911, and they got there really fast. Ginny, I was afraid she was already dead."

His voice was so shaky it scared her. "Oh, Beemer, this can't be happening. Are you with her now?"

"No, the doctors are examining her. They won't let me in. I'm going crazy waiting out here in the hall, wondering what's going on in there. Pray, Ginny—pray she'll make it."

"I'm coming, Beemer." She glanced at her watch. "I should be there by six thirty. You're at the medical center?"

"Yes, but, Ginny, maybe you'd better fly. You're in no condition to drive. Why don't you check to see if there's a red-eye from St. Louis to—"

"Hendersonville? Not likely. I'd probably have to fly into Nashville and take a cab the rest of the way. I can drive to Hendersonville faster than that."

"Drive carefully. Make sure you have your seat belt fastened, and lock your doors. You have plenty of gas?"

"I filled up as soon as I got here." Her heart pounded fiercely. "I'll be out of here in five minutes."

"What about that sworn statement?"

"Right now that's the least of my worries. I'll call the attorney. It'll have to wait. Under the circumstances, I'm sure they'll understand. I'll have my cell phone turned on so call me, please, if you hear anything. Anything at all. Okay?"

"You know I will. I'll—I'll be waiting."

She told him a hurried good-bye, then while sending a quick prayer to the Lord begging Him to be with her aunt, rushed into her bedroom to dress. She had to get to Aunt Margaret as soon as possible.

195

Though Beemer called her at least once an hour during her long drive, he had nothing more to tell her, other than the fact that they had moved their aunt to an intensive care unit and she was still alive.

"I've been praying God would be with her and spare her life, Beemer," she told him, tears rolling down her cheeks the last time he phoned her. "I love her so much. Other than you, she's my last living relative."

"I know. She's my last living relative that I know of. Though we've never heard from them, who knows, my real mother and father may still be alive. Someday I'd like to try to find out who I really am."

"Maybe, when all this is over, I can help you find them." His words and the sadness in his voice broke her heart. What a tragedy for a young boy to experience. Even though it had happened not long after Aunt Margaret and Uncle Harold met and married, he no doubt still bore the emotional scars of rejection. She squinted at the road sign ahead. "Only ten miles to go, and I'll be there."

"I'll be waiting for you at the main door. That way I can take you right to where she is. I can hardly wait to see you, Ginny. It seems like you've been gone for days."

"I know. It seems like that to me, too. See you in a few minutes."

As promised, Beemer was waiting for her at the main entrance when she turned into the lot and parked. He rushed to her van and nearly yanked her out the door, pulling her into his arms and holding her close, his chin resting in her hair. "You made it."

She smiled up at him. "Yes, I made it, and you have no idea how happy I am to be back." On impulse she stood on her tiptoes and kissed his cheek.

Touching his fingertips to her hair, Beemer grinned. "And I'm happy to have you back. Let's go see our aunt."

Dr. Mechan was waiting for them when they approached the intensive care desk. "I'll be straight with you. Things don't look good. Margaret's cancer has been out of control for some time, and she's been bleeding internally. She didn't want you to know how bad her condition was, and as her doctor I had to abide by her wishes. We've done everything we can. It's only a matter of time."

Ginny grabbed onto Beemer's arm for support. "How much time?"

"Probably only a few hours."

Both Beemer and Ginny gasped.

"Is she conscious?"

Dr. Mechan gave her a slight smile. "Yes, but very weak. She'll know you're there, but don't be surprised if she doesn't respond to you." He nodded his head toward a nearby glassed-in room. "Come on. I'll take you to her."

Ginny clasped her hand in Beemer's, and together they followed the doctor into the small room, the sound of monitors beeping rhythmically, breaking the uncomfortable silence.

Sadness and the impending threat of loss tugged at Ginny's heart as she gazed at her aunt and began to cry.

Beemer slipped his arm about her waist, drew her close, and whispered, "Don't, Ginny—don't cry. She might hear you."

Ginny nodded then wiped at her tears with her sleeve.

Releasing his hold on her, Beemer leaned over the bed and kissed his aunt's pale cheek. "Hi, my little sweetheart. I'm here. So is Ginny."

Taking her aunt's bony hand in hers, Ginny leaned close and whispered, "I love you, Aunt Margaret. These past few weeks, being with you and Beemer, living in your beautiful home with you, have been some of the happiest moments of my life."

"Shouldn't you pray for her?" he asked in a hushed whisper, his face racked with concern.

Surprised by his words, Ginny looked at him. "You really want me to?"

"I want you to do anything that will keep her here with us." He blinked hard. "I think she'd want you to pray for her."

Ginny reached for his hand, twined her fingers with his, and began to pray. She asked God to allow Aunt Margaret to stay with them a little longer if it would be His will and thanked Him for the wonderful days they'd spent with their beloved aunt. When she said amen and opened her eyes, she found Beemer staring at his aunt, tears streaming down his cheeks. It was obvious he loved her as much as she did. As she gazed at this strong man who was built much like a linebacker, she realized that inside he was a loving, tenderhearted marshmallow with a heart of gold. She had an even greater respect for him.

A nurse hurried into the room and began checking the various monitors that continued to beep away then gestured toward her aunt. "Go ahead—talk to her. She might hear you."

Beemer leaned even closer. "Hey, little sweetheart, can you hear me? You gave me quite a scare, falling and hitting your head like that." He lovingly pushed a lock of silvery hair from her forehead. "You're beautiful. Did you know that?" He motioned for Ginny to come closer. "Ginny's right here beside me. She hurried back from St. Louis to be with you."

"There's no place I'd rather be than right here with you."

No response.

Ginny sent a quick glance toward Beemer who rubbed at his forehead then shrugged. "You've got to get better so we can take you home. Would you like that? It's a lovely day outside. I was thinking of getting some perennials we could plant along the driveway, but I'll need you to show me where to plant them."

Again no response.

Ginny lowered her head and closed her eyes, her fingers cradling Aunt Margaret's frail hand. "Lord, I come to You asking You to be with our precious aunt Margaret at this difficult time. Even though Beemer and I want her to stay with us, we know her body is worn out, life is hard, and she longs to be with You and her dear husband. I can't thank You enough for letting me be her niece. She's been my rock, my encourager, and a mother to me since my own mother died. Her life and her generosity have touched so many people."

She paused, her heart aching with sadness. "Only You know how many folks will spend eternity in heaven because of her steadfast witness to them. She loves You, God. She loves You with her whole heart. What an inspiration she has been to all of us. I've felt her prayers so many times, times when it seemed the whole world was against me. I know Beemer feels the same way. He loves her, too. Aunt Margaret is the most loving, godly woman I've ever known."

She sneaked a quick peek at Beemer and found him clutching Aunt Margaret's other hand, his head bowed, his eyes closed. "And, please, God, speak to Beemer's heart. Make him see how lost he is without You and how he will never see our beloved aunt again unless he admits he is a sinner like the rest of us and makes things right with You. Nothing would make Aunt Margaret happier. You're a wonderful God and can do great and mighty things." Ginny swallowed hard before adding "amen." She was almost afraid to look at Beemer, fearing she might have offended him by praying openly for him.

But when she opened her eyes, she found him staring at Aunt Margaret's face with such intensity it frightened her. Finally, without looking at her, he reached out and took her hand, his gaze still pinned on his aunt's face, and in an almost whisper said, "Thank you, Ginny. That was a wonderful prayer. I'm sure Aunt Margaret appreciated it."

Although relieved he hadn't seemed offended, she wondered if he'd even been listening or if his mind had been focused on the soon loss of the aunt he dearly loved.

Ginny kept vigil by her aunt's side with Beemer until noon, hoping for some sign that showed she knew they were there, but it didn't happen.

"I noticed you attached a sticker to my aunt's bed, with DNR printed on it in big letters," Beemer said to one of the nurses as she came into the room. "Does DNR stand for what I think it does?"

The nurse sent a glance toward the sticker then back to Beemer. "DNR means Do Not Resuscitate. Many times, when patients know they are terminal, they decide ahead of time that they do not want to be resuscitated. Your aunt had already signed a statement saying she did not want resuscitation under any circumstances. We have to follow the patient's wishes."

Suddenly one of the machines began to make a loud, steady shrill-like sound, causing them both to flinch. Almost instantly two more nurses and an orderly rushed into the room, motioned Ginny and Beemer aside then huddled over Aunt Margaret, speaking in low tones.

Finally the head nurse backed away. "I'm sorry. She's gone."

Ginny screamed out at her. "No! She can't be! Not yet! You have to do something!"

Tears rushing from his eyes, Beemer grabbed onto Ginny's hand, holding it so tightly she feared her bones might break. "Gone? Just like that? Are you sure? We didn't even get to say good-bye!"

The nurse gave her head a sad shake. "I'm sorry. There was nothing we could do. With your aunt's DNR request, our hands were tied. Just remember it was her wish."

Ginny felt as if she'd been punched in the stomach. "What do we do now?"

"Dr. Mechan left instructions that we were to call the Garden of Prayer Mortuary. There's nothing else for you to do here. I suggest you go home and get some rest. You both look as if you could use it. You might want to phone the mortuary in an hour or so and set up a time for one of their representatives to meet with you."

Beemer grabbed onto his aunt's hand and held it fast. "Do—do we have to leave? Can't we stay with her for a while?"

The nurse gave him a kindly smile. "Will five minutes be enough?"

He nodded. "Yes, thank you." Wrapping his free arm around Ginny he tugged her close. "I need to say good-bye."

Through a rush of tears she smiled up at him. "Me, too."

Slowly Beemer leaned over the bed, hugged his aunt, told her how much he loved and appreciated her then kissed her and said a tearful good-bye before moving to the foot of the bed, where he stood gazing at her still figure.

Ginny's stomach churned, and her body felt weak. Aunt Margaret was gone? Really gone? She grabbed onto the bed's railing, clutching it with all her might for support, and stared at her aunt's frail body. "I—I don't know how to begin to tell you how much you mean to me," she finally managed to say in a voice she didn't even recognize as her own. "How will I ever get along without you? You were always there for me." Uninvited sobs racked her body as more of the tears she'd been holding back for her aunt's sake took over and flowed freely down her cheeks. "I love you. I know you're with our heavenly Father now, and I know you've longed to be with Uncle Harold again, but it hurts. I want you here."

She leaned into Beemer, absorbing his strength as she felt his arm circle her waist and pull her close.

"I'm really going to miss her."

"Me, too." Ginny dabbed at her eyes with a tissue from the box on her aunt's serving table. "She was the most beautiful person I ever knew. As beautiful on the inside as on the outside. I'll never forget her."

He planted a kiss in Ginny's hair. "I won't forget her either. She truly was my little sweetheart."

Pulling free from his grasp, Ginny bent and kissed her aunt's wrinkled cheek. "Good-bye, Aunt Margaret."

"Come on, Ginny. It's time to go." Taking hold of her hand, Beemer walked her across the room. When they reached the open doorway, they paused, giving one last look at the woman whose life had impacted them more than anyone else's.

Ginny smiled up at him. "Look, Beemer—her face is so peaceful. The pain and misery she's had to endure are over. Her frail body is in that bed, but Aunt Margaret is where she's longed to be. In the arms of Jesus."

A small smile broke out across his tense lips. "Next I guess she'll be looking for Uncle Harold."

Ginny grinned. "I'm sure of it. What a reunion that will be."

Beemer stopped at a fast-food drive-through on the way home, picking up sandwiches and salads they could take with them, though neither felt hungry.

Weary of body and mind, Ginny had just stretched out across her bed, hoping for a few hours' sleep, when the phone rang. Thinking perhaps Beemer had dozed off while resting on the sofa, she snatched up the phone on her nightstand.

It was Della Hawkins, her aunt's nearest friend who lived a little over an hour away in Clarksville. "Dr. Mechan's nurse phoned me. I can't believe Margaret is gone. I'd hoped she'd be with us a little longer, but she was ready to go. She asked me if I would assist you with the funeral arrangements, help you go through her things and sort them out, and in any other way I could help—if that's acceptable with you." She paused. "I feel a little ridiculous saying this, but your aunt was afraid you might feel—awkward—staying alone in her house with Beemer. Not that he isn't a gentleman, she just knew—with you being a Christian—you—well. . . What I'm trying to say is, she suggested I move in with the two of you until after the funeral. If you don't want me to, I'll—"

"I'd love for you to stay here with us, Mrs. Hawkins." Ginny smiled to herself. It was so like her aunt to think of something like this. "You can take the spare bedroom. It's all ready for you whenever you want to come. Neither Beemer nor I have any idea how to plan a funeral, the dinner they usually have afterward, or any of it. I'm sure I'm speaking for both Beemer and myself when I say your help would be most appreciated."

"Good. Then it's settled. I'll be there by eight o'clock this evening. Don't you worry about a thing. I'll take over and do exactly what I know Margaret would want me to do, and don't be concerned about meals. A committee at her church takes care of things like that. They'll be bringing more food to the house than you can eat." She paused again. "I know how hard this is on you, Ginny, and on Beemer, too. Just remember your lovely aunt is in heaven now, walking on streets of gold."

"I know she is, but I still hurt. Thank you, Mrs. Hawkins. We'll be looking for you around eight. Be careful driving."

Between Mrs. Hawkins's help and the kind consideration of the man at the mortuary, everything pertaining to the funeral was taken care of quickly and in good order. Ginny was amazed as more food showed up at the house than they could ever eat. Facing life without Aunt Margaret was difficult, but with the Lord's help, she tried to find ways to cope with her loss by focusing on the good years they'd had together.

The day they'd been dreading, the day Aunt Margaret's body would be put to rest, finally arrived. With tears of sadness flowing down her cheeks and an ache in the pit of her stomach, Ginny sat close to Beemer, his arm wrapped tightly around her, as Pastor Peterson spoke the words her aunt had requested, admonishing the hundreds of friends and members of her church who had assembled to make sure they were ready to meet their Maker when their own day of death arrived.

Ginny prayed silently that Beemer was listening. So many times he'd heard the gospel. So many times he'd seemed to be on the brink of making a decision for God; yet it hadn't happened. It broke her heart to think of him floundering his life away without choosing to have a close relationship with God. If only he would come to his senses.

Again at the graveside service, the pastor spoke of everyone's need of a Savior, and again Ginny prayed for Beemer.

"Your aunt was such a lovely woman and such a beautiful Christian," so many well-wishers told them afterward. "And so unselfish. She was always ready to say a kind word and help anyone who needed it."

Ginny basked in the praises. Those descriptions fit her aunt exactly. What a treasure her aunt had been.

"I've been dreading going through the things in Aunt Margaret's room," Ginny confessed to Beemer late that afternoon, "but it needs to be done."

"Want me to help?"

She gave him a grateful smile. "Would you? Mrs. Hawkins offered to help, but I thought maybe the two of us should do it."

"Of course I will. I don't want you to have to do this by yourself, and I know Mrs. Hawkins has to be worn out with the busy day she's had."

Ginny gestured toward the huge jewelry box on the chest of drawers. "Why don't we start there?"

Beemer lifted down the box then opened one of the little drawers. "Wow! I had no idea she had so many pieces." He held up a large, sparkly broach. "Suppose this thing's real?"

"Probably. You know how much your uncle loved her. He was always buying nice things for her."

He pulled a tiny gold ring from a velvet box. "This is small. I can't even get it on the end of my pinkie."

Ginny took the ring carefully from the tip of his finger. "Look—there's an inscription inside. The letters are so tiny I can hardly read them. It looks like N-a-t-a-s—Natasha! Do you know anyone named Natasha? I don't."

Beemer shook his head. "Nope. I wonder why she'd have someone else's ring in her jewelry chest?"

"I have no idea."

He let out a snort. "Maybe we can list it on the Internet, and someone named Natasha will see it and bid on it."

She swatted at him. "Only you would think of that."

They went through the remains of the large chest, sorting her aunt's lovely jewelry into what Ginny wanted to keep, what Beemer wanted to keep, and what they would give to Aunt Margaret's friends.

When they finished, Beemer rose and stretched his arms one way and then the other. "Whew! That took longer than I expected. Now what?"

Ginny stood and placed her palms on her hips, stretching forward from her waist then backward. "Why don't we put the rest of it off until tomorrow? I'm beat, and you must be, too."

"Want me to check on Tinkerbelle and Ding Dong and the other kitten?"

She frowned. "Ding Dong? Who's Ding Dong?"

He huffed. "Tinkerbelle's biggest kitten. She's taken a real liking to me, too. But she keeps wandering off, and her mama has to nudge her back. Good thing their eyes are beginning to open. Maybe Ding Dong will learn to stay with the crowd."

"I'll check on them. You took care of them while I was gone. Oh, don't forget we have an appointment with Aunt Margaret's attorney in the morning at ten. Wonder what he wants."

Beemer shrugged. "You got me. Guess we'll find out."

∞

Ginny awakened early after a fitful night of tossing and turning. Even though three of them were there, the house seemed so empty. Life would never be the same without her dear aunt. Mrs. Hawkins was up early, too, and had breakfast ready when she walked into the kitchen. "I need to call my boss before I eat."

"I'll slide the bacon and eggs into the oven to keep warm for you."

"Thanks. I won't be long." Ginny sat down at the table and after flipping open her cell phone hit the number on speed dial. "Hi, this is Ginny. I need to speak with Mr. Larsen," she told the receptionist.

Mr. Larsen answered right away. "Ginny, I was so sorry to hear about your aunt. Did you get the flowers we sent?"

She smiled into the phone. "Yes, they were beautiful. Thank you so much. It was very thoughtful of you to send them. Roses were my aunt's favorite flowers."

"I hope this call means you're ready to come back to work. We really need you. We're going into our busy season, and no one can handle our clients like you."

"I still have a few things to take care of here, but I should be back to work by Monday. I need to make that sworn statement."

"I'll understand if you need more time. Ginny, are you sitting down?"

"Yes. Why?"

"You'll need to clean out your office when you get back. I've given your job to Kevin Swartz."

The wind went out of Ginny's sails. "I—I didn't know."

"Ginny! I gave your job to Kevin because I'm promoting you to junior investment counselor, the job you've been wanting."

Ginny jumped to her feet and let out a shriek. "What? Are you serious? I'm going to be a junior investment counselor?"

"Yes, it's true. You'll be moving into a new office. Congratulations, Ginny. You deserve it. Of course this means unlimited income. With the way you're able to work with our clients, in a few years you'll probably be our top producer."

She felt breathless. Though she'd had her eye on the position and the additional income it would bring, she hadn't expected to have a chance at it for at least two more years. "I'm in shock, Mr. Larsen. I promise I'll do a good job for you. I've loved working for Larsen Investments."

"So I'll see you Monday?"

She grinned, her excitement uncontainable. "Yes. I'll be there." She hung up the phone.

"You're going back to St. Louis that soon?"

Ginny turned to see Beemer standing in the kitchen doorway, his hands braced against the doorjamb.

"I have to, Beemer. My boss has been great about my being gone, but I need to get back to my job."

"You could stay in Hendersonville. I'm sure you could get a job here."

"Beemer! I've been promoted! I'll be making more money than I ever dreamed of. Besides, I like working for Larsen Investments. I'll miss seeing you, but you can come and visit me in St. Louis, or I can come and visit you here."

"I didn't think you'd leave this soon."

"At her request I came here to take care of Aunt Margaret. Now that she's gone, I no longer have a reason to stay."

He gave her a mischievous smile. "I know a reason. If you leave you're going to break up a couple who were meant to be together."

Ginny's eyes opened wide. Surely he didn't mean the two of them!

"You know—Mortimer and Tinkerbelle. You won't believe the way those two are getting along. Mortimer is enamored with those kittens. He's even taken a liking to Ding Dong. You wouldn't want to separate them, now that they're one big happy family, would you?"

Unable to resist a smile, Ginny wagged her finger in his face. "You're impossible. I'm going to miss you and that warped sense of humor of yours, but I have to go."

Beemer planted one of his famous cousinly kisses on her cheek. "I'm going to miss you, too. I'll try to get to St. Louis as often as I can and take you out to dinner at some of those fancy restaurants."

Mrs. Hawkins pointed to the clock on the wall then picked up the coffeepot and began filling their cups. "If you two are going to get to the attorney's office on time, you'd better eat your breakfast."

∞

"You're right on time." James Barlow extended his hand as Beemer and Ginny walked into his office an hour later. "It's nice to meet you, but I wish it would have been under more pleasant circumstances." He fanned his hand toward the two empty chairs in front of his massive oak desk. "Your aunt was one of my favorite people and a real lady. I highly respected her."

After a few pleasantries, they settled down to business. "From what your aunt told me, I doubt she ever discussed her financial condition with you, but she did leave you a letter. I've made copies for each of you. For the sake of time, though, let me read it to you." Mr. Barlow pulled his reading glasses from their case and put them on.

" 'Dear Ginny and Beemer, I'm sure you're both wondering why I asked the two of you to give up your lives to come and care for me when I could have hired a live-in nurse and housekeeper. Being the two wonderful people you are, though, you came willingly without question. I'll always love you for that.'"

Beemer reached over and gave Ginny's hand a squeeze.

" 'I had a reason for asking you. You see, a few years ago I got to thinking about the two of you, the two most wonderful people in my world. Neither of you had found that special someone—the person you would love and spend the rest of your life with. I got this bright idea that I feel came from God Himself. I think you, Ginny, would make the perfect wife for Beemer.'"

Taken by surprise, Ginny uttered an "Oh, no! Whatever was Aunt Margaret thinking? That's ridiculous."

"She told me that, too. Gave me a real sales pitch about you." Beemer jabbed at her arm playfully. "Who knows? You might make a fairly decent wife if you'd ease up a bit and not be so stuffy. You're actually pretty cute."

His jovial response set her somewhat at ease, but she was still embarrassed speaking of such things in front of him and Mr. Barlow.

"Perhaps we'd better get on with it." A slight smile touched the attorney's somber expression as he lowered his head and continued to read. " 'And, Beemer, I think you would make the perfect husband for Ginny.'"

Ginny smiled slightly but remained silent, still fazed by her aunt's suggestion and Beemer's reaction to it.

" 'If I could get the two of you together, figure out a way for you to get to know one another, what would happen? I tried dozens of times to work out a plan. But Beemer was overseas serving his country, and you, Ginny, were working at a job you loved in St. Louis. Then my liver cancer flared up again. The news that I was probably not going to live more than a few months and would suffer much pain frightened me, but I realized my illness could be the perfect opportunity I'd been looking for to get you two together.'"

Beemer dabbed at his eyes with his sleeve. "That sweet old conniver."

" 'At the time of this writing, though the two of you are getting along famously, the romance I'd hoped to see blossom between you hasn't developed. Perhaps that is because Ginny loves the Lord and would never consider marrying a man who doesn't. Beemer, as much as I love you both, unless you make your peace with God, I would not want to see the two of you married. Keep your heart open, my dear nephew, please. God has the perfect plan for your life. I pray you will trust Him before it is too late.'"

Sure her face had turned a deep crimson with all this discussion of such personal things, Ginny dropped her head shyly.

"There's more." Mr. Barlow adjusted his glasses. " 'I've made out a will. My attorney will be giving you each a copy, but I wanted to explain it here. God has been good to me. So was Harold. I've had everything I ever needed and most of the things I merely wanted. Now I'm leaving a big portion of what I have accumulated to the two of you. Everything I own, with the exception of this wonderful house at 223 River Road, is to be divided equally three ways, with a third going to you, Ginny—'"

Ginny's eyes widened as she let out a gasp. "A third to me? I don't deserve anything!"

"That was your aunt's wish. 'And a third to you, Beemer.'"

Beemer shook his head in disbelief. "I didn't expect anything either. I figured she'd give it all to her church."

" 'The remaining third is to go to Natasha Reynald.'"

"Natasha?" Ginny and Beemer exchanged glances.

"Natasha! The name on the little gold ring!" *But who is Natasha Reynald?* Ginny wondered. *And why would Aunt Margaret be leaving one-third of her estate to her?*

" 'Natasha's portion is to be held in trust until she can be located.'"

"Surely Aunt Margaret knew where to reach her if she was leaving one-third of her estate to her."

"If she did, she never gave that information to me." Mr. Barlow pulled off his glasses, rubbed his eyes, then locked his gaze on the two of them. "As to the River Road house? It was your aunt's fondest desire that one day the two of you would marry and it would become your home."

Ginny gulped hard, her heart pounding in her chest, as she and Beemer exchanged questioning glances.

After looking from Ginny to Beemer and back again, the attorney continued. "Because of that dream, your aunt specified that the house and all its furniture and contents must be left intact, exactly as it was at the time of her death, for the period of one full year, to give time for Beemer to get his heart right with God and the two of you to become better acquainted and perhaps fall in love and marry."

Ginny's mouth fell open. "She actually said that in her will?"

Mr. Barlow nodded. "Yes, she was quite meticulous in her demands. If by the end of a year nothing has developed between you, the house and all that goes with it are to be sold and the proceeds divided equally between you two and Natasha Reynald."

Ginny shook her head in disbelief. "Amazing. I should have known she had something in mind, other than needing to be cared for, when she insisted I drop everything and come to Hendersonville. Especially after I realized Beemer was already here and she'd done the same thing to him."

Mr. Barlow raised his hand as if to silence her. "There's more. She wanted you to know how much she loved both of you and how she wished you a good life filled with happiness. The next paragraph is meant for you, Mr. Douglas."

Beemer straightened in his seat and waited.

"In this part her words are almost pleading. She asks you to come to grips with your life and your eternity and accept Christ as your Savior. She wants more than anything to meet you both in heaven one day. She warns you to face your mortality head-on, consider where you will spend eternity, and not put off the most important decision of your life."

Ginny blanched at his words but remained silent.

Beemer sat gazing at Mr. Barlow, his hands folded in his lap, his face emotionless.

The silence in the room was palpable.

God, speak to Beemer. Reach into his heart and melt the indifference he's harbored toward You. May Aunt Margaret's love and concern and these final words she's left just for him touch him in a way that will bring him to You.

Mr. Barlow pulled off his glasses. "That's basically it. There are a few other minor things in her letter, but you can read those for yourselves. Now I have a question for you. Do either of you know how to reach this Natasha Reynald? Your aunt left no address and no information as to where she is or how to reach her."

Ginny shook her head. "No, neither of us had ever heard of her until we found a little ring with the name Natasha engraved in it."

The attorney pulled a sealed envelope from the corner of his desk and handed it to Ginny. "She left this for you. Maybe it contains more information."

Ginny took it and inspected the handwriting. It was her aunt's. "Should I open it now?"

"That's up to you."

She pulled out the letter, then, deciding it might be too personal to read with an audience, slid it back into its envelope. "Maybe I'd better wait and read it when I get back to her house."

"Your decision." He gave them each a large manila envelope. "Here is your copy of the will and a copy of your aunt's letter." Removing a large shoe box from the credenza behind him, he handed it to Ginny. "She left this box for you, too. I have no idea what it contains."

Beemer took the box; then he and Ginny thanked the man for all the years he'd capably represented both Aunt Margaret and Uncle Harold and headed back to the house.

"This whole thing is amazing," Ginny told him as they turned onto River Road. "Surely Aunt Margaret didn't expect her plan to work."

After Beemer adjusted the rearview mirror, he glanced over at her. "Why not? We're both red-blooded Americans with the same desires and urges other folks our age have."

Ginny glared at him. "It sounds pretty crude when you put it that way. Marriage is not to be taken lightly. It's a lifetime commitment, or should be. Just because people have urges and desires, as you put it, doesn't mean they should run out and marry the first person who pays them any attention."

"That hardly describes us. Neither of us has exactly operated on impulse. If I'd married the first person who paid any attention to me, I'd have been married in junior high. I agree with you, Ginny. Until a man says 'I do', I think he should keep his hands to himself."

"Beemer!"

Taking his eyes off the road, he gave her a guarded grin. "Well, I do. Marriage should be between a man and a woman who love each other and are serious enough about the vows they take at that altar to live by them until death do they part." The grin turned into one that stretched from ear to ear as he added, "Even if it kills them."

Ginny couldn't help but laugh. "You're incorrigible. I don't know why I even try to talk to you."

The house was eerily quiet when they entered. Mrs. Hawkins had left a note saying she had gone to the market, so she wasn't there to greet them.

"Which are you gonna do first? Read her letter or open the box?" Beemer asked after they'd checked on Tinkerbelle and finally settled down at the kitchen table for a cup of freshly brewed soothing coffee.

Ginny stared at the box on the table then picked up the letter. "Read the letter, I guess." Carefully she unfolded the piece of paper. "It looks as if this is to both of us."

"Really?" He scooted his chair a little closer.

She nodded. "I'll read it aloud." Setting the envelope aside, she began to read. " 'Dear Ginny and Beemer: What I'm about to tell you, no one else knows. Not my attorney, not my closest friends, not the pastor, and not even Harold, my dear husband of many years.' "

Looking shocked, Beemer leaned toward her, rested his elbows on his knees, and propped his chin in his palms. "What's she talking about?"

Ginny shrugged. "I have no idea." Staring at the letter, almost fearful of what secrets it might contain, she continued. " 'From the time I was a little girl, long before I became a Christian, I was consumed with the desire to become a famous dancer. At sixteen I ran away from home and went to New York City, hoping to get a job in the chorus line of one of the off-Broadway shows. But, like so many girls with stars in their eyes, I met a good-looking, talented man, Antonio Reynald, and went gaga over him. He was a bit older than me and already a dancer in a troupe, and I was in awe of him and his talent. To make a long story short, I ended up pregnant. Antonio wasn't ready to get married, but he said he loved me and loved our baby. Everything was going along fine, I thought, until one day, a few months after our baby was born, he put little Natasha in her stroller and took her for a walk. He never returned. I was frantic! I looked everywhere for them without success. I called the police, but they did little to try to find them. Their attitude seemed to be, with me a young, unmarried, nonworking mother, that it might be best for the baby to be with the father, who had been willing to support us. At that time if a young woman turned up pregnant, it usually meant she had been promiscuous. They would have notified my parents, but by the time that happened, I was eighteen.'"

Ginny lifted her eyes to meet Beemer's. "Aunt Margaret had a baby? All this time I thought she was childless."

"I thought that, too." Beemer let out a big sigh. "What a terrible time that must have been for her. Can you imagine having your baby taken away from you like that, with no idea how to find her?"

"I would die if it happened to me." Ginny felt heartsick as she lifted the letter and read on. " 'To this day I haven't heard a word about Natasha's or Antonio's whereabouts. I don't even know if she's alive. I was too ashamed to admit what had happened, that I'd had a baby out of wedlock, so I kept quiet about it, moved to Nashville, and never told a soul. Later I met and married Harold and was too ashamed to tell even him.'"

Beemer let loose a low whistle. "Uncle Harold never knew. I wonder if she tried to find her daughter later on."

"I wonder that, too. What a difficult time that must have been for Aunt Margaret. I can't imagine going through life, knowing somewhere out there you have a child. I wonder if that little girl ever knew she had a mother."

"What else does she say?"

Ginny blinked back a tear and read on. " 'After the police wouldn't help me, I pretty much gave up trying to find my precious baby. I was broke, discouraged, and not much interested in going on with anything, until I met someone who changed my life.'"

Beemer's eyebrows rose. "Uncle Harold?"

Ginny continued. " 'That man was Jesus Christ. Confessing my sins and accepting His grace and forgiveness made life worth living again.'"

Beemer gave his head a shake. "All this time I'd thought she was nearly perfect."

"None of us is perfect, Beemer. That's why God sent His Son to—"

"To die on the cross for us? Aunt Margaret was always trying to tell me about that and how I needed a Savior, but I wouldn't listen. Now that she's gone, I wish I had." He gestured toward the letter. "Go on."

Ginny wanted so much to tell Beemer about the night when, as a child, she had given her heart to Jesus, but right now it was time to finish reading Aunt Margaret's letter. " 'I want you and Beemer to try to find Natasha for me, give her the contents of the box, and make sure she gets her share of the inheritance. I know it's a lot to ask, but you two are the only family I have now.' "

Beemer shot a sudden glance at Ginny. "But how could *we* find her? You're going back to St. Louis."

Ginny pressed the letter to her chest. "Maybe I could put off going back for a few more days. Mr. Larsen told me to take whatever time I needed. Aunt Margaret asked so little of us yet gave so much—we can't refuse her final request. We have to try to find Natasha."

"You're right about that, and we have some tools at our disposal she didn't have."

Ginny smiled. "The Internet."

"Right. Who knows? Maybe Antonio Reynald is still around? Maybe even made a name for himself in the entertainment field. It's worth a try."

"Yes, definitely. Let's see. Aunt Margaret said he was a few years older than she was. That would make him at least eighty-seven or eighty-eight? Right?"

"Maybe even older. Or dead."

Ginny frowned. "Beemer!"

"Well, he could be."

"So if Aunt Margaret gave birth to Natasha when she was sixteen or seventeen, that would make Natasha around sixty-eight or sixty-nine?"

"Or dead."

"Beemer, don't be so negative."

"I'm not being negative. Just stating a fact."

She shook her head. "I prefer to think she's alive and well and will be excited to hear from us."

He nodded toward his bedroom where he kept his computer. "Let's see what we can find on the Internet."

Beemer sat down in his desk chair and motioned Ginny to a chair beside him. "Where should we start?"

She hesitated. "Why don't we try the white pages first? Want me to type in his name?"

"Naw, now that I've got those clumsy splints off my fingers, I can type well enough. I just have to be careful." He typed in the words—Antonio Reynald—hit ENTER, then leaned back and waited. Six results showed up almost immediately, stating there was no Antonio Reynald, but listing two Albert Reynalds, one William Reynald, one Carson Reynald, one Xavier Reynald, and a Jean Reynald. "Well, that didn't work."

"But someone on that list could be one of his children or even grandchildren," Ginny countered.

Beemer rubbed his chin. "Could be. Think we ought to contact them and see?"

"Um, maybe later. Let's try some other avenues first."

Beemer pressed CONTROL and the letter P, and the printer started humming. Almost instantly the printed copy of the names emerged. Ginny pulled the paper from the printer and placed it on the desk. "Try one of the search engines."

Beemer typed in the Internet address then the word *Reynald*. Up popped an amazing number of references. "Looks like we've got our work cut out for us. It's showing 129 responses, but most of those are duplicates or probably the ones we have on the list. Why don't we print out the first two or three pages and divide them up between us? I doubt we'll find phone numbers, but we might find e-mail addresses. If those don't work, we'll try the others."

"Good idea. At least it gives us a starting place."

"Think it would help to type Natasha Reynald into the search engine? Maybe she never married."

Ginny thought over his suggestion. "Wouldn't hurt. Do it."

He typed in the name, but nothing promising came up. "If we don't get anywhere with the things I've printed out, I'll go back to the white pages and enter her name."

Ginny pulled the additional printed copies from the tray, kept two, and handed one to Beemer. "I'm going to my room and start checking on these. Maybe we'll get lucky and come up with her e-mail address. I'll let you know if I find anything."

Beemer began to peruse his list. "Okay. I'll start checking mine out, too."

They looked at one another when they heard the front door open, and Mortimer, who was once again allowed in the house now that he and Tinkerbelle had become good friends, barked and ran toward the front hall.

"Beemer? Are you here?" a woman's voice sang out. "We brought you some food."

He glanced at Ginny. "Sounds like Mitzy."

"Looks like *you* won't get any calling done." She followed him to the front hall, and there, reflected in the mirror over the fireplace, stood Mitzy, Dora, Patti,

Deirdre, Gloria, and two other women Ginny hadn't met, holding an assortment of carry-out sacks from a variety of local fast-food restaurants. "Hail, hail, the gang's all here," Ginny said in a mocking singsong fashion, pointing toward the mirror. "I'll be on the phone in my room if you need me, but I doubt you will. Have fun."

Beemer grabbed onto her arm. "Aw, Ginny, this wasn't my idea. I didn't ask them to come."

She pulled from his grasp. "Your dedicated entourage is waiting for you to grace them with your presence. It must be nice to be so popular with the ladies that they can't leave you alone for even a day. I'll bet you're the envy of your male friends."

"Ginny, wait."

"Wait? For what? So I can watch them fawn over you? I think not. I've got work to do."

"I'll tell them to leave—that I'm too busy to talk to them now."

"Oh, no, you don't. They'll think it was my idea."

He jutted out his chin. "Wasn't it? You're the one who's making such a big deal of them coming."

"I am not making a big deal of it!"

"Oh, no? It looks that way to me. I think you're jealous."

She felt the scruff on the back of her neck rise, or was it that she'd been around Tinkerbelle so much she only imagined she had a scruff? "Jealous? Jealous of what? A bunch of would-be little princesses who think they've found their Prince Charming? You're being ridiculous. Not one of those girls has anything I want!"

Beemer glared at her, meeting her icy stare. "Ginny, sometimes you can be a real handful, you know that?"

Her patience growing thin, she scowled at him, her hands going to her hips and planting themselves there. "No, I didn't know that, but you just told me. Thanks for enlightening me."

Lifting his hands in the air, he headed for the living room. "You're impossible! We'll talk about this later."

Frustrated and incapable of speech, Ginny watched him go. She hated to admit it, but he'd hit the proverbial nail on the head. She was jealous.

Chapter 8

Discouraged with the lack of information she'd found and still upset with Beemer for calling her jealous, Ginny pushed back in her chair and stretched her arms first one way and then the other. She'd completed nearly ninety percent of her list and hadn't found a single promising bit of information. How were they supposed to find a girl who was probably in her late sixties, who could have married several times and be living under another name?

"Ginny, I need to talk to you."

She glanced toward the doorway and found Della Hawkins standing there, dish towel in hand. "Is there a problem?"

Smiling, Mrs. Hawkins strode across the room. "Oh, my, no. No problem. But now that your aunt's funeral is over and you and Beemer will be going back to your lives, I thought it was time for me to go home. I'm kind of anxious to get back to my house and my pets. I'm sure my neighbors are getting tired of caring for them."

"We hate to see you go. It's been wonderful having you here." Ginny latched onto her aunt's friend's hand. "I can't tell you how much we appreciate your taking time out of your busy life to help Beemer and me through this difficult time. I don't know what we'd have done without you."

"It was my pleasure. I loved your aunt more than I can tell you. She was a delightful woman and more in love with the Lord than anyone I know. I thought I'd leave right away, as soon as I tell Beemer good-bye, if that's agreeable with you."

Ginny nodded. "Of course it's agreeable with me. Just promise to keep in touch. You have my phone number."

"Yes, I do, and I'll be calling you from time to time. Thank you for giving me your aunt's precious music box and all those other things. I'll think of her every time I hear that little melody."

"She would have wanted you to have the things. You were very special to her. Take care of yourself." She watched as Mrs. Hawkins gave her a little wave then disappeared down the hallway. Though she hadn't wanted to say anything to her about it, her leaving that suddenly *did* present a problem. As a Christian she didn't feel it was right for her and Beemer to be staying in the house alone. Since her apartment was way off in St. Louis and Beemer had kept his Hendersonville apartment while he'd been staying at Aunt Margaret's house, the logical option was for him to move out. It would only be for a few days. Just long enough for them to try to locate Natasha, finalize everything, and close up the house.

"What?" Beemer nearly shouted, waving his arms at her several hours later when she suggested he move back into his apartment. "You afraid I'm going to attack you or something?"

Ginny suppressed a slight feeling of irritation. "No, Beemer, that's not it at all. I trust you completely. In fact I feel safe with you."

He dropped onto one of the chairs at the kitchen table, his intense gaze anchored on her face. "Then what's the big deal? You're only planning on staying a few more days at most."

"It doesn't look right."

There was a heartbeat of silence. "You and I are relatives! We're cousins. What's the big deal?"

"Cousins in name only."

"Is that what Mrs. Hawkins was doing here? Chaperoning us? Don't you think we're a bit too old to need a babysitter?"

"We both have good reputations to maintain."

"And you're afraid your precious reputation would be jeopardized if someone found out the two of us were living in the same house—alone?"

Ginny sighed. "I—I guess that's it."

"Okay, if that's the way you want it—I'm out of here." With a scowl on his face he stood and, shoving his hands deep into his pockets, headed for the door. "You're the only woman I know who's afraid of me. Most women go out of their way to try to get me alone."

Ginny sighed again. This whole conversation was getting out of hand. "I'm not afraid of you. Surely you know that. It's just—"

"Just that you have to protect your lily-white reputation? Well, I sure don't want to do anything to arouse suspicion or give old ladies cause to gossip. You'll be much better off if I leave right now."

"What about Natasha? I thought we were going to find her."

He shrugged. "Maybe we can meet in a restaurant or some other public place to decide what to do about her, a place where you won't have to worry about me molesting you."

"That's not fair!" Ginny struggled to hold back tears. The death of her aunt was so fresh on her mind, and she didn't want to offend Beemer, who was taking their aunt's loss as hard as she was. "I'm sick about this, Beemer. I had supposed she'd stay until we both left, and we wouldn't have this problem. I never anticipated having to ask you to move out. I'd never deliberately do anything to hurt you. I thought you knew that. You mean more to me than anyone I know."

Beemer stood staring at her for a moment then stepped forward and slipped his arms about her. "Now I feel like a heel."

She leaned her head against his shoulder. "Besides losing the aunt we love, so much has happened these past few days. I think we're both a little edgy. I know I am."

He nestled his chin in her hair. "Yeah, I guess I am, too. I should never have torn into you like that. I even barked at Mitzy awhile ago over nothing. She stormed out of here mad at me."

"It's been a trying time for both of us."

"You have every right to be concerned about appearance. If I were any kind of man, I'd have offered to leave on my own. You're not like the other women I know. You have high morals and scruples. I should, and do, respect that. I'll pack up my things and be out of here by evening."

Relieved by his change in attitude, she lifted misty eyes to his. "Thanks, Beemer. You and your feelings are important to me."

"And you're important to me. You're"—he kissed her forehead—"sweet."

He kissed her cheek. "Pretty."

His lips grazed gently across her face to her other cheek. "Fun to be with."

He kissed her chin. "Smart. A good listener. The best friend I ever had and—"

Ginny's heart was pounding wildly.

"And—kissable."

She thought she'd go crazy as his lips claimed hers in the sweetest kiss she'd ever had, leaving her breathless and totally in awe of this man.

When they parted she stood there, as still as if she'd turned to stone, her mind in a whir, her heart doing cartwheels.

"Ginny?"

"Hmm?"

"It's hard to think of you as my cousin."

"I know."

"Ginny?"

"Hmm?"

"You know what? I want to kiss you again."

She smiled up at him. "What's stopping you?"

Without answering, he kissed her a second time. When he stopped, she wanted to beg for more. But suddenly she remembered her vow, and she remained silent.

"Wow," Beemer said, slowly releasing his hold on her. "Wow, wow, and triple wow. I could make a steady diet of that."

She wasn't sure what to do next, but she knew she couldn't let their relationship go any further, no matter how much she wanted it to. She smiled and backed away. "Maybe we'd better talk about Natasha and make plans on how we should proceed."

He gave her a mischievous grin. "I'd rather kiss you again, but I guess it's time we settle down to business."

"Yeah, I guess we'd better." For want of something to do to avoid looking at his handsome, teasing face, she moved to the kitchen sink and filled her water glass, taking a few sips. The cool water felt good to her throat. Why was it her throat always felt dry when she was nervous? "I didn't have any success with my phoning. None of those people ever heard of Natasha, her father, or Aunt Margaret."

"Me either."

"So, where do we go from here? Should we try typing Natasha's name into whitepages.com?"

He gave her a grin. "Sure, but wanna pray first? Ask God to make her name appear as if by magic? Maybe even her picture, and she'll look like Aunt Margaret?"

Grinning back, Ginny rolled her eyes and gave her head a slight shake before starting down the hall toward the computer. "I've already prayed about it, and I certainly don't believe in magic."

Beemer followed her then settled himself in front of the keyboard. "Here goes."

She leaned over his shoulder for a better view of the monitor as he typed in Natasha's name then leaned back in his chair. "Nothing."

"How about N. Reynald?"

Using the backspace key he eliminated the last six letters of Natasha. "Still nothing."

Ginny nibbled at her lower lip. "I thought sure we'd find something in the white pages."

"Got any other ideas?"

Pulling up a chair beside him, Ginny sat down and stared at the screen. *Please, Lord. We have to find her.* "We didn't try that other search engine, did we?"

"Naw, but if there was anything on the Internet, the one we used should have located it."

"It might be worth a try."

Beemer typed in the Internet address. "Nothing on Natasha Reynald."

Ginny's heart plummeted. "Oh, Beemer, other than the Internet, I have no idea where to start looking for Natasha."

Cradling his head between his palms, Beemer let out a long sigh. "Me either."

"Try Antonio Reynald again. Maybe this search engine will catch something the other one missed."

"Don't count on it." He typed in the letters then let out a yelp. "Look! There's his name!"

Her heart throbbing with excitement, Ginny leaned toward the monitor and began to read aloud, " 'The Willow Creek Senior Care Center's birthday party was well attended last Thursday with four of its senior residents celebrating birthdays. After listening to the "Happy Birthday" song being sung by the other residents of the Willow Creek Home, birthday honorees Joe Miller, Lettie Morgan, Bill James and'"—Ginny clapped her hands—" 'and Antonio Reynald—joined together to blow out the candles and enjoy the delicious birthday cake and ice cream provided for their special occasion.'"

Beemer grabbed Ginny's hand and tugged her into his arms, squeezing her so tightly it nearly took her breath away. "Antonio is in a care home! Ginny, we've found him! Wow! Am I thankful someone took time to put that notice on the care home's Web site!"

"I just knew the Lord would lead us to someone in Natasha's family!"

He tilted her face upward with his hand. "Looks like you were right. Next time you talk to God, thank Him for me, will you?"

"You could do it yourself if you wanted to. He'd love to hear from you."

"Naw, if I started talking to Him, He'd say, 'Beemer who? I don't know you.'"

"You've got that backwards, Beemer. He knows you—you don't know Him."

He shrugged. "Whatever. Now let's go to the care center's home page and see if they've listed their phone number and address." He punched a few more keys, and not only the information they were looking for appeared but also a full-color photograph of the home itself. "Looks like they're located in Wyoming."

Ginny groaned. "That far away? I was hoping Antonio was closer."

"Maybe we could call and talk to him. After all, the guy was able to blow out his candles; he can't be too bad off." He copied down the phone number and handed it to her. "You're better on the phone than I am. Why don't you call?"

Ginny dialed the number and, after being transferred several times, finally reached a nurse. "This is Nurse Borden. They tell me at the desk you are inquiring about one of our residents? Antonio Reynald? Is there something I could help you with?"

"Yes. We've been trying to locate Mr. Reynald to ask him about his daughter. My aunt, her mother, passed away last week and left his daughter a sizable inheritance, but no one knows how to reach her or if she is dead or alive. We were hoping Mr. Reynald could tell us where she is." *Please, God, let this man be lucid enough to give us the information we need.*

"I'm sorry, but Mr. Reynald passed away a few days ago."

Ginny wanted to cry. They'd come so close to finding Natasha, but with her father gone, they'd reached a blank wall.

Chapter 9

B ut," the woman went on, "I can get in touch with his daughter and ask her to call you. We know her quite well. She's been coming to visit him at least once a week during the five years he was here."

Ginny gasped. "Natasha's alive?"

The woman laughed. "Alive? That one is more than alive. She's one of the bubbliest people I've ever known. All our residents' eyes light up when she comes to visit, and you should hear her sing. She has a voice like a nightingale. I'll be seeing her later today. Even though her father has passed away, she'll still volunteer a number of hours here each week. In addition to singing and entertaining our residents, she reads to those whose eyesight is waning. We all love Natasha."

His brows raised, Beemer poked Ginny in the arm. "What? What's she saying?"

Ginny covered the mouthpiece with her hand. "Natasha is alive, and the nurse is going to have her call us!"

"Give me your phone number, and I'll make sure Natasha gets in touch with you, Miss—"

"Markham. Ginny Markham." Ginny gave the woman her number then thanked her for her help. "We've found her, Beemer. We've found Aunt Margaret's daughter!"

Both Ginny and Beemer watched the clock impatiently, waiting for Natasha's call. When it came, Ginny answered, then, after exchanging greetings with the woman, advised her she would be putting her on speakerphone so Beemer could join in the conversation.

"I've always wanted to find my mother," Natasha told them, and it was obvious she was crying. "Now I'll never have a chance to see her. My father was a wonderful man, but he was very tight-lipped when it came to my mother. All he would say was that she didn't want me. I guess, knowing I wasn't wanted, I never put forth the necessary effort to find her. Now that it's too late, I wish I had."

"She loved you, Natasha," Ginny told her, remembering how lovingly her aunt had mentioned her name. "Your birth came at an awkward time in both your father's and mother's lives. I don't know how much he told you, but Aunt

Margaret ran away from home at a very young age, with stars in her eyes and high hopes of becoming a dancer on Broadway. That's where she met your father. He was older and wiser and extremely talented, and she fell head over heels in love with him. Then you came along."

"I guess I ruined her career," Natasha said sadly.

"From what we learned in the letter our aunt left," Beemer explained, "you were only a few months old when your father put you in your stroller and said he was going to take you for a walk." He glanced at Ginny then cleared his throat. "He—he never came back, Natasha. Aunt Margaret never saw or heard from you or your father again. It nearly killed her not knowing where you were."

"She said he took me and left? Without telling her?"

Ginny winced. She hated saying anything that would mar this woman's saintly image of her father, but Aunt Margaret had a right to have her side told, too. "It's all documented in a letter she left for us. We also have a shoe box full of letters she wrote to you over the years, but she never knew where to mail them."

"You need to come here to Hendersonville, Tennessee, Natasha, read these letters, and talk to the attorney who is handling your mother's will." Beemer's voice echoed the irritation Ginny felt that Natasha's father had kept the truth from her. "Perhaps you grew up believing your mother didn't love you and didn't want you, but she loved you enough to leave one-third of her estate to you."

"She even kept a tiny baby ring engraved with your name in it, in hopes of one day finding you and giving it to you," Ginny added, hoping Natasha would accept Beemer's invitation.

"I'll come," Natasha said resolutely. "I'll get the first plane out that has a seat available. You said Hendersonville, Tennessee?"

"Yes, but plan on flying into Nashville, and Ginny and I will pick you up. Just give us the time your flight will arrive."

Ginny smiled at Beemer. For sure, he was one of the good guys.

"You said you were my mother's niece and nephew?" Natasha asked.

Beemer chortled. "Yes, we're all cousins, just not blood cousins. Harold, who was really my uncle, took me in when my parents, his brother and sister-in-law, decided they didn't want me, so I know how you feel. I barely remember my parents, not that it's any loss." He gestured toward Ginny. "Ginny's your mom's sister's child. This whole thing's kind of complicated. Does what I'm saying make any sense?"

A slight laugh sounded on the other end. "I think I've got it."

"Aunt Margaret asked Beemer and me to come and take care of her so she could die at home," Ginny added. "We've been here for nearly a month. She was a wonderful woman, Natasha. We loved her very much. I just wish you could have known her."

"I do, too, especially after hearing all you've told me about her. I guess any story always has two sides." Natasha hesitated. Ginny thought perhaps she was crying. "I'll call the airline and then call you right back. I babysit my three great-grandchildren while their parents work, so I won't be able to stay long. Thank you both for being there for my mother when she needed you, and thank you for going to all the trouble to track me down. I'm looking forward to meeting you."

They told her good-bye, then closed the connection.

At ten o'clock the next morning, Ginny and Beemer stood at the exit gate at the Nashville airport waiting for Natasha. They recognized her the moment she entered the gangway. Other than being nearly twenty years younger than their aunt, she was the image of her.

After they hugged one another, Beemer picked up her bags, and they drove to the house on River Road.

"I love this house," Natasha told them after they'd given her a tour of all the rooms in the stately old redbrick home. "It's decorated exactly as I would have decorated it. Isn't that uncanny?"

"Naw, it's in the genes." Beemer slipped his arm around her shoulder and steered her back into the living room. "You look and act so much like her that it almost seems she's here with us. Even your voice sounds like hers."

"He's right. You are like her." With tears in her eyes and a heart filled with gratitude toward God for leading them to her, Ginny motioned Natasha to a chair then placed the shoe box filled with letters in her lap. "Once you read these, I think you'll feel as if you knew your mom."

Ginny took the ring from the box on the table where she'd set it earlier and stared at it. Her aunt, the woman she'd thought of as perfect, had given birth to a baby out of wedlock and then had to let her go. What a horrible secret to have kept all those years. What guilt she must have carried. Ginny could only imagine how many times Aunt Margaret had held that precious little circle of gold in her fingers, weeping and wondering if her baby had lived or died, if she was happy, maybe even had children of her own.

"I hope so. You have no idea how I've longed to see her. I've had so many questions. I loved my father, but I always wondered if he was telling me the whole truth."

"Your mother was a wonderful woman. At that time she had little money, but she purchased this precious ring for you right after you were born and had your name engraved in it." Blinking hard, trying to suppress the tears that ached to be released, Ginny reached out and touched the circle of gold. "You were too small to wear it safely then, so she was saving it for you until you were older. She never got to give it to you, but she kept it all these years, hoping one day she'd find you."

Natasha tenderly took the ring and slipped it onto the tip of her little finger. "I wish she had found me. I love it and will keep it always."

Catching Ginny's eye, Beemer nodded toward the kitchen. "I don't know about you ladies, but I'd like a good cup of coffee. Ginny, why don't you help me put the pot on to brew so Natasha can have a little time to read her mother's letters. Maybe she'd like some privacy."

Dabbing at her eyes with a tissue from her pocket, Natasha gave Beemer a weak smile. "Thank you. I'd like that."

That evening they ate dinner together at a nice Italian restaurant. "Don't forget we have an appointment at your mother's attorney's office at ten in the morning," Beemer reminded Natasha later when they were back at the house. "This has been a long day. You ladies are probably both tired so"—he winked at Ginny—"I'm going to my apartment. I'll pick you up about nine thirty."

Both Ginny and Natasha walked him to the door. He kissed each one on the cheek, said good night, and left.

"We've been so busy talking about Aunt Margaret, I'm ashamed to admit I haven't even asked you about your family," Ginny said, showing Natasha to the room Mrs. Hawkins had so recently vacated. "You mentioned great-grandchildren?"

Natasha's expression brightened. "Yes. I have four sons and four lovely daughters-in-law and six of the most beautiful, intelligent grandchildren the world has ever known, plus three equally brilliant great-grandchildren." Sobering she added, "I only wish my family could have known my mother."

Ginny sighed as she turned back the covers on the bed, remembering all the wonderful times she'd had with her aunt. "So do I, Natasha—so do I."

The attorney had the paperwork lined up on the desk when they walked into his office the next morning. After introductions he reread the same parts of the will he had read to Ginny and Beemer then explained in layman's terms exactly what it meant, even the part about the house going to Beemer and Ginny if they decided to marry.

Natasha gasped at his words. "You two are engaged?"

Beemer held up his hand. "No! Ginny and I are—good friends at this point. We—"

He seemed to be struggling for words, so Ginny explained. "This marriage thing was our aunt's idea. Since we were her only living relatives, and knowing we weren't cousins by blood, she came up with the idea of playing matchmaker and getting the two of us together."

Having apparently gathered his thoughts, Beemer jumped back in. "She asked us both to move into her house and care for her so she could die at home. She needed the help all right, but the matchmaking was the most important part of her plan."

A smile played at Natasha's lips. "Her plan didn't work?"

Ginny felt heat rise to her cheeks. "We've become good friends, and we have a great time together, but that's about it. Beemer and I—well, we've both been hurt in the past by those we thought loved us, so at this point neither of us is ready for a serious commitment." *That was an evasive, clumsy answer,* she told herself, avoiding a glance at Beemer. She hoped Natasha would let the subject drop.

"If at the end of a year Beemer and Ginny do not marry, the house will be sold and the proceeds divided equally among the three of you," Mr. Barlow told Natasha. "Your mother was quite specific as to her wishes."

After asking a few more questions and signing several papers, Ginny, Natasha and Beemer thanked Mr. Barlow and headed back to the River Road house.

Once inside, Natasha pulled a handkerchief from her purse and dabbed at her eyes. "Why would my mother be so generous with someone she barely knew? From what you've told me, and what I read in those precious letters she left me, I was probably only two or three months old when my father took me away from her."

Ginny clasped Natasha's hand in hers. "You were her baby. Her own flesh and blood. The only child she ever had. Wouldn't you feel the same way if one of your sons had disappeared when he was three months old?"

Natasha nodded. "Yes, of course I would, but one thing puzzles me. Why did my father do such a thing? From all that you've told me, and the things I've read, my mother was a wonderful person. What happened between them that made him do something so irrational? Was it her fault? His fault? I wish I knew."

"Maybe it's best if you don't know," Beemer said.

Ginned nodded. "Beemer's probably right. It all happened so long ago. They were both young and immature. People change over the years. Sometimes regretting what they did in the past, yet not knowing how to make up for it. Maybe that's what happened with them."

Natasha gazed off in the distance. "I missed so much, not having a mother."

"Your dad never married?"

Natasha looked at Beemer. "No. He raised me alone. So many times I wanted to sit him down and demand to know what really happened, but I never did. Then he developed Alzheimer's, and what past he could remember was muddled up in his mind. By the way, how did you locate him?"

Beemer explained about their attempts using the Internet. "Then my cuz suggested we try a different search engine, and there he was. Featured in an article on the Willow Creek Web site about four people celebrating their birthdays. One phone call, and here you are."

"Praise the Lord for the Internet," Ginny added. "I'd prayed and prayed we'd find you."

Natasha grabbed hold of Ginny's arm. "You're a Christian?"

Ginny nodded. "Sure am. I turned my life over to God years ago. So was Aunt Margaret. She was one of the godliest women I know."

"I am, too! I tried to lead my father to the Lord so many times, but he wouldn't have any part of it. I'm afraid he died without making his peace with God." She turned to Beemer. "I guess that means you're a Christian, too."

Ginny drew in a breath.

"Not exactly." Beemer cast a glance her way. "But I've been thinking a lot about it lately."

That's progress, Ginny thought, hoping Beemer was serious and not making small talk.

"You can't just think about it, Beemer. You have to make a decision." Natasha's voice was firm yet kind. "God wants us to come to Him, but He never forces anyone to do His will. No one can make that decision for you. I learned it the hard way."

Ginny frowned. "What do you mean?"

"I was always a good person. You know, a good wife, good mother, good and helpful friend. I couldn't believe, no matter what the Bible said, that God would keep me out of heaven if I didn't become a Christian. I'd seen people who claimed to be Christians who weren't half as good as I was. Then, when I was forty-three, I was diagnosed with breast cancer and was terrified. I suddenly realized I knew all about God, but I didn't know Him. What if, since I hadn't committed my life to Him, He didn't hear my prayers? A verse I'd learned as a child kept niggling at my brain. I couldn't remember the entire verse, but I did remember the part about His knowing His children, hearing their voice and calling them by name. As I faced the fact that I might die from my cancer, I began to see things in a different light. Almighty God created the world, He created me, and He made the rules. Who was I to defy them? Not to follow them? Even a famous ballplayer gets thrown out of the game if he doesn't follow the rules. Weren't God's rules so much more important than those?"

Ginny sneaked a peek at Beemer, fully expecting to see a disgruntled look on his face with all this talk about God. Instead his gaze was fixed on Natasha, as if he were hanging on her every word.

"I'd never thought of it that way," he finally said, still looking at Natasha. "Though my aunt and Ginny were always talking about God and why I should accept Him, no one ever explained it that way before."

Ginny felt her heart pound against her chest. Maybe there was hope for Beemer after all. This was the most interest he'd ever expressed in anything having to do with God and the Bible.

Beemer glanced at his watch. "If we're going to get you to Nashville in time for you to go through security, we'd better move along. Is your overnight bag packed?"

Natasha nodded. "Yes, it's in the front hall, but I hate to leave. There's so much I want to know about the two of you. You must come and visit me in Wyoming. I want you to meet my family and them to meet you." She grinned toward Beemer. "Maybe, if anything develops between the two of you during this year, you can come to Wyoming for your honeymoon."

Ginny, embarrassed by her words, forced a laugh. "Don't count on it. We're both pretty stuck in our ways."

Natasha smiled back. "I'll pray about it."

"I wish you lived closer. I really miss Aunt Margaret. Being with you is like having her here. The resemblance is uncanny." Beemer picked up her bag and started for the door. "We'll have to keep in touch."

Natasha touched his arm fondly. "Yes, we will. Now that we've found one another we'll have to make up for lost time. Maybe you two could come and spend Christmas with us."

Ginny looped her arm through Natasha's. "I'd love to spend Christmas with you. I'll bet Beemer would, too."

Beemer nodded as he held the front door open. "Yeah, I sure would. I've never been to Wyoming. Maybe your sons could teach me to snow ski."

"Then it's a date. Mark it on your calendars. We'll have a great time together."

Ginny's heart sang as she followed them to Beemer's truck. Though she'd lost Aunt Margaret, she still had family.

"Well, kiddo, we found her." Beemer wrapped his arm about Ginny's shoulders as they walked across the Nashville airport parking lot after seeing Natasha off.

"Aunt Margaret would be proud of us." Ginny climbed in his truck and fastened her seat belt while he rounded the front and stepped into the driver's side.

"You know, I've been thinking about what Natasha said. That woman has a good head on her shoulders." Beemer fastened his seat belt then turned the key in the ignition. "That Pastor Kenneth Peterson is a good guy. I've been thinking a lot about some of the things he said at Aunt Margaret's funeral. You know, about being ready to face eternity and accepting God on His terms. Then when Natasha explained about God making the rules, it all came together and made sense to me. You've said many of the same things, just not in the same way."

Ginny's heart leaped. Was this the beginning of the answer she'd been praying for?

They drove a few miles before he pulled the truck to the side of the road, bringing it to an abrupt stop on the shoulder. After shifting into park, he turned to face Ginny, his expression more serious than she'd ever seen it. Tilting her face toward his, he stared into her eyes. "Ginny, I'm tired of fighting the tug I've felt on my heart. I've decided it's time I accept Christ as my Savior like you and Aunt Margaret did."

Excited and about to burst with happiness, Ginny wanted so much to say something, to shout with joy, but a voice deep within seemed to tell her to keep silent, to let Beemer talk.

"Seeing the way our aunt joyfully faced death and looked forward to spending eternity in heaven touched my heart deeply. I want to be as sure as she was, so that when my time comes I'll be ready."

Her heart overflowed with delight and praise to God and the way He had used the tragedy of her aunt's death to speak to Beemer. She cupped his hand in hers and held on tight. This was the moment she'd been praying for. "One of my favorite verses is from First John. It says, 'If we confess our sins, he is faithful and just to forgive us our sins, and to cleanse us from all unrighteousness.' That says it all, Beemer. We have to have faith and trust to accept Him and His word."

"It's that simple? Do I have to confess my sins out loud?"

Ginny couldn't help but smile. "No, just in your heart. God can hear your innermost thoughts."

Shedding tears, Beemer lowered his head and, mouthing the words inaudibly, began to talk to God. Ginny watched quietly, her joy exceeded only by her expectations for his future as a Christian.

When he finished, he smiled at her, his face aglow. "Thanks, Ginny. I've needed to do that for a long time. I guess my pride kept me from it. I can't tell you how relieved I am to have things settled with God. I honestly want Him to take over and rule my life."

God, thank You, thank You, thank You! Ginny cried out within her heart.

But her enthusiasm was short-lived.

Chapter 10

A horrible thought struck her, and seeds of doubt crept in, snatching away her joy.

What if Beemer was only saying these things because he knew she'd vowed to never again have any kind of relationship with a man who didn't share her faith?

Had he actually felt God's tug on his heart, or was this all some kind of playacting? Something he could laugh about later with his groupies?

Was he only pretending to be a Christian? To have accepted the Lord? But why would he do such a thing? She was going back to St. Louis. They wouldn't be spending any time together once she was gone.

"What? Why are you looking at me that way?"

She'd been so caught up with her negative thoughts that she hadn't realized she'd been staring at him.

"Ginny, what is it? You were always talking to me about God. I thought you'd be happy I've made a decision for Christ, but your face looks anything but happy. Have I offended you in some way? If I have, I'm sorry."

Though her mind was in a quandary, she forced a big smile. "My thoughts wandered, that's all."

She didn't want to risk saying something she shouldn't and upsetting Beemer, perhaps even taking away *his* joy. So she prattled on about Natasha and her family and some of the lighter things the two of them had discussed after Beemer had gone to his apartment.

"I'm hungry, and I think my decision to live for God deserves a celebration. Why don't we go to that Chinese restaurant you like for dinner?" Beemer asked as he pulled into Aunt Margaret's driveway. "I'll go to my apartment, take a shower, and pick you up about seven. Dress up. Let's make it a fancy night."

Ginny's eyes widened. "Good idea. Dressing up will be fun."

Beemer threw back his head with a boisterous laugh. "Let's make it a real date. I'll even bring flowers."

"Umm, the last of the big spenders, huh?"

His smile narrowed. "Thanks to Aunt Margaret's generosity, I could buy you a whole carload of flowers."

She gave his hand a gentle pat. "I know. It's going to be weird having all that money. I'm used to cutting corners. With that coming my way and getting the money back my exfiancé stole from me, I guess I'll finally be able to get the larger apartment I've been wanting."

"And a van that runs better than that junk heap you drive."

Ginny pointed at him. "You think you have girlfriends now—wait'll they find out how much you're worth. You'll have your pick of the litter."

He grabbed her hand and linked his fingers through hers. "My pick of the litter, huh? What if I chose Ding Dong?"

"I'm talking about women, not cats."

"Would you believe me if I told you I don't want any of those women?"

"You'd rather settle for a mischievous kitten?"

Leaning over the console, he kissed her cheek. "No, I'd rather have you. There's nothing to keep us apart now, Ginny. I've accepted your Lord."

Ginny felt as if two dogs were battling in her heart. One saying, "Yes, he's a Christian now. Go for it!" The other one, mean and ugly and looking for a fight, saying, "Huh! Don't believe him. He'd say anything to get you where he wants you. Make you vulnerable."

Pulling her hand away, she reached for the door handle, gave it a quick turn, and slipped out of the seat. "I'll see you at seven."

Inside Aunt Margaret's house Ginny closed the door then leaned against it. "Beemer Douglas, you drive me crazy! I'm so in love with you it hurts. Yet I'm afraid to trust you!"

She barely recognized him when he appeared at the door at exactly seven. With his black suit and starched white shirt, his short hair slicked back with gel, a lovely bouquet of freshly cut flowers in his hand, he looked like an Adonis. "You're positively handsome," she told him, meaning every word. He looked great!

His gaze running from head to toe, he handed her the flowers then stepped back, letting out a low whistle. "And you are gorgeous! Is that what women call their little black dress? Whatever you call it, I like it." He touched her upswept hair with the tips of his fingers. "Wow! Is this beautiful creature really my date for the evening?"

She let a girlish giggle escape her lips. "You flatterer. No wonder women love you."

"Yeah? I'll bet the St. Louis men flock around you, and you're just too bashful and shy to tell me." He held out his hand. "Come on, Miss Universe. Let's go to dinner."

Still not convinced Beemer's profession of faith was sincere, Ginny guarded her heart as best she could. But then Beemer, without any prodding on her part, bowed his head. And in the words of a newly born Christian, he asked God to bless their food and their time together and thanked Him for their aunt's exemplary life and for leading them to Natasha. Ginny felt sure he had been born again. God had answered her prayer, and she hadn't been discerning enough to recognize the change in him and his attitude toward God.

They laughed their way through dinner, each talking about their childhood and their high school crushes. She felt like a queen as they walked across the parking lot to his truck, her hand tucked into his arm and Beemer smiling down at her.

"This has been a night to remember," Beemer told her as he walked her up the steps to their aunt's house. "I can imagine Aunt Margaret smiling down from heaven, happy to see the two of us getting along so well."

"I can just imagine she is. I really miss her. . .and always will."

He opened the door then handed her the keys. "You must be beat. Try to get a good night's rest, okay?"

She nodded. "You, too. You've done as much as I have."

His hand rested on the doorframe above her. He looked at her for a moment then lowered his face to hers. Ginny could feel his warm breath on her cheek as her heart filled with anticipation. Finally his lips sought hers, and she melted into his arms. When he released her, she felt dizzy and giddy with happiness.

"I'll stop by in the morning," he whispered softly into her hair. "Be sure to lock the door. I don't want anything happening to you."

As she gazed into his face in the moonlight, she let out a sigh of contentment. "And you be careful driving home."

He kissed her once more then backed away. "You make a great date."

She grinned. "So do you."

Ginny had a hard time falling asleep. She had to go back to St. Louis. There were no two ways about it. With what her aunt had left her, she'd have enough money so she wouldn't have to work for a number of years, but money had nothing to do with it. Her job and her accomplishments at Larsen Investments meant everything to her. They were like milestones in her life. And hadn't she been promoted? To a job she had thought would be years away in the future?

She couldn't let that much-sought-after opportunity slip through her fingers. Just because Beemer had gotten right with God and they had an attraction to each other didn't mean the two of them would end up together, as Aunt Margaret wanted them to. If they decided they wanted to spend time together, they could do it. There was no rush. It wasn't that far from St. Louis to Hendersonville. She could still drive down once a month, and Beemer could drive up there.

There was so much to do in St. Louis.

Yes, her mission in Hendersonville was over. There was no need for her to stay any longer.

Tomorrow she would go home.

She watched the hours tick by on the clock, finally falling asleep about four. By six she was wide-eyed and ready to get out of bed.

"Are you and those kitties of yours ready to go home?" she asked Tinkerbelle as the cat strode from the bathroom into her bedroom with two little kittens trying to nuzzle up to their mother's belly. "We'll have to find a nice box for the three of you to ride in."

After rummaging through the garage, she found the perfect box and lined it with several old towels she located in the back of the linen closet. "There, that should do it. Now keep those babies out of my way. I have packing to do."

By the time Beemer rapped on the door at ten, Ginny was packed and had loaded everything into her van, including the sentimental items she wanted to keep from her aunt.

"What's all that stuff in your van?" He stepped inside the house. "You're not leaving yet, are you? I figured you'd at least stay a day or two. I—I don't want you to go."

She closed the door then entered the living room. "I have to. I promised my boss I'd be back as soon as possible. I've already overstayed my time."

"But I thought—"

"You knew I had to go back, Beemer. There's nothing to keep me here now, with Aunt Margaret gone. We've already sorted through her things and given most of them away to her friends. We can't do anything about the furniture and the other things in the house for a year. You know that. My mission here is finished."

"But I was going to take you to a concert. I've heard you talk about Michael W. Smith. He's going to be in town next weekend."

Out of habit she plumped the pillows on the sofa. "The concert sounds wonderful, but I can't wait here all week for it. No, I have to go back. I've already phoned Mr. Larsen and told him I'd report for work in the morning. I'm driving back today."

Beemer slammed his fist into his palm. "Well, terrific. Now that all the crises are over, you're out of here."

The tone of his voice irritated her. Didn't he realize the importance of her job? "Beemer, I came here to care for Aunt Margaret. Now she's gone. I stayed so we could find Natasha. We found her, and she's been here and gone. There's nothing else to keep me here."

"I'm here."

"So? I like being around you. We have a great time together, but I can't stay here just because you're here. I have a life to live, too. Your life is here. Mine is in St. Louis. Everything I've worked for is there."

He grabbed her arm and turned her around to face him. "I can't let you go, Ginny. You can't leave me. I—I—"

Ginny stared at him. "You what?"

"I—I—" Still clinging to her, he gulped. "This is so hard to say. I've never said it to another woman, except the one who let me down. "I—I love you!"

She gasped. The words he'd said were the ones she had longed to hear.

"Did you hear me, Ginny? I said I love you! I don't want you to go. I want you here with me. Aunt Margaret was right. We belong together."

"I—I love you, too, but are you sure? I mean, do you really love me, or is it that you loved our aunt and you want to do what she wanted you to do?"

He gathered her up in his arms. "No, that's not it at all. I thought about this long and hard last night. In fact, I barely slept a wink. I can't let you go. You're the most important thing in my life. If you don't stay, I'll follow you to St. Louis. Please say you'll stay."

Ginny pushed away from him and threw her hands in the air. "Stay and do what, Beemer? Stay in Aunt Margaret's house, find a menial job somewhere, and share you with Mitzy, Dora, Rosie, and who knows how many others? That's not my style. With me, it's all or nothing. I'll never compromise again."

He grasped her wrist and held on when she tried to pull away. "Don't you get it, Ginny? Do I have to spell it out for you? I'm asking you to marry me! I want us to spend the rest of our lives together!"

Ginny's mouth fell open as the full significance of his words penetrated the fuzziness of her brain. Did Beemer say what she thought he said? "Marry you? Are you serious? Don't kid around, Beemer. In God's eyes, marriage is a lifetime commitment."

Beemer stepped forward, his gaze locked with hers, and pulled her into his arms, drawing her close. "Say you'll be mine, Ginny. Say you'll marry me, become my wife, and share my life with me. I'm offering you the love I've been saving for the right woman. You, my darling Ginny, are that woman. I want to love you, provide for you, protect you. I want us to live together as one, attend church together, raise a family together. Come on, Ginny—say yes. I love you."

Suddenly her job, her apartment, the promotion, all the things she'd worked for, paled into insignificance, losing their luster, their appeal that had beckoned her back to St. Louis. Beemer's change of heart was what she'd been praying for. And, praise the Lord, that change had included her. "You're sure about this?

You're really sure? If you're not, please, for both our sakes, tell me now. There's still time to back away because, if I commit to you, it will be forever."

Beemer gently brushed his lips across hers. "Ginny, with God as my witness, I love you and want to marry you. I want you to be my wife. Sweetheart, the house we both love, the house filled with wonderful memories, is waiting for us. Please say you'll share it with me until we part in death."

Reeling from his nearness, Ginny leaned into him, relishing his scent, his strength and, yes, his gentleness. She wanted so much to say yes.

Haven't I answered your prayers? a still small voice from deep inside her asked. *Hasn't Beemer turned his life over to Me? He now shares your faith. Can't you trust him? Trust Me?*

"I'm waiting, Ginny."

Ginny looked up into his gaze of love. A gaze that told her she could trust Beemer with her life, her heart, anything. Suddenly all the fear and anxiety she felt disappeared. God *had* answered her prayers. Everything she'd prayed for had happened. Was she so blinded by fear she couldn't see it?

Lovingly touching her fingertips to his cheeks, she stood on tiptoe and gazed into his eyes. "I love you, Beemer Douglas. You're everything I've ever prayed for. I know God has brought us together, and with His help I'll be the wife you deserve. Yes, I'll marry you. Whenever and wherever you say. Nothing would make me happier than becoming Mrs. Beemer Douglas and sharing this house on River Road."

His lips sought and found hers as he kissed her. "I can't tell you how happy this—"

A horrible meowing sound followed by several loud barks drove the pair outside. There, up in the same tall tree, through the covering of dense leaves, was a small cat that looked very much like Ding Dong, mewing a mournful meow, with Mortimer staring up at her, his front paws braced against the tree trunk, barking his most ferocious bark.

After reprimanding Mortimer and assessing the situation, Beemer backed away, holding his hands up defensively, his palms spread wide between himself and Ginny. "No, don't even ask. I am not going to climb that tree one more time. I refuse to rescue that stupid cat. I broke my fingers rescuing her mother. I'm not going to take a chance rescuing her. Ding Dong can just stay up there."

Ginny touched his arm and gazed up at him, tears welling in her eyes. "Please, Beemer. She's just a baby."

Beemer rolled his eyes then headed for the tree and, grabbing onto one of the lower branches, began to shinny up its trunk, holding on tightly to each branch. "If this doesn't prove my love for you, Ginny Markham, I don't know what will."

Within minutes, his arms scratched by the tree's unyielding branches, he reached the cat. "This isn't Ding Dong. It's some mangy stray!"

Shielding her eyes, Ginny called out, "It's not Ding Dong? Are you sure?"

"Ginny, of course I'm sure. Aren't I the one who took care of her while you were gone? Take it from me—this cat is not Ding Dong."

"But you are going to bring it down, aren't you? The poor thing's probably terrified. And it was your dog who chased it up there."

Beemer parted the leaves and peered down at her. "You're not serious, are you? This cat doesn't know me. She might claw me."

"Could you try?"

"Okay, for you, but if she claws me you're going to have to nurse me back to health."

She watched as he moved slowly toward the errant cat, finally taking off his shirt and throwing it over its head, wrapping the cat in its folds, rendering it helpless.

"Be careful, Beemer, please," Ginny cautioned, wishing she hadn't asked him to go up after the cat. She should have realized Ding Dong was much too small even to think about climbing a tree that size. "I don't want anything to happen to you."

Parting the branches again, he smiled down at her. "Now you tell me."

A few seconds later he reached the ground, safe and sound, sporting only the few scratches from the tree's branches. Unwrapping his shirt from around the cat, he turned it loose. They stood and watched as it scampered away and disappeared into a neighbor's yard.

Beemer brushed his hands against his pant legs. "Hope that mangy cat appreciated my efforts. I should have realized it wasn't Ding Dong. Tinkerbelle would never let her baby out of her sight."

Wrapping her arms around Beemer's waist, Ginny pressed her head against his broad chest and gave him a big hug. "My hero!"

He gazed down at her. "Hero? I like that."

Reaching up and linking her fingers behind his neck, Ginny kissed him. "You'll always be my hero, Beemer. Whether you're rescuing a cat from the top of a tree or lovingly cradling one of our children in your arms."

Together they walked back into the house on River Road, the house they would live in when they became husband and wife.

"I love you, Ginny. I hope you'll always remember that."

Ginny smiled up at him. "I love you, too."

"Do you think we'd ever have gotten together if it hadn't been for Aunt Margaret and her conniving?"

Ginny nestled her cheek against his. "I'm sure of it. I think God created us for one another. Aunt Margaret's part was to bring us together."

"I'm sure glad she listened to Him."

"Me, too."

Epilogue

Dressed in a beautiful gown of snowy white satin, Ginny stood at the altar, her fingers twined with Beemer's, listening as he pledged his life to her. Never had she been so happy.

Pastor Peterson nodded toward Ginny. "Ginny, would you say your vows to Beemer?"

For that moment Ginny nearly forgot about the church filled with friends and well-wishers. Nothing was on her mind except the fact that Beemer, the man she loved and adored, was standing beside her and within minutes they would become husband and wife. Bringing her hands up to capture his face, she gazed into his eyes. "Beemer, my friend, my love, my hero. I pledge you my life, my admiration, my worldly goods, my love, everything I am or ever will become. You are the personification of all I've ever desired or could ever want in a husband. You're caring, gentle, yet manly. You treat me like a lady, always putting my needs before your own. Most of all, you love God and have dedicated your life to Him. With God as the head of our home, and you as its spiritual leader, our marriage cannot fail. I promise to honor you, to keep myself only unto you and to love you in sickness and in health, in good times and in bad, so long as we both shall live." It wasn't part of their wedding rehearsal, but Ginny reached up anyway then and kissed Beemer with a long, loving kiss that sent chills down her spine.

Someone in the audience began to clap. Soon everyone was clapping.

Smiling, Pastor Peterson waited a few seconds then motioned the applause to cease. "This is the kind of wedding I like to perform. One where it is obvious the bride and groom truly love one another, pledging to make their marriage last a lifetime."

Turning to Beemer and Ginny, he added, "Never be embarrassed or ashamed to express the purity of your love for one another, either in private or in public. Our God is the God of love. He wants and expects us to express our love to one another and to Him. Our young people need to see husbands and wives outwardly showing their love and respect for each other, instead of the bickering and name-calling many of them see. God is not only the God of love, but He is love. Ginny and Beemer, keep your eyes centered on Him. He is the glue that will hold your marriage together. As your pastor I challenge you to say with Joshua, as for me and my house we will serve the Lord."

His chin tilted high, Beemer smiled at Pastor Peterson. "Pastor, since I've only recently accepted Christ as my Savior, I don't know much about the scriptures, but I intend to read my Bible and learn all I can. I want to be all that God wants me to be."

His eyes becoming misty, Beemer pulled Ginny close. "I'm sure I can speak for Ginny, too, when I say we are accepting your challenge. As for me and my house, I promise we will serve the Lord."

Her heart so full of love for this man that she thought she would burst with joy, Ginny smiled up at Beemer.

Thank You, Lord.

Thank You.

Thank You.

Thank You.

Secondhand Heart

Dedication

I dedicate this book to my two beloved pastors:

Jim Congdon, Topeka Bible Church, Topeka, Kansas, where my husband and I attended for many years and John Henry, Central Community Church, Wichita, Kansas, which has become my home church since Don passed away in 2004.

Both of these men have had a tremendous impact on my life, not only as a pastor but as a friend. They already know, so I'm not telling any secrets, but the ideas for many of the stories I write in my books have come directly from some comment, illustration, or truth they expressed from the pulpit. Thank you, Jim and John, for being the godly, obedient, gregarious men you are. You are each truly an example for the rest of us, and I thank God for you.

Prologue

I hate this scar!" Sammy stood in front of the hall mirror in her Denver apartment.

Her mother frowned at her daughter's reflection. "One in four people dies waiting for a donor heart. Having that scar is a small price to pay for your life. Besides, most of that redness will leave with time."

"I know, and I don't mean to complain. Words can't express how thankful I am. I'll be eternally grateful for the loving person who donated my wonderful, amazing heart, but this scar is so—ugly."

"What difference does it make, dear? Other than you and me, who else sees it?"

"No one—for now. But I'd be lying if I said I wouldn't like to get married someday." Sammy continued to stare into the mirror, her fingertips tracing the long scar that wove its way from the natural indentation in her neck down the center of her chest to an area just above her navel. "But what if, someday, I meet the man of my dreams and fall head over heels in love? Then what am I supposed to do? If I tell him about my surgery and my scar, he'll freak out. If I don't tell him and ceremoniously unveil it on our wedding night, the poor guy will probably pass out from shock. I can't win either way. I'm afraid not many men could handle it."

After filling two cups with coffee in the kitchen, her mother handed one to Sammy then shook her head. "Sweetie, aren't you being a little too self-conscious? You waited for nearly two years for that heart, and you certainly aren't the first young woman to have had a heart transplant. Others out there are just like you."

Sammy stared into the cup. "I'm sure you're right. I remember how frightened I was the first time I heard that word—transplant. To think a doctor could actually insert someone else's heart into another human being was mind-boggling, and I never thought it would happen to me." She sniffed at the coffee's delicious aroma then blew to cool it. "Face it, Mom. What man is going to want a woman who has an ugly scar like this and a life expectancy of ten years, maybe less? Most men want children. Maybe a guy could get past the medication I have to take and seeing this ugly scar every day of his life. But what man would want to live with the idea of losing his wife, knowing unless he remarried, he'd probably have to raise his children alone? Certainly no man I know."

Mrs. Samuel slipped her arm around her daughter's shoulders and gave her a hug. "You may not know a man like that now, but if God wants you to marry, He's probably already preparing some man's heart to accept you the way you are."

Sammy looked toward her apartment's small living room where the TV blared out her nephew and nieces' favorite cartoon. "But what about these precious children, Mom? Even if a man could circumvent the heart thing, what about them? They're a part of me, at least until their mother comes back for them. Any man who would accept me would also have to accept these children who are living with me."

"Oh, honey, have faith. God will give you the understanding and strength you need. In the meantime, we have to pray your sister will wake up, realize what she is missing, and come back for them."

"I feel so inadequate. Other than the books I read, I know practically nothing about parenting. I may be feeling my way along as I go, but I'm doing the best I can. Honest I am."

"You're doing a wonderful job. You have more patience with those children than I had with you and your sister."

Sammy gazed at her silver-haired mother. Though the events of the past few years had aged her, to Sammy she was still beautiful. "I'm glad she left them with me instead of expecting you and Dad to care for them. With his poor health and your having to work to make up for the loss of his income, the two of you could never have taken them in. And I couldn't have made it these last few months since my surgery if you and Daddy hadn't offered to come to Denver and stay with me."

Her mother settled back in the chair with a sigh, folding her hands in her lap. "I wish we could have done more."

"You've already done more than you should. It breaks my heart to think Tawanda would desert Simon, Tina, and Harley as she did, especially since she was aware of my heart problem. But I'm sure she knew you and Dad would jump in and help me."

Tears misted over her mother's eyes. "I thought for sure she'd only be gone a couple of weeks and then come back."

"I can't imagine a woman leaving her children for any reason, especially some motorcycle-riding, tobacco-chewing, jobless guy, just because he paid her a little attention."

"I don't know where your father and I went wrong with your sister."

Sammy gave her mother's shoulder an appreciative squeeze. "You and Dad were the best parents ever. It was Tawanda who went wrong."

"Even though they drive your father crazy and his nerves are frazzled, we've enjoyed being here with you and our grandchildren. His declining health has really taken its toll. I've worried about him. He seems to be getting weaker every day. I'm afraid it's time to take him home."

"I know, and it makes me cry to see him this way. He's always been so strong. I'm sure the six of us being cramped up in my tiny apartment hasn't helped." Sammy gestured toward a photo magnet on her refrigerator. "Sad, isn't it? I doubt little Harley would remember her mom if she walked in that front door. What kind of mother would name her sweet baby girl after her boyfriend's motorcycle?"

Mrs. Samuel shook her head. "At least she didn't choose Gold Wing as her middle name. I love Tawanda as much as I love you, but her actions and her uncaring attitude break my heart. Only the Lord can bring her to her senses. We just have to keep praying for her."

Sammy nodded, well remembering the day her sister left and the trauma it had brought. "I pray for her constantly, Mom. I love these children, and I know they love me, but like most kids, they want their mom. I enjoy having them here and would be happy to keep them always, but they're *her* children. It'd be just like Tawanda to turn up unannounced on my doorstep, ready to waltz right back into their lives, expecting them to go with her as if nothing ever happened. As much as I'd like to see her little family reunited, I couldn't stand the idea of seeing them uprooted and hurt again."

"Then there's the other side of the coin, Sammy. What if Tawanda never comes back after them? Are you prepared to care for them until they're old enough to be out on their own? Honey, I think you need to face the fact that your sister was never cut out for motherhood. I hate to say it, but I suspect each of those darlings was the product of an evening of nothing more than lust and carelessness."

Sammy let out a deep sigh. "I've thought that, too. I feel sorry for my sister and try to keep her memory alive by talking about her and showing her pictures to the children so they'll remember her, but how can I explain her absence to them? The lack of phone calls and letters? She has no idea how much she's giving up by not being with these amazing children."

"They're amazing because of you, Sammy, and the love and care you've given them since she left. Good thing you thought to get her to sign temporary custody over to you so you'd have the power to take care of any emergencies that came up." Mrs. Samuel took Sammy's hand and gave it a gentle squeeze. "When your heart doctor gives you your final release, sweetie, why don't you come back to Nashville to live? We have excellent doctors there. I know you're happy living here in Denver and you like your job, but you're still recuperating and will be for a while. You need help. I'd like to stay in Denver and continue to care for you and the children, but your father needs to be back in his own home and near his doctors. And I can't expect my boss to hold my job much longer."

Sammy drank the last of her coffee, making a face when she realized it had turned cold. "Your offer is tempting."

"It's going to be some time before you'll be operating at full speed. If you come back to Nashville, I can continue to help you and the children until you're able to take on a new job. There's plenty of room in that big old house for all of us. You and the kids can have the entire second floor. Moving back would be better for everyone."

Sammy sent another glance toward the living room. "But if I quit my job here, how will I support myself and the children? Their mother hasn't sent a penny since she's been gone. If Uncle Mort hadn't put Tawanda's and my names on that insurance policy, I don't know what I would have done, but that money isn't going to last forever."

Mrs. Samuel rose and filled their cups. "Well, getting a job in Nashville shouldn't be too difficult for you, not with your exemplary employment record. Dozens of companies could use a good customer service director. With your experience and the kind of references your boss would give you, I'm sure you'll have no trouble finding a job when you're ready to take one on. Meantime, your dad and I can help with finances. I've been saving what Mort left me for a rainy day. I can't think of a better way to spend that money."

Sammy thoughtfully twisted a lock of hair around her finger. "It would be nice to live closer to you and Dad and to get back to my home church."

Mrs. Samuel smiled at her daughter. "Then it's settled. Your father and I will go home this week. But as soon as the doctor gives you the okay, I'll fly back to help you pack up, and we'll all head for Nashville. Agreed?"

Sammy pondered her question before answering. Moving back to Nashville would be the best solution for everyone, but did she really want to move back? Give up her apartment, the Denver church where she worshipped, and the job she loved and had worked so hard to get?

Raising her brow in question, her mother gave her a gentle nudge. "Say yes, dear. It's the best answer for everyone."

A job and an apartment are just things, Sammy reasoned as she considered her options. *Being with those you love is what's important. And even though I love my church here in Denver, I love my home church in Nashville even more. Once the children get used to it, they'll love it, too.* "You're right, Mom. Moving back is the best answer. With all that's happening in our lives now, the children and I need to be nearer you and Dad. God has given me the awesome privilege and responsibility of taking care of Simon, Tina, and Harley by making sure they are loved and have a solid Christian upbringing. It's my mission in life, my God-appointed mission."

A sudden peace came over her as she lifted her face and gazed into her mother's eyes. "But if I go, you have to promise not to baby me like I'm an invalid, and I don't want to have to discuss my operation or my new heart with anyone. The less said about it, the better. I want to get over this thing as soon as possible and get on with my life, whatever may be left of it. I don't want anyone feeling sorry for me."

Her mother smiled and raised her right hand. "I promise."

Sammy felt a slight tug on her shirt. "Well, hi, little sweetheart. Did you have a good nap?"

Tina grinned up at her. "Yes, Mommy."

Kneeling beside the child, Sammy wrapped an arm about her tiny waist. "You mustn't call me Mommy, sweetie. I'm your aunt." She bobbed her head toward the shelf above the gas fireplace. "Mom, would you please hand me Tawanda's picture?"

Once she had the photograph in hand, she pointed to the image of her sister's face. "See, that's your mommy. She's beautiful just like you."

Tina gave her a puzzled look. "But why can't I call you mommy? My friend Lacy calls the lady she lives with Mommy."

"That's because that lady *is* her mommy. Your mommy is away for a while, that's all—but she's still your mommy."

"Where is she? Why isn't she here with me the way Lacy's mommy is with her?"

The wide-eyed innocent look on Tina's face ripped at Sammy's heart. "I don't know exactly where she is at this moment, but we have to keep praying for her that God will bring her back to us, safely and as soon as possible."

Tina lowered her lip in a pout. "I want you to be my mommy."

"I'd like to be your mommy, but you already have a mommy. And you know what? You look very much like her."

Tina glanced at the picture. "But I don't want that mommy. She never comes to see me. I want you."

Sammy pulled the irresistible child onto her lap, lovingly brushing a curl from her forehead. "Please try to understand, precious. Mommy is busy right now. I have an idea. Why don't you draw a picture for her? Then, when she sends us her address, I'll mail it to her." She leaned toward the coffee table, picked up the tin of crayons she kept there for the children, and handed them to Tina. "Maybe when Harley wakes up, she'd like to draw a picture for your mother, too."

Tina showed little enthusiasm, but she took the crayons, scooted off Sammy's lap, and padded toward the bedroom.

Sammy's mother sat down beside her and took her hand, giving it an affectionate squeeze. "I'd say you handled that just fine."

"I hope so, Mom. I want the children to think well of their mother, but it's hard when she never writes or calls them. I couldn't even give Tina a straight answer when she asked where her mother was."

"God knows where she is, sweetie. We have to give Tawanda over into His hands. She's out of our reach."

"I know, Mom. I know."

Chapter 1

Three years later

S ammy spotted a couple of empty chairs next to the railing at the far end of the upper deck of Nashville's famous *General Jackson* riverboat. She made her way toward them and seated herself, closing her eyes and lifting her face to the sun. What a glorious day it was, and she had it all to herself. "Don't worry about anything, Sammy," her mother had told her when she'd arrived at her apartment that morning to care for the children. "They'll be fine. Just enjoy yourself. You deserve a break."

Sammy adjusted her sunglasses then smiled. *I don't know about deserving a break, but it is nice to have an entire day to myself.*

Her smile disappeared. She hadn't heard from her sister in nearly a year, and then it was only a postcard. For all she knew, Tawanda could have disappeared off the face of the earth. She wondered if the man she'd left with was treating her well. It seemed every man Tawanda had ever dated had been an abuser of some sort, by either taking everything he could get from her or tiring quickly of her company and shoving her around, blacking her eyes, or doing even worse.

Nearly four years since his mother disappeared, Simon still talked about some of those beatings. Cowering in the closet and frightened out of their wits, he and Tina had witnessed many of them, and those experiences had left emotional scars on them both, especially Simon. Being the oldest, he remembered things more vividly than Tina. Fortunately, since Harley had been a baby, Sammy was sure she wouldn't remember and have the emotional baggage to carry around the rest of her life as her siblings would.

"This seat taken?"

Startled by the voice, she sat up straight and opened her eyes, shielding them from the morning sun, which made her intruder nothing more than a dark profile against its glare. "No, I don't think so." She'd hoped no one would decide to sit in that chair. It would have been nice to be alone for a change. To someone whose life was filled with work, kids, doctor appointments, and church activities, the solitude had sounded inviting. "At least no one was sitting there when I came up here."

The man moved past her and placed his soft-drink cup on the small table between them before sitting down. "The music got a little loud down there." He gestured toward the stairs leading to the lower deck. "I enjoy music, but my ears can take only so much of it at those decibels."

"I know exactly what you mean. It was loud for me, too."

"Have you done this riverboat thing before?"

For the first time since he'd become a full-fledged person and not a silhouette against the sun, she looked up into his face. "No. Even though I've lived in Nashville most of my life, this is my first time." Glancing sideways while trying not to be too obvious, she sized him up. Tall, but not too tall. Nearly average build, but muscular enough to look as if he worked out. Well-coordinated shirt and trousers, better than most guys his age. Maybe his mom helped him pick out his clothes.

He pulled his sunglasses from his pocket and slipped them on. "First time for me, too."

Her next glance went to where she usually looked when meeting a man for the first time, though she didn't know why. Habit probably. No wedding ring, but that didn't mean anything. Some men never wore a ring, even if they were married. What difference did it make anyway? The guy was only looking for an empty chair. She leaned her head back against the tall deck chair and closed her eyes again.

"You like country western?"

So much for closing her eyes! She'd hoped shutting them would put an end to their conversation. "Music?"

He grinned, causing the indentation in his chin to show prominently. "Yeah, music. I like most of it, but the guys where I work play it constantly. I get a little tired of it, especially the songs where some gal is moaning because her boyfriend is two-timing her or vice versa. I like the more toe-tapping ones. What kind do you like?"

"I can't remember the title, but my favorite country song is the one about a truck driver out on the road, thinking about his family and how he loves his wife and children and wishes he were home with them. Not many songs like that." *What's the matter with me? I should have simply nodded and kept quiet. I didn't have to give him a full answer.*

A smile brightened his handsome face. "I know exactly the song you mean. It's one of my favorites, too." He picked up the plastic drink cup he'd brought with him to the upper deck. "Would you like a cold drink? Ah—I don't know your name, and I hate to call you 'hey-you.'"

Not sure she wanted to share such personal information with a stranger,

Sammy tugged her collar up closer about her neck and paused before answering. She decided it wouldn't hurt to let him know the nickname her parents and friends called her instead of Rosalinda, her real first name. She gave him a guarded smile. "My friends call me Sammy."

He stuck out his hand. "Hi, Sammy. I'm Ted. Now what will it be? Iced tea? Lemonade? What? I need to go after a refill anyway."

"Iced tea will be fine, thank you. Unsweetened."

His face contorted into a playful frown. "You're a Southerner, and you want unsweetened tea? Didn't your mama teach you better than that? I thought all Southern ladies drank sweet tea."

She shrugged. "Guess Mom failed in her duty. I've never liked sweet tea."

He rose and gave her a teasing wink. "Unsweetened it is. I'll be right back. Save my seat."

She watched as he crossed the deck and disappeared down the stairwell. Ted. What a nice old-fashioned name. She hadn't met anyone named Ted since Ted Maxwell sat behind her in the fourth grade. But, nice or not, she would have preferred spending the rest of the day alone. Oh, well. He'd leave after a while. Surely he hadn't come alone. His friends were probably on the lower deck. She'd barely settled back in her chair when he returned, carrying two glasses of tea.

"Unsweetened for you. Sweet for me. Can't help it. I'm a typical Southerner."

She thanked him then took a long sip of the cool drink. It tasted good. She hadn't realized she was so thirsty.

"Hope I didn't take your boyfriend's seat."

Sammy nearly choked. "I'm here alone."

He gaped at her. "Alone? Really? A pretty woman like you? That's hard to believe."

Embarrassed at having admitted such a personal thing, Sammy felt a flush rise to her cheeks. "Yes, really. Believe it or not, some people enjoy doing things alone."

He lifted his hands in surrender. "Sorry. I guess my question sounded a bit flippant. It's just that you're so—beautiful—well, I figured some lucky man had escorted you here. Actually"—he paused with a bashful grin—"I came alone, too."

As good-looking and well mannered as he was, Sammy found his statement hard to believe, too.

"Someone gave me two tickets. My buddy was supposed to come with me, but he had to cancel at the last minute. I almost didn't come but then decided, why not? I was off today and had nothing better to do, and I love being out on the river."

Without responding, after taking another sip of tea, Sammy leaned her head back again.

"Actually I was kinda glad for a chance to spend the day alone. I moved into my new apartment about six months ago and was enjoying it until I invited my older brother, his wife, and their kids to move in with me while he looks for a job. The company he worked for in Miami is downsizing, and he got the ax. The two weeks they originally said they'd be staying with me have turned into six weeks. I hate to say it, but those kids are driving me up the wall. I used to think I'd like to get married and have a houseful of them; now I'm not so sure."

Sammy wanted to speak up in defense of growing children and their sometimes loud, unruly exuberance for life but decided not to. The last thing she wanted was to get into a conversation about childrearing, which would inevitably lead to having to explain that her sister had abandoned her children. She simply nodded.

"I had no business saying those things about my nephews. The kids aren't to blame. My brother and his wife believe in permissiveness. You know, without discipline, ground rules, penalties for misbehavior, the whole enchilada."

Sammy nodded. "I think every child needs parameters. It gives them a feeling of security."

He wagged his head approvingly. "Like a lot of guys my age, I've filled my apartment with all sorts of electronic gadgets. The first thing I did after I offered to let them stay with me was to make space for all my computer stuff in my room and put a lock on my door. I figured that would save a lot of hassles. I even bought a used computer from a friend, set it up in the living room and let them have at it, which made them happy and kept me happy, too. Unfortunately, one of them wiped the hard drive clean the first day. But good ol' Uncle Ted reloaded everything, and they were back in business within minutes."

"Adding that used computer sounds like a great idea."

He nodded. "Yeah, it's worked out well and keeps them occupied. Don't get me wrong. I'm glad to help my brother out. . . . But enough about me." Smiling and tilting his head toward her, he lifted his brow. "Other than going on riverboat cruises alone, what else do you do for fun, Sammy?"

"Me? Work. Go to church. Teach a Sunday school class." She almost added she was the temporary custodian of three children but decided not to mention it.

"What's your job?"

She gave her mock turtleneck collar another tug. "I'm the customer service manager for a large national company."

"I'll bet you're good at it."

"I like to think so. How about you?"

"Fireman. At one of the smaller neighborhood fire stations. You know. On one day, off two. Today is one of my days off."

About to melt under the sun's rays, Sammy took off her jacket and draped it over the back of her chair. "It'd be nice to have two days off every third day like that. You like being a fireman?"

"Yep, wouldn't want to be anything else."

She could tell by his smile he meant it. "It's nice when people enjoy their jobs. I love my job, too, though I have to deal with many disgruntled people. Sounds crazy, but I actually enjoy working out their problems for them. It's a challenge."

"Do you ever have any customers who are simply impossible to work with?"

"I wish I could say no, but we're highly trained and know what to do, what not to do, and how to do what we can. That helps. After you've been there as long as I have, your reactions become second nature."

The loudspeaker crackled, and then a heavy male voice announced, "The luncheon buffet is now being served on the main deck."

Ted rose and extended his hand. "Wanna humor a lonely guy and have lunch with him? I hate eating alone."

Sammy's grip tightened on her tea glass.

"Oh, come on. I'm harmless. Besides, there are a lot of people on board to protect you."

"Maybe it wouldn't—"

Lowering his hand, he backed away. "You don't have to explain. It's okay. I understand. You don't know me. If I were a woman I'd probably say no, too. It's been nice meeting you, Sammy. Enjoy the rest of your day." Spinning around on his heel, he moved in line with the others who were making their way down the stairs leading to the lower deck.

Sammy watched him go, wishing she'd accepted his invitation. Surprising herself, she leaped out of the chair and made her way to join him, breathlessly telling him, "If the invitation still stands, I'd love to have lunch with you."

Grinning, he motioned for her to step in front of him. "You bet it still stands. Thanks for changing your mind. You really deflated my ego. No one likes to be rejected."

"I wasn't rejecting you."

His grin widened. "I know. I'm just teasing, but I am glad you changed your mind."

They made their way through the abundant buffet line, taking small samples of nearly everything and laughing about the silly face the chef had carved into a watermelon, and then climbed the stairs to the upper deck.

"Ah, our seats are still there." Ted nodded toward the places they had temporarily vacated. "I guess when folks saw your jacket draped over the chair, they thought it'd been left there to save it."

Sammy's eyes widened. "I did leave my jacket. Where was my brain?"

He gave her a sheepish grin. "It was busy thinking up reasons you shouldn't have lunch with me."

She rolled her eyes. "No, it wasn't."

"Oh, yes, it was. Admit it."

"Okay, I'll admit, it did seem a bit awkward for me to have lunch with a man I'd just met. Satisfied?"

They enjoyed their lunch while discussing calories, carbohydrates, polyunsaturated fats, and other topics, laughing and talking like two old friends.

"Sit right there, and I'll go get us two big wedges of cheesecake." Ted stood. "Want strawberries or blueberries on yours?"

"Um, strawberries, but you don't have to get it for me."

"I want to get it for you. Not every day I have the privilege of serving such a lovely Southern lady."

"Even if she doesn't drink sweet tea?"

"Even then."

He was back in a flash as promised, with two large wedges of cheesecake topped with fresh strawberries. "One for you, madam, and one for me."

Sammy stared at the huge piece of cheesecake. "I could never eat that much cheesecake, even on an empty stomach. I'm already full. That's the biggest lunch I've eaten in a long time."

"Eat what you can. It really looks tasty."

Tasty? Wasn't that an old-fashioned term? Her father was the only man she knew who used that word to describe the foods he liked. She took the plate from his hand and sampled the delicious-looking concoction. "Oh, my. Just what I was afraid of. It's marvelous."

"I figured it would be. Now aren't you glad you tried it?"

Sammy licked at her lips. "Promise you'll stop me if I try to eat the whole thing?"

He raised his brow. "Me, stop you? No way. You're on your own. Me? I intend to eat every bite, every tiny morsel. This is a real treat. I'm used to cupcakes, cookies, and other things out of a package. Sara Lee and I get along real well in the kitchen. If it weren't for her frozen foods at the supermarket and the cooking the guys do at the fire station, I'd die of starvation."

Sammy ate until she could eat no more, then placed her fork on her plate. "I'm stuffed, Ted, and every bite of this fantastic lunch is going to show up on my hips." She realized it was the first time she'd called him by name. Did that mean she was finally comfortable with him? But as nice as he was, who wouldn't feel comfortable with him?

"But worth it, right?"

She rubbed at her tummy and let out a sigh. "Absolutely."

"We'll be getting off in an hour or so. Want to take a spin around the deck to walk off some of our lunch? I'd like to step out on the back of the lower deck and watch that big paddle wheel go around. This boat is amazing. Makes you think how different life must have been years ago when the river was filled with paddle wheelers."

Sammy had to admit she was tired of sitting in the same place so long, and what harm could a walk around the boat do? "Sure, a walk would be nice." After slinging her purse strap over her shoulder, she stood. "Lead the way."

The two strolled leisurely around the deck, talking about the intense growth of trees and the cabins along the shore-line, pausing now and then to watch a bird soar overhead. Eventually they walked down the staircase and out onto the lower deck, ending up leaning on the railing that separated them from the gigantic paddle wheel. They enjoyed the fine mist kicked up by its movement and listened to its rhythmic *swish, swish* as it rotated on its huge axis.

"I can't tell you how much I've enjoyed this day, Sammy," Ted shouted over the loud noise as the wheel whapped against the water. "I'm glad I didn't cancel when my buddy couldn't come."

"I've enjoyed it, too." And she had. More than she cared to admit. How long had it been since she'd carried on a conversation with a man, other than her father and a few male acquaintances at her church? It'd been nice talking with Ted. No commitments. No need to put on a façade. No reason to have to explain about her nieces and nephew being in her care. Thanks to him, it had been a lovely, refreshing day. One she would remember for a long time.

"We're pulling into the dock," the heavy male voice boomed out over the loudspeakers. "For your safety, please remain on board until the boat is secured to its moorings and the gangway lowered. Thank you for spending the day with us on Nashville's famous *General Jackson*. We hope you've had a good time and will come and visit us again soon."

"Bummer. Looks like our boat ride is coming to an end." Ted cradled his hand about her elbow and nudged her toward the crowd assembling at the exit gate.

"Looks that way. I've really enjoyed it. It's been a great day."

"Ted! I didn't know you were on this boat."

The couple turned to take note of a man several yards behind them, waving and wearing a broad smile.

"Pete, hey—I didn't know you were on here either."

Letting go of her arm, Ted made his way back to the man whom Sammy assumed to be a close friend and gave his hand a hearty shake.

Grasping Ted's arm, the man tugged him toward several other passengers. "I want you to meet my fiancée, Carla; my mother, Gladys; my dad, Robert—"

"Move along, folks," the crewman standing near the exit gate told the crowd in a friendly manner, motioning to the gangway. "For your safety and the safety of those near you, be sure to use the handrail."

The passengers around Sammy eased their way forward, moving her along with them. She glanced back at Ted. Finding him engaged in deep conversation with his friend's family, she stepped onto the gangway with the others and then onto the dock. When she turned and looked back at the departing crowd, Ted wasn't among them. He was still visiting with his friends, apparently oblivious to the fact that she wasn't still waiting for him and they hadn't said a proper good-bye. But what difference did it make? Why should he be concerned whether she'd waited or not? They'd never see each other again. They'd simply been two strangers who had spent a pleasant few hours together. That was all. But she had hoped he would leave his friends, catch up with her, and at least say good-bye.

Pushing aside her disappointment, she edged along the narrow dock and headed toward her car. Her day with Ted had been a good one, exactly what she'd needed to give her self-confidence a much-needed kick start. But the day was over, never to be repeated. She'd go her way and he'd go his, and life would move on.

Ted the fireman, one of the nicest men she'd ever met, would be just a pleasant memory.

Chapter 2

Ted had hoped to see Sammy waiting for him when he excused himself and left his friend's family, but she was nowhere in sight. Most of the passengers had disembarked and were heading across the dock to the parking lot. *You're an idiot*, he told himself as he trudged down the gangway. *You spent most of the day with one of the nicest and prettiest women you've ever met, and you didn't even get her last name. Dumb. Dumb. Dumb.*

He'd nearly reached the landing when a thought occurred to him. Sammy had draped her jacket over a chair. Had she picked it up before they left the upper deck? He couldn't remember if she had. Turning quickly, just as the deckhand prepared to fasten the chain across the open section of the railing, he explained about her jacket, located the rear stairs, and hurried to the upper deck. Sure enough, there it was, exactly where she'd left it.

Now what? He had no address or phone number, no way to return it to her. As he lifted it from the chair, an idea struck him. Rushing back to the main deck, he thanked the deckhand, exited down the gangway, and headed toward the boat's ticket office.

"My friend left her jacket on the boat and will probably be calling about it." Picking up a pen that was lying on the counter, he wrote the word *Ted* and his phone number on a nearby scratch pad. "Her name is Sammy. Just tell her Ted has it and to give me a call, and I'll bring it by her apartment."

A slight frown creased the woman's brow. "You sure you don't want to leave it here? We have a lost-and-found box."

"Naw. It'll be a lot easier if I deliver it, rather than have her drive all the way back here."

"Why don't you just call her yourself?" She gestured toward the phone on the wall.

Clinging tightly to the jacket, he shook his head. "I doubt she's home yet. When she calls, just tell her I have her jacket." No way was he going to leave it behind. That jacket was his only link to Sammy.

After pulling a piece of transparent tape from its dispenser, the woman taped the information he'd given her on the wall next to the phone. "There you go. If she calls, I'll give her your message."

From time to time, Ted glanced at the jacket lying beside him in the front seat as he drove back to his apartment, grateful Sammy hadn't remembered to take it with her. When he reached home, he hung it carefully in his entry closet, smoothing out the sleeves to avoid wrinkles. It smelled pleasant. Like freshly cut flowers on a spring day. The fragrance hadn't overwhelmed him like the perfume of some of the women he'd dated, but he'd noticed it the moment he sat down beside her on the boat. It was one of the nicest fragrances he'd ever smelled. In fact, everything about her was nice.

There were no two ways about it.

He had to find Sammy, his mystery woman.

He should have gotten her last name.

He worked until dark, helping his brother change the oil in his car then ran the washer and dryer, folding several loads of laundry. Next, since it was nearly impossible to avoid the endless array of questions from his nephews, he closed himself in his room, going through the stack of mail that had accumulated all week, doing anything he could to avoid thinking of Sammy.

Ted checked his phone at least once an hour to make sure it was working properly, but no call came from Sammy. Try as he may, though, even without her call, he couldn't get her off his mind. Something about that woman had drawn him to her the moment he'd sat down beside her on the paddle wheeler. Had it been her reserved attitude? Her reluctance to talk to a stranger?

Though he himself was shy by nature, his occupation as a fireman attracted women to him whether he showed any interest in them or not. Something about a man in uniform, whether military or civilian, seemed to have universal appeal to women. He grinned as he thought about it. Most of his single coworkers laughed about that well-known fact and bragged about how they'd used their uniform to its best advantage whenever they were around a woman they'd like to meet.

"We're their protectors," one of the guys on his shift had told him. "They trust us. We're the guys who come to their rescue when they're in need. If I'm in uniform and I see an attractive woman, all I have to do is give her a smile and she's mine."

With an exaggerated chuckle, Ted had poked his finger into the man's slightly pudgy stomach. "Even with that gut of yours?"

His coworker protruded his stomach out even further. "Yep, even with this, but when she gets a load of these biceps"—he paused long enough to strike a muscleman pose—"she forgets all about the gut."

Ted sobered. Unfortunately, what the man had said was true. He'd seen it too often. Women *did* gravitate to men in uniform, especially firemen, law-enforcement officers, and pilots. Spending twenty-four-hour shifts at the firehouse, he and his buddies had plenty of time for talking, and talk they did.

Though he often figured much of what they said was nothing *but* talk, exaggerated to impress one another, some of it was probably true. A high percentage of the men he worked with had been divorced at least once, some several times.

Some of their conversations were a little on the shady side, but most were okay, and since he wanted to fit in, he participated with exuberance when he could. He could hold his own with the best of them when it came to sports, cars, motorcycles, world events, and other topics of general appeal, but not when it came to women. As far as he was concerned, that subject was taboo. He hated it when men bragged about their conquests and discussed things that were too personal even to mention. Times like that, he quietly slipped away and went to his bunk to read.

By the time Ted turned in at half past eleven, he still hadn't heard from Sammy.

Maybe he never would.

He had barely crawled into bed and switched off the light when he heard a crash from somewhere in his apartment. Jumping up, he rushed out into the living room to find the lamp from the credenza shattered into a million pieces. "What happened?" he asked his sister-in-law who was standing there in her robe with some sort of green goop on her face.

"Both Robbie and Billy were having trouble going to sleep, so I told them they could watch TV for a while," she explained, cuddling her eight- and ten-year-olds to her side. "I guess your lamp got bumped somehow."

Ted stared at her in disbelief. "Bumped? How? It was clear on the other side of the room."

"Billy was running around the room messing with the remote control, so I threw a pillow at him," Robbie explained, pointing at his brother. "I guess it hit your lamp."

Ted shook his head. "That lamp was inexpensive and can be replaced, but you boys shouldn't have been throwing pillows in the living room."

"And you shouldn't talk to my boys that way," his gooped-up sister-in-law railed at him, scowling and grabbing hold of Robbie's hand. "It was an accident."

Ted felt his dander rise. "Accident? You call throwing pillows in a living room at midnight an accident? If they wanted to roughhouse, they should have waited till tomorrow and taken it outside. That's what my parents always told me."

Her eyes narrowing, she glared at him. "Maybe that's the reason you and your brother are so messed up. Your parents never let you play like normal children."

"Us, messed up? Since my brother has been married to you, he's changed from a happy-go-lucky, carefree guy to an introverted scarecrow of a man who rarely speaks."

"What do you know about marriage? You can't even find a wife!" she flung back.

If Ted hadn't been so upset with the woman, he might have laughed. Standing in the middle of his living room in his pajamas and her in her tattered robe with that green stuff smeared all over her angry face made him think of a cartoon he'd once seen. He sucked in a breath and faced her again, this time his voice soft and low. "Look, Wilma—I'm sorry for what I said. I know it's hard on all of you with Albert out of a job and having to move in here with me, but it's hard on me, too. Since I've been out on my own, I've never lived with anyone else. Having your family here is an adjustment for me, as well."

Wilma turned in a huff, dragging her sons toward the bedroom they shared. "We'll find another place to live," she called out over her shoulder, her voice continuing to hold its angry edge. "And don't worry about your precious lamp. As soon as Albert gets a job, we'll pay you for it."

"Forget it. It was only a lamp, an object for supplying light. I shouldn't have gotten so upset about it."

As he crouched, grabbed the wastebasket from under his desk, and began to pick up the remains of the lamp, his thoughts went to the lovely, soft-spoken woman with whom he'd spent the day. And he wondered, if he were married to her, or someone like her, would life be wedded bliss? Or, in time, would it, too, lose its luster and turn as sour as his brother's marriage seemed to be?

∞

Since her mother had volunteered to keep the children overnight, Sammy decided to take advantage of the time by playing the CDs a friend from her church had loaned her and doing some much-needed cleaning in the kitchen. But as she listened to a Southern gospel artist sing her favorite songs, visions of the handsome man she'd met on the riverboat filled her thoughts. Why hadn't she asked his last name? Or given him hers? Not that it would make any difference. He probably had no further interest in her anyway, and she'd never go after a man, no matter how nice he seemed, even if he shared her faith. It wasn't her style. She might have done something that gutsy when she was younger, before it became obvious her heart wasn't going to last much longer, but not now. Especially not now.

Now, as far as she was concerned, she was damaged goods, and very few men would want her if they knew. It was a subject she'd rarely discussed with anyone. She'd warned her friends that talking about her heart transplant was forbidden. The last thing she wanted was to be pitied, pampered, and looked at as an invalid who needed special attention. Her deepest desire was to live a healthy life, as normal as possible, for whatever days God allotted her before taking her home to be with Him.

It would be nice to see Ted again, though. We had such a great time together. But I have to face reality. Having a good time with him doesn't give me reason to believe our newfound friendship could develop into something more serious. She pulled a can of cleanser from beneath the sink and began scrubbing at the rust stains around the drain. *But maybe, if I could find him again, the two of us could simply be good friends. Spend time together. A lot of relationships never get past the friendship stage. Isn't that the purpose of dating? To get to know a person before a real relationship develops?*

Her thoughts sounded reasonable and would maybe work with someone else, but she might as well forget about their working for her. The likelihood of the two of them running into each other, even in a city Nashville's size, was pretty slim. *There might be a way, though.* She smiled to herself. *Maybe I could set my apartment on fire, and he'd be one of the firemen to respond.*

"I should be so lucky," she reminded herself aloud with a giggle. "With all the fire stations in town and Ted working only one out of every three days, the odds he'd be one of the responders are definitely not in my favor."

Sammy mentally pictured Ted dressed in his uniform, fire extinguisher in hand, rushing into her apartment to put out the fire and rescue her. "I have to forget about that man. Even if I could find him and he was as interested in spending time with me as I am with him, he'd be repelled by this scar on my chest. Besides, he'd be freaked out to discover the remainder of my life span may be no more than that of a Labrador retriever, not to mention the three children living with me. Hadn't he mentioned his brother's kids drove him crazy and made him decide he didn't want kids?"

As she always did when she felt frustrated and needed to talk to someone about it, Sammy lifted her face heavenward. *Father, it looks as if I already have three strikes against me, and I'm not even up to bat yet! Help!*

Pulling the stopper from the sink, Sammy watched her dreams disappear as they circled down the drain with the bubbles.

Chapter 3

Sammy's mother arrived at nine the next morning with all three children showered, dressed, and ready for Sunday school. "They were little darlings," she told her. "Even Simon. Your father and I enjoyed having them spend the night. We'll have to do it more often. So how did your day go?"

Before answering, Sammy kissed each child, reminded them she loved them, then sent them off to watch cartoons until time to leave. "It was nice, really nice. Thanks, Mom, for keeping the kids for me."

"You don't have to thank me, sweetie. I just wish we could have them more often. Did you take that ride on the riverboat as you'd planned?"

She smiled. "Yes, it was a wonderful ride. I can't believe I'd never gone on it before. Someday I'll take the children. They'd love it. Maybe, if Dad feels like it, you two can come with us."

"I'm sure we'd enjoy it, but wasn't it kind of lonely? Being by yourself like that? You should have invited one of the women from your Sunday school class to go with you."

Sammy wondered how much she should say. Her mother was such a worry-wart, but she had to tell her about Ted. "I—I wasn't exactly alone. I met someone. We had a marvelous day together."

Smiling, her mother grabbed her arm. "Oh, sweetie, I'm so glad. Was she your age? What was she like?"

"She wasn't a she."

"I don't understand. What do you mean?"

"She was a he." Feeling ridiculous at the choice of words she'd used, Sammy muffled a snicker. "I mean, the person I met wasn't a woman. He was a man."

Her mother frowned. "You spent the day with a man? Oh, honey, I've heard of guys who go places like that in search of vulnerable women."

"I'm not as vulnerable as you think, but don't worry. I didn't give him my full name or address." *But I wish I had. I'd like to see him again.* She took hold of her mother's arm and leaned close to her. "He was so nice, Mom. You would have loved him. He's a fireman."

Her mother's eyes widened. "Aren't you the girl who—not too long ago—told me—"

258

"That no man would ever want me? Yes, and I still feel that way, but I can't tell you how nice it was to be with a man like Ted. He's—"

"Ted? That's his name?"

Sammy felt a flush rise to her cheeks. "Yes, Ted. In some ways he reminds me of Dad. Not that he looks like him, but in other ways. He even called his cheesecake 'tasty.' Dad is the only other man I know who uses that term."

"You don't know many men," her mother reminded her.

"But, Mom, he's kind and gentle, considerate—"

"Maybe he was that way to impress you."

"No, Ted was for real. I could tell," Sammy snapped back, slightly miffed that her mother doubted her words.

"I'd love to see you find a nice man, but you were only on the boat with this stranger for how long? Maybe five or six hours? What makes you think *you* know him that well? He could be an ax murderer for all you know. At least a stalker. I just want you to be careful, that's all."

Rather than argue about it, Sammy lifted her hands in surrender. "You may be right, and I appreciate your concern, but my female intuition tells me otherwise. I wish you could have met him; then you'd understand why I liked him. I think he liked me, too."

"Of course he liked you. You're a lovely person." Her mother's eyes narrowed. "You're sure you didn't give him your phone number or address?"

"Yes, I'm sure. As I said, we didn't even exchange last names."

Mrs. Samuel sighed with relief. "Good, then maybe he won't be able to find you."

"I wish he *could* find me," Sammy whispered so softly her mother couldn't hear. "If only I'd been like Cinderella and left my slipper behind."

∞

"Hey, you. Ted Benay. Get your head out of that newspaper. Lunch is ready."

Ted looked up from the sports section of the Sunday morning paper and smiled at Captain Grey. "Thanks, Cap. Just checking on the Titans. They're having a pretty good season this year."

"About time. With all the muscle power that team has, they should finish in the top three, maybe even higher. Of course, they have to get that quarterback settled down. The guy's too unpredictable. Up one game, down the next. I'd like to see them go all the way to the play-offs, but then I'm biased."

Ted followed his captain down the hall toward the fire station's dining area. "Guess I'm kinda biased, too. I sure wish I could attend all their games."

"Hey, Benay, whatcha think about those Titans?"

Ted smiled at a man already seated at the table then, after nodding at the other guys at the big table, scooted in beside him. "They're doin' real good. You watch that game Monday night?"

"Yeah, that was some game all right. Wasn't that pass McGregor made something? Went right into his receiver's hands slick as a whistle." Reaching across the table, Ted's coworker grabbed the bowl of mashed potatoes and scooped out a big spoonful, plopping it onto his plate with a snap of his wrist. "Did you see Arkansas play yesterday?"

"Naw, I was, ah, busy."

"Finally got those new hubcaps put on your truck, huh?"

Ted took the bowl from his hands. "Nope, put those on last week. I did something I've wanted to do for a long time—took a ride on the *General Jackson* riverboat."

"Sounds like fun. My wife's been bugging me to take her on that thing." He nudged Ted's arm with his elbow. "You take some purty little gal with you?"

Ted nonchalantly spooned a scoop of potatoes onto his own plate then doused them with a ladle full of thick brown gravy. "Yeah, I guess you could say that."

Jake, one of the guys who loved to needle Ted every chance he had, reared back with a boisterous laugh. "Hey, Benay, you actually had a date? What was the occasion?"

Ted grabbed up a biscuit and pelted the man with it, hitting him on the nose.

Chuckling, the man picked up the pieces and disposed of them in his empty coffee cup. "Good shot!"

Cal, one of Ted's favorite firemen, reached for the platter, took off a luscious-looking piece of fried chicken, then passed it on to the next man. "Come on, Ted. 'Fess up. Did you really take some gal on that riverboat? Enquiring minds want to know."

"No, I didn't *take* anyone with me. I went alone when my friend had to cancel on me at the last minute. But I did meet someone, a really nice woman."

"Ted's—got—a—girlfriend," Jake sang in singsong fashion, making up his tune as he went.

"And—it's—about—time," a second man joined in, albeit off-key, as they laughed and jeered at Ted's expense. But he didn't mind. The men he worked with had become like family. He knew they meant well.

Jake speared a piece of chicken then handed Ted the platter. "So you picked up some little gal on the boat?"

Ted wished he'd kept his mouth shut and let them think he'd gone alone and stayed that way. They constantly teased him about being the most eligible bachelor on his shift and challenged him to go out and find himself a woman. Though he didn't mind the teasing, he hated having to explain himself.

"I didn't pick her up, as you so crudely put it, Jake. We just sort of ended up sitting next to each other. That's all. I don't even know her last name." *But I wish I did!*

"But you got her phone number, right?"

Ted turned toward Cal, who was shoveling food into his mouth as if it were his last meal. "No, I didn't."

Jake snorted. "Either you were a fool, or she was a real dog. Which was it?"

"Fool, I guess. She was one of the nicest, prettiest women I've ever met, and I let her get away. I have no idea how to find her."

The laughter ceased as every man eyed Ted.

"You're serious?"

Ted nodded. "Yeah, Cal, I'm dead serious. As we were getting off the boat, I ran into one of my friends, and he wanted to introduce me to his family. In the confusion of everyone heading for the gangway, I lost Sammy in the crowd. By the time I got to the exit gate, she was already gone."

Jake wiped his chin with his napkin. "Bummer. Too bad, guy. Next time make it a priority to at least get the gal's phone number."

"I'd hoped to hear from her, but so far she hasn't called me."

"You gave her *your* number? That was pretty smart. Maybe you're not as dumb as we thought you were."

Ted sent Cal a feeble smile. "You give me too much credit. I didn't give her my number, at least not directly." He explained about the jacket and leaving his number with the lady at the ticket office. "I'm hoping she'll call."

"There're plenty of fish in the sea, Ted," Captain Grey said sympathetically. "If one gets away, there's always another."

Again Jake snorted. "Yeah, but some of those fish are scrawny little unattractive minnows who aren't the kind you want to keep; some are pretty trout and the best fish a man could catch"—he paused for effect—"and some are dangerous piranhas, the kind you should stay away from, unless you're lookin' for big trouble. From my experience, that sea of women has far more piranhas in it than trout. You might want to throw the minnows back. The piranhas may be pretty, but don't forget they're deadly. The trout? When you find one of those babies you know you've hit pay dirt. From the stars in old Teddy-boy's eyes, I'd say the one he let get away was a trout. If it was me, I'd keep right on fishing in that same sea until I found her again."

Ted pondered his words. No doubt about it, the fish he'd hoped would end up in his net had, through his own carelessness, gotten away. That jacket was the only bait he had to find her. But the sad thing was, unless the ticket office lady gave Sammy his number and she called him, he had no idea where to fish.

"Hey, Cal, you gonna eat those mashed potatoes all by yourself, or are you gonna share that bowl with the rest of us?" Before Cal could respond with a snappy retort or shove the potatoes in Jake's direction, the alarm sounded, and the dispatcher's voice boomed vital information throughout the station. Every man headed toward the fire trucks and their waiting gear, leaving their half-eaten lunch on the table.

∞

Sammy stuck her arm out of the covers long enough to hit the snooze button when the alarm went off at its usual time on Monday morning. "Just five more minutes, please," she groaned, turning over on her side. "I'm not ready to get up yet."

When the shrill sound ripped through her bedroom a second time, she begrudgingly flipped off the covers, stood, and went through her usual waking-up routine, stretching first one arm then the other, then bending and touching her toes. Like it or not, it was time to face the day. She decided she had time to add a load of dirty weekend laundry to the washing machine before putting breakfast together. She quickly emptied both hers and the children's hampers and began sorting things into piles by color when it occurred to her that her jacket was missing. She'd purposely taken it with her on the riverboat, but where was it now? Had she left it in the car? No, she would have seen it when she'd gone to church.

Disgusted with herself, she shook her head. *I left it on the riverboat. I hope someone turned it in, or they found it when they cleaned the upper deck.* She glanced at her watch. *Too early to call now. I'll call them later.*

"Up, up, up!" She clapped her hands then gently tugged off the quilts that covered the three little munchkins with whom she shared her apartment. Getting two children off to school, little Harley to the babysitter, and herself ready for work each morning was no easy task. "Rise and shine, kidlings. Open those little eyes."

By ten o'clock, with everyone safely deposited in their proper places, Sammy picked up the phone on her office desk and called the riverboat ticket office.

"Yes, someone did bring in a jacket that had been left on the upper deck last Saturday. He left his name and number on a piece of paper, said for you to call and he'd bring the jacket by your apartment," the woman explained.

Sammy's heart soared. Ted had left his number?

"I taped it up here on the wall by the phone"—the woman paused—"but it's gone now. Don't know what happened to it, but since he was a friend of yours, I guess you know the number."

Her heart plummeted as quickly as it had risen. "No, I don't know it. If he calls again, would you have him call me? I'd like to get my jacket back." *And I want to see him again.*

"Sure—give me your number. This time I'll write it on the inside cover of our phone book so it won't get lost."

Though Sammy gave the woman both her home and work numbers, she doubted Ted would call the riverboat again. When she didn't call him, he'd probably think either the jacket wasn't of value to her or she didn't want to see him again—or both. She thanked the woman then hung up. It seemed her life was one long series of ups and downs.

Mostly downs.

Her thoughts still filled with visions of the handsome fireman, she tried to imagine what it would be like to date Ted. Maybe even marry him. She'd be Mrs. Ted—ah—what? She didn't even know his full name. And though he had a great personality, was well mannered, and seemed like an all-around nice guy, was he a Christian? Did he share her faith? To her, that would be the most important part of any relationship.

∞

Two weeks passed, and the phone call from Sammy didn't come. Though Ted had nearly given up on hearing from her, each time he passed his closet he couldn't resist opening the door and glancing at her jacket.

Another week went by. Still no call.

"Hey, Benay, what happened to that girl you met on the riverboat?" Without even turning, Ted knew it was Jake. "She give you the boot? Find herself another boyfriend?"

Ted shrugged. "We kinda lost track of each other."

"I got the impression you really liked that girl," his captain chimed in.

"I did."

"And you're going to give up on her, just like that?"

"I didn't exactly give up on her."

"She dumped you, right?"

Ted swung around toward Cal. "No, she didn't dump me. I think she actually liked me."

Jake waved the popcorn bowl in Ted's face. "If she liked you and you say you haven't given up on her, what's your problem?"

"I hoped she'd call, but—"

The alarm went off for the third time in less than two hours, ending their conversation and sending the men scurrying toward the truck.

"I'm thankful it isn't that nursing home again," Cal yelled out over the sound of the motor as Jake revved up the truck's big engine. "I love those old people, but

I sure hate it when we can't help them or we're too late."

Like two others they'd had in the past two hours, the call was a near false alarm. The fire was out by the time they got there. All it had taken was a neighbor's borrowed fire extinguisher to put out the small fire that had started in a garage.

"You'd think people would invest a few bucks in a home fire extinguisher," Cal quipped with disgust, sliding out of his boots and outer pants and then placing them next to the fire truck. "They invest most of their income in their home and its contents but won't buy an extinguisher."

Jake gave his arm a playful nudge. "Why should they when they have us? Most folks think all we do is watch TV and play dominoes. Face it, man. We've got the kind of job most men only dream about."

Cal rose quickly as the shrill alarm sounded again, echoing throughout the station. "There she goes! We've got another one. Surely it's not another false alarm."

Ted felt a rush of adrenaline as he pulled on his pants, boots, and jacket and swung himself up into his seat. Maybe it was the fear of the unknown, the anticipation of putting out the fire and keeping everyone safe. Whatever it was, the thrill of being a firefighter was always there, surging through his blood, and he loved every minute of it. It was as if his calling in life had been to be a fireman.

Within three minutes, they pulled up in front of one of the larger office buildings in their district and began their standard procedures. The police arrived on the scene at nearly the same time and took charge of the scores of employees who were rushing out of the building in a panic.

"It's in the furnace room!" shouted a man who looked to be one of the building's maintenance crew, pointing to the back of the large building. "Not sure what caused it, but it's really burning in there!"

The engine from another fire company pulled up, followed by a third engine. Knowing exactly what to do and how to do it, the firemen from the three companies worked together until the fire was out. It wasn't as serious as they'd first thought, but if they hadn't arrived when they did, with that many people working in the building, it could have been a lot more serious.

∞

Sammy stood on the sidewalk, her heart pounding in her ears, her hands trembling. She'd never been in a building when it caught on fire. Just the sound of the fire alarm going off had terrified her. Along with the other people who worked there, she'd made her way down the stairwell and out onto the street, watching in amazement as the firemen methodically went about their business.

Tiffany, her company's receptionist, poked her in the arm as they stood a half hour later watching the activity playing out before them. "Aren't they cute in their uniforms?"

Sammy blinked hard. "The firemen?"

Tiffany nodded then popped her gum. "Yeah, the firemen. Who'd you think I meant? Wonder if they'd let me take one of those guys home with me? Maybe that one over there. The tall one. He'd look real fine in my apartment."

Sammy turned to see which man Tiffany was talking about. "I don't know how you could tell. In those uniforms, they all look alike."

Tiffany let out a chuckle. "No problem. I'd take any one of them, sight unseen."

I'd take one of them, too, if his name were Ted.

The young woman ran her fingers through her bleached, spiked hair then tugged at her short skirt. "Come on, Sammy. Don't tell me you wouldn't like to have one of those hunky guys living in *your* apartment. Surely you have blood flowing through those veins of yours."

Sammy hoped her thoughts about Ted hadn't made her blush but then realized the fast trip down the stairs had already done that job. "If he was the right guy I would, but only if we were married."

Tiffany wrinkled up her face then popped her gum again. "Right guy? Surely you don't believe in that one-special-man-created-just-for-you stuff."

Sammy hadn't expected to get into this type of conversation while standing in the parking lot surrounded by fire trucks and police cars, but she had to let this young woman know where she stood. "Yes, Tiffany, I do believe that. I don't know if God intended for me to marry or not, but if He did I'm sure He has the right man out there—somewhere."

Tiffany sighed, her long chandelier earrings swaying from side to side like the pendulum on a clock. "How're you going to find him? The world is full of men."

"I don't know how, but God can bring us together. I'm sure of it."

"Meantime you're gonna save yourself for him? That special man you're expecting God to send you with a sign on his back saying he's yours?"

Sammy didn't like the ridiculing tone of Tiffany's voice or the way she was making fun of something of vital importance to her. But the girl was young and more interested in men than she was in God's will for her life, so Sammy answered as kindly as she could. "That's exactly what I'm going to do, and I hope he's saving himself for me."

Tiffany's eyes widened. "That's about the most absurd statement I've ever heard. You really think some guy is saving himself for you? Maybe they did stuff like that in the Dark Ages but not in today's world. If you want a man, you've got to do like the rest of us. Go out there and find him. Go where men congregate.

Pick out one you like. Flirt, throw yourself at him—do whatever it takes to get his attention."

Sammy crossed her arms over her chest and scrunched up her face. "No, thanks. I'd never be that desperate."

"Are you insinuating I'm desperate?"

"I'm not insinuating anything, Tiffany. I'm simply telling you how I feel."

An officer moved up between them and motioned toward the double doors. "You ladies can go back into the building now. Everything is under control."

Relieved at having a reason to bring their awkward conversation to an end, Sammy turned in the man's direction. But it wasn't his face that caught her attention; it was the familiar face of a fireman standing alongside one of the big red vehicles.

"Ted?"

Chapter 4

Cal jabbed Ted in the shoulder as the two stood by the fire truck waiting for their captain to come back from his final walk-through. "Hey, old buddy, you get a load of all those good-lookin' women standing over there by those double doors?"

Ted sent him an amused grin. "Nope. Never noticed."

"Man, you'd better get yourself to the doc for a checkup as soon as possible. Somethin's wrong with you. You're not still pining over that little gal you met on the riverboat, are you?"

Ted snorted, not about to tell Cal that Sammy was the subject of nearly all of his waking thoughts and sometimes his dreams. "Only thing wrong with me is I'm too picky. I don't want just any woman; I want the right woman."

"You ain't gonna find her sittin' on your duff. You gotta get out there and circulate." Cal latched onto Ted's arm. "Why don't I take you over there and introduce you to one of those pretty gals?"

Ted let out a chuckle. "You don't know any of those women."

"Hey, don't need to know them. Women are always impressed with a man in uniform. I guarantee you—if the two of us walked over there and said hello, we'd have those women falling all over us. I'd even give you first choice."

Ted frowned. "And then you'd pick one? I don't think that sweet little wife of yours would approve."

Cal wiggled his eyebrows. "I won't tell if you don't."

With a roll of his eyes, Ted tugged his arm away. He hated it when the married guys at his station talked that way, even if they didn't mean it. "You go wow them if you want. I'll stay and finish up here."

Cal shrugged. "Don't say I didn't offer. Man, if I was your age and as good-lookin' as you, I'd—"

"Ted?"

Ted glanced up at the sound of his name.

It was Sammy!

It was actually Sammy!

Without a word of explanation to Cal, Ted hurried over to her. But when they met halfway, he stopped. He wanted to take her in his arms and hang on

267

tight; he wasn't about to lose her a second time. But, being a gentleman and not wanting to come on too strong and frighten the poor girl, he simply gazed down at her awkwardly, his arms dangling at his sides. "Hi," he finally managed to say. "I've been thinking about you." She was every bit as attractive as the first time he'd met her.

Sammy gazed up at him. "I've been thinking about you, too."

"I tried to catch you that day, but by the time my friends and I left the boat, you were already gone. I'd hoped you'd wait for me."

"I—I didn't want to intrude. And, after all, our ride was over. One of the crew members opened the gate and motioned for all of us to exit, so I just moved along with the crowd."

Though he didn't want to stare, he couldn't help himself. Her shoulder-length brown hair glistened in the sun, and her eyes, as blue as he'd remembered them, held him captive. "I found your jacket."

"I know. I called the ticket office. They told me you'd taken it with you, but somehow the note with your phone number on it disappeared from the wall where the lady had taped it. I didn't know how to reach you."

"I didn't know how to reach you either. I—I still have your jacket. It's hanging in my hall closet. I could bring it to you." *Get her phone number and address and her last name!*

"That's asking too much of you. Why don't I come by the fire station and pick it up?"

He was tempted to say yes so his firefighting buddies would know he truly had met a real live girl on that riverboat. But he wasn't taking any chances. He wanted to make sure he could find her again. "No, give me your address. It'd be a lot simpler if I brought it to you."

Though her smile lingered, Ted noticed that she pulled back slightly at his suggestion. "Or maybe we could have lunch tomorrow, and I could bring it to you there," he added quickly. "You name the place."

∞

Sammy's heart raced. Wonder of wonders! The fantastic man she'd met on the riverboat was standing in front of her, and he was asking her to meet him for lunch. She was glad he'd suggested lunch. She didn't know him well enough to invite him up to her apartment or go to his. "That's a great idea, Ted. I do need to get my jacket back. There's a terrific soup and sandwich shop about a block down from here. Maybe we could meet there. About noon?" His smile made her heart flutter.

"I know the place. Noon would be great."

"But it has to be my treat. After all, you are returning my jacket."

His smile broadened. "I'll arm wrestle you for the check. But I warn you, firemen are good arm wrestlers. It's an Olympic sport at the station."

She loved his warm smile, his boyish ways, and his sense of humor. They were what had attracted her to him in the first place. "No way! I appreciate your taking care of my jacket. It's one of my favorites. The least I can do is buy you lunch." Sammy hoped she wasn't grinning like some starstruck teenager, but she was so glad she'd found him, and not just because she wanted her jacket back.

"Hey, Ted. We're ready to roll."

"Sorry. Got to rush off. The captain is ready. See you tomorrow?" Sending her another grin, he backed away.

"Yeah, tomorrow. 'Bye."

" 'Bye."

Sammy watched until he'd climbed into the cab and the big truck disappeared around the corner before heading back into the building, her heart doing cartwheels. Ted was back in her life, even if only for one more day, and she still didn't know his last name.

She took care of a number of customer service calls the next morning, but time seemed to stand still. Sammy found herself checking the clock every five minutes. At eleven thirty, purse in hand, she headed for the ladies' room to comb her hair and freshen up her lipstick.

As she passed the reception desk in her company's foyer, Tiffany popped her chewing gum, then cocked her head to one side and gave her a once-over. "You're lookin' good today, girl. Where you going? The man upstairs call you from heaven and tell you that special man He created for you was waiting here in the lobby to take you to lunch?"

Unable to resist, Sammy donned a big smile. "You should know. Wouldn't God have had to go through your switchboard to reach me? What's the matter? Didn't you recognize His voice?"

Apparently unfazed by her question, Tiffany smiled at her. "Next time you talk to that God of yours, ask Him to send me a man about six foot tall, black hair, blue eyes, with a great personality and lots of money. Tell Him if He does, I'll go to church on Sunday."

Sammy gave her a wink then hurried toward the double doors, calling back over her shoulder, "Too bad you didn't recognize His voice. You could have asked Him yourself."

Despite the time it took for her little repartee with Tiffany, Sammy was still five minutes early when she strolled into the soup and sandwich shop. Ted was already there and seated at a booth near the wall.

"Over here!" Rising, a grin broke out across his face. "I got here early."

She smiled a hello then noticed her jacket neatly folded on the opposite side of the booth and seated herself next to it. "I'm early, too."

He picked up a menu and handed it to her. "I know you like iced tea. I've already ordered it for you. I hope that's okay."

"Iced tea is fine." She gestured toward her jacket. "Thanks for bringing it, Ted. I was afraid it was lost forever when they couldn't find the phone number you'd left."

"I thought I'd lost you—" He lowered his gaze and almost seemed nervous. "I mean, without your phone number or last name, I had no idea how to reach you—to give you back your jacket."

The waitress arrived with two tall glasses of iced tea. "What'll you have, folks?"

Sammy closed the menu and handed it to her. "I'll have the Minnie Pearl, please."

Ted looked up from his menu. "The Minnie Pearl? What's that?"

She reached across the table and pointed to a spot at the far right side of his menu. "I guess you haven't had a chance to look at it yet. Every item on the menu is named for a country music star. The Minnie Pearl is actually broccoli cheese soup and a small shaved ham sandwich. I order it nearly every time I come here."

Ted scrunched up his face and stared at the vast array of selections. "Um, let me see. I guess—I'll have—the Garth Brooks."

Sammy had to laugh. "Oh, you like Reuben sandwiches, too? The Garth Brooks is my second favorite."

"Great minds think alike!"

"Mind if I pray?" she asked when their lunch arrived.

"I'd be disappointed if you didn't."

What did that mean? Slightly confused by his answer, she bowed her head and uttered a quick thank-You-for-our-food prayer before picking up her spoon and plunging it into her soup.

They laughed their way through lunch, talking about the way they'd met, the fun they'd had on the riverboat, her jacket, and the uncanny way they'd met again at the fire.

"I can't let you pay for my lunch," Sammy told him, reaching for her purse when the waitress brought the check.

"Oh, so you do want to arm wrestle me for it. I'm only kidding. Put your money away. No woman I take to lunch is going to pick up her tab. My daddy raised me right."

Though she felt awkward letting him pay for her lunch, she was impressed by his determination to do what he considered the gallant thing. Actually, she considered it gallant, too.

"Looks like we were destined to meet," Ted told her as he walked her back to her building. "Don't you think it's about time we officially introduced ourselves?" He reached out his hand. "I'm Ted Benay. Nashville firefighter extraordinaire."

Sammy smiled up at him. "Hi, Ted Benay. I'm Sammy Samuel. Waggoner Enterprise's super-experienced customer service director."

He raised his brow. "How about giving me your phone number? I'd like to give you a call sometime. Like maybe tomorrow when I'm at the station."

Why not? What harm could it do? She gave him a bashful grin. How long had it been since a man had asked for her phone number? "It's 555-2172."

Ted patted his shirt pocket. "I don't have a pen."

"I have one." Sammy unzipped the clutch bag she carried to work each day and fished around inside, pulling out a small spiral pad. "Um, a pad, but no pen. I must have left it on my desk."

"That's okay. I have a good memory. You did say five-five-five—twenty-one-seventy-two, right?"

"You do have a good memory. That's exactly right." After sliding the pad back inside, she zipped the bag shut.

He opened one of the double doors to her building then tipped his imaginary hat. "Thank you for the pleasure of your company, Sammy Samuel. I'll call you tomorrow."

"And thank you for a pleasant lunch, Ted Benay. I'll look forward to your call."

"Any special time be best?"

Remembering how noisy it was in her apartment before the children went to bed, she considered his question carefully. "Best after nine in the evening. I'm—busy—before then."

He tipped his imaginary hat again. "Nine it is."

She felt his eyes pinned on her as she moved through the open door and toward the elevator. Could this really be happening? Could this handsome man be interested in her enough to call her? *Calm down, girl. He was only talking about a single phone call, not a long-term commitment. Don't get your hopes up. You may never hear from him again. And, at this point, you're not even sure he's a Christian.*

"Well, you're looking rosy." Tiffany's voice carried its usual mocking tone as Sammy passed the reception desk. "That must have been some lunch, or did you drink too much wine?"

Sammy hated to dignify Tiffany's comment with an answer, but she felt she needed to respond. "The lunch was terrific. No wine needed. And, yes, God sent that special man to take me to lunch." *I hope it was God who sent him.* "He's a fantastic guy. Maybe someday I'll bring him to the office so you can meet him, but you have to promise—hands off! He's mine." *I can't believe I actually said that! Now she'll be expecting me to bring Ted here.*

Tiffany's face sobered. "You're serious? A man really did take you to lunch?"

"Of course a man did. A real hunk of a guy." Sammy lifted her chin and put on a mischievous smile then headed for her office, leaving Tiffany with her mouth hanging open.

∞

The next evening nine o'clock came, then nine thirty, then ten, and still no call from Ted. He'd seemed so sincere when he'd promised to call. Sammy fingered the tip of her scar. Surely he hadn't noticed it. As was her custom, she'd worn a high-necked blouse. *Maybe he's too busy to call.* She shook her head to clear her thoughts. Why was she making excuses for him? He hadn't called as he'd said he would, plain and simple. She'd been a fool to believe she'd ever hear from him again.

∞

Ted stared at the phone. How could he have forgotten Sammy's number? He'd been so sure he'd remembered it correctly; yet each of the three times he'd dialed it, the same man had answered the phone, obviously irritated. Great! Sammy was expecting his call, and he had no way to reach her. He tried checking the phone book, but either her number was unlisted or listed under another name. If he had her address, he would go right over there and tell her his addled brain had somehow transposed her number. But, since he didn't know it, he could only wait until morning and try to catch her at her office.

He arrived shortly after nine at the reception desk. "I'd like to see Sammy Samuel, please."

Popping her gum, the receptionist gave him a sideways tilt of her head and blinked her long lashes seductively. "You the guy who took her to lunch the other day?"

Startled by her question and wondering how she knew, Ted frowned. "Yeah, I am. Would you please call her and tell her I'm here?"

"Be happy to." The flirtatious smile she gave him as she picked up the phone made him uncomfortable. "Wait here."

Within seconds of her call, Sammy appeared, looking businesslike in pretty dark blue pants and a white shirt. Ted felt as tongue-tied as a schoolboy as he gazed at her. Something about her was different. Her hair, maybe? Whatever it was, she looked good.

"Well, hello. I didn't expect to see you here this morning." She eyed him a bit coolly and then, after a glance in the receptionist's direction, motioned toward two chairs along the wall. "We can talk over there."

Once they were seated, Ted smiled, hoping she wasn't upset that he hadn't called as he'd said he would. "You must think I'm a real dodo. I thought for sure I'd remember your phone number, but somehow I got it messed up. Some man kept answering, and he was none too happy." He grinned. "I really wanted to talk to you last night. All I can say is I'm sorry."

Her face softened into a demure smile. "I thought maybe you didn't mean it when you said you'd call."

"Oh, I intended to call you all right. I just didn't know how." Ted couldn't keep his eyes off her. It seemed each time he saw her, she was more beautiful than the last. "I have to know something, Sammy. Do you have a steady boyfriend? Are you engaged? Married?" What a dumb thing to come right out and ask, but he had to know. He was attracted to this woman, but he sure didn't want to tread on some decent man's toes.

She burst out laughing at his impromptu question. "No, none of the above. Are you?"

"Am I what?"

"Married or engaged or have a steady girlfriend?"

"Oh, I get it. Turnabout is fair play, true? I guess you have as much right to know the answer to those questions as I do. Like you, none of the above!" He never blushed, so why did his cheeks feel hot?

∞

Sammy froze as Ted reached his hand across and cupped hers.

"I enjoyed our time together on the *General Jackson*. If I'd had my wits about me and gotten your address, I would have sent you flowers to show my appreciation for allowing me to share the day with you."

Be still, my heart. "I had a great time, too, but as much as I love flowers, you needn't have sent them. You barely know me."

He gave her hand a gentle squeeze. "Not by choice. I'd planned on inviting you out to dinner so I *could* get to know you. But, dumb me, I left you standing on the deck when I ran into my friend and his family and let you get away. Do you think you could ever forgive me?" A grin tilting at his lips, he let go of her hand and shifted his body toward the edge of his seat. "I'll even get down on my knees and beg your forgiveness if it'll help."

"No, don't! I mean, there's nothing to forgive. We'd just met. You owed me nothing. I'm the one with the debt. I owe you for taking care of my jacket."

His face brightened. "Does that mean if I asked you out on a real date, you'd accept?"

She nibbled at her lip, fighting the gigantic smile that begged to erupt. He was asking her for a date! "What kind of date?"

"Dinner at a nice place, then a movie. A chick flick, if that's the kind you like. Hot fudge sundae at the ice cream parlor afterward. Whatever you want to do. Wherever you want to go. Your choice."

His hand cupped hers again. It felt warm. Safe. Strong. "I do like you, Ted," she began, wondering if she should blurt out the reasons that would send him running the other way if he knew her background and what her life was like or if she should drag it out slowly. "And I'd love to accept your invitation, but—"

"But what? I promise I'm trustworthy. We can even take someone with us if you're concerned about going out alone with me when you don't know me any better than you do."

She swallowed hard. "It isn't that I don't know you. It's that *you* don't know me."

His grip tightened on her hand. "That's the whole point of it, Sammy. That's why you should go to dinner with me. I want to get to know you. I'm sure there's nothing you could tell me that would make me *not* want to know you better. I have a feeling you and I think alike."

"I'd like to go—really I would—but there's—"

With a teasing smile, he put his finger on her lips. "Shh, not another word. If either of us has any skeletons in our closets, we'll deal with them later. But at this moment, let's concentrate on the here and now." He laughed. "Who knows? Maybe once we get to know each other, we won't like one another and won't even have to deal with those skeletons."

Sammy evaluated his words carefully. Though he was saying it in jest, what he was saying was true. Maybe they wouldn't like each other, but it would be fun dating him to find out. And he was a great guy. What harm could it do? She didn't have to tell him about the children now and certainly not that she had a transplanted heart. And she was sure her next-door neighbor would stay with the children if she asked her. "Okay, if your invitation still stands, I'd love to have dinner with you." From the look on his face, it seemed he was as pleased with her answer as she was.

"Thursday night work for you? Unless you'd rather go someplace else, how about having dinner at the Opryland Hotel?"

Her heart raced with excitement. "Isn't it a bit pricey?"

"Have you ever eaten there?"

"No, believe it or not, I've never even been in the hotel, but I've heard it's nice."

"You've never been to the Opryland Hotel? Then I have to take you there.

That's where I took my mom for Mother's Day, and she loved it. What time shall I pick you up?"

Pick me up? "Maybe I could just meet you somewhere."

"Hey, this is an official date, remember?"

"Yes, I remember. Would seven be okay? That'll give me time to get home from work and change into something more suitable." Her heart pounded against her chest. Perhaps she could have her neighbor keep the kids over in her apartment for the evening so he wouldn't be flabbergasted by their presence when she opened the door. Yes, that would work. She'd just have to make sure their toys and belongings weren't left scattered around.

"Seven it is, but you'd better write your address down on a piece of paper along with your phone number. I've already proven how bad my memory is."

After asking Tiffany for a pen and paper, Sammy wrote down the information and handed it to him, watching as he folded it and stuck it in his shirt pocket.

"See you Thursday night at seven." He gave her a slight wave then hurried to catch the elevator before the doors closed.

"Hey, if you don't want that guy, I'll take him. He's cute!"

Sammy tried to appear casual as she made her way past Tiffany's desk, although inside she was a bundle of nerves. "Thanks for the offer, but I think I'll keep him."

"Where'd you meet him? I've never seen him around here before."

Sammy smiled. "Would you believe me if I said God sent him?"

Tiffany's eyes rounded. "You really think He did?"

The smile still etched on her face, Sammy shrugged. "Only God knows the answer to that question."

∞

"Thanks, Edna, I owe you one." Sammy closed the door of her neighbor's apartment Thursday evening and then hurried back across the hall to her own apartment.

Her place looked strangely unfamiliar without the toys, books, crayons, and videos that normally adorned her living room. She scanned her surroundings one more time, making sure all the evidence of living with three children had been removed. After one final glance in the hall mirror, she sat down to wait for Ted's arrival. *I actually have a date, a real date, and with a very nice man! I hope I don't spill food or knock my glass over and embarrass myself. Or Ted!*

He arrived on the stroke of seven, a small bouquet of flowers in his hand and the dazzling smile on his face that always made her heart beat faster. "Hi, these are for you."

Sammy clasped her fist against her pounding chest. "Oh, Ted, how thoughtful. I love flowers, but you—"

"Shouldn't have? Ah, but I should. I wanted to. By the way, you sure look nice. I like that scarf thing you have around your neck. Nice colors."

"Thank you. It was a gift from my mom." She fingered the scarf to make sure it was covering what she'd intended. "I'd better put these roses in water so they won't wilt."

When she realized he was following her into the kitchen, she panicked. Had she made sure all traces of kid stuff had been removed from the kitchen? She couldn't remember, but, much to her relief, the kitchen was in perfect order, without a crayon, lunch box, or child-sized garment in sight.

He summed up the area. "Nice place you have here."

"Thanks. It's a little crowded with"—she paused, quickly rethinking her choice of words—"with everything. I can't seem to throw anything away."

His brows rose. "You, too, huh? That's the way I am. Always sure I'll need it again someday."

The traffic was unusually heavy for a Thursday evening as they made their way up Gallatin and turned onto Briley Parkway toward the Music Valley section. "You lived in Nashville long?"

Sammy smiled up at him. "I lived here growing up, left to get an education, took a job in Denver, and moved back here about three years ago, so I guess you could say this is home. How about you?"

"My family moved here before I went into the service, so when I was discharged I decided to come back here. I like Nashville. It has a lot to offer."

"I think you said you like working as a fireman, right?"

Without taking his eyes off the road, he nodded. "Yeah, I do. Good pay, good benefits, and I like the idea of having one day on and two days off. Good retirement program, too. You said you like being a customer service director, too, didn't you?"

Sammy gazed out the window, taking in the scenery. She rarely got to this part of town. "Yes, I really do. I like working with people and their problems. It's such a great feeling when you're able to solve them and they walk away happy."

"Sounds like a tall order to me. People can be so cantankerous sometimes. I had a woman so mad her face turned red when I had to use the fire extinguisher to put out a fire in her kitchen because of the gray residue it left, and she's the one who called 911 asking for help. Guess some folks you can never please."

"I have one of those occasionally, but most of the people I deal with only want satisfaction. If I'm nice to them, let them know I sincerely care about their problem and can work things out to where they're happy with the solution, they'll stay a customer. That's my goal. I try to tell everyone in my department it's much easier to keep an old customer than it is to find a new one."

"Sounds smart to me." He gestured toward the Opryland Hotel as he turned into the parking lot. "Hope you're hungry."

She allowed a grin to tilt her lips. "Starved."

Since Ted had called in their reservation to the restaurant located in the hotel's atrium, they were taken in right away and seated at a table for two near the railing, overlooking the spectacular cascades and courtyard.

"Wow!" Sammy gazed at each of the two glassed-in walls surrounding them.

"Nice, isn't it? I thought you'd like it."

"Those waterfalls are incredible, and the gardens! I've never seen such lush growth."

"The entire hotel is like this. We'll take a walk around it when we're finished. This area is only a small part of it."

Her gaze wandered upward to the high domed glass ceiling that towered over them and gave light to the thousands of plants. "This is amazing!"

"That it is. I know I was impressed the first time I came here." He handed her a menu then scanned his own. "How about Australian lobster tail for dinner?"

"I've never had lobster tail."

"Then it's settled. You must have it tonight."

They commented on the many iron balconies that clung to the walls around the atrium and discussed the various types of plants in the gardens and a myriad of other things as they munched on their salads and waited for their entrées. Finally their dinners arrived.

Sammy's eyes widened. The lobster smelled delicious and looked phenomenal, but she had no idea how to eat it.

"Madam? May I?"

She looked up into the smiling face of the waiter then nodded as he, tools in hand, poised himself over her dish. She was relieved for him to do what was needed to get to the meat in the lobster tail. Just watching him and his routine was a treat.

But Ted declined when the man offered to assist him. "Thanks, but I like to do it myself so I can get every tiny morsel. I love this stuff."

"It does look good." As was her habit, Sammy wanted to pray before her meal, but she wasn't sure how he would feel, especially in such a nice restaurant. She sat patiently waiting until their server left. She couldn't help but smile. When she was a child, her grandmother always told her she would get indigestion if she didn't thank the Lord for her food.

"Guess it's my turn to pray. You prayed last time." The words rolled off his tongue as easily as if he'd asked her if she wanted a glass of water. Without waiting, he bowed his head and prayed in a way that let her know he had a personal relationship with God. Ted was a Christian!

After he said amen, Ted waved his fork and gestured toward her plate. "Go ahead. Try it. Take a small piece and dip it in that little container of drawn butter."

Still touched by the way he'd prayed, she did as he'd instructed, being careful not to dribble the warm butter on her chin. "Mmm, it *is* good and so mild. I thought it would taste strong or fishy, but it's not like that at all."

He grinned. "See, I told you you'd like it. Now try the vegetables. They really know how to fix zucchini. I guess it's roasted or something."

"It's delicious," she told him after taking a mouthful. "I've never had it seasoned this way. I like it."

They giggled their way through the rest of the meal, teasing and visiting like old friends.

"How about caramel cheesecake for dessert?"

Her hand on her tummy, Sammy stared at him wide-eyed. "Surely you're kidding. After that meal? No way!"

He lowered his lip and frowned. "Guess that means I can't have any. Next time we come here, we'll have to save room for dessert."

Next time? Did that mean he liked her? That he was truly enjoying her company? She was certainly enjoying his.

They lingered over coffee, and then Ted paid the check. "How about a boat ride?"

She gave him a blank stare. "Now?"

"Yeah, right here in the hotel, complete with a guide. It's not exactly the *General Jackson*, but they have five nice twenty-five-passenger Delta River flatboats. I think you'll like it."

His enthusiasm was contagious.

"A boat ride sounds wonderful."

After strolling through several lighted lush green walkways and over a bridge, they eventually came to the landing where the boats loaded. "They call it an indoor river," Ted explained, taking her hand and helping her into one of the seats. "It winds through the hotel's four-and-a-half-acre indoor garden."

Sammy had never been in such a romantic setting. It was like a movie, and she was the star. Chills ran down her spine when she felt Ted's arm slide around her shoulders and draw her close. She didn't know if she should scoot closer or pull away.

He leaned toward her, his forehead nearly touching hers, and whispered, "You're a great date. I'm sure glad you said yes."

"I'm glad, too. This beautiful hotel, the lobster, now this boat ride." She shivered as she felt his warm breath on her cheek. "This—this has been a magical evening."

"It's been magical for me, too. Good thing you left your jacket on the riverboat. Otherwise I may never have found you."

"I'm glad I left it, too."

"Maybe the man upstairs wanted us to find each other."

Sammy sucked in a deep breath. *The man upstairs? He calls God "the man upstairs"? I thought he shared my faith!*

"Well, I guess I shouldn't have said 'the man upstairs,'" he went on, apparently oblivious to her repulsion at that name. "I know a lot of folks call God that, but it's disrespectful. I guess I'm around the guys at the fire station so much I automatically pick up their lingo and use it without even thinking sometimes. God is much too important to be called by such a frivolous name."

Though slightly relieved by his explanation, Sammy was reminded of Tiffany's comment. "I know what you mean. I hear that kind of talk every day. God is the most important part of my life. Like you, I hate to hear Him called by that name. It's so disrespectful."

"I won't say it again. To be honest, the Lord is the most important part of my life, too, but right now I'm having trouble understanding His will. He allowed something to happen that changed my life forever, and I'm still struggling to understand why."

"His plan and will for our—"

Frowning, he pulled away a bit. "My mom has given me all those arguments and quoted dozens of scripture verses to me, but I can't see what good could come out of what He allowed to happen." His frown eased, and he smiled as he leaned toward the side of the boat. "If you keep an eye on the water, you might get a glimpse of Danny."

"Danny? Who is Danny?"

Ted laughed. "The hotel's eighty-pound catfish. I'm sure the guide will be telling us about him soon."

Though Sammy wished their conversation could have continued, she couldn't help but laugh, too. "An eighty-pound catfish? Wow! Now that's a fish." She kept smiling, but inside she was aching for Ted. Something had hurt him—enough to cause him to doubt God's will. What was it?

At that exact moment, the guide began to tell them the story of Danny. "But, folks, I haven't seen Danny all evening. He must be taking a nap."

"Too bad," Ted told her, his gaze scanning the river. "I hoped you'd get to see him." He smiled and pointed. "Around that curve up ahead is Delta Island's eighty-five-foot waterfall. Can you imagine building a place like this?"

"No, I can't. I never dreamed this hotel was so large and so beautiful. I'd like to see it at Christmastime. It must be spectacular."

Ted moved a little closer and gave her a nudge. "We can always come back again. I'm sure the restaurant has other items on its menu we can try."

Sammy gave him a bashful grin. "Come here again? You have to be kidding. I saw the prices on that menu."

"You let me worry about those prices. It'll be my Christmas treat. That is, unless you forget all about me by Christmas."

"How could I forget the man who brought me to this wonderful place? But maybe you'll forget all about me."

"Not a chance! It's not every day a man meets a woman who's not only attractive but nice and fun to be with." As the boat came to a slow stop, Ted took Sammy's hand and assisted her up onto the dock. "In fact, I'm off again tomorrow. How about dinner again tomorrow night?"

I can't keep up this charade. I like this man, and he seems to like me. He deserves to know the truth. Well, at least part of it. "Ted," she began slowly, wishing she didn't feel compelled to be honest with him, "I'd love to have dinner with you tomorrow night, but the only dinner we can have together is if you want to come to my apartment and"—the words caught in her throat—"and eat hot dogs with three rambunctious kids." There—she'd said it.

Chapter 5

K ids?" Ted let go of her hand as if it were suddenly on fire, his jaw dangling nearly to his collarbone. "I thought, I mean—you said you weren't married. I didn't know you had kids—maybe—" He wanted out of there—fast. A woman with kids usually meant an ex-husband was in the picture, and he surely didn't want to find himself in the middle of a nasty triangle.

Sammy grabbed hold of his arm. "They're not my children, Ted. They're my sister's."

He felt ashamed at the way he'd backed away from her when she'd dropped what he thought was a bombshell. "Your sister's kids? She lives with you?"

Sammy shrugged. "No, she left her three children with me four years ago and took off with her boyfriend on his motorcycle. I have no idea when, or if, she's ever coming back. Meantime, her children are living with me."

"What a rotten thing to do." He shook his head. "Didn't she realize you have a life, too?"

"Oh, I don't mind. I love my nieces and nephew, but I'm not the one who should be raising them. They need their mother. I keep pictures of her around my apartment, and we talk about her a lot."

"Where were the kids tonight—when I picked you up?"

She gave him a sheepish grin. "Across the hall at my neighbor's. She's baby-sitting them. I should be getting back soon. She has an early day tomorrow."

Three kids? He hadn't realized she had children in her life. "Ah, yeah, sure. You wait by the door while I go get the truck."

During his walk across the parking lot, Ted evaluated the situation. In some ways, Sammy having three children in her life was a definite turnoff. In other ways, her taking care of her sister's children made her even more attractive. Only an unselfish, loving woman would want to care for three young children who weren't hers. Surely they wouldn't be with her forever.

What if he fell in love with this woman and she ended up keeping those children until they were grown? Was he prepared to be a father—to someone else's children?

Ted shook his head then sucked in a deep breath of the night air. *Hey, man, what are you thinking? You met this attractive woman on a boat, took her to lunch, and now you two have had dinner together. That's not exactly a long-term commitment. Why don't you let life see where it leads you? Get to know her better and then decide how far you want this relationship to go. At this point, nothing is carved in stone. You might even like those kids.*

"I'm sorry, Ted," Sammy told him as she crawled into the front seat and reached for the seat belt. "I should have told you up front about the children."

He gazed at her pretty face. He liked her. He honestly liked her. This was the kind of woman he'd thought he'd never find—yet here she was. "Don't worry about it, Sammy. I think it's admirable of you to take on those children as you have. If the invitation still stands, I'd love to have hot dogs with all of you tomorrow night."

"You would? You're sure?" The surprised look on her face nearly made him laugh.

"I'm sure. I'll bring the ice cream. All kids like ice cream. What's their favorite? Chocolate? Strawberry? Chocolate chip?"

"They love chocolate chip, but you really don't—"

"I want to, Sammy. If I didn't, I'd say so. What time?" The smile she gave him made it worthwhile.

"Seven?"

"Seven it is."

∞

At exactly seven o'clock the next evening, Ted knocked on the door, two ice cream cartons in hand. But it wasn't Sammy who opened the door.

Before Ted knew what happened, someone tackled him about his waist, nearly bringing him to the floor, but fortunately he was able to grab hold of the doorframe and catch his balance.

"Simon! Stop! Let go of him!" Sammy moved to tug the young boy off Ted's legs. "I'm so sorry, Ted. Simon has more energy than he knows what to do with."

Stunned by what had just happened, Ted found himself speechless.

"Are you okay?"

"Uh, yeah, I guess so."

Taking hold of the boy's arm, Sammy lowered herself to his level. "Ted is our guest, Simon. You had no business tackling him like that."

The boy frowned. "I was only playing."

"That may be true, but you don't play that way with company, and Ted is our company. Tell him you're sorry."

"Why? I didn't hurt him."

"That may be true, but you could have hurt him. Apologize, Simon. Please."

Simon frowned and lowered his lip. "Don't want to."

Sammy sent Ted a look of embarrassment. "Then please go to your room. We need to talk about this in private."

"It's okay, really. Boys will be boys." Ted felt almost sorry for the boy. "No harm done." He bent and picked up the two cartons of ice cream from the floor. "Except for a little damage to the boxes. Someone from the Tennessee Titans ought to sign up that boy." *And maybe I should just cut and run. I'm not at all sure I'm up to this.*

"Please forgive Simon, Ted. I guess he was more excited about your coming than I realized, but that doesn't excuse his actions. I'd planned to greet you at the door with all three children lined up on the sofa, faces scrubbed until they shone, their hands folded in their laps, with gigantic smiles on their faces. Looks like my plan failed."

For the first time since arriving, Ted took a good look at his hostess. Sammy, in her pink knit shirt and jeans, looked fabulous. He wished he could sweep her up in his arms and carry her off somewhere, away from the responsibility of taking care of her sister's children.

"You look great," he finally mumbled, in awe of her wholesome beauty. She wasn't like the other women he'd met. They'd been—plastic. Not at all real, and out to impress him. Sammy was—Sammy. Nothing more. She seemed genuine to the core.

She smoothed a lock of hair that had fallen onto her forehead. "I don't feel great. Not after the welcome we gave you."

"Can we come in now?"

Ted turned to find two little girls peeking around the corner.

"Yes, you may come in." Sammy hurried toward them, taking each one by the hand and bringing them to stand before him.

"You've already met Simon. This," she said, pulling one of the girls forward, "is my sweet Tina. She's six."

Tina dipped her knee in a slight curtsey.

Ted reached out, took her small hand in his, and gave her a smile. "Hello, Tina. It's nice to meet you. You're a pretty little thing. You look a lot like your aunt."

"And this is Harley. She's nearly four and a half."

Harley wrapped her arm around Sammy's leg and clung to her, burying her face in her jeans.

Sammy stroked the young girl's silky blond hair. "Sometimes she's bashful, but she'll warm up to you when she gets to know you."

Ted felt as awkward as a blindfolded tightrope walker on a poorly stretched wire. He'd rarely been around children, except for his brother's kids. "Hi, Harley.

I'll bet you like ice cream. I brought you some."

"She loves ice cream," Tina volunteered, speaking up for the first time since she'd entered the room.

Sammy took the cartons from his hands. "I'll put these in the freezer, and then, if you'll excuse me for a few minutes, I need to have a talk with Simon."

When he felt a tug on his pant leg, he looked down into Harley's big blue eyes.

"Would you read me a story?"

"Uh—why don't we wait for your aunt? She'll be right back."

"Aunt Sammy told you not to ask." Tina took hold of her sister's hand and led her to the sofa, helped her up, and then sat down beside her.

"But I want him to read me a story."

Ted appraised the situation and decided, even though he'd never read a story to a little girl before, he could probably manage it. "Where are your books?"

Tina gestured toward a magazine rack at the end of the sofa. Ted scanned the selection, finally pulling out a book about a fireman, then seating himself beside Harley.

Before he could stop her, the little girl climbed onto his lap, wiggling around until she was comfortable. "Did you know I'm a fireman?" He opened the book and pointed to the picture on the first page. "Like him. I wear a uniform just like that."

Tina tugged on his sleeve. "Is it fun to be a fireman?"

Ted quirked up his face. "Most of the time. I like helping people and making sure they're safe."

She frowned. "I don't like the sirens. They scare me and make my ears hurt."

He couldn't help but laugh. "Sometimes they make my ears hurt, too."

Harley gave him a nudge with her elbow. "Read, please."

"Yes, ma'am." Ted opened the book and began to read. "Fireman Tom works at fire station number 5. He wears a blue shirt and blue pants. But when the alarm sounds, he hurries to the fire truck, slides his feet into his boots and then pulls on his big fireman coat, hat, and gloves before climbing onto the truck."

Tina scooted closer to him. "Firemen are nice. Simon said they came to our house and put out a fire when our mother dropped her cigarette in our couch."

Ted shuddered at the thought of what could have happened to those children through their mother's carelessness. He'd seen it happen before. "I'm glad the firemen got there in time," he said, shaking his head before turning his attention back to the book.

"As you've found out, the children love to be read to." Sammy sat down in a chair opposite them. "The book you're holding is one of their favorites."

Looking up from the book, Ted could tell Sammy was upset. "You okay?"

She nodded. "Just a little frustrated with Simon. I don't know what's happening to him. He seems to get mouthier every day. I've taken away his TV time, cut off his allowance, and quit letting his friends come to visit, but I'm running out of options."

"I wish there was some way I could help." *Did I say that?*

"Thanks, but there's nothing you can do."

Harley nudged Ted again. "Read, please."

"No more reading, young lady. It's time to cook our hot dogs. I imagine Ted is hungry." Sammy pulled Harley from Ted's lap and straddled the child's legs over her hip before using her free hand to latch onto Tina's arm.

"Want me to go talk to Simon?"

Sammy gave Ted an incredulous look. "You want to?"

"Sure. I might not be able to accomplish anything, but I could try."

She nodded toward the hallway. "Go ahead. Just don't expect too much."

Squaring his shoulders and lifting his chin, he sent her a guarded smile then moved toward the closed door. "Simon, can I come in?"

No answer.

"I thought we could talk. Man-to-man."

Still no answer.

"Go on in," Sammy called out from the living room. "There's no lock on the door."

After sucking in a deep breath, Ted turned the knob and stepped into the semidarkened room. "Did you pull down the shades like that? It's kinda dark in here." Ted moved toward the boy who was sitting on the side of the bed, his arms crossed defiantly over his chest, a deep scowl etched into his forehead. "I'd like to be your friend, Simon."

"Don't need any friends."

Using caution, ready for any kind of response, Ted lowered himself onto the bed beside the boy. "You like baseball?"

The boy's belligerent expression showed a slight softening. "Yeah, sorta."

"I loved baseball when I was your age. Ever been to a game? I mean a real game?"

Simon shook his head.

"My dad used to take me out to Greer Stadium when I was a kid. Bet you didn't know the Nashville Sounds are a triple-A farm team for the Milwaukee Brewers."

The boy gave him a blank stare.

"The Nashville Sounds are Nashville's home team. Boy, my dad and I've seen some really good games out at that stadium. You ever play T-ball?"

Simon shook his head again.

"Do you own a bat?"

Again the boy's head slowly rotated from side to side.

"How about a baseball?"

"Nope."

Ted searched his brain for something else to say. It appeared he was striking out with the baseball subject.

Simon's scowl lessened. "I had a ball once, but it got lost."

"You like to play catch?"

"I tried with my mom's boyfriend when I was little, but he got mad at me when I threw the ball over his head so I quit."

He scooted a bit closer to the boy. "Tell you what. Next time I come over I'll bring my ball, and you and I can play catch."

Sad eyes stared back. "No, don't want to."

"Why? It'll be fun."

"You'll get mad at me."

"No, I promise I won't. I remember how awful I was when I first started playing catch with my dad." He gave the boy a grin. "Once I hit him right between the eyes."

"Did he yell at you and call you names?"

"No, he didn't yell at me. He laughed." Ted slipped his arm around Simon's shoulders. "He knew I didn't mean to do it. You know what he did? He put his strong hand around mine and showed me how to grip the ball and throw it so it would go where I wanted it to. With a little practice, I got pretty good at it."

"I don't have a dad."

"You don't have to have a dad. All you need is a friend who is willing to show you how to do it. I'd like to be your friend, Simon. I still have the ball glove my dad gave me for my seventh birthday. It should fit you just fine. Want me to bring it over and teach you how to hold the ball and throw it?"

Simon's piercing eyes zeroed in on Ted. "Aren't you mad at me?"

"Mad at you?" Ted let out a chuckle. "For tackling me? No, I'm not mad, but I do have to admit I was a little surprised when you did it. You caught me off guard."

"I didn't mean to hurt you."

He tousled the boy's hair. "I know you didn't. Why don't we forget about it and go help your aunt fix those hot dogs?" Ted rose. "I don't know about you, but I'm starved."

A slight smile curved at the corners of the boy's mouth as he stood and walked toward the door. "Me, too."

Not a victory but a good first start. Ted followed Simon into the kitchen and through the sliding glass door to where Sammy and the girls were setting the table on the patio outside her apartment.

Sammy looked up as they joined them. "Everything okay?"

Ted gave her a wink. "Yeah, Simon and I had a good talk. I think we're going to be good friends."

Sammy mouthed the word "thanks" then added aloud, "I hope you don't mind hot dogs cooked on the electric grill. I don't have an outdoor cooker."

Ted nodded toward her nephew. "We men are hungry. We like hot dogs cooked any old way, don't we, Simon?"

∞

She couldn't believe it. Simon was actually smiling! "The hot dogs are nearly ready. Why don't you sit there, Ted, next to Simon, and I'll sit between the girls."

When they were seated, Sammy bowed her head and thanked the Lord for their food and asked Him to take care of the children's mother.

"Our mother is off riding on her boyfriend's motorcycle," Simon explained as he smeared mustard on his hot dog. "Do you have a motorcycle, Ted?"

"Nope, but I ride my friend's occasionally. I'm more into trucks. Maybe I can take you for a ride in mine sometime, if your aunt doesn't mind. I think you'll like it. It's got those shiny hubcaps that keep spinning even after my truck has stopped moving."

"I saw those on TV once. They're neat. Can I go, Aunt Sammy?"

Sammy continued to stare at Simon in amazement. He was not only smiling but also carrying on a conversation with Ted. "If Ted wants to take you, it's fine with me."

"And he's gonna show me how to throw a ball. He said he wouldn't even get mad if I threw it over his head."

She shot a grateful glance toward their guest. "That's really nice of Ted."

Ted winked at her. "Hey, every boy should know how to throw a ball. Simon and I might even take in a game out at Greer Stadium sometime."

"Ted and his daddy used to go to games there," Simon related with authority. "His dad taught him how to throw a ball like he's gonna teach me."

The five enjoyed their dinner as Ted related story after story about his own childhood. He was such a nice man, good-looking and apparently a good worker. He'd been at the fire department for a number of years and seemed to love it. It was hard to believe some woman hadn't snatched him up before now. Other than having trouble understanding God's will for something that happened in his life, was there another flaw she was missing? A hot temper maybe? No, if he'd had a hot temper or a short fuse, he would have exploded when Simon tackled him at the front door.

"What're you thinking about?" Ted nudged her elbow as he reached for the last hot dog on the plate.

"Just—things. Sorry. My mind wandered for a minute. It looks like the girls are finished. Maybe I'd better dip the ice cream."

He grabbed her arm as she stood. "I don't know how you do it, Sammy. Work a full-time job during the day and take care of these children nights and weekends. Don't you ever have time for just plain fun?"

"She plays games with us," Tina volunteered. "That's fun."

Ted let out a good-natured snort. "That wasn't exactly the kind of fun I meant, but knowing your aunt, I'm sure she enjoys playing games with you."

∾

After the ice cream had been eaten, Sammy sent the girls into the living room to watch the video she'd rented for them and Simon to play with his handheld video game while she and Ted carried things back into the kitchen. "I've never seen Simon so agreeable," she told him, pulling open the refrigerator door and placing the mustard and catsup bottles on the shelf.

"It seems to me he has every right to be disagreeable. Oh, you're a great substitute mother, and I'm sure he enjoys living with you, but everyone knows a child longs for that perfect home and family."

"I wish these children had that perfect home and the love they deserve."

Ted moved toward her and encircled her in his arms. She smelled good. Like flowers. "They love you. I can tell."

Sammy's eyes widened. "And I love them. What I do for them, I do willingly and count it a privilege."

He responded with a sigh, in awe of her dedication.

"How much longer is your brother's family going to be with you?"

Ted shrugged his shoulders. "As long as they need to stay, I guess."

"I'm sure they appreciate your willingness to take them in as you have."

"Yeah, I guess they do, but I wish they'd show their appreciation by doing a better job with their kids. Those boys need the same kind of loving discipline you're giving Simon." Ted backed away then glanced at his watch. "Guess I'd better be going. I don't want to overstay my welcome. Besides, I have to work tomorrow."

"I do need to get the children bathed and to bed."

He hated to see the evening come to an end. "I've got an idea. They're having a Christian concert at the old Ryman Auditorium next weekend. I heard them advertise it on my car radio. I'm off Saturday. I'd like to take you." He was disappointed when she shook her head.

"Thanks for the invitation, but I can't go. My mom works every other Saturday and is dead tired when she gets home. I couldn't think of asking her to babysit after such a long day."

"What about your neighbor?"

"Saturday night is her bingo night. She plays every Saturday."

"Then we'll take the kids with us." *Did those words come out of my mouth?*

Sammy nodded toward the living room. "I—I don't know, Ted. They behave well in church." She chuckled. "Most of the time, anyway—but a concert? I wouldn't want to embarrass you."

"If they get bored, we'll leave." He grabbed her hand. "Come on, Sammy. Say yes."

"Ted, you're such a nice man, and I appreciate your offer, but you really don't have to do this."

He tightened his grip on her hand. "Have to? I want to. I'm sure the kids'll do fine. The concert starts at eight, so I'll pick you up about seven, okay?" He loved it when her face brightened.

"If you're sure—"

"I'm sure." Bending, he planted a quick kiss on her cheek and released her hand. "Thanks for the great supper."

"Great supper? Hot dogs?"

"The hot dogs were good, but it was the company that made it special." He reached out his hand and was pleased when she took it. "I'll tell the kids good-bye and be on my way."

The pair walked into the living room where two sleepy-looking little girls huddled together in the corner of the sofa, their brother sitting on the other end, his full attention focused on the video game in his hand.

" 'Bye, Tina. 'Bye, Harley." Ted leaned over them and gently wiggled his fingers through their silky curls then reached out his hand toward Simon, who looked at it as if he wasn't exactly sure what he was supposed to do. Reaching his hand out even farther, Ted said, "Put it there, pal."

Simon grinned then grabbed Ted's hand and gave it a vigorous shake. " 'Bye, Ted."

Ted was happy when Sammy walked him to the door. He wanted to kiss her good night, but this was only their second date, so maybe he'd be overstepping his mark. In fact, it wasn't even a date. She'd simply invited him over for dinner. "See you Saturday about seven." The smile she gave him made him want to kiss her even more.

"I'll understand if you change your mind."

"No way, and you can't change your mind either, okay?" To his surprise she stood on tiptoe and kissed him on the cheek.

"Okay."

He backed awkwardly out the door. *Wow, what a woman!*

∞

"Hey, Benay, what's up with you?" Captain Grey sat down at the table next to Ted, coffee cup in hand. "You've been spacey ever since you came to work this morning."

"Spacey? Me?"

The captain nudged him with his elbow. "Yeah, you, Mr. Confirmed Bachelor. Anything happening between you and that little gal you met on the *General Jackson*?"

"I had hot dogs with her and her sister's three kids."

Jake sat down on the other side of Ted, his coffee cup coming down with a *kerplunk* on the table. "Hot dogs? That's it?"

Ted nodded, grinning. "Yeah, but we have another date next weekend."

Cal, who'd been listening but hadn't added to the conversation, leaned back in his chair, a smirk on his face. "A real date? Sure you can handle that? You aren't going to take those kids along, are you?"

Ted flinched. "Actually, yes. She doesn't have a babysitter for them."

Jake sputtered and nearly choked on his big swig of coffee. "Babysitter? What about the kids' mother?"

"She ran out on them. Went off with some bozo on his motorcycle."

Cal shook his head. "Kinda hard to romance a gal with three kids."

Jake grabbed a doughnut from the sack in the middle of the table, broke off a chunk, and stuffed it into his mouth. "Hey, couldn't you find you some nice girl without kids?"

Cal nodded in agreement. "Kids can sure complicate things. Ask me. I married a woman with two of them. Between their needs and her ex-husband butting in where he's not wanted, life can be pretty miserable."

Captain Grey rose and placed his hand on Ted's shoulder. "Back off, guys. Give him a break. You've been bugging Ted for months to get himself a girlfriend. Now he has one."

As the fire alarm sounded throughout the station, drawing every man's immediate attention, Ted breathed a sigh of relief. He hated talking about himself and wondered why he'd even mentioned his upcoming date. He should have realized they'd make a big deal of it. Well, he wouldn't have to worry about that now. Duty called.

∞

"Let me come over there and take care of the children Saturday night. I love spending time with them," Sammy's mother said when Sammy phoned her the next morning and told her about Ted's visit and his invitation. "I feel bad I can't help you out more with them."

"No, Mom, I can't ask you to do that. Besides, Ted wants them to go with us." Sammy smiled. "He's terrific, Mom. I've never met anyone like him. Even Simon likes him. But don't worry about the children. They'll be fine. I'm sure Ted wouldn't have invited them if he hadn't wanted them."

"Maybe it's you he wants, dear. Did you ever think of that? A man willing to invite three children along on a date must want to spend time with you."

Sammy glanced at her image in the mirror and adjusted her neckline. "I haven't told him about my—surgery."

"You've only had a few dates, sweetie. I doubt he's told you everything about himself. Maybe he has athlete's foot. Don't worry about it. If things develop between you, you can tell him then. Meanwhile, just enjoy yourself."

Sammy snickered at her mother's choice of words. "Athlete's foot is hardly the same as having someone else's heart beating in your chest."

"Everything in its time, sweetheart. Do what you think best, but if I were in your place, I'd wait and tell him later, when the two of you know one another better."

"What you're saying is, don't scare him off any sooner than necessary, right?"

"I guess you could say that. Ever hear the phrase 'don't borrow trouble'? Telling him now may be pointless. At this stage in your relationship, you two barely know one another."

"You're probably right, but I don't want you worrying about us. We're definitely taking the children along. You spend the evening with Dad. With his physical problems, he needs you more than we do. Give him a big kiss and hug for me, okay?"

"Okay, but if you change your mind, I'm more than happy to keep the children for you."

"I won't change my mind, but thanks for the offer. Talk to you later, Mom."

Sammy thought over her mother's words. Maybe she was being needlessly concerned. Who knew? Their Saturday date could be their last one. Maybe he'd never invite her out again. Why go into detail about something unnecessary? She'd wait and see what the weekend held before deciding when she should tell him.

She was tempted to buy a new outfit for the concert but decided she had plenty of appropriate things hanging in her closet. Besides, shopping with three children was hardly worth it. After trying on at least six outfits, she selected her navy blazer and off-white skirt topped with a lightweight red turtleneck shirt.

By the time the doorbell rang the following Saturday night, she was a bundle of nerves. Harley had resisted taking a much-needed nap, Tina spilled orange juice on her best dress and had to change it at the last minute, and Sammy couldn't locate one of the earrings she'd wanted to wear. To her amazement, the only person who seemed in control was Simon, and he'd been dressed and playing with his video game for over an hour.

"Wow, you look beautiful," Ted told her when she pasted on a smile and opened the door with little Harley in her arms and Tina by her side.

Before she could respond with a thank-you, Simon shot past her, his hand extended. "Hi, Ted."

"Well, hi, yourself, Simon." Ted gave his hand a vigorous shake then reached out a ball glove. "Didn't think I'd remember, did you?"

The boy's eyes shone. "This is the one your dad gave you?"

Ted bobbed his head. "Sure is. I thought you could keep it here, and next time I come over we'll play catch. That okay with you?"

"Yeah." Simon took the glove and slipped it onto his hand. "Hey, look! It fits!"

Ted grinned. "I told you it would. Take good care of it, okay?"

"Maybe you shouldn't—"

Ted put his finger to Sammy's lips. "Don't worry about it. If I hadn't wanted Simon to have it, I wouldn't have brought it. Everybody ready to go? We're going to have to ride in my truck, but it has an extended cab so there should be room for everyone."

After carefully placing the glove on the sofa, Simon raced to the door. "Your truck. Wow. Now I can see your hubcaps."

"You have to sit quietly," Sammy told the children later as the usher led the five to their seats in the big historic auditorium.

"I want a drink."

All eyes turned toward Harley. Sammy gave her niece a slight frown. "Not now, baby. You had a drink just before you left home."

Ted smiled at the little girl. "Maybe we can get something to drink after the concert."

"I want one now."

Sammy brushed a lock of hair from Harley's forehead. "No, Harley. Not until after the concert is over." She gestured toward the stage. "In a minute those curtains will open and—"

"I need a drink, too."

With a frown, Sammy turned toward Tina who was sitting on the other side of her. "You and your sister are going to have to wait. I warned you before we left home that—"

"Want me to take them?"

Her frown disappearing, Sammy smiled. "No. Thank you, Ted, but it's important that I follow through when I've told the children something. Don't worry about them. I doubt they'll go into dehydration before the concert ends." She'd barely gotten the words out when the lights dimmed, the curtains opened, and the concert began. Sammy glanced from child to child, each one's attention focused on the sight and the sounds of the music. Then she looked at Ted, who smiled at her approvingly and gave her a thumbs-up. But by the time an intermission was announced, all three children, especially young Harley, were getting fidgety.

"I have to go to the bathroom," Simon announced the moment the auditorium lights came on.

∞

Ted leaned toward Sammy. "Why don't I take him?"

"If you don't mind, that'd be great. That way I can take the girls to the ladies' room and then get them a drink."

"Sounds good to me. We'll meet you back here." He stepped out into the aisle, making way for Sammy and the girls to pass, then motioned toward the boy. "Come on, Simon. We'd better hurry if we don't want to stand in a long line."

Apparently it was too late. The line extended into the hallway. Just as they were about to enter the men's restroom, another man exited, a former classmate of Ted's. "Brian! Long time no see."

"Hey, Ted. Where've you been keeping yourself?"

"You go on, Simon," Ted told the boy as he reached out to shake his friend's hand. "I'll wait for you out here." He watched until Simon disappeared inside then moved to join his friend.

"That your kid?" Brian asked, nodding toward the doorway.

Ted laughed. "Nope, 'fraid not. Simon's the nephew of a friend of mine. How about you? You got kids?"

"Yep, three of them. I heard you were a fireman. That true?"

For the next several minutes the men conversed, laughing and catching up on the more than eight years since they'd seen one another. Ted noted the crowd around them was thinning out. "Well, I'd better go find Simon so we can get back to our seats. Good to see you, Brian."

"Yeah, good to see you, too."

Ted walked into the men's room, which was nearly deserted, but Simon was nowhere in sight. "Simon," he called out, stooping to check beneath the stall doors. "You in here?"

No answer.

His heart racing, he rushed out into the hall. "Simon?" But Simon wasn't there either. *He probably went back to his seat,* Ted reasoned, as he made his way to their section. But as he reached their aisle the lights dimmed, and the second half of the concert started. Narrowing his eyes, he finally located their seats. There sat Sammy and the two girls, but no Simon. His heart pounded in his ears. *Where could Simon be?*

He hurried back out into the hall, retracing his footsteps to the men's room. Still no Simon. Should he go back and tell Sammy he'd lost the boy? Contact security? Surely the theater had some kind of security set up. *I don't have kids! I have no idea what to do!*

"Are you having trouble locating your seat, sir?"

Ted spun around and found a lady wearing a badge with the word USHER printed on it staring at him. "No, I've lost someone, a nine-year-old boy."

"Was he wearing a red sweater?"

Ted nodded. "Yes, have you seen him?"

She placed a consoling hand on Ted's arm and smiled at him. "Yes, he couldn't remember where he was sitting, so I walked him up and down the aisles until we located his aunt. He's in his seat."

"Whew! You have no idea how relieved I am. I was so afraid something had—"

"He's fine. Nice little boy. He even thanked me for helping him."

"And I thank you, too. Guess I'd better get back to my seat before they send out a posse to find me."

Sammy leaned across Simon and touched Ted's wrist as he sat down. "Where were you? I was beginning to worry when Simon said he couldn't find you."

"*He* couldn't find *me*?" Deciding it wouldn't be polite to carry on a conversation and disturb those seated around them, he shrugged and whispered, "I'll tell you later."

By the time the concert ended, Harley was sound asleep in Ted's arms with the sleeping Tina curled up in Sammy's lap. Ted had to laugh to himself as he gazed at his little group. To anyone who didn't know them, they probably looked like the average American family. Mom, Dad, and three kids. All they needed were a minivan, a dog, and a house with a white picket fence. And though those things had scared him in the past, somehow now they didn't seem half bad.

"We had a great time, Ted," Sammy told him once she'd tucked the children in bed.

After one final glance at the eleven o'clock news, he hit the off button on the remote, leaned back against the sofa, and motioned her to sit beside him.

"I had a great time, too."

"You never did tell me how you lost Simon."

Ted sucked in a deep breath and circled his arm across the sofa's back. "I didn't lose him. I was waiting for him in the hall right outside the restroom door, visiting with an old school friend. He managed to get past me without my seeing him."

Smiling, she leaned back into his arm. "No harm done. That nice usher helped him find me, but I started to worry when Simon said he couldn't find you."

"Guess he just missed me in the crowd. I really felt bad." Ted gave her a hesitant grin. "Actually, I panicked. Here you'd entrusted him into my care, and I'd let him get away. I was so afraid something had happened to him."

"Well, it didn't. Take it from me. Simon has a propensity for wandering off. I have to keep my eye on him. He's curious about everything."

Ted tightened his arm around her shoulders, enjoying the delicate scent of her hair. "You sure you're not saying that to make me feel better?" What was it about her that drew him to her? He'd dated other women, without the family entanglements she had; yet he hadn't felt the same vibes with them as he did when he was with her.

Tilting her head slightly, she smiled at him. "No, it's the truth. He's always wandering off. I don't think he does it on purpose. As I said, he's just curious, and his curiosity gets him into trouble."

For a moment Ted stared into her beautiful eyes, eyes that reminded him of a Tennessee sky on a cloudless day. "I was kinda like that myself when I was a kid. I was fascinated by anything that worked, made a sound, or took batteries. I had to know what made them tick."

"Guess it's a man thing." Sammy tugged her collar up about her neck.

"You cold?" Ted used his question as an excuse to pull her even closer.

"No, I'm fine. Are you cold?"

"No, just right. What are your plans for tomorrow?"

Sammy's brow creased. "Tomorrow?"

"Yeah, I'm off again tomorrow. I thought maybe we could do something together."

She turned to face him with a look of surprise. "Are you serious? I thought after spending the evening with three rowdy kids, you'd want to run for the door and I'd never see you again."

He huffed. "It wasn't so bad, although I admit Simon disappearing gave me a few anxious moments. The kids were much better behaved than I thought they'd be. My nephews could learn a lot from them."

A smile returned to her face. "Back to your question. Since tomorrow is

Sunday, the kids and I will be going to church, but you could come along."

"I usually drive to where my parents live and go to my home church with them."

"Maybe they wouldn't mind if you missed this one time." Sammy took his free hand and folded it in hers. "We'd like for you to come with us."

How could he refuse that beautiful face? The pleading of those big blue eyes?

"The children are in Sunday school during the worship service, and my substitute is filling in for me and teaching my class, so it'll be just the two of us."

"Just the two of us? You mean I can have you all to myself for one whole hour?"

She gave him a childish giggle that set his heart singing.

"Maybe longer. I might be able to persuade my mom to take them home with her, and we could have the afternoon to ourselves. That is, if you *want* to spend the afternoon with me."

"You drive a hard bargain."

"Only because I enjoy your company." Sammy glanced at the clock. "I hate to say it, but I think we'd better call it a night. I need to get to bed. I'll have to be up by six to get my shower and make sure the children are bathed, fed, and dressed in time." She stood and reached out her hand.

He took it, stood, then slipped his arm around her waist and guided her toward the door. "Makes me tired thinking about all the work you have to do just to get to church."

"So are you coming with me?" she asked, pulling the door open before gazing into his eyes.

After wrapping her in his arms, Ted grinned down at Sammy. "On one condition."

She eyed him warily. "Condition? What condition?"

"That you let me kiss you good night."

∞

Sammy's heart did a cartwheel. She'd longed for Ted's kiss since the day he'd shown up at her office, but she'd never expected it to happen. Now here she was being held in his arms, and he was asking to kiss her. Not only that, their kiss was the condition that would bring Ted to her church. He had to be joking.

"What's your answer, Sammy?" he whispered, his chin nuzzling her hair as he drew her nearer to him. "Are you going to let me kiss you good night?"

She sent him a timid smile. "I do want you to go to church with me, Ted, but I can't trade you a kiss for it. It wouldn't be right."

"Does that mean I can kiss you whether I go to church with you or not?"

Her smile widened. "That's not exactly what I said."

Using his forefinger to tilt her face upward, Ted slowly leaned toward her until his lips brushed hers.

The touch of his lips, the scent of his aftershave, the tender way his arms held her close, made her almost giddy. She held her breath, hoping just by holding it, her throbbing heart would settle down.

Though Sammy tried to hold back, she thought she would explode with joy as his lips pressed against hers and she was enfolded in his strong arms, his fingers splayed across her back. Their kiss was pure ecstasy. When it finally ended, she leaned into him, reveling in the moment, one she would treasure forever.

Slowly Ted released her, his gaze locking with hers as they parted. "What time should I pick you up?" he asked, seeming as dazed as she felt.

"Ten," she answered weakly, not even sure her words were loud enough to be heard.

"Ten it is." He started to step out the door but stopped, gazing at her with eyes that told her their kiss had been special to him, too. "One for the road?"

Feeling more feminine than she had in a long time, Sammy gave him a demure smile, then stood on tiptoe and kissed his cheek.

"Nice, but not exactly what I had in mind." Wrapping his arms about her again, his lips sought hers, and his kiss made her head spin. "Good night. Thanks for a great evening."

Dipping her head to avoid his gaze, Sammy backed away, her legs trembling and threatening to crumple beneath her. "Good night, Ted."

After gazing at her for a few more seconds, he stepped outside, closing the door behind him. Sammy turned and leaned against it, her fingers gently touching her lips, as if by touching them she could preserve the kisses he'd bestowed upon them.

Her moment of overwhelming joy collapsed as her hand went to her heart. *I have to tell him. Soon. Though our attraction for each other may never go beyond where it is now, it's not fair to keep something like this from him. It seems that, just by being my friend, he has the right to know the heart beating within me is not my own.*

Her mother's words came racing back. *Don't borrow trouble. Telling him at this early stage of your relationship may be pointless.*

"You may be right, Mom," Sammy said aloud, glancing at her mother's photograph on the mantel. "The last thing I'd want, though, would be to hurt Ted by keeping the truth from him. But I can't take the chance of having him turn away now, especially since he's agreed to go to church with me. The truth will have to wait a little longer."

∞

Ted crawled into his truck and turned the key in the ignition, visions of the lovely

Sammy rotating through his mind. She was the kind of woman he'd hoped to find one day, and he'd just kissed her. Giving his head a wake-up shake, his hands came thudding down on the steering wheel. *Man, what are you thinking? She may be everything you ever wanted, but what about those kids? From the sound of it, that sister of hers may never come back. Do you want to be saddled with three kids who aren't even yours? Especially when you almost decided you don't even want children?*

He shifted into drive and nudged the truck slowly forward. *Who knows? Maybe her sister will come back. I can't let her guardianship of those children stand between me and the first woman I've been truly interested in. I think I'll hang around for a while at least and see what happens.* ∞

Sammy was up a full thirty minutes before her alarm sounded, despite the fact that thinking about the unexpected kiss had kept her awake half the night. Nonetheless, she was excited about the day that was about to unfold before her—until she showered and caught a glimpse of her image in the mirror. Though most of the redness had long since faded, to Sammy, the nasty scar was as ugly as ever. *But without this scar and what it represents, I'd no doubt be a dead woman by now.*

"Up, up, time to get up," she told Simon while rousting him out of bed an hour later. "Guess what! Ted is going to church with us!"

Simon, who was always the hardest to get out of bed, peeked out from under the covers. "He is?"

"Yes, and guess what else! I talked to Grandma, and she wants you guys to spend the afternoon with her and Grandpa. Isn't that great?"

Simon eyed her suspiciously. "Are you and Ted going to Grandma's, too?"

"No, I'm spending the afternoon with Ted."

Simon threw back the covers, sat up in bed, and crossed his arms over his chest. "I wanna stay with you and Ted. He promised he'd play catch with me."

Sammy reached for the boy's hand and tugged him to his feet. "And I'm sure he will. Just not today."

Pulling away from her grasp, Simon dropped back onto the bed, a scowl marring his face. "Then I'm not going to church."

Her first impulse was to order him out of bed and into the bathtub, but she remembered how he'd unexpectedly taken to Ted and smiled at him instead. "I'm sure Ted will play catch with you as soon as he gets time. You wouldn't want to disappoint Grandma and Grandpa, would you? They're looking forward to your visit. Now hurry up and get your bath. You *are* going to church."

She smiled as she said it but added a firmness to her voice, which she hoped would settle the matter. To her relief, Simon slid to his feet and padded quietly toward the bathroom.

While he bathed, Sammy awakened the two girls and gave them their breakfast. By nine thirty, all three children were lined up on the sofa, dressed in their Sunday best, waiting for Ted while Sammy hurriedly tidied up the kitchen.

The parking lot was nearly full by the time they arrived at the church. After delivering the children to their Sunday school classes, Sammy led him through the welcome center toward the sanctuary, stopping briefly along the way to introduce him to Pastor Day and other friends and acquaintances.

"Oh, look—there's my mom. I want you to meet her." Taking hold of his hand, she led him toward a group of women who were engaged in conversation. She touched her mother's elbow. "Mom, this is the man I've been telling you about. Ted Benay. Ted, this is my mom."

Ted extended his hand. "Hello, Mrs. Samuel. I've heard a lot about you, too."

Mrs. Samuel wrapped her arm about her daughter's shoulders and smiled. "It's nice to finally meet you, Ted, but don't believe everything this girl says. She's biased. By the way, Sammy, you needn't pick up the children this evening. Your father and I will drive them home."

"Are you sure? I know Dad doesn't like you driving after dark. I could come—"

"I'm sure. Besides, it's not that far. We'll plan to have them home about seven. You two have a great day and don't give the children a second thought. They'll be fine."

After thanking her mother, Sammy linked her arm in Ted's, and they stepped into the sanctuary.

"Nice church. It's much bigger than the one I go to," Ted admitted after he and Sammy were seated in a pew near the front. "God's probably looking down and saying, 'What's Ted Benay doing here? This isn't his home church.'"

Sammy gave him a playful nudge. "I'm sure He's glad you're in church, even if it isn't the one you usually attend."

"You think so?"

"I know so."

"I only came here today because I wanted to be with you."

"And I asked you because I wanted to be with you. I'm glad you're here."

The sound of the church's mighty organ filled the sanctuary as the organist began playing the prelude, temporarily ending their conversation. Sammy was delighted when Ted sang the hymns and worship choruses along with her and was surprised at the richness of his voice.

"You must have sung in the choir, right?" she asked him as they made their way through the double doors toward the parking lot when the service ended. "You have a great voice."

He nodded. "Yep, used to every Sunday. Even did a few solos, but since I work so many Sundays now, I'm not able to anymore. Though I don't go regularly, I still love the Lord. But I sure don't understand the way He does things."

"He never promised we'd understand. I know there are things in my life I don't understand, but I have to trust Him."

"It isn't that I don't trust Him—though maybe that's part of it. I just wish I understood Him."

She couldn't be sure, but she thought she heard a note of despair in his voice, a sadness. What could have happened to make him question God's will?

His demeanor suddenly changed to one of happiness, and he spun her around to face him. "Enough of this gloom and doom—where shall we eat lunch? They have a fabulous Sunday buffet at Martha's at the Plantation Restaurant on the grounds of the old Belle Meade mansion. Or we could go to Calhoun's and have their famous ribs. Or maybe to Mario's for Italian or the New Orleans Manor for seafood. Your choice. You name it."

Sammy's eyes widened. "Aren't those all a bit expensive?"

"Not when you're taking your best girl out to dinner."

Her breath caught in her throat. "Best girl?"

Ted winked then pulled open the door of his truck and, with a grand swoop of his arm, motioned her inside. "Best and only girl."

She moved past him, accepted his hand to assist her into the truck, and then winked back. "And you're my best and only guy. Today."

After closing her door he hurried around to the driver's side and crawled in. "Today? Does that mean you have another guy warming up in the wings to take over my spot tomorrow?"

Tilting her head coyly, she gave him a teasing smile. "That's for me to know and you to find out."

He twisted the key in the ignition, revved up the engine, and turned to face her, his expression serious as his hand went to the gearshift. "I wasn't joking, Sammy. You *are* my best girl. If you feel the same way about me, I'd like for us to spend time together and get to know each other better."

Stunned yet excited by his words, she gaped at him. "You really mean that?"

He smiled. "Wouldn't have said it if I didn't. Seems like all I do lately is think about you."

"I—" She lowered her head, her fingers working nervously at the mock turtleneck of her shirt. "I—think about you all the time, too."

His smile turned into a full-fledged grin, and he shoved the gearshift into drive then fell in line with the other vehicles waiting to exit the parking lot. "Now that that's settled, tell me where you want to eat and what you would like to do for the rest of the afternoon."

"Can we go anywhere I'd like? We don't need to go to such expensive places. My tastes are pretty simple."

"Believe me, price makes no difference, but, as I said, you name it. This is your day. We'll do whatever you want."

"Then I'd like to pick up a bucket of the Colonel's chicken, mashed potatoes, and slaw, rent a couple of movies, then kick off our shoes and eat a leisurely meal at my apartment."

Ted took his eyes off the traffic ahead of him long enough to eye her suspiciously. "You're kidding, right?"

She shook her head. "No, I'm absolutely serious. I can't remember when I last sat down to a meal at my house without having to jump up every few minutes to wipe up spilled milk, refill a plate, referee a spat, or take a child to the bathroom. Eating a meal at home today, without the patter of little feet, would be a real luxury. And watching a movie? An entire movie not designated for viewers under thirteen? I can't even remember the last one I saw in its entirety. It doesn't even need to be a chick flick. A comedy or an action movie would be fine. A treat indeed."

Ted maneuvered his truck out onto the street and into the line of traffic then reached across the seat and grabbed her hand, giving it a squeeze. "Lady, you are my kind of woman. A bucket of chicken and a couple of movies it is."

Sammy let out a sigh of satisfaction. "So I'm a cheap date. What can I say?" Her heart pounded furiously at the thought of spending the entire afternoon with him.

After nearly thirty minutes giggling over the movie selections and finding two they agreed on, they picked up the chicken. It was well after one o'clock when they entered her apartment. They'd scarcely closed the door when Ted's cell phone rang.

"Hello." He paused. "Yes, I have it. Why?"

The expression on Ted's face told Sammy not only was something wrong, but Ted was upset about it. When he finally hung up he said, "It seems my nephews found my bowling ball in the back of the hall closet in a box under some magazines where I'd hidden it from them. They were rolling it across my living room floor and hit the sliding glass door leading onto my balcony and shattered it. That was my sister-in-law wanting to know if I had homeowner's insurance."

Sammy's eyes widened. "Was anyone hurt?"

"No. I thought sure I'd hidden it so they wouldn't find it. I probably should have locked it in the storage container in my truck bed, but that's hindsight."

Sammy watched as he put the phone back into its belt holster. "Do you have to go home and board up the opening?"

"Not now. It's nice outside. I'll do it later. I'm not about to let a little broken glass ruin our day. I told her where to find the phone number for my insurance company and to go ahead and call them. I hope she and my brother will clean up the mess. If not, I'll do it when I get home."

She smiled and patted the cushion next to her on the sofa. "Maybe some nice tender chicken will make you feel better." She reached into the carryout sack, pulled out its contents, and placed them on the coffee table in front of them. "If, after we pray, the chicken and the mashed potatoes have cooled off, I'll zap them in the microwave."

"Good. Those things are so much better hot." Ted accepted the plate then bowed his head and remained silent while she prayed, echoing her amen.

After their meal, he helped her clean up before they went back into the living room to watch their first movie.

"How about some popcorn?" she asked when the movie ended and the credits began to roll.

"With lots of butter and salt?"

She wrinkled up her nose. "I guess this one time wouldn't clog up our arteries too much."

He followed her into the kitchen. "I hope I didn't sound grumpy earlier. You know, about the bowling ball."

"I thought you took the news fairly well." She pulled the popcorn bag from the cabinet, placed it in the microwave and hit the button marked POPCORN.

Ted rubbed at his temples. "Okay. We've talked a lot about me but very little about you. Tell me something about yourself, Sammy, something I don't already know."

He gave her a playful nudge. "Have you always been as perfect as you are now? Surely you have a few flaws."

Yes, one huge one running right down the center of my chest. "Perfect? That's the last word I would use to describe myself. I'm impatient with the children, put off my bill paying until the last minute, let my laundry go until the hamper is running over, hate to clean the bathroom, forget where I left my cell phone, drive my car until the gas peg is on empty—"

Ted laughed. "Those are the worst flaws you can think of? Sammy, those are nothing, not even worth mentioning. Come on—surely you can do better than that. Give me one big flaw."

She trembled at his question. *This is the perfect opportunity to tell him. Maybe I'd better just blurt it out and get it over with.*

The dinger sounded as the microwave shut off. Ted carefully lifted out the hot bag then rubbed his hands briskly together. "Mmm, hot popcorn. Looks like you're off the hook, momentarily anyway. Let's take this into the living room and eat it before it gets cold."

Sammy's body went limp. She felt like a prisoner getting a last-minute reprieve from the governor. "Ah, good idea."

"I know you have a brother. Do you have any other siblings?" She hoped to change the subject and avoid talking about herself once they were seated again on the sofa, sharing the popcorn directly from the opened bag.

He stopped eating, his hand poised in midair. "Why did you ask me that?"

Did his voice have a sharp edge to it, or was it her imagination? "I'm curious, that's all. You said we should get better acquainted."

A deep sigh seemed to come from the pit of his stomach as he stared at her. "Sorry, Sammy. I didn't mean to snap at you. In answer to your question, no, other than my brother I don't have any other siblings. Not now. Tiger—that's what I called my twin sister—died several years ago in a car accident. She never regained consciousness."

Startled by his revelation, she grabbed hold of his arm, nearly knocking the popcorn bag out of his hand. "Oh, Ted, I'm so sorry. She was your twin? That must have made her loss even harder."

Closing his eyelids tightly, he bit at his lip. "Tiger and I were close. I—I still can't believe she's gone. She was such a beautiful woman, inside and out."

Sammy slid closer and wrapped her arm around his neck, her head resting against his. She wanted so much to comfort him, but other than "I'm sorry" what could she say? "Is—is that why you question God's will? Because He took your sister?"

His misty eyes turned cold. "Wouldn't you question God if He took your sister in the prime of her life or one of those children you're caring for?"

"Without going through the experience I can't honestly say, but I don't think I'd *question* His will. I'd be upset at their loss and wonder *why* He took them, but God knows best. God created us. He has every right to take us when He chooses."

Ted pointed an accusing finger in her direction. "You're right about one thing. *You* can't say without going through the experience, but I can. I've been there. I've felt the horrible pain of losing someone I loved."

Her heart went out to him. "We've all lost someone we love. Maybe not a twin sister, but that doesn't mean we should blame God. We see only our side and the grief we feel. God sees the whole picture. It's never easy to lose a loved one under any circumstance, whether by old age, natural causes, illness, or an accident. Though losing someone that close to you, without a chance to tell them good-bye, has to be one of the worst horrors a human being can endure."

A visible tremor racked through Ted's body. "Especially if *you* were the one driving the car!"

A jolt of surprise raced through her body like a sudden electric shock. "*You* were driving the car?"

The pain of remembrance showed on his face. "Yeah, me. Her very own brother. I tried to stop in time when that fool's car came barreling through the intersection, but I couldn't. If only I'd sped up or slowed down or had been ten seconds earlier or ten seconds later, he wouldn't have hit us, and she might have—"

Placing her palms on his cheeks, Sammy swiveled his face toward hers. "Look at me. Listen to me. You can't blame yourself, Ted. It was the other person's fault. Not yours. Though I didn't have the privilege of knowing your sister, I'm sure she wouldn't have blamed you. You can't go on letting that accident eat you up like this."

Tears rolled down his cheeks. "She wasn't wearing her seat belt, and that was my fault, too. I'd asked her to get my sunglasses out of my jacket, which I'd left in the backseat. She'd taken off her seat belt to reach for them just before that car hit us. If she'd had it on, maybe she would have survived."

With her thumbs, Sammy gently brushed away his tears. "And maybe it wouldn't have made any difference. That's something you'll never know. You told me that even though you're questioning God, you still love Him. Surely you haven't forgotten the scripture that says all things work together for good to them that love God. I know it's hard to believe any good could come from your sister's death, but we can't second-guess God's will. From the sound of things, your life could have been taken, too. He spared *your* life. He must have a purpose for you."

"I understand that, and I'm thankful I'm alive. But why would He take my beautiful, talented sister and leave me behind? It doesn't make sense." Ted pulled one of the paper napkins from the stack the store had given him when he'd picked up the chicken and wiped at his eyes. "Losing her was bad enough, but what the rest of my family agreed to do really upset me."

Chapter 6

Sammy's eyes widened. Unless he was talking about his sister being cremated, which many people didn't want for their loved ones, she had no idea what he was talking about.

"They wanted her heart to be removed from her body and given to someone else!"

His words struck Sammy with such force they nearly rendered her helpless. She felt sick to her stomach, as if she was going to throw up. Pushing away from him, she leaned back against the sofa, clutching its arm for support, struggling to catch her breath.

"I guess my sister had signed a donor card, but she hadn't told me about it." He was apparently so absorbed in telling about the accident that he hadn't noticed her reaction. "Can you imagine loving parents giving permission to do something like that to their daughter? I couldn't. I fought them on it, but I was overruled. They were for it, and Tiger had signed that card. I still haven't forgiven them for it. According to that card, she donated her eyes, liver, and other organs, too. They took them all. I still wish my sister had asked me before someone talked her into signing that stupid card."

"But—but—" Her borrowed heart pounded so loudly she could barely hear him. Sammy struggled for words, any words, but they wouldn't come. Finally she managed to say faintly, "But that heart—gave someone else life. Doesn't that make it worthwhile?"

He held up his hand to silence her. "Don't even try, Sammy. Believe me, I've heard all the arguments, and I still disagree. It's my opinion that if God wanted a person with a bad heart to live, He would heal them. I've heard heart recipients only live a few years anyway."

"But a few years could mean a world to the person who needed that heart."

"Losing my sister was the most devastating thing that ever happened to me, especially since I was driving the car, but the idea of having Tiger's heart beating in someone else's body was the crowning blow. If God wanted that other person to live, why didn't He just keep their heart from going bad?"

"I—I don't know."

"I hope I never meet the person who has her heart. I could never look them

305

in the eye, knowing it took my sister's death to keep them alive."

"But, Ted, if your sister was a Christian, her spirit went to be with the Lord, leaving her body behind. That body was only the shell in which she lived."

"That may be true, but that body she left behind was the part of her that I, and everyone else who loved her, saw and loved, and I didn't want anything to happen to it."

For the first time since beginning his upsetting disclosure, Ted looked directly at Sammy. "Your cheeks are flushed. Aren't you feeling well?"

Tugging at her collar, she lowered her head, avoiding his penetrating gaze. "I do feel a little woozy."

He placed his flattened palm on her forehead and frowned. "You feel warm. Can I get you a drink of water?"

"I think I have a headache coming on." She slowly rotated her head from side to side, her fingertips massaging her temples. "Sometimes lying down helps."

"Do you want me to go?"

"No. Go ahead and watch the other movie. I just need to shut my eyes for a while." *And absorb what you said and decide if this is the time I should tell you about my heart or if I should wait until you're not already upset.*

He pushed a lock of hair from her forehead. "I hope my ranting and raving didn't cause your headache."

With great effort she lifted the corners of her mouth into a weak smile. "You only said what you felt. Your words helped me understand you better."

"I've never spelled it out like that to anyone except my family and the man from the mortuary. But with you I felt I could open up, that maybe you'd be the only one to understand my feelings."

I'm the last person who would understand your feelings!

He impatiently grabbed his cell phone when it rang again. Sammy watched him answer it, her insides still churning.

"A toothache, huh? That sounds pretty miserable." Ted's eyes darted toward her. "Yeah, I can come. You'd do the same for me. I'll be there in twenty minutes." He flipped the phone shut. "A buddy of mine, one of the firemen on B shift, has a doozy of a toothache. He wants me to come and finish out his shift for him. I hope you don't mind. I hated to tell him no."

Though it upset Sammy to see him leave so soon, in some ways she was relieved. "But aren't you working tomorrow?"

"Yeah. I keep some extra clothes and shaving gear in my locker at the station, so I'll be fine. But I hate to leave you, especially since you're not feeling well." Cupping her hands in his, he gave her a look of concern. "Take something for that headache, okay?"

"I will."

He glanced at his watch. "I'd better scoot. Can I call you later?"

She nodded. "Yes, that would be nice."

He said a quick good-bye then closed the door, leaving Sammy standing in the middle of the living room, her head throbbing, her heart pounding furiously, and her mind in a whirl.

"A lot of people feel that way about donating their loved one's organs, Sammy," her mother told her three hours later as they stood in Sammy's kitchen preparing mugs of hot cocoa for the children. "Literally thousands of people have signed donor cards and want their organs donated, but Ted's feelings are not that unusual. No one likes the idea of having their loved one's body desecrated." She shrugged. "Even knowing how important it is that someone donated their heart to you, if I lost your father I'd have trouble giving permission for the same reasons Ted has. Maybe I've watched too many of those reality shows on TV where they show parts of an autopsy. Even though I know it's staged, I couldn't bear the thought."

"Neither could I!" Sammy grabbed her mother's arm. "That's what makes me so thankful my donor and their family had the courage to do what they did. Otherwise I might not be here now."

"You must tell him, dear, now that he's poured out his heart to you. You know that, don't you? For his sake *and* for yours. I know I said earlier you should wait, but the time has come. The longer you put it off, the harder it's going to be for both of you. He may not take the news as badly as you expect him to."

"Hey, what's taking so long?" Sammy's father called out from the living room. "These kids are clamoring for their cocoa."

"Be right there, Dad." Sammy circled her arm around her mother and gave her a loving squeeze. "Pray for me, Mom. I want to do the right thing, but it's so hard. I don't want to lose Ted."

"I will, sweetie. God has a plan for your life. If Ted is to be part of that plan, he will be."

Those words echoed over and over in Sammy's mind as she lay curled up beneath the quilt that night, waiting for sleep to overtake her. Finally, after burying her face in the pillow, she released the flood of tears she'd been working so hard to hold back. *Oh, Ted, what have I done? What have I done? If I'd been upfront with you at the beginning, I would never have fallen in love with you, and this wouldn't have happened. But I am in love with you, and I can't stand the thought of losing you. I'm so confused. Only God can get me out of the mess I've made!*

∽

Sammy stared aimlessly out her office window the next morning, sipping the cup of hot coffee she'd purchased from the vending machine in the hall, wondering what kind of night it had been at the fire station. Her phone rang once, twice, then a third time before she turned to answer it.

"Good morning," Ted's voice called out cheerily. "Headache gone?"

Her fingers tightened on the receiver. "All gone. I'm feeling much better. How'd your night go?"

"Biz–zee, in and out of bed all night, but nothing too serious. Mostly minor stuff. I'm hoping to catch a couple of catnaps today. Think you could get an extended lunch hour? I thought maybe I could con you into picking up a couple of burger baskets and bringing them over to the station."

She glanced at her desk calendar. "Sure, I guess I could do that."

"Good. I talk about you all the time, but none of these guys I work with thinks you're real. I want them to meet you."

"You're kidding, right?"

"No, that's the truth. See you about twelve?"

"Ah, sure. Twelve will be fine, Ted. I'll be there."

∞

"I'm here to see Ted Benay," Sammy told the fireman who opened the door when she rang the outside buzzer at noon.

With a congenial smile he eyed her then motioned her inside, closing the door behind her. "So you're Sammy?"

She nodded awkwardly. "Yes, is he here?"

"Sammy!" Ted rushed into the waiting room and latched onto her hand. "You made it."

Three other firemen hurried in and gave her the once-over as the first one had done. "Well, I'll be," one of them said, nudging Ted's arm. "She *is* real. You've got yourself a girlfriend."

"A good-lookin' girlfriend," the third one added.

"Too good-lookin' for the likes of this ugly guy," the fourth one added, ramming his fist into Ted's arm. "Must be all that great fireman's pay you're hoardin' in your attic that attracted her."

"Actually it's my animal magnetism that attracted her." Slipping his arm around her waist and drawing her to him protectively, Ted rolled his eyes. "Don't listen to this bunch of old windbags, Sammy. They've been here way too long, heard too many fire bells, and it's affected their thinking."

Grinning, Captain Grey joined them. "I have to admit, Ted, I never expected such a beautiful young lady to take up with the likes of you."

Unable to think of a thing to say and overwhelmed with all their undeserved flattery, she simply smiled at each one before turning her smile on Ted.

He drew her closer. "See what I have to put up with, Sammy? Can you imagine having to spend twenty-four-hour shifts with this bunch of characters?"

"Come on, fellas." The captain motioned them toward the day room. "Might be a good idea if we gave them some privacy. Looks like Sammy's brought their lunch."

"Nice to have met you," she called out as the smiling group trooped out of the room.

"Sorry. I hope they didn't embarrass you. I'm kinda their pet-pick-on project. They meant no harm." Ted gestured toward a small desk along the wall. "Why don't we sit over there?"

She handed the carryout sack to him then scooted into a chair. "I wasn't embarrassed, and I hope you weren't either. I could tell they really like you."

He ripped the bag open, distributed their burger baskets, then pulled up a chair beside her. "They're a great bunch of guys. I'm used to their ribbing. Mmm, this smells good."

"I know you like grilled onions. I had them add a few extras."

He gave her wink. "You're my kind of woman. Thanks." Without asking, he bowed his head and simply said, "Thank You, God, for this food and Sammy's willingness to bring it."

How good it felt to know that, despite the way Ted felt about his sister's heart, he was still on praying ground.

"I was hoping you'd come," he said finally, breaking the silence that seemed to wedge itself between them. "I owe you an apology. For ranting the way I did yesterday. I had no right to lay my feelings on you like that. You were a real sport about it."

You still can't see how unreasonable you are? Your sister wanted to donate her heart. It was such an unselfish thing to do. Because of her and others like her, there are people like me who are able to live and breathe and enjoy life for a few more years than we may not have had otherwise. You should have respected her for it.

"My mom and I can't even be in the same room without getting into a disagreement over—well, you know what."

Sammy picked a dill pickle slice off her burger and placed it on her plate. "Don't you think that's a bit sad? You said it's been over three years since you lost your sister. You can't unring a bell, Ted. What's done is done."

"That may be true, but I want to make sure they don't volunteer my organs when *I'm* gone. I want my body to remain intact. I still get the willies when I visit Tiger's grave, just thinking about it. But no more of this unpleasant talk, okay? Subject finished. As you said, you can't unring a bell. Tomorrow's my day off. Got any plans for supper?"

"Not plans exactly, but I was going to stop by the store and pick up a small ham. The children love ham and beans. I usually put them on to cook before I leave for work and let them simmer all day."

"Ham and beans? I love ham and beans!"

"Does that mean you're trying to wheedle an invitation?"

"Would it work if I said yes?"

His silly expression made her laugh. "Only if you stay to help with the cleanup."

He stuck out his hand. "Deal."

"That means you'll have to put up with the three munchkins again, and you'd better come prepared to play catch with Simon."

"I'll be there. Six?"

"Six."

∞

All the next day Sammy watched the clock, wondering if she'd added enough water to the beans, turned the oven up too high, sprinkled on too much seasoning. But when she rushed into her apartment at five thirty, lifted the lid, and tasted a spoonful of the perfectly cooked and seasoned ham and beans, she knew she had done everything right. The ham was tender enough to fall apart, the beans were just the right texture, and the aroma was inviting.

With Ted's old ball glove already on his hand, Simon parted the curtains and peered out the window. "How come he's not here yet?"

Sammy gave the boy a hug. "Because it's not six."

"He can't play ball with you, Simon," Tina told him from her place on the sofa. "He's gonna read a book to me and Harley."

"No, he's not! He said he—"

"Whoa, you two. If Ted heard you arguing like that, I doubt he'd play catch *or* read a book." Sammy lifted Harley, straddling the child's legs over one hip. "I'm glad you kids like Ted, but when he gets here let's give him some space, okay?" When the children gave her a reluctant nod, she quickly placed Harley on the sofa beside Tina and hurried into the kitchen to prepare the cornbread, mince the raw onion, and set the table.

"Mmm, mmm. Ham and beans. Does that ever smell good."

Surprised to hear Ted's voice behind her, Sammy swung around quickly. "I didn't know you were here yet."

"Simon was standing in the doorway when I arrived. He let me in." He glanced around the kitchen. "What can I do to help?"

"Not a thing. Everything's ready."

The five of them laughed their way through dinner as Ted told story after story of things that happened to him when he was growing up. Sammy was filled with both joy and regret as she listened and watched the happy expression on the children's faces. Joy because they were having so much fun with Ted and regret when she realized how much they'd missed by not having a father figure in their lives.

"Tell you what, Simon," Ted told the boy once their last bite of dessert had been consumed. "Give me fifteen minutes to help your aunt clean up the kitchen, and we'll go out onto the parking lot and play some catch."

"But Harley and me wanted you to read us a book."

With a consoling smile, Ted turned to Tina. "I'll read to you as soon as Simon and I finish playing catch, okay?"

Sammy was relieved when Tina didn't fuss and simply nodded. She was sure Ted had his fill of bickering when he was home. He didn't need any more.

∞

"Are you gonna move in and live with us?" Simon asked Ted as the two walked out to the parking lot.

Taken aback by the boy's question, Ted stared at him. "Move in with you and your aunt? Why would you think something like that?"

The boy gave a nonchalant shrug. "All my mom's boyfriends moved in with us."

Ted ached for Simon. What a sad, confused life that boy must have had before he and his sisters came to live with Sammy. "No, I'm not going to move in with you. I'm not going to live with any woman unless we're married."

"Are you gonna marry Aunt Sammy?"

Ted's jaw dropped. He'd been put on the spot by a nine-year-old, and he had no idea how to answer.

"If you married Aunt Sammy, *then* you could live with us."

Deciding to sidestep the question, Ted reached out and tousled the boy's hair. "Did we come out here to talk or play ball? It'll be dark soon."

Simon smiled up at him. "Play ball."

Ted backed away, pulled a brand-new, shiny white ball from his jacket pocket and gently tossed it to Simon. "Okay, let's play ball."

∞

Sammy braced her arms on the window sill and gazed dreamily at the game of catch going on in the parking lot. She tried to imagine what it would be like if she were married to Ted and stood watching him play ball with their own son. *Come on, girl. Get back to reality,* she told herself, shaking her head to dismiss the thoughts. *Dream all you want, but don't expect your dreams to come true. There are far too many obstacles in your way.*

Ted burst through the door with Simon at his heels. "Whew! Simon and I worked up a sweat. Got any of that iced tea left?"

Sammy hurried toward the kitchen. "Coming right up."

Ted took the glass from her hand then sat down on the sofa, squeezing himself between two giggling little girls. "Okay, which book are we going to read?"

Still giggling, Tina pointed to a book on the coffee table.

He reached for it and gazed at the cover. "*The Little Engine That Could?* Sounds like a good book to me. Is this your favorite?"

Both girls nodded.

"As soon as Ted finishes the book, it's off to bed for all three of you." As eager to hear him read the story as the girls were, Sammy sat down in the wooden rocking chair she'd rescued from the Dumpster and waited.

Ted glanced her way as he opened the book. She was so beautiful, so sweet. Suddenly Simon's question popped into his head. Though he had to admit he felt a real attraction to Sammy, he hadn't thought seriously of marrying her. But now, sitting there with her across from him, smiling at him with that smile that drove him crazy, the idea of being married to her had great appeal. Just then Harley crawled onto his lap and leaned her head against his chest, and he remembered that marrying Sammy could mean a package deal. The idea of spending the rest of his life with Sammy—and possibly three children who weren't his—lost some of its luster.

"I'm not in any rush to get away," he said when he finished reading. "Is there anything I can do to help you get them ready for bed?" He closed the book and put it back on the table.

"Not really. They're all old enough to get into their jammies by themselves. I just need to make sure they brush their teeth and—" She paused. "It won't take long. I—I have something important to tell you. Why don't you relax and wait for me?"

"Good idea." Glad for the opportunity to spend more time with her, Ted told the children good night then leaned back against the sofa, closing his eyes.

Sammy appeared again fifteen minutes later. "All tucked in. Thanks for being so patient." She sat down beside him and smiled. "For someone who never wanted kids, you're pretty good with children. Those three adore you."

He shrugged. "Funny thing is, I enjoy being around them. Especially Simon. Tiger loved children. She always wanted a big family, a whole houseful of kids." Ted slipped his arm about her shoulders. "Since you're the children's caretaker and your sister might never come back after them, if the right man came along, would you consider marrying him?"

She let out a sharp breath. "Do you honestly think any man would want to

312

take on a wife and three children who weren't even hers?"

"I was asking you a hypothetical question."

"Hypothetical, huh? Okay, then my hypothetical answer would be yes—*if* the right man came along and *if* he loved me and shared my faith and *if* he was willing to help me provide a good, loving, stable home for them. But I doubt that's going to happen. Not many men would be crazy enough to take on that kind of responsibility."

"Yeah, you may be right." He wanted so much to be able to tell her how attracted he was to her, but getting seriously involved with Sammy would mean a bigger commitment than he might be prepared to give. Yet he couldn't walk away from her. *Face it, buddy. You're not only attracted to Sammy, but you're in love with her! You're even thinking the M word.*

"Oh," he said, snapping his fingers and hoping to change the subject, "you said you had something to tell me. What is it?"

Sammy sucked in a deep breath. *No need to tell you about my transplant now. It looks as if our relationship is doomed since you just agreed with me that any man would be crazy to take on my unconventional little family.* "Never mind. It wasn't important."

He eyed her suspiciously. "You sure? You made it sound important."

"Trust me. It's nothing you need to know."

His shoulders rose in a nonchalant shrug. "Okay."

Sammy winced as his arm tightened around her. *Now what do I do? Try to end things as quickly as possible to avoid the agony of putting off the inevitable? Or simply let things take their course and enjoy the ride until it blows up in my face? Either way I'm going to be miserable when this sweet relationship with Ted comes to an end.*

He cupped his free hand over hers, his thumb gently massaging her knuckles. "I'm pulling an extra shift again tomorrow. That means I can't see you for two whole days. I may have withdrawal pains."

Sammy gazed at their joined hands, enjoying his touch. If only it could be that way forever. "Someone sick?"

"Naw, one of the guys needs time off to go to his folks' fiftieth wedding anniversary celebration. Fifty years with the same person—wow! Think you could spend fifty years with the same guy?"

"If I were married to the man of God's choosing."

"I'm in awe of your faith, Sammy. You seem to trust God for everything. Don't you ever get mad? Throw things? Pout?"

She pulled her hand away and fiddled with the neck of her shirt, checking to make sure the top button had remained firmly lodged in its buttonhole. "I'd be lying if I said I didn't." She managed a slight snicker. "Well, I don't throw things, but I do get pretty upset sometimes, and I have been known to pout when things haven't gone my way. But God is faithful. He always sees me through." *I'm counting on Him to see me through whatever happens with you.*

"He's seen me though all my troubles, too, except for one. I don't know where He was when that one happened. He sure wasn't listening to me."

"Your sister?"

"Yeah, God really let me down on that one."

"Maybe *you* let *Him* down."

"Me? How?"

"By making such a big issue out of something that seemed important enough to your sister that she signed a donor card." The frown and look of almost despair he gave her made her wonder if she'd overstepped some invisible line.

"Look, Sammy—I know you mean well. But you've never had a loved one's heart taken from them as I have, or, believe me, you'd feel differently about things. I did the research. I've seen the pictures. I know what that type of surgery looks like. Until you've walked in those shoes—"

"I *have* walked in those shoes!" she blurted out.

Ted spun around to face her. "What do you mean, you've walked in those shoes?"

Her heart racing and her fingers trembling, with tears she unfastened the top button on her shirt, spreading the tips of the collar far apart. "See! See this scar? You should recognize it, Ted. You said you did the research!"

All color drained from his face as he stared at the scar. "You've had a—a heart transplant?"

Lifting her chin to allow him a better view, she wept openly, nearly shouting her words. "Yes, I've had a heart transplant! Thanks to people like your sister, who unselfishly donate their organs, I was able to receive a donor heart, and it saved my life. I waited over two years for this heart, Ted. Two long, scary years. So, yes, I *do* know what it's like to have your heart taken from you. But, praise God, mine was replaced with a healthy one someone was no longer able to use!"

Visibly shaken by her revelation, Ted stood and began to pace about the room, raking his fingers through his hair. "Why didn't you tell me? I had no idea—"

"Tell you? After the way you've carried on about your sister's heart?"

His face drawn and contorted, he stopped pacing and spread his arms open wide. "So now what am I supposed to do? For all I know, that could be my sister's heart beating in your chest."

Brushing away tears with the back of her hand, she shook her head firmly.

"That's not likely, Ted. I was living in Denver at the time."

"That's a relief." He grabbed up his ball glove and headed for the door. "This is maddening. I've got to get out of here."

She hurried after him. "I'm sorry this is upsetting you, but I'm glad you know. I've hated keeping it a secret."

"That was no secret you were keeping, Sammy. It was a bombshell!" With that, he yanked open the door and disappeared. A few seconds later, she heard the tires on his truck squeal as he left the parking lot.

Ted was gone.

Probably for good.

Chapter 7

Two weeks passed, and still no word came from Ted. Though Sammy wore a pleasant smile around the children, she ached inside. There was no excuse for what she had done. She knew how strongly Ted felt. She should have told him the day she'd learned about his sister's death and faced up to his reaction, no matter how upsetting it might be. Instead of waiting and blurting it out as she had, with no warning or forethought leading up to it to soften its impact.

But that was hindsight, and she had to admit the few weeks she'd had with Ted were the best weeks of her life. She thought they'd been good for him, too, but apparently not good enough for him to put aside his feelings of resentment and anger.

"When is Ted gonna come and play catch with me?" Simon asked late one evening as Sammy knelt beside his bed. "He said he'd come back, but he hasn't."

Swallowing at the lump in her throat that seemed to have become a permanent fixture, Sammy bent and kissed the boy's forehead. "I don't know when Ted is coming back, Simon. I miss him, too."

Turning away from her, he flipped over onto his side, tugging the quilt with him. "People never come back when they say they will. That's what my mom said, too, and she never came back."

"I wish I had an answer for you, honey, but I don't. But I love you, Simon, and I promise you the only reason I'd ever leave you is if your mother comes back. But even if she doesn't, I'm going to be right here beside you. You do believe me, don't you?"

"I guess so," he barely whispered.

"God will never leave you either. No matter what. Simon, do you hear me?" She nudged his shoulder lightly, only to find he'd fallen asleep. She wasn't even sure he'd heard what she said.

∞

"Phone call," Tiffany told her the next afternoon as Sammy passed by the reception desk. "They asked for Rosalinda Samuel. I'd nearly forgotten your real name since everyone calls you Sammy. You can take it here if you want."

"Thanks, but I'll take it in my office."

"You not feeling well, Sammy? I've never seen you so down in the dumps before. You and that boyfriend of yours break up?"

Sammy pasted on a fake smile. "Just been busy, that's all." She hurried past Tiffany's desk, made her way through the maze of cubicles that lined the walls and stepped into her office. "This is Rosalinda Samuel. How may I help you?"

"Miss Samuel. This is Dr. Bettenburg's office in Denver. We keep hearing from the doctor's office of the person who donated their heart to you. It seems your donor's mother wants desperately to meet you and see how you're doing. Her doctor had explained the anonymity clause to her, but the woman refuses to take no for an answer. Dr. Bettenburg and her doctor have finally agreed that our office should phone you to see if you have any interest in meeting with this person."

Sammy tapped her pencil idly on the desk. "I wouldn't mind meeting with her—in fact, I'd like to thank her—but as you know, I no longer live in Denver."

"Oh, she doesn't live in Denver either. She lives in Tennessee. Smith Springs, Tennessee. Is that anywhere near Nashville?"

"I think so. I'm not sure."

"Do you want us to call her and give her your number, or would you prefer to call Barbara McCoy directly?"

Pulling a fresh sheet off the notepad, Sammy poised her pencil. "Give me the number. I'll call her." She wrote down the number then added the name Barbara McCoy.

"By the way, Miss Samuel, how are you and that heart of yours getting along? We miss seeing you here in our Denver office."

"It's doing just fine. I can't tell you how grateful I am to the donor and to Dr. Bettenburg. I can hardly wait to talk to Mrs. McCoy. Thank you for calling. Give my best to the doctor."

Before she could dial the number, her phone rang again. This time it was her mother.

"Hi, sweetie. Any word from Ted?"

"No, nothing, not that I expected to hear from him."

"I know I warned you not to tell him, but I was wrong. Perhaps it would have been better if you'd told him earlier."

"I know, Mom, but that's hindsight."

"Telling him at the very beginning could have saved you both a lot of grief."

"But if I'd told him, then we wouldn't have become acquainted, and I wouldn't have had all those wonderful times with him. I wouldn't give those up for anything. Those times will stay with me forever."

"I'm glad you had those times, too, but I worry about you, dear. You *are* taking your medication, aren't you? You know how important that is."

"Yes, Mom, I'm taking my medication. You worry too much. I do have something to tell you, though." She explained the call she'd received from Dr. Bettenburg's office.

"You're going to call her? That Mrs. McCoy?"

"Yes, I was about to dial her number when your call came in."

"Let me know what happens, okay?"

"You'll be the first to know."

"I love you, Sammy. Give the kids a kiss and a hug for me."

"I will. Love you, too, Mom. 'Bye."

Sammy broke the connection and sat staring at the phone for several minutes. Finally she dialed the number then sat back and waited while it rang. One ring. Two. Three. Then, gasping for breath, a woman's voice answered. "McCoy residence."

"Mrs. McCoy, this is Rosalinda Samuel. The nurse in Dr. Bettenburg's Denver office called and said you were trying to reach me." Was that weeping she heard on the other end of the line?

"I can't thank you enough for calling. We lost our precious daughter a little over three years ago. She'd signed a donor card. We've always wanted to find the person who received her heart, but there are rules of anonymity about those things. I can't tell you how happy I am to finally be talking to you."

Sammy clutched the phone tightly, her own eyes filled with tears. "I'm glad to be talking to you, too, Mrs. McCoy. I've wanted to thank you. I can only imagine how hard all of this has been on you. Losing a child has to be one of the worst ordeals a person would have to endure. The nurse who phoned me said you lived at Smith Springs?"

"Yes, we live on the lake. It's such a beautiful spot. I'm sure you're busy, but I was wondering if you might be able to come down and spend a little time with my husband and me? Maybe Sunday afternoon. We're about twenty miles southeast of you. The Murfreesboro Pike will bring you right to us. I'd offer to come up to Nashville, but I recently had a knee replacement and am not getting around too well."

"I think I could work that out. What time should I be there?"

"Anytime will be fine."

Sammy glanced at her watch. If she left right after church on Sunday, she could be there by no later than one o'clock, maybe even earlier, depending on the traffic. "I'll try to be there around one, but you'd better give me directions."

The woman gave her specific instructions, even telling her the color of the paint on the houses at the intersections, then added, "You have no idea how grateful I am to God for bringing us together. If it weren't for His love and mercies, my husband and I couldn't have made it through our tragedy."

Sammy felt an instant kinship with Mrs. McCoy. "That's the way I feel, too. My faith in God is the most important thing in my life."

"I think you and I are going to be the best of friends, Rosalinda. We'll see you on Sunday."

"Yes, Sunday." An overwhelming joy filled Sammy's heart as she hung up the phone. At last she was going to meet her donor's family.

∽

His brother was sitting on the couch wearing a stained T-shirt and a pair of tattered jeans, looking bored and staring at the TV when Ted strolled into the living room at the end of his shift. "Hey, bro, what's happening? Had your breakfast yet?" When Albert slowly turned in his direction, he caught sight of an overgrowth of beard that appeared to be about three days' worth. "What's the matter? Your razor on the fritz?"

"Nope, it's working fine."

Ted sat down beside him. "So what's with the beard?"

"Just figured it was a good time to grow one."

"What's the matter, Albert? You still having trouble finding a job? I know you've been out on a bunch of job interviews."

Albert glanced toward the kitchen then leaned toward Ted. "Nobody wants me. I'm either too old or too qualified. I may end up flipping burgers. But please don't say anything to Wilma about it. She's upset enough with me already."

"What's happened to you, Albert? You used to be top salesman every month, won a car for your outstanding sales record, then took over the management of that car dealership in Miami."

His brother shrugged. "Lost my zip, I guess. I can't seem to do anything right anymore. My wife thinks I'm a loser. My kids are out of control. My bank account is depleted. My credit card maxed out. I just don't care."

He reached for the can of beer he'd left on the coffee table, but Ted stopped him. "How long has that been going on? The drinking?"

Albert's brows rose. "I may drink, but I don't have a drinking problem."

"Hey, buddy, this is me you're talking to. Ted, your brother. I'm not here to condemn you. I'm here to help you." He gently placed his hand on Albert's wrist. "Is this the real reason you lost your job?"

After a few moments of silence, Albert lifted his face to Ted's, his eyes filled with tears. "Yeah, I kinda let my drinking take over my life. I'm not sure you ever noticed because you were so grief stricken, but our precious sister's death was hard on me, too. I think I took it harder than anyone realized. Me included."

"And I shut you out, didn't I?" Ted slipped his arm around his brother's shoulders. "I wish you'd confided in me sooner. You need help, man. I'm here for you now."

Albert rubbed at his eyes with his sleeve. "I couldn't ask you for help. You're already letting my family live here with you and paying for most of the groceries. That's far more than I deserve."

A lump rose in Ted's throat, and he felt like a heel for criticizing his brother and his family. "What I'm doing for you doesn't amount to a drop in the bucket. Together we'll see this thing through. Whatever I have, whatever you need, is yours."

Weeping like a baby, Albert buried his head in his hands. "Thanks, Ted."

"As I said, man, I'm here for you." He paused. "I assume you and your family haven't been attending church, right?"

Albert nodded. "We dropped out some time ago. I haven't prayed in years. I figured God didn't want to hear from me. Somehow it seemed arrogant to get drunk all week then go to church on Sunday and pretend everything was right between me and the Lord."

Ted gestured toward his brother's dowdy apparel. "From the looks of things, I'd say you don't have any plans for today. How about going to see Pastor Day with me? I've heard they have a great twelve-step program at his church. Not just for those who have trouble with drinking but also for anyone whose life is out of whack. And don't worry about a place to live. You can stay with me as long as you like. And as to finances? I've got a little money saved up. You can have what you need now and pay me back when you get a job."

"You'd—you'd do that for me?"

"Sure I would. You're my brother. We brothers have to stick together." Ted took the half-empty beer can from the table and carried it to the bathroom, emptying it in the sink, then brought it back and placed it in the metal waste-basket by the desk. "Go get you a cup of coffee while I phone the pastor."

∞

In some ways it seemed the week would never end; in other ways it almost flew by. But still no word from Ted. Three times Sammy drove by the fire station, and three times she saw his truck parked in the lot, but she never stopped. It was obvious she was out of Ted's life for good. To make matters worse, the children kept asking for him.

"Maybe you should call him," her mother said as the two stood in the church's welcome center on Sunday morning. "Men are the world's worst when it comes to admitting they've made a mistake. Perhaps Ted is missing you as much as you miss him, but he's having trouble admitting it."

Sammy shook her head. "No, Mom. You don't know him the way I do. He was adamant about his opinion on his sister's heart being taken from her and given away. You should have heard him talk about it. He even researched the procedure."

"Somehow that doesn't sound like the Ted you've told me about. You described Ted as being compassionate, kind, gentle. I can't imagine his getting so upset he'd walk out on you."

"I'm convinced it was because he knew each time he looked at me, he'd be reminded of his sister and what had happened to her."

Her mother shrugged. "The whole thing is so sad. I just hope he comes to his senses. I hate seeing you like this."

"Could we not talk about it anymore, please? Are you sure you don't mind keeping the children this afternoon?"

"Of course I don't mind. We'll have fun. Don't you worry about a thing. Just concentrate on having a good time with Mr. and Mrs. McCoy."

Since the church service ended a little earlier than usual, Sammy decided to stop long enough to pick up a sandwich and fill her car's tank at the convenience store before driving on to Smith Springs. But as she headed for the door to pay for her gas, someone called out her name.

Chapter 8

I t was Captain Grey. "Well, hello, Sammy. How've you been?"

Though Sammy was glad to see him, she knew their pleasantries would eventually turn to Ted. "I'm doing okay. How about you?"

"Me? Other than covering an extra shift today, I'm doin' just fine." He took hold of her arm, pulling her to one side to let a customer pass, then asked quietly, "It's none of my business, but did you and Ted break up? He's been like a bearcat for the past couple of weeks. Barks at everyone. Stays to himself. Grumbles about everything. That's not Ted's style. All the guys are worried about him. I even asked him about it, but all he did was shrug."

"I guess you could say we broke up. He pretty much walked out on me."

"*He* walked out on *you*? That's strange. He'd told some of the guys he was thinking about asking you to marry him."

Sammy's jaw dropped. "He did?"

"You didn't know? He never said anything about it to you?"

"No. I was half hoping we were heading in that direction, but—" She paused, wondering if she'd said too much already.

"I know it's none of my business, but I'd like to see the two of you get back together. I'll keep you both in my prayers."

"Thanks. I'd appreciate it."

He held up a carton of milk then gestured toward a red truck parked in front of the store, bearing the Nashville Fire Department emblem on its door. "I'd better get this to our cook, or we won't have any lunch. He needs it for the gravy. Want me to tell Ted hello for you?"

She shook her head. "No, I doubt he would care, but it was nice to see you. Have a good day."

He nodded. "You, too."

She watched until his truck disappeared around the corner. He said Ted was thinking of asking her to marry him? She was that close to winning the heart of the man she'd hoped to marry and lost him? *Lord, why? Why couldn't Ted see the good his sister's act had done? Why couldn't he be proud of her instead of being upset with her and her decision? And with me? And why can't he stop questioning You?*

Blinking back tears, Sammy selected her sandwich from the refrigerated case, added a soft drink, and paid for her purchases. *Forget about Ted. Think of something pleasant,* she told herself, squaring her shoulders as she headed toward her car. *Smile. Be thankful. You're going to meet some wonderful people today—people who are proud of the fact that their child was willing to donate her organs to someone who needed them.*

By following the directions Mrs. McCoy had given her, Sammy found their place with no difficulty, even though it was located in a densely wooded area on a road high up on a hill overlooking the lake. The McCoys were standing on the deck, smiling, waiting for her when she arrived.

Barbara McCoy, a slight woman with graying hair who looked to be in her midfifties, threw her arms around Sammy and gave her a hug. "I can't believe you're actually here!" Then, turning to her husband, she added, "Isn't she beautiful, Carl?"

"She sure is." Extending his hand, he greeted Sammy with a warm smile. "Nice to meet you, Rosalinda."

Bracing herself with her cane, Barbara McCoy took hold of Sammy's arm and limped toward the door. "Come on inside. Let me get you a nice glass of iced tea."

Once the three were seated comfortably in the living room, Barbara gestured toward a photograph prominently displayed on the mantel. "I remember the day my precious daughter told me she had signed a donor card. Tanny was so afraid I'd be mad at her for doing it without asking me."

"Tanny? How beautiful. That was your daughter's name?"

"Yes, Tanny. She always liked it." The woman paused, as if to gather her emotions before going on. "I—I told her I wasn't mad at her. I was proud of her for doing it. I told her Carl and I had signed one, too."

Carl took his wife's hand, gently cradling it in his own. "Barbara and I figured we'd be the ones to go first, but I guess God had other plans."

Barbara's face brightened somewhat. "Tell us all about yourself, Rosalinda. We want to hear everything."

For the next few minutes, Sammy told them about the trouble she'd had as a child with rheumatic fever and how it had affected her heart and weakened it. "I was on a waiting list for two years before I got the call to"—she stopped midsentence, aware of the impact her next few words would have on Tanny's parents—"to report to the hospital."

"That was the night our daughter lost her life." Barbara pulled a tissue from her pocket and dabbed at her eyes. A gentle smile tilted the corners of her lips. "I know this sounds silly, but may I feel your heart beating? Tanny's heart?"

So touched by the woman's request she could barely speak, Sammy nodded, took her hand, placed it next to her heart, and held it there. Her heart seemed to thunder in response, as if just by being Tanny's heart it could sense Barbara's presence.

Barbara's eyes widened. "I can feel it! I'm actually feeling my daughter's heart beating. Oh, this is a true miracle!"

Sammy struggled to contain the pent-up tears, but they spilled down her cheeks. "Yes, it is a miracle. If your daughter hadn't signed that card—"

"But she did, Rosalinda, and I was so proud of her for doing it. In many ways you remind me of her. I'm thankful her heart went to you. I have a feeling you're as kind and unselfish as she was." Slowly Barbara pulled away her hand. "Thank you for letting me feel the beating of her heart. It's a moment I'll treasure forever. We must stay in touch. I can't tell you how good it is to have you here with us." She turned to her husband. "Isn't it, Carl?"

He nodded then smiled at Sammy. "My wife has been hoping and praying for this day ever since Tanny left us. There's no way we can tell you how thankful we are that you agreed to meet with us."

"And come all the way to Smith Springs to do it," Barbara added. "Carl is driving me up to Nashville in a couple of weeks to see my doctor. Maybe the three of us could have lunch together."

"I'd love it. You have my phone number. Just give me a call." Sammy liked these two. They were such a nice couple. What a warm, loving home they must have provided for their daughter.

"Carl, why don't you take Sammy's picture with that new digital camera I gave you for your birthday?"

"Great idea." Carl hurried to the bookcase. "Maybe I can get a picture of the two of you together."

Sammy held up her hand, a grin etched on her face. "You can only take my picture if you e-mail me copies."

Carl nodded. "You got it. Now smile for me."

Once the flash had gone off, he motioned Sammy to scoot closer to Barbara. "Oh, that'll make a nice picture."

Again Sammy's heart seemed to thunder in her chest.

After Carl had taken several more pictures, he put the camera back in its place. "You ladies sure looked good together."

From somewhere in the direction of the kitchen, a door slammed. "Hey, anybody home?"

Chapter 9

The smile on Barbara's face widened.

"We're in the living room, son," Carl called out, glancing at his wife.

Sammy sucked in a breath and then held it. *That voice! It couldn't be!*

"I know it's been awhile, and I should have—" Their visitor stopped midsentence, his startled gaze going to Sammy then to Barbara, to Carl, and back to Sammy as he entered the room.

Barbara reached out her hands. "I had no idea you were coming today. Come here. I want you to meet someone."

No, no, it can't be! Sammy, feeling as if her breath had been knocked out of her, managed a faint smile as the pieces of an unknown puzzle suddenly fit together. "Ted?"

Barbara turned to face her. "You two know each other?"

"Sammy?" Ted rushed across the room. "I don't get it. What are you doing here? How do you know my parents?"

"Sammy? I thought her name was Rosalinda."

"It is," Sammy confessed with a nod toward Carl, her gaze still fixed on Ted. "Rosalinda is my given name, but almost everyone calls me Sammy."

Carl leaned forward in his chair, his attention going back to his son. "You mean she didn't tell you?"

"Tell me what?"

Barbara latched onto Sammy's hand, holding it tight. "That she's the one who received your sister's heart."

The color drained from Ted's face. "What? No. That can't be. What are you talking about?"

"I'm as surprised as you are!" Sammy thought for a moment before speaking. "It's true, Ted. I *am* the recipient of your sister's heart. But, until I saw you walk through that door and I put two and two together, I had no idea the heart that was keeping me alive belonged to your sister."

Ted dropped down in a chair, his long arms dangling at his sides, his voice tinged with anger. "This is too much."

Barbara's arm circled Sammy's shoulders protectively. "Don't you dare be upset with this sweet girl. I believe her when she says she didn't know whose heart she had. I'm the one who contacted her when I finally convinced the doctor who operated on your sister to get in touch with the recipient. He told her we'd like to meet her, and asked her to contact us. Sammy, being the kind, gentle, understanding person she is, called me. We talked, and she agreed to meet with us. If I'd thought you would have behaved yourself and not gone into a tirade, I'd have invited you to be here when she came, but you'd made your feelings perfectly clear. I had no idea how you'd treat her."

Carl motioned toward Ted. "But you still haven't told us how the two of you know each other. I'm sure your mother is as curious as I am."

"We've been dating."

Barbara's eyes widened. "You have? You and Rosalinda?"

"Yeah, we met on a riverboat ride." Ted sent Sammy a sheepish nod. "I thought she was about the prettiest and nicest girl I'd ever met."

"I wish I'd told you in the beginning, Ted." Sammy fingered her collar. "Then maybe we would never have—" She took a breath. "But having a second-hand heart isn't something you casually bring up in conversation. A lot of emotional baggage comes along with knowing you're alive only because someone else died—not to mention the terrible scar it leaves, the medication, the frequent trips to the doctor for checkups, the limited life span. As you once told me, some people consider the whole procedure unacceptable—you being one of them. But I honestly had no idea of all this." She nodded toward his parents.

"I hope you didn't behave as badly about it in front of Rosalinda as you did with us," Barbara said, her voice wavering with emotion. "Your words hurt me, Ted. They hurt your dad, too. We only did what your sister wanted."

"You could have intervened."

"And go against Tanny's wishes? No! When she signed that donor card, she made it clear that's what she wanted. As her mother, I felt compelled to let her have her way."

For a moment Ted stared at his mother without speaking. When he rose, his gaze traveled to Sammy. "I'm glad you were able to have a heart transplant, Sammy, but it should never have been my sister's." He turned and rushed out the front door.

Sammy started to go after him, but Barbara grabbed her hand. "No, leave him alone. You'll only get hurt."

"If I'd had any idea you were Ted's parents, I wouldn't have come without telling him. But I didn't know. Honest, I didn't." Sammy shook her head. "I'm so confused. Ted's name is Benay. Yours is McCoy. You live in Smith Springs. He lives in Nashville. Your daughter died in Nashville, but I received her heart in Denver."

Carl gave her a kindly smile. "I'm Ted's stepfather. His real father was killed in an industrial accident when Tanny and Ted were barely two. Barbara and I were married a couple of years later. Though I'm the only father the children have ever known, we decided they should keep the Benay name in honor of their father. We lived in Nashville until the company I worked for went bankrupt a few years ago and I got a job here in Smith Springs."

"Didn't Ted ever mention his sister?"

Sammy rubbed at her eyes. "Yes, Barbara, he did, but he always called her Tiger, not Tanny."

"That was his pet name for her from the time they were little, when he first began to talk."

"If only I'd known. I'm sure Ted loves the Lord, but he's having a hard time getting past God taking his sister."

Barbara sighed. "I know. Losing his twin has been agony for him. I think the real problem is the guilt he feels because he was driving the car. He's always felt responsible for her death. I'm not so sure it's God he's upset with. I think he's mad at himself and can't understand why God would have let that accident happen."

Carl nodded in agreement. "That boy has really struggled with his part in his sister's death. You know what they say. There's a special bond between twins. I think the day Tanny died, a bit of Ted died, too. He's never stopped blaming himself."

Sammy considered both Carl's and Barbara's words. "So many things have confused me about Ted, but what you've told me of his terrible inner struggle over the accident helps me understand him better."

"We pray constantly for him, that he'll wake up and see how unreasonable he's been and how many people he's hurt by shutting them out. It wasn't Ted's fault the accident happened. It was the driver of the other car's fault." Barbara gestured toward the picture on the mantel. "Our lovely daughter's life was snuffed out that day, but in some ways she's still with us because of you and your need for a heart. How many people can say that of a loved one they've lost? If Ted could only see that, he'd be proud to know the woman he's become fond of is alive and well because of his sister."

"But I still don't understand how I ended up being the recipient of your daughter's heart when she died in Tennessee and I lived in Denver. Since Denver is such a large city, I always assumed my heart came from there."

Barbara clasped Sammy's hand in hers. "That part confused me, too, so I asked the surgeon's office about it. They said it's best to get a donor's heart to the recipient as quickly as possible. So donor hearts are flown all over the world and don't always stay in the area where the donor lives."

"That's why I ended up receiving a donor heart from Tennessee even though I lived in Denver? Amazing."

"Yes, it is amazing. I look at it as another one of God's miracles." She sighed. "We have to continue to pray for Ted."

In awe of what had just happened, Sammy turned to stare at the front door. "Yes, we have to."

∞

Ted drove like a madman, his foot pressing harder on the gas pedal than it should as he made his way back to Nashville. Why did it have to be Sammy who had his sister's heart? How could he bear to see her again? And why hadn't she told him earlier about her heart? He could understand her reluctance to tell him when they first met, but how about later when they got to be friends? Would it have been so hard to have told him? He was a reasonable sort of guy. Easygoing. Not normally upset by unexpected things. Most of the time, anyway. But the thought of her having someone else's heart beating in her chest, and now finding out it was his sister's—it was more than he could take. He would never forget the accident he'd tried so hard to erase from his memory.

When he reached Nashville, he pulled into the gym out on Nolensville Pike to work off some steam, *Funny*, he thought as he pulled on his shorts and headed for the exercise equipment, *when I got out of bed this morning, my goal was to go visit my folks and make peace with them. That's a far cry from what happened. They're probably more upset with me now than they were before I got there.*

He yanked a towel from the shelf and tossed it over his shoulder. *And I had hoped she was the right woman for me. Now I don't know what to do. Every time I look at her, all I'll be able to think about is Tiger's heart.* Lifting his eyes heavenward, he whispered, "Why, God? Why did You have to let this happen? You could have performed miracles—let Tiger live *and* healed Sammy. What was Your purpose in all of this? I just don't get it."

"Don't get what?"

Ted spun around, embarrassed that someone had overheard him. "Oh, hi, Jake. I didn't know you worked out here."

"I do, but not as often as I'd like. For some reason, my girlfriend can't understand why a guy my age would enjoy lifting weights and running on a treadmill." Jake gave Ted a playful jab to his shoulder. "You and Sammy make up yet?"

Ted frowned. "No, I'm afraid not."

Jake looked at him. "Take it from me—if you like that little gal, tell her you're sorry for whatever happened between you two and get on with it. Looks to me like that Sammy of yours is one fine woman. You'd better hang on to her."

"I wish it were that simple."

"Simple? Not much of life is simple, my friend. Surely you've learned that by now." Jake stepped onto a treadmill and flipped the switch. "But some things are worth fighting for. Why don't you just suck up that pride of yours and patch things up? I can't think of a single thing, short of her cheating on you, that would be worth losing her for." Jake's brow furrowed into a frown. "She didn't cheat on you, did she?"

Ted shook his head. "No, nothing like that."

"You cheat on her?"

"No!"

"I rest my case." Jake gestured toward the door. "You're wasting time, my friend. A good woman is hard to find."

Ted watched as Jake sped up the treadmill and began to jog. *Oh, Sammy, how quickly things can change. I had convinced myself I could accept the fact that those three precious children might be with you until they were grown. Then all this happened. Now what? Where do we go from here? Is there any future in store for you and me?*

∞

"You look awful," Captain Grey told Ted when he reported for work the next morning. "Don't tell me you're coming down with something. We're already shorthanded."

Ted rubbed at the back of his neck. "I'm okay. Just didn't sleep well last night."

The captain motioned toward two chairs along the wall in the day room. "I get the feeling your problem is more complicated than losing a few hours' sleep. You seem preoccupied. Wanna talk about it? I'm a good listener."

Ted moved into one of the chairs, leaned back, and locked his hands behind his head. "Because of my pigheadedness and know-it-all attitude, I've hurt the three people I love most in this world, and I don't know what to do about it."

"How about confessing you were wrong and saying you're sorry? If those people love you, surely they'll forgive you."

"Saying I'm sorry would be the same as admitting I *was* wrong."

"Were you?"

"I didn't think I was, but now I'm beginning to wonder."

Captain Grey moved to the coffeepot, poured two cups, and then handed one to Ted before seating himself. "You want to tell me what you're talking about?"

Ted stared into the cup then took a slow sip. "Sure you want hear about it?"

"Wouldn't have offered if I didn't. Does this have anything to do with Sammy?"

"Yeah. A lot to do with Sammy, but let me start at the beginning. Remember how I ranted and raved when I found out my sister had signed that donor card?"

"How could I forget?"

"For a while I guess I let my disappointment and anger about her decision consume my life."

"I'd say that fairly well sums it up."

Ted took another slow sip. "Sammy has my sister's heart."

The captain sputtered and choked on the swig of coffee he'd just taken. "What? Sammy has your sister's heart? How can that be, and why didn't you tell me about it before now?"

"I didn't know until yesterday. Neither did she."

"Man, I'm totally confused."

"If you're confused, you can imagine how I felt when I walked into my parents' house down at Smith Springs and found Sammy sitting in their living room." Ted went on, filling the captain in on everything from the day he'd met Sammy, found out about the three children living with her, learned she'd had a heart transplant, to when he'd discovered her with his parents and that his sister's heart was keeping her alive. "I'm afraid I behaved pretty badly and said a few things I now regret. I doubt she'll ever forgive me."

Captain Grey thoughtfully rubbed at his chin. "Let's do some evaluating here, but first, let me ask you a question. Do you love Sammy?"

"I thought so."

"All I want is a simple yes or no."

Ted gazed at the ceiling, searching his heart. "Yes."

"*If* Sammy hadn't needed a heart transplant to live, would you want to marry her, spend the rest of your life with her as your wife?"

"But she—"

"Only yes or no, Ted."

"Yes, of course I would. She's the only woman I've ever wanted to marry."

Looking directly into his eyes, Captain Grey placed his hand on Ted's wrist. "Then what's the problem? You're both Christians. You both love the Lord. From my vantage point, I'd say you're one lucky man. Think about it, Ted. If it weren't for the accident, you may have never met Sammy. If your considerate sister hadn't signed that donor card, the heart you've been so concerned about, the heart that has caused a rift between you and your parents and you and the woman you love—that heart would have been buried with your sister. Is that what you wanted? Is it that hard for you to accept the fact that Sammy's life is the result of your sister's unselfish gift?"

Captain Grey's words hit Ted as hard as if he'd whopped him with a sledge-hammer, and they hurt. For the first time, he could see himself for what he really was. Stubborn, selfish, and arrogant. He'd wanted things his way, not God's, and without even considering the validity of the opinions of the other people who loved his sister as much as he did.

"Each time you look at Sammy, you should feel happy and grateful to God. Only He could have caused Sammy, who was living in Denver at the time, to be the recipient of a heart donated in Nashville, and then the two of you to meet on a riverboat and fall in love. Remember what Romans 8:38 says? 'All things work together for good to them that love God.' *God* took your sister. In His plan, her time had come. You could have been taken just as easily in that accident, but you weren't. He still has things planned for you that haven't been fulfilled."

Captain Grey moved his comforting hand to Ted's shoulder. "You may have been driving that day, Ted, but none of it was your fault. God was in control. You're a great guy, one of the best. Take my advice. Life's too short to dwell on the past."

The fire bell clanged out loudly, making it impossible for Ted to respond, which was fine anyway. He needed time to mull over Captain Grey's words.

The fire was a big one—a three-story apartment building in an old, run-down part of Nashville. "Looks like they're trapped!" Cal pointed to a window on the upper floor where a woman with a baby in her arms and several small children stood waving and screaming at them.

"These old apartment buildings are nothing but tinder boxes. I'm surprised they haven't been condemned." Jake shook his head as the men quickly began to pull the heavy fire hoses from the truck and attach them to the fireplug near the front of the building.

Ted grabbed hold of the captain's sleeve. "I'll go up after them, Captain."

Captain Grey motioned toward Jake and Cal. "Cover him." The men maneuvered the hoses into place then trained the nozzles on the rusty iron fire escapes on the outside of the blazing building. "Don't take any chances, Benay," the captain called out as Ted began his ascent. "You know the rules."

Ted moved carefully up the iron rungs. Though it was difficult with all the gear strapped to him, he finally reached the third floor. "Can you make it to the fire escape?" he yelled to the woman, trying to make his voice heard above the roar.

She leaned out the window, her face contorted with sheer terror. "No! I can't carry all three of them and the baby, too!"

"I'll have to go in, Captain!" Ted was relieved when his captain waved him on. After a quick prayer for protection, he crawled through the window above the landing and, crouching, carefully made his way through the thick wall of smoke in the hall.

"Help! We're here!" he heard the woman cry as she and the children, coughing and gasping for air, moved out into the hallway. "Help us! Please help us. We don't want to die!"

Ted took the baby from her arms then grabbed hold of the oldest child's hand. "I'll take him. You hold onto my jacket and bring the others with you. Don't let go!" The woman did as she was told, and soon they were through the window and out onto the fire escape landing, near where the ladder from the truck had been moved into position.

"We need to get out of here as quickly as we can. You and the children let the firemen help you onto the ladder. I'll take the baby down the fire escape." To his relief the woman, though panicked, shoved the children toward the ladder. As one of the firemen helped the four, Ted, with the baby held safely in his arms, carefully climbed down the fire escape to where the paramedics were waiting to check them over and assist in any way they could.

Ted smiled through his mask, then placed the baby in the mother's waiting arms. "You and the children are safe now—that's all that matters."

The woman began to weep hysterically. "We would have died up there if you hadn't come up after us. Thank you—thank you so much."

Ted smiled at her through his face mask. "All in a day's work, ma'am. Just glad to have been of service."

Captain Grey pulled him aside. "That's everyone, Ted. Good job."

"Thanks, Captain. I'd better go help Cal. Looks like that hose is about to get the better of him."

It was nearly four hours before they returned to the firehouse and another hour before the truck was cleaned and back to its shiny self. They made a few routine calls to a couple of the homes in their district and extinguished the fires quickly. Otherwise, they had no other major catastrophes the rest of the day, for which Ted was thankful. After what the captain had said to him, he had plenty of thinking to do.

As he headed for his bunk a little after ten that night, Captain Grey pulled him aside. "Come on in my office." He sat down behind his desk and smiled. "I've been thinking a lot about your situation, Ted. I saw the way you responded when you thought that woman and the children were in jeopardy. You didn't know those people. You'd never seen them before; yet you were concerned enough about them to go into that burning building without hesitation. Yes, you were covered with protective gear, and, yes, you had been trained and knew what to do. But, as you and I both know, fire of any kind is an unpredictable monster and can turn on us at any time. Explosions happen, roofs collapse, walls crumble—but did that stop you from wanting to help them? To save their lives?"

"But, sir," Ted countered, "what I did was routine."

"That may be true, but even so the element of danger was there—and you faced it head-on, without the slightest pause. Which makes me think about your sister. Didn't she do the same thing? Have a concern for those she didn't know who might be in trouble and need a heart, even though it meant going against the wishes of the brother she loved and hated to upset? I'm sure your mother would prefer you be anything but a fireman; yet you go against her wishes every time you report for work because you care." He grinned. "It sure isn't because of the fantastic money you make."

Ted nodded. "That's true. I could pull in a much better paycheck working at construction or selling used cars, though I doubt I'd be much of a salesman."

"What I'm trying to say, Ted, is that we each have to do what we have to do. Your sister did what she wanted to do by donating her heart. Sammy did what she had to do by going through the agony of the surgery and the many months of recuperation that followed. She's caring for her sister's three children because that's what she wants and needs to do. And you? You have to do what you have to do—*if* you want the woman you love to be your wife. The choice is up to you. Don't blow it. You're a Christian. Pray about it. Seek God's will for your life."

Ted leaned toward the captain's desk and rested his elbows on its surface. "What you say makes a lot of sense."

"I'm only saying these things because I respect you. You know, Ted, God is a God of miracles. He could have come down from that cross and struck His enemies dead with a swoop of His hand, but He didn't. And He could have kept your sister alive, but He didn't. He could have kept Sammy's rheumatic fever from damaging her heart, but He didn't. But He did perform a miracle by bringing the two of you together. We don't know His will for our lives, and we certainly don't understand why He allows things to happen the way they do. But we do know this—God is in control, and we must trust Him. We have to make sure our hearts are right with Him at all times. Times both good *and* bad."

Captain Grey slowly moved his hand across the desk and cupped it over Ted's. "Just make sure your heart is right with God. If it is, all the other things will fall into place."

"Thanks, Captain. I value your counsel. As usual, you've given me a lot to think about."

Though his body was weary, Ted's mind was restless as he lay in his bunk that night and thought over the things the captain had said, especially the part about his heart being right. *Who am I kidding? My heart hasn't been right since*

Tiger's death. It was easy to walk with God when everything was going right, but things changed the day I lost my sister. My faith was shaken. Now, looking back, it all seems so foolish. Tiger's heart was hers to do with as she pleased. I had no right to object, and I certainly had no right to turn on Mom and Dad for supporting her decision.

He dabbed at his eyes with the hem of the pillowcase. *How I must have grieved their hearts. How I must have grieved God's heart! And look what I did to Sammy.*

His insides ached with sorrow and regret for his thoughtless actions and words. He threw back the covers and fell to his knees beside his bunk, pouring out his heart to God, pleading for His forgiveness.

∞

Sammy struggled to pull on her pajamas. Never had she been so miserable. She'd found the man of her dreams, only to lose him almost as quickly as she'd found him. "Why?" she called out to God from the depths of her heart. "Why did this heart have to be Ted's sister's? I don't mean to sound ungrateful, Father, for this extended life You have given me. But of all the hearts donated each year in the United States, why couldn't it have been someone else's?"

When the phone rang near midnight, Sammy sleepily snatched it up. It wasn't likely Ted, and she wasn't in the mood to talk to anyone else, but she didn't want it to awaken the children. "Hello."

"Hi, sis! It's me. Tawanda. Guess what? I'm going to Alaska. Did you know that in Alaska you can—"

Suddenly wide awake, Sammy sat straight up in bed. "Tawanda, where have you been? We haven't heard from you since we got that last postcard. Aren't you even interested enough in your precious children to ask about them?"

"Oh, I knew they'd be fine with you. I have to tell you where I've been. I've been to Denver, Las Vegas, Santa Fe, San Antonio, Houston, Miami, Atlanta, Chattanooga, Philadelphia—"

Sammy bit back the words she'd like to say. "When are you coming home, Tawanda? As much as I love these adorable children, you're their mother. They need you. You can't just keep disappearing like this. You know, with my physical condition, there's a good possibility I may not be around 'til they grow up."

"Oh, don't be silly. I'll bet you're the picture of health. You should see the new motorcycle we bought with the money he won in Las Vegas. It rides like a dream. We're headed toward—"

"I don't care about your motorcycle or your boyfriend. What I want to know is when you're coming back. Your wonderful children ask about you every day."

There was a pause on the other end. "I'm not coming back, Sammy. I've never told my boyfriend I have children. If he knew, he'd leave me."

"You're not coming back? *Ever?*" Sammy wished she could go right through that phone line and strangle her sister for not caring about her children.

"No. We're getting married when we get to Anchorage. That's what I was trying to tell you. If you live in Alaska for two years, you get to share in the money the state takes in on the sale of their oil. With that and what the two of us can make picking up part-time jobs here and there, we'll be able to stay there. I know it sounds callous of me when I say it, but you can have my kids. They're yours. They probably love you more than they do me anyway, and you already have their guardianship papers."

Sammy gasped for air. "I can *have* the kids? Just like that? Like they're an old pair of shoes you've tired of? As much as I'd like it if I were their mother, I'm not. You are! You have to come back, Tawanda. *Now!*"

"You know what a free spirit I am. I wasn't cut out for motherhood."

"You should have thought of that before you had those adorable babies."

"I always thought I was being careful. I guess I wasn't, but that's okay. I'm sure they're happy staying with you. When I get a job, I'll try to send you a little money now and then to help with their expenses, but don't count on it. I've heard it's pretty expensive living in Alaska."

Sammy shook her head in bewilderment. "Have you no shame, Tawanda? To leave the precious children God gave you to run around the country with some guy you met in a bar?"

"God didn't give them to me. Those three no-good men did. Got me pregnant then deserted me—that's what they did. If I could find them, I'd give them a piece of my mind."

"Isn't that exactly what *you're* doing? Running off and deserting them? What am I supposed to tell your children, Tawanda? That their mother didn't want them? That she gave them away because they didn't fit into her vagabond lifestyle?"

"Tell them *you're* their mother now. I'm sure they'll be pleased. Especially Simon. That boy never liked me."

"It wasn't *you* he didn't like, Tawanda. It was the constant trail of men who traipsed through your house. He was filled with rage when you left like you did. He's just now beginning to get over it."

"See? What'd I say? They're better off with you. Have your lawyer draw up the adoption papers. When my sweetie and I get settled in Alaska, I'll call you with my new address, and you can send me the papers to sign."

Sammy grabbed hold of the table for support. She was so upset by her sister's uncaring attitude, she was weak. "What about Mom and Dad? Aren't you going to ask about them? Dad's health is getting worse by the week."

"Mom'll take good care of him. Tell them I said hi."

"What if something happens to Dad? How can we reach you to let you know? Do you have a cell phone?" She could almost see Tawanda's shrug of indifference on the other end of the line.

"Nope, don't have one. Maybe I'll call you when we get to Alaska. Gotta go. My honey has our motorcycle all gassed up and ready to roll. 'Bye."

A *click* sounded in Sammy's ear.

Tawanda had hung up the phone.

Sammy quietly pushed the door open to the bedroom and stood staring at the sweet, innocent faces of the three sleeping children. She hoped they hadn't been awakened by the ringing of the phone and heard her side of the conversation with their mother. "Looks like we're a family, kids. Your mom doesn't want you," she said in the faintest of whispers.

Simon lifted his head and opened one eye. "Did you say something, Aunt Sammy?"

She stepped to his bed, leaned over him and kissed his cheek. "Just that I love you, precious. Go back to sleep."

As she crawled back into bed, Sammy lifted her eyes heavenward. "Is this why You spared my life, God? So I could raise these three special children and teach them to love You? You know I'll do my best. I already love them as if they were my own. Please let me live long enough to see them through high school and out on their own before You take me. I feel humbled, yet so unworthy of being their mother. I'll never be able to do it alone. I need Your help."

Her heart filled with both joy and sadness, Sammy cried herself to sleep, only to dream about Ted and the unpleasant way they had parted at his parents' house.

She'd barely reached her office the next morning when Ted rushed in the door, sweeping her up in his arms and kissing her to the hoots and hollers of all those in the office area.

"What was that for?" she was finally able to say when he quit kissing her long enough to gaze into her eyes.

"I love you, Sammy Samuels, and I want the world to know it."

Confused, she pushed back and stared at him. "I thought you and I were through."

He wrapped his arms about her so tightly she had to gasp for air. "That was before I saw myself for what I was and begged God for His forgiveness. I was wrong, Sammy. So wrong. Can you ever forgive me?"

She glanced nervously about the room and found dozens of people staring at them. "We can't talk about this here, not with an audience."

"How about lunch?"

"I can't. Our annual employee luncheon is today. I have to be here. Can you come by my apartment tonight? About six?"

"You bet I can." Ted kissed her cheek then released her and headed for the elevator.

She watched until the doors closed behind him then, trying to maintain some composure, turned with a grin of embarrassment to the crowd of onlookers who had assembled and gave them a dismissive wave. "Show's over, folks. You can go back to work now."

Though she tried to appear calm on the outside, inside her heart was racing wildly. *Did Ted actually say he loved me? And asked for forgiveness? If only we could have talked, just the two of us, but not with everyone standing around gawking at us, listening to our every word.* She glanced at her watch. *Nearly ten hours before I see him again? I'll never make it!*

By the time Ted arrived, she had a nice supper waiting for him, with the table set for two and candles lit. "Where are the kids?" he asked, his gaze scanning her apartment. "I brought them a new video."

"Mom came by after them. I thought it would make it easier to talk." A ripple of joy ran down Sammy's spine as Ted moved toward her, pulled her into his arms, and kissed her with a long lingering kiss. She'd thought of this moment all day, and it was as delicious as she'd imagined.

"I meant what I said this morning, Sammy. I love you," he whispered softly as their lips parted. "And I'm begging for your forgiveness. I was such an arrogant fool, thinking everyone was out of step but me. Now, thanks to God and Captain Grey, I realize I was the one who was out of step."

Sammy frowned. "Captain Grey? I don't understand."

"We had an apartment fire yesterday. A bad one. A woman and her four children could have easily lost their lives, but we were able to get them out in time."

"We? You were involved in their rescue?"

"Yeah, sorta."

By the way he dipped his head, as if wanting to avoid any praise, she was sure he had been an important part of it.

"After we got back to the station and the trucks had been washed and parked inside, Captain Grey invited me into his office, and we had a talk. He was pretty direct. He pointed out my pious attitude and other things in my life that I'd been too blind to see. Oh, I was upset with him at first, but I respect him, not only as an honorable man but also as a Christian. I knew he was only saying those things for my good. A lot of what he said was what you, my parents, and others had been saying, but for the first time I saw myself for what I really was. Stubborn, selfish, and vindictive, and that's just the beginning of the list."

"But—"

"As I listened to his words, God spoke to my heart, reminding me of something your pastor said in his message the day I went to church with you. I remember each word as clearly as if he'd said them only moments ago. 'God's children should never put a question mark where God has placed a period.' I've tried so many times to forget those words, but I couldn't. Those words really convicted me."

He took Sammy's hand, lovingly cradling it in his own. "Although I didn't want my sister's heart taken from her, that decision was hers, not mine. And the worst part was that I was upset with God for taking my sister from me. It's a wonder you, my parents, and God want anything to do with me. What a knucklehead I've been. God has forgiven me. Now, sweetheart, I'm begging for your forgiveness."

Sammy felt like pinching herself to see if this was a dream. "Of course I can forgive you. I—I love you." Tears welled up in her eyes. "I'm glad you're no longer upset with your sister's decision, but—"

"How do I feel about Tiger's heart being your heart?"

She nodded, fearing what his answer might be.

"I've given that much thought. I'm ashamed to admit it, but I think I said something to you like, 'I hope I never meet the person who has my sister's heart.' I am so sorry for those words, sweetheart. I no longer feel that way. Knowing my sister's heart is *your* heart makes our relationship that much more special." He lifted her hand to his mouth and kissed her fingertips. "I know I don't deserve it after the way I behaved, but, please, Sammy, know that my heart is right, and I'll never say anything like that again. I promise you."

Her heart nearly exploding with love for this man, Sammy gazed up at him through misty lashes. "You have no idea how happy your words make me. I've longed for this moment—"

Ted put his finger to her lips. "Then say you'll marry me, Sammy. I want you to be my wife. I want us to be together forever."

Sammy stared at him. "Did you say m–m–marry you?"

Scooping her up in his arms, he whirled her about the room. "Yes, I said marry me! I love you, sweetheart. You mean everything to me. We belong together."

Suddenly her sister's phone call came to mind, and she pulled away from his grasp, her newfound joy turning into a terrible ache in the pit of her stomach.

"I can't—we can't do this. I love you with all my heart, Ted, but—"

He reached for her hand, his questioning eyes fixed on hers. "But why? We both love each other, and you said you'd forgive me."

Sammy swallowed at a lump in her throat that threatened to choke her. "My sister called. She's not coming back for the children."

"Not coming back now?"

"Not ever. She gave them to me."

"Gave them to you? Permanently?"

Sammy nodded. "She told me to have a lawyer draw up the adoption papers." As much as she loved Ted, she loved the children, too. They were, and would continue to be, her first priority. They had to be. "Tawanda had no interest in them at all. She didn't even ask about them. It broke my heart. Those children need their mother."

Ted wrapped her tightly in his arms again. "They don't need her, sweetheart. They need you. The love you have for them and the care you give them are far more than their mother ever gave them. I'd say God gave them to you for that very reason."

"But that means they'll always—"

"Always be with you?"

"Yes, as long as God gives me breath."

He tilted her face up to meet his. "And you think I might not want to marry you because of them?"

"Yes," she answered in a mere whisper.

"You're worrying needlessly, dearest. True, I haven't spent a great deal of time around the children, but I've seen the look of excitement in Simon's eyes when we play catch. That boy needs a father figure in his life. I'd like to be that father figure. And Tina? What a joy that little girl is. Her smile and her sweet, gentle ways are so like yours. She even looks like you." He gestured toward a photograph on the end table. "And little Harley? Who wouldn't love that precious child, with her cute little button nose and those big blue innocent eyes? I've grown to love those children, Sammy. I'd be proud to become their uncle and help you with them. I'm sure at times it'll be hard, but doesn't anything worthwhile take time and effort?"

Sammy savored his words, words she'd never expected to hear when she'd told him about Tawanda's call. But she was still filled with uncertainties. Did Ted have a realistic idea of what he might be getting into? From being a confirmed bachelor to becoming a husband and sharing the raising of three children was a considerable leap. "Are you sure you mean that, Ted? Living with three children isn't easy. You've already complained about living with your nephews. Maybe you'd better give this considerable thought before committing yourself to what could be a long-term task."

Smiling at her, Ted brushed an errant lock of hair from her forehead. "I've already thought about it. I've spent quite a bit of time with my brother and his family lately, and you know what? I've actually enjoyed being around them. The children are a little rough around the edges, but they're pretty good kids. I'm getting along well with my sister-in-law now, and my brother and I are closer than we've ever been."

"Oh, Ted, I'm glad for all of you."

"Me, too. Now all I need is for you to say you'll marry me." Reaching into his pocket, he pulled out a small gold ring. "I was hoping you'd forgive me, so I stopped by the jewelers this afternoon. I'm waiting, dearest. What's your answer?"

How she longed to let Ted slip that ring onto her finger as a symbol of their love and commitment, but she couldn't. "You need to consider something else," she confessed with a heavy heart, her hand touching the neckline of her blouse. "Your sister's heart has given me new life, but there is no assurance how long that life will last. I may have one more year, maybe five, maybe ten. As a heart transplant recipient, my life span isn't as long as most folks' might be, and there's always the chance of complications. You've already lost your sister. Do you want to take a chance on marrying someone who may not have many years of life left? Who takes medication every day of her life? Who constantly has to go to the doctor for checkups?"

Ted gazed into her eyes with love. "According to the law of averages, Tiger, who was in excellent health, should have lived at least into her seventies, but she didn't. Her life was taken in that accident. None of us knows how long we're going to live. Only God knows. Whatever time either of us may have, my darling, I want us to spend it together. So—my answer is yes, I *do* want to marry you, knowing all those things."

His words made her heart soar with anticipation, but she knew she had to bring up one other thing. She paused then reached up to her neckline, unfastened the top two buttons of her blouse and spread the collar tabs open wide. "Though you've only seen the tip of this unsightly scar, it runs all the way to my waist. I'm not the beautiful unblemished wife you deserve, Ted. Are you sure you want to live with a woman disfigured like this? See this jagged, ugly scar every day? Be reminded of your sister's thoughtful act?"

Ted studied the scar for a moment then bent and kissed the indentation area slightly above her collarbone, the area where the scar began. "Your scar isn't ugly, sweetheart. It's beautiful. Beautiful because it gave you life. I won't mind seeing it and touching it. In fact, I'll consider it an honor because, without it, there would be no you, the woman I love." Tenderly he kissed the scar again. "Will you marry me, Sammy, be my wife?"

Her hand flew to cover her mouth as an overwhelming love rushed to the surface and spilled down her cheeks in the form of tears. Unable to speak, she simply bobbed her head.

Ted let loose an enthusiastic laugh. "I take it that's a yes?"

She threw her arms about his neck. "Yes, it's a yes! Oh, Ted, I can't tell you how much I love you. Words can't express how happy you've made me."

Taking her hand in his, he gazed into her eyes. "Sammy Benay. I like the sound of that. Or how about Rosalinda Benay? That has a nice ring to it. Hmm, Mrs. Ted Benay. I like that even better. Now are you going to let me put this ring on your finger or not?"

"Yes, oh, yes, Ted. I'd love to wear your ring." Sammy couldn't help but stare at the ring as he slipped it onto her hand. It was the most beautiful ring she'd ever seen. "I love it. This ring is precious because it symbolizes the life we plan to have together. I'll treasure it always." She leaned into him reveling in the warmth and strength of his embrace as Ted circled his arms around her and pulled her close.

"So when should we get married?"

"When?" Lifting her face to his, she gazed into his clear blue eyes, delighting in the love she saw reflected there. "I don't know. Don't you want time to get better acquainted with the children first? Make sure you'll be comfortable living with them?"

"I don't need time, Sammy. I love those kids and have already wasted too many years of my life. I'd like us to get married as soon as possible. Of course we'll have to find a house first. I don't think your apartment could hold one more person, and I told my brother he and his family can stay at my place for as long as they need."

Her eyes widened. "You have?"

"Yep."

"So we're going to look for a real house? Not an apartment?"

"Yes, a real house. One big enough for the five of us and any children we'll be adding to our family."

Her jaw dropped. "*Adding* to our family?"

"Sure. Even though we love your sister's children, we'll want children of our own, won't we?"

"I've always wanted children, but I wasn't sure you would. Especially after adopting Tawanda's children."

"I want kids, too, Sammy. Our kids—yours and mine."

Both Sammy and Ted turned as the outside door opened and Simon came bursting in, throwing his arms around Ted's waist. "Did you come to play catch with me?"

Releasing his hold on his bride-to-be, Ted slipped his arm around Simon's shoulders. "Sure did, buddy. From now on, you and I are going to be playing a lot of catch."

Mrs. Samuel and the other two children appeared in the doorway. Little Harley took one look at Ted then raced across the room and leaped into his waiting arms. "Will you read me a story?"

"Sure, honey, as soon as Simon and I play a little catch." Ted reached out his free hand to Tina. "Would you like to hear Uncle Ted read a story, too?"

The little girl gave him a wide grin. "Yes, I like your stories."

Their grandmother frowned then walked over to stand by Sammy. "Uncle Ted? What's going on? Did I miss something?"

Sammy felt herself beam. "Only the happiest moment of my life. Ted and I are going to be married."

Taking on a guarded smile, her mother leaned even closer. "He knows everything?"

Sammy let out a sigh of contentment. "Everything and more. I'll tell you all about it later."

Epilogue

Three months later

Ted took his place at the front of the church. From the looks of those seated in the pews, nearly everyone he and Sammy had invited had turned out for their wedding.

"You're a lucky man, Benay," Captain Grey said as he walked up and shook hands with Ted. "That Sammy is one great woman, a real gift from God. Good thing you got your head on straight before you lost her."

"I know. I was a real jerk." Ted touched his bow tie and smiled at Captain Grey. "Thanks for your wise counsel."

"I only pointed out a few things I'm sure you knew already. You just needed a little reminder."

"There's someone I'd like you to meet." Ted gestured toward the man standing on his other side. "Captain Grey, this is my best man, my brother, Albert."

The captain reached out and gave Albert's hand a hearty shake. "Nice to meet you, Albert." Then, glancing around, he backed away. "Guess I'd better find my seat. Looks as if your wedding is about to begin."

Albert leaned toward Ted. "We look pretty handsome in these black tuxedos, don't we? You're not nervous, are you?"

Ted held out his hand. "Me? Nervous? Naw, my hand always shakes like this."

Albert's face took on a somber expression. "Thanks to you and your willingness to attend that twelve-step program with me, things are going much better now. The marriage counseling Pastor Day is giving Wilma and me has helped, too. Our relationship is improving every day. Even the kids are settling down. I owe you a lot."

"You owe me nothing. I'm not a drinker, but I probably got as much out of that twelve-step program as you did. I see a lot of things more clearly now."

"I hope I'll have a job soon and we'll be out of your apartment."

"Don't worry about it. Now that Sammy and I have purchased a home, I won't be needing it. You're welcome to it."

"Wow! Thanks, Ted."

Ted glanced around the room. "I wish Tiger could have been here. I know she and Sammy would have been the best of friends, and Tiger would have loved being around the children."

Albert nodded. "I wish she were here, too. Our sister was one in a million. You suppose she's looking down at you? Watching your wedding?"

Ted grinned. "I know she is."

The two men turned their attention to the double doors at the back as the sound of the big organ filled the sanctuary. Within seconds the doors parted, and Sammy's mother emerged, followed by Ted's parents, all escorted by Ted's fireman buddies who had eagerly agreed to be ushers.

Next came two of the cutest little girls Ted had ever seen. His heart swelled with pride as Tina and Harley, in their long white dresses, slowly walked up the aisle toward him, dropping rose petals from the baskets they were carrying. Next was Simon with the ring pillow, looking quite dashing for a nine-year-old in his black tuxedo, his hair slicked down with the goop Ted had generously applied.

Ted waited anxiously as several bridesmaids came up the aisle, followed by Sammy's next-door neighbor and babysitter whom she had asked to be her maid of honor. "Sammy has to be next," he whispered to Albert, his nervousness rising to the surface.

He'd barely gotten the words out when Sammy appeared beside her father. Ted had never seen a lovelier sight. He didn't know much about fashion and what women looked for in a wedding gown, but he did know she looked like an angel in that full, filmy white dress as she floated up the aisle toward him. Her hair was tucked up under a circle-like piece covered with flowers and some kind of net attached. She looked beautiful, and the best part was—she was going to be his.

"Was she worth waiting for?"

Without taking his eyes off his bride, Ted leaned toward his best man. "You bet she was! Wow!"

When Sammy reached him, instead of waiting for her father to place Sammy's hand in his, Ted impulsively grabbed her and pulled her into his arms. He couldn't wait to hold her. So when the pastor asked, "Who gives this woman to be married to this man?" Mr. Samuel stepped forward and said, "Her mother and I."

Ted tried to keep his mind on the service, but all he could think of was the woman standing beside him who was about to become his wife. When the pastor asked each of them to recite their vows to one another, instead of saying the vows he'd rehearsed, Ted spoke directly from his heart. He ended by saying, "I promise to cherish you always, my love. I know God led the two of us together, and I praise Him for it. As for me and my house, we *will* serve the Lord. With

God as my witness, I vow to do all I can to be the husband you deserve and the man you can trust with your very life. I love you, Sammy."

The pastor nodded toward Sammy. "Now, Rosalinda, you may say your vows to Ted."

Ted was sure he was the happiest man alive as Sammy gazed into his eyes and began to say her vows. He hung on to her every word, completely amazed that this moment had finally arrived after the trials and troubles they'd been through.

"I, too, promise to be the mate you deserve," she said in closing. "My heart—your sister's heart—is filled with love for you, my dearest. It is my desire that every beat of it will bring us closer together. Never doubt my love, sweetheart. I give it all to you."

Pastor Day reached out and placed his right hand on Sammy's shoulder, his left on Ted's. "Your family and friends have gathered together today to support you and help celebrate your union. May God have His hand on your marriage and may you remember the vows you have made before Him. By the power vested in me by the state of Tennessee, I now pronounce you husband and wife. Ted, you may kiss your bride."

Ted gazed into Sammy's adoring eyes as he lifted her veil. Beginning this day, he would do all he could to protect her and shield her from any harm that might come to her or threaten her life. They were a team now, and together, with God as the head of their home, they were unbeatable. He drew her close and placed his lips on hers, tasting their sweetness and enjoying the scent of her perfume.

When they parted, Sammy gazed into his eyes. Then, lifting her face heavenward, she said, "Thank You, Lord, for being patient with me and giving me this wonderful, caring man."

"And thank You that my sister signed that donor card." Ted also looked upward before smiling at his beloved.

Then, hand in hand, they made their way down the aisle past family, friends, and loved ones, eager to begin the life God had given them, thanks to his sister's thoughtfulness and Sammy's secondhand heart.